PRAISE FOR THE MINDHUNTERS SERIES
BY KYLIE BRANT

WAKING THE DEAD

"Get ready for lots of twists and turns with an abundance of suspense in this thrilling romance." —*Fresh Fiction*

"Once again Kylie Brant kept me awake until three in the morning to finish her book . . . a really impressive series. She reminds me of a few great writers. If you love Kay Hooper's writing you will love Ms. Brant's writing, too."
—*A Romance Review*

"If you have been reading this Mindhunters series, you will not want to miss out on this next installment. If you haven't picked up one of these intriguing romantic suspense stories, what are you waiting for? I recommend reading them all from the beginning!" —*Fallen Angel Reviews*

"An electrifying and infinitely gripping novel . . . Kylie writes excellent dialogue, creates engaging characters, vividly detailed investigation, and action scenes. The smooth process in which she moves the story along keeps the pages turning, allowing the reader to immerse themselves in the novel from start to finish." —*The Romance Studio*

"Terrific." —*Midwest Book Review*

"Provided a thrill and plenty of romance and forensics-based action!" —*Errant Dreams Reviews*

WAKING EVIL

"Enjoyable . . . a superb police procedural . . . enhanced by the supernatural and the romance."
—*Midwest Book Review*

continued . . .

DEADLY INTENT

THE MINDHUNTERS

KYLIE BRANT

BERKLEY SENSATION, NEW YORK

THE BERKLEY PUBLISHING GROUP
Published by the Penguin Group
Penguin Group (USA) Inc.
375 Hudson Street, New York, New York 10014, USA
Penguin Group (Canada), 90 Eglinton Avenue East, Suite 700, Toronto, Ontario M4P 2Y3, Canada
(a division of Pearson Penguin Canada Inc.)
Penguin Books Ltd., 80 Strand, London WC2R 0RL, England
Penguin Group Ireland, 25 St. Stephen's Green, Dublin 2, Ireland (a division of Penguin Books Ltd.)
Penguin Group (Australia), 250 Camberwell Road, Camberwell, Victoria 3124, Australia
(a division of Pearson Australia Group Pty. Ltd.)
Penguin Books India Pvt. Ltd., 11 Community Centre, Panchsheel Park, New Delhi—110 017, India
Penguin Group (NZ), 67 Apollo Drive, Rosedale, North Shore 0632, New Zealand
(a division of Pearson New Zealand Ltd.)
Penguin Books (South Africa) (Pty.) Ltd., 24 Sturdee Avenue, Rosebank, Johannesburg 2196,
South Africa

Penguin Books Ltd., Registered Offices: 80 Strand, London WC2R 0RL, England

This is a work of fiction. Names, characters, places, and incidents either are the product of the author's imagination or are used fictitiously, and any resemblance to actual persons, living or dead, business establishments, events, or locales is entirely coincidental. The publisher does not have any control over and does not assume any responsibility for author or third-party websites or their content.

DEADLY INTENT

A Berkley Sensation Book / published by arrangement with the author

PRINTING HISTORY
Berkley Sensation mass-market edition / November 2010

Copyright © 2010 by Kim Bahnsen.
Excerpt from *Deadly Dreams* copyright © by Kim Bahnsen.
Cover art: *Red Liquid* by Paul Taylor/Stone/Getty, *Girl Against a Wall* by Antoine Rouleau/Getty,
Man Walking in Snow by Elan Cumming/Axiom Photography Agency/Getty.
Cover design by Rita Frangie.
Interior text design by Laura K. Corless.

ISBN: 978-0-425-23853-0

BERKLEY® SENSATION
Berkley Sensation Books are published by The Berkley Publishing Group,
a division of Penguin Group (USA) Inc.,
375 Hudson Street, New York, New York 10014.
BERKLEY® SENSATION and the "B" design are trademarks of Penguin Group (USA) Inc.

PRINTED IN THE UNITED STATES OF AMERICA

10 9 8 7 6 5 4 3 2 1

For Lindsey,
who deals with the acquired large extended family
with grace and aplomb.
We love you!

Acknowledgments

As usual, I'm grateful to so many for filling the gaping holes in my expertise. A very special thanks to Kevin and Mary Ann Welter for the suggested locales, maps, and pictures of areas in Colorado. Next visit we are definitely going to have to take in some of those sights! And thanks to Edd Catfish Kray, musician extraordinaire, for information on the Arapaho Forest and Conifer areas.

Much appreciation to Karl Wilmes, deputy director of the Colorado Bureau of Investigation, whose generosity of time and incisive assistance stand in stark contrast to a certain character in the story ☺. The details about Coplink were especially helpful, although I immediately took a bit of fictional license with it! And to Dr. Carole Chaski of the Institute for Linguistic Evidence and ALIAS Technology LLC, a huge thank-you for the intriguing explanation of your work as a forensic linguist. One of the best parts of this writing gig is getting glimpses into new worlds.

For all things computer related, thanks are owed to Patrick Murray who has an enviable knack for explaining technology in layman's terms. Kyle Hiller, captain with a special response team, once again came to the rescue regarding tactical response. Lee Lofland supplied necessary DNA-related details. Matt Tragna introduced me to eye-opening facts about mask-making. Vickie Taylor provided the fascinating information on air-scent dogs. Kyle Christian of Smarter Security Systems Ltd. helped devise my fictional estate's security so my villain could proceed to circumvent it ☺.

Many, many thanks to you all! With the wealth of expertise provided, any inaccuracies in the story are mine alone.

Prologue

She could hear him breathing.

Icy talons of fear shredded the fabric of sleep and brought Ellie Mulder instantly awake. Old habits had her keeping muscles lax, her eyes still closed as she strained to identify what had alerted her. When she did, her blood ran as cold as the frigid Colorado wind beating against the windows.

The sound was the same snuffle snort that warned her whenever he was coming for her. He'd returned, just like he'd threatened. He'd snatch her from her bed, from her house, and this time, she'd never get away. Not ever.

Her eyes snapped open, a scream lodged in her throat. The old terrors were surging, fighting logic, fueled by memory. It took a moment to see through the veils of the past and notice her familiar surroundings.

She was home. In her own room. In her bed. And Art Cooper wasn't here. He would die in prison.

A long sigh of relief shuddered out of her. The bright illumination of the alarm clock on her bedside table said one eighteen A.M. The sleep scene on her computer lit the corner of the room that held her desk. And the large aquarium on the opposite wall was awash in a dim glow. She often "forgot" to turn it off.

The items had been chosen because of the light they afforded. Her mom and dad had worried when she'd needed doors open and lights blazing to go to bed at night. But they'd been happy when she'd casually mentioned wanting a computer. Had expressed an interest in tropical fish. Had selected things to decorate her bedroom like the brightly lit alarm clock. Those things were *normal*, the psychologist said. And Ellie knew it was important that she seem normal. Even if it was a lie.

The slight noise sounded again and she tensed, her hand searching for the scissors she kept on the bedside table. But even as her fingers gripped the handle, her mind identified the sound. It was the gurgle of water in the overflow box for the aquarium. Not Cooper's asthmatic breathing.

The realization relaxed her, but she didn't replace the scissors. She kept them clutched in her hand and brought them close to her chest, the feel of the small weapon comforting. Learning her daughter slept with a knife under her pillow had made her mother cry. So Ellie pretended not to need that anymore.

She had become very good at pretending.

So good that her mom and dad had been thrilled with her new interest in kirigami several months ago. She'd heard the psychologist tell them that the act of creating, of folding and cutting paper into pretty shapes, would be very therapeutic for her. So there was never any fuss about the constant paper scraps on the floor. Fresh supplies appeared on her desk without her ever having to request them.

Only she knew that the new hobby was an excuse to keep a sharp pair of scissors with her at all times. And the psychologist was right. That part, at least, was very therapeutic.

The initial flare of panic had ebbed. She listened to the blizzard howl outside the windows and found the noise oddly soothing. Bit by bit, she felt herself relax. Her eyelids drooped. She had the half-formed thought that she needed to replace the scissors before her mom came in the next morning to check on her. But sleep was sucking her under, and her limbs were unresponsive.

It was then that he pounced.

The weight hit her body, jolting her from exhaustion back to alarm in the span of seconds. She felt the hand clamped over her mouth, the prick of a needle in her arm, and fear lent her strength beyond her years. Rearing up in bed, she flailed wildly, trying to wrest away, trying to strike out. She tasted the stickiness of tape over her lips. Felt a hood being pulled over her head.

There was a brief flare of triumph when the scissors met something solid, and a hiss of pain sounded in her ear. But then her hand was bent back, the weapon dropping from her fingers, and numbness started sliding over her body. She couldn't move. The hood prevented her from seeing. A strange buzzing filled her head.

As she felt herself lifted and carried away, her only thought was that she was being taken.

Again.

Chapter 1

The sleek black private jet sat waiting, its motors idling. It looked impatient somehow, looming dark and silent in the shadows, as if it had somehow taken on the personality of the man inside it.

Needles of sleet pricked Macy Reid's cheeks as she hurried across the tarmac at the Manassas Regional Airport. Adam Raiker, head of Raiker Forensics and her boss, had demanded she be there within the hour. Her home in Vienna, Virginia, was nearly twenty miles from the airport. Since the usual DC traffic was light at four A.M., she'd made it in less than forty-five minutes.

An attendant took her suitcases and stowed them for her as she wiped the frigid moisture from her cheeks and made her way up the steps to the aircraft. Her satisfaction at arriving early dissipated when she recognized the man seated in the roomy black leather seat next to her boss. Kellan Burke. Fellow forensic investigator. And the man she'd been avoiding for months.

Her stomach gave one quick lurch before she ordered it to settle. She gave Raiker a nod. "Adam." She spared barely a glance for the other man as she chose the free seat next to her boss and buckled in. "Burke."

"The inimitable duchess Macy." Kellan gave her a sleepy smile that she knew better than to trust. "Been a while since we've been paired on an investigation. Miss me?"

"Like a case of foot rot."

"A comeback," he noted admiringly. "You've been practicing."

She could feel a flush heating her cheeks and damned yet again the fair complexion that mirrored her emotions. Almost as much as she damned the man for being right. Experience had taught her that it paid to have a ready repertoire of witty replies if she was to spend any length of time in Burke's presence. Unfortunately, those replies usually occurred several hours after they were required, leaving her at the crucial moment as tongue-tied and frustrated as an eight-year-old.

It also paid to have her guard up and her hormones on a tight leash. *That* experience was more recent, and the memory much more devastating.

Adam pressed a button on his armrest that would alert the pilot to ready for takeoff. "Any squabbling and you'll ride in the luggage compartment. Both of you." He leaned forward to withdraw two file folders from the pocket of his briefcase and handed one to each of them as the jet began its taxi down the runway. Macy seized it, grateful to have something else to focus on.

"Stephen Mulder." Burke was studying the first sheet inside the folder, his expression thoughtful. "Why is that name familiar?"

"Maybe because he's the owner of the discount stores that bear his name." Raiker's voice was dry. "A quick Google check shows there are two thousand Mulders in the country, with several hundred more operations in Europe, Asia, and South America."

The name had also struck a chord of recognition with Macy, but not for the same reason. "Stephen Mulder? His daughter was one of the girls rescued when you broke that child swap ring a few years ago." The case wasn't one she was likely to forget. Her testimony had helped put one of the perpetrators behind bars. It had also brought her to Raiker's attention.

"That's right." For Burke's benefit, he explained, "Ellie Mulder was seven when she was snatched while attending a friend's birthday party. FBI took control of the investigation almost immediately. She was found incidentally when one of my cases overlapped a couple years later. I broke up a child auction, and her kidnapper was among those looking for a trade-in. By that point, she'd been missing twenty-two months."

Macy's gaze dropped to the opened folder in her lap. A moment later she froze in the act of scanning the information he'd put together for them. "She's been abducted . . . again?"

"Sometime between eleven and two A.M. this morning." Raiker's expression was grim. "The entire Denver area was having a hellacious blizzard, and Ellie's mother went in to check on her. She discovered her missing from her bed and looked around the house. Woke her husband when she didn't find her, and they searched the estate. He called me an hour after they discovered her gone."

"But not the FBI," Burke guessed shrewdly.

Macy caught Raiker's gaze on her and followed it to where her fingers lay against the folder. Her fingers were beating a familiar tattoo against the surface. *Tap-tap-tap. Tap-tap-tap. Tap-tap-tap.* Throat drying, she deliberately stilled them and refocused her thoughts.

"The feds failed her before." She met Raiker's stare, knew she was right. "They had nearly two years to find her the first time. But you're the one responsible for bringing her home to them. So her father contacted you."

Her employer inclined his head. "If the Mulders had their way, no law enforcement would be involved at all. They're pretty devoid of respect for LEOs after the last incident. But I convinced Stephen that he has no choice but to report Ellie's disappearance. He has a personal relationship with the governor and both Colorado U.S. senators. He'll use his influence to bring in the Colorado Bureau of Investigation as leads."

"Elbowing aside the Denver PD," Kellan muttered, still studying the contents of the file.

"The Mulder estate is located near Conifer. It actually falls under the jurisdiction of the Jefferson County Sheriff's Office. Mulder is still bitter at the way the feds kept him out of the loop on the first kidnapping. He's insisting we stay on his estate so he can be updated as often as possible. CBI isn't going to like that. Without proper management, this could turn into a territorial tug-of-war of monumental proportions."

Macy considered the ramifications. Being hired by a family member rather than the investigating law enforcement entity made their appearance on the scene a bit more tenuous. In a case like this, suspicion fell first on the family and those in closest proximity to the child. The CBI would worry that their allegiance to Mulder would take precedence over their commitment to teamwork. Without Raiker running interference, they could be shut out of the investigative end of things almost completely. He was going to have his plate full handling the politics of this one.

She glanced at Burke. Found him watching her through a pair of trendy dark-framed glasses that were new since the last time she'd seen him. "They're going to want to bring in their own people."

"Of course. But it's my job to convince them they don't have anyone who can match the experience the two of you bring. Don't make a liar out of me."

It took her a moment to realize Raiker was joking. It was always difficult to tell with him. "You've checked on Cooper's whereabouts?"

"Art Cooper is still in prison in Sussex, fulfilling his thirty-year sentence for the kidnap and rape of Ellie Mulder."

"And . . . the others?" It took all her resolve not to fidget under the shrewd look Raiker aimed her way.

"All accounted for, still inside serving their time."

She wouldn't have asked. Couldn't have formed the words. But in the next moment, he added deliberately, "Castillo has been bounced around some. He's currently housed at Terre Haute in Indiana."

"So are we looking at the original group you rounded up in that first case?" Burke demanded. "Do any of them have the cajones to reach out this way from prison?"

"Every avenue will need to be explored." Adam outstretched his injured leg, nudging aside the cane he was never without. "We can't afford to overlook the possibility that Ellie's disappearance this time is somehow connected to that first kidnapping. I'll line up the interviews for each with the prison wardens and make personal visits."

There was a sick knot of dread settling in the pit of Macy's stomach. With an ease born of long practice, she pushed it aside and looked at her boss. "And then we have to decide who the real target of this crime is. Ellie Mulder, or her father."

There were more than a dozen SUVs and vans parked in the wide drive that looped in a half circle in front of the sprawling Mulder estate. Additionally, what looked like a black oversized ambulance set on a sixteen wheeler was pulled up next to the house. It didn't look like Stephen Mulder had been successful in limiting the scope of the LEO presence. The still-heavy snowfall had already buried the vehicles and had slicked the roads here from the airport. A drop in temperature would make them treacherous.

Macy stepped out of the SUV and scanned the grounds. They'd been detained at the iron gates at the base of the drive, more than a quarter mile back, until the CBI agent posted there had scrutinized their IDs and waited for permission from someone inside to admit them. That had given her plenty of time to eye the twelve-foot stone walls that surrounded the property. Discreetly placed security cameras topped them at regular intervals. The security station in front of the gates was meant to be manned by a live operator. If a stranger had gotten in and out of the estate undetected, he wasn't an amateur.

The front door of the home swung open as they got out of the SUV. From the grim-faced visage of the man in the doorway, Macy knew immediately he was another CBI agent.

He waited until they'd ascended the stairs to demand their IDs again. It occurred to her that the extra precautions were a bit late. Ellie Mulder was *gone*.

"Assistant Director Cal Whitman is waiting for you in the study with Mr. Mulder. This way."

They were led through a marbled-floor hallway that was lined with paintings and punctuated by large abstract sculptures. Macy recognized some of the artists, had no doubt the pieces were original. With Mulder's billions, there was little he couldn't afford. Except the one thing his money apparently couldn't buy.

His daughter's safety.

"Not too shabby," Kellan said in an undertone as he strolled along at her side, casting an appraising look at the place. "What do you figure? Fifteen million? Twenty?"

"I wouldn't know." It was usually best to ignore Burke. But the man made it difficult. Even now she could feel his pale green eyes on her, alight, no doubt, with amusement. It seemed to be the primary emotion she elicited from him.

The hallway seemed endless. They trailed Raiker and the CBI agent who had let them in. "Pretty easy to get lost in a place this huge," Burke said, unzipping his navy down jacket and shoving his hands in its pockets. "How long do you think it would take them to locate us?"

"Why don't you find out?"

He gave her a lazy grin. The prism of lights from the crystals on the overhead chandeliers shot his thick brown hair with reddish glints. She'd bet money he'd been auburn-haired as a youngster. And probably incorrigible even then.

"If you promise to lead the search and rescue party, I might consider it. I can imagine it now. Me, weak from lack of food, maybe injured. You, bending over me in concern, wiping my brow, the strap of your lacy camisole slipping down one satiny shoulder . . ."

She resisted an urge to smack him, which was the most frequent reaction she had around him. "Why would I lead a search and rescue mission clad in a camisole?"

His smile turned wicked. "Why indeed?"

"Burke."

They both jumped at the crack of Raiker's voice. He was several feet ahead of them. They'd been speaking too quietly for him to have heard. Hadn't they? "Yeah, boss?"

"Shut up."

He slid a sideways glance at Macy and winked at her, clearly unabashed. "Shutting up, boss."

And those, she noted, as they were ushered into a large dark-paneled room, were the most promising words she'd heard all day.

The man who rose to his feet to step toward Raiker, his hand outstretched, was immediately recognizable. Stephen Mulder. He hadn't appeared at the Castillo trial Macy had testified at, but there'd been plenty of news stories devoted to his family since his daughter's first disappearance. He was prematurely gray, with a long lean runner's build outfitted in a tailored suit. Its cost likely exceeded two months of her very generous salary. As the two men clapped each other on the shoulder and leaned forward to murmur a few words, her gaze went beyond them to the others seated behind a long polished conference table. It was easy enough to guess which one was Whitman.

The assistant director had a decade on Raiker, she estimated, which would place him in his mid-fifties. It was difficult to tell his height while he was sitting, but she'd bet well under six feet. He had a shaved head and thick neck. His ill-fitting suit pulled across his beefy chest and shoulders. When his flat brown gaze flicked over them, Macy had the impression they'd been sized up in the space of an instant. There was nothing in his expression that gave away his thoughts about their inclusion in this case.

Mulder stepped away from Raiker and inclined his head in the direction of her and Burke. "Thank you for coming. I have tremendous respect for your boss. He performed a miracle once." There was a barely discernible break in his voice. "I'm hoping he's got another one up his sleeve."

"Where Raiker is concerned, achieving the impossible is

a daily expectation," Burke assured him soberly. Macy remained silent. She was always leery about issuing assurances to victims' families. Life didn't come complete with happy endings.

Mulder turned away. "Assistant Director Calvin Whitman"— he gestured to the man she'd pegged as CBI and then to the second man—"and my attorney and friend, Mark Alden. He's also Ellie's godfather."

Alden was impeccably dressed, but his dark hair was slightly mussed, and his eyes were as red-rimmed as Mulder's. He gave them a nod but said nothing.

"Why doesn't everyone sit down, and I'll catch you up." Whitman waited for them to take a seat at the table. As they shrugged out of their coats, he continued. "Since the Mulders insist you all need to reside here on scene in case a ransom demand comes in, he's agreed to extend his hospitality to a few of my team members, as well. As per Mr. Mulder's request to the governor, I brought a small team of agents, and we arrived around five thirty. My people are completing the search of the house and beginning to go over the grounds. An AMBER Alert was issued before I arrived on the scene by the governor's office." There was a flicker in the man's eyes at this breach of protocol. "I'll be coordinating the interagency involvement on this case. The Jefferson County Sheriff's Department will handle the calls regarding the alert and fully investigate each. I've been assured the Denver Police Department will offer personnel and resources if any leads overlap into their jurisdiction."

"Has the alert elicited any calls yet?"

Whitman didn't appear to appreciate Kell's interruption. "There's been no trace of the child reported so far. I have an agent taking Mrs. Mulder's statement. The live-in help have been interviewed and the other employees contacted. Many have arrived already. We're preparing to question them."

"Stephen just finished his statement for Agent Whitman when you arrived." It was the first time the lawyer had spoken. "We'll expect a copy of it, and of all the case notes, to be shared with Mr. Raiker's team members in an expedient manner."

The tilt of Whitman's head could have meant anything. But it was telling, Macy thought, that he had made no verbal agreement.

Mulder obviously thought so, too. "Just so we're clear on this, Agent." He placed his palms on the table and leaned forward, his tone fierce. "Raiker's unit is here with the blessing of the Colorado governor and our U.S. senators. They *will* be a full part of this team." He gave a humorless smile. "I've been through this before. I know how it works. Althea and I are suspects until proven otherwise. So is everyone else in this house. I realize that effectively shuts me out of most of the details in this investigation. But the person I trust won't be shut out. He's here to be sure other aspects of the investigation don't stall while you're wasting your time eliminating us as suspects." When the CBI agent would have spoken, he waved aside his protest. "I'm not waiting two years to bring my little girl home this time."

He made a slight gesture, and Alden got to his feet, as well. "I recognize there's information that you won't share in my presence, so Mark and I will leave now. I want to be there for Althea when they've finished with her."

The room was silent as the men left, shutting the door behind them. Upon their exit, Whitman eased his bulk back in his chair and eyed Raiker. "Your inclusion here puts us in a dilemma. You have to realize that."

"The thing about dilemmas is they always have solutions." Adam's voice was no less steely. "Consider those solutions, Agent. You can't afford not to utilize us."

The other man rubbed the folds at the back of his neck. "We don't have grounds to force the Mulders out of their home for the duration of the case, but I would if I could."

Adam's smile was feral. "No one is making you take up residence here. That was your idea."

"If you're here, we're here. You have to . . ." He paused then, seemed to choose his words more carefully. "I'm *sug-*

gesting that you avoid any conflict of interest by waiting for
my people to complete the search of the premises. So far, this
floor has been cleared. I've got a crime scene evidence recovery unit going over the girl's room right now."

"And once they're done, we have free access to the property and copies of any and all reports as they're formulated."
Raiker clearly knew how to play the game. "My people will
be included in all briefings and task assignments."

"The information is a two-way street." The agent looked
at Macy and Kellan, making no attempt to mask his expression now that Mulder had gone. The man was plainly unhappy with their presence. "If I learn that you've withheld
something from me, you're off the case and I'll have you
detained for obstruction."

Macy noted Raiker's fingers clenching around the intri-
cately carved knob of his cane. It was his only sign of temper. His voice, when it came, was even. "Threats are the
realm of the unimaginative. You've got some very powerful
people lined up behind Stephen Mulder. They were summoned
because the investigation into the previous kidnapping of
Ellie Mulder went nowhere."

"And you were the superstar there. Yeah, I got that." Curi-
ously, the squaring off seemed to have eased something in
the other man. "I knew your rep when you were with the
bureau." His gaze lingered on Raiker then, as if taking in the
eye patch and the scars on his throat and hands. "Got another
earful about your outfit from my director. As long as we
understand each other, I think we ought to get along well
enough."

His focus traveled between her and Burke. "Which of you
is the forensic linguist?"

"I am."

His gaze settled on Macy then. "We don't have a ransom
note. At least nothing's been found yet. But if the offender is
going to reach out, I'd expect it to be fairly soon. Give him
time to see the girl secured and then turn his attention to the
next matter."

"I have a few contacts in the penal department." Macy

was certain Adam's words were a gross understatement. The man seemed to know people everywhere. "Everyone scooped up in that last case where Ellie was rescued is accounted for in his respective prison."

"And there's no one else out there that maybe slipped by you guys?" The gibe was nearly hidden in Whitman's words. "How can you be sure you got everyone affiliated with that case?"

Raiker lifted a shoulder. "I had no reason to suspect otherwise, but anything is possible. That's why I'm arranging another round of interviews with each suspect involved. I've got phone calls in to each warden to set them up."

"Video?"

"In person."

The special agent grunted. "That'll save us some serious time and manpower."

"When will we have access to the scene? And the rest of the house?"

Macy caught the barely discernible note of frustration in Kell's voice. She seconded it. As private forensic consultants, it was rare to be called to a fresh crime scene. This was one of the quickest callouts she'd ever participated in, and they were effectively being shut away from the scene for several more hours, if not longer.

"When the crime scene evidence recovery unit is finished. It'll be evening at the earliest. Until then, you can participate in the interviews of the employees. They've already started and will probably take us most of the day."

"How many people are we talking about?"

Whitman glanced down at a sheet of paper in front of him. But before he could answer Macy's question, Adam said, "Mulder employs over thirty full- and part-time employees in the winter months. That would include the daughter's teacher and various instructors: piano, dance, whatnot."

"How many live on the grounds?"

"None live in the house," the special agent said, "but the teacher has an apartment over one of the garages. A mechanic, two stable hands, and a couple groundskeepers have places above various other outbuildings. Everyone else lives off-site." He consulted his notes again. "Half a dozen security officers, six maids, two drivers, three cooks, one personal assistant—a sort of secretary to Mrs. Mulder—a hairdresser, masseuse . . . it's like a damn village around here."

"And how many of those people were on the grounds yesterday?" Kell asked.

"In addition to the family, there were thirty on the property at some point." He lifted a shoulder. "A few never made it in because of the weather. Others left early. All have been notified that they're wanted in for questioning. About three-quarters have arrived so far. A couple business associates were on the property yesterday, too, as Mulder was working from home. His lawyer, Mark Alden, who you met. Lance Spencer, the firm's accountant, and Tessa Amundson, Mr. Mulder's executive secretary. By his account, which was verified by Alden, they worked through lunch and dinner, with everyone departing by seven thirty."

"You would have looked at the tapes first," Macy noted. She wondered if the agent had been getting to that or if he wouldn't have brought it up if she hadn't asked. "They've got live video feed, right? That means a security station inside the property with someone manning the cameras. Something had to have shown up on them."

"Nothing that we've found yet. But we've only been at it a couple hours. I've got some of the best techs in the agency going over that feed. Whatever is there, we'll find it."

"How many of the security officers have arrived?"

Macy shot Kell an approving glance. They were on the same page. Right now, she was most interested in the interviews of the security officers. One of them had to know something or at least have ideas. No one knew the ins and outs of the estate's safety precautions better.

"Two were on-site when we got here. All but one of the others has arrived."

"Tell us about the security specs." Raiker had assumed a careless slouch. Macy recognized that the position relieved the cramps that frequently seized his leg. She knew better than to call attention to it.

"Well, you saw the twelve-foot walls around the perimeter," Whitman said dryly. "The grounds are secured by cameras mounted every seventy feet, and motion detectors. Two criteria are required for an alarm to sound—pixel change on the camera and motion on the sensors. The guard station is manned twenty-four, seven. Gates don't open without keycard ID and thumbprint identification. Then the vehicles and their undercarriages are inspected before they're allowed through. The same procedure is followed when exiting."

Raiker's voice was sharp. "But the guard out front has override powers."

"No. Override can only be done from the inside. But we've found no record of that yesterday. We're looking deeper."

Burke was exuding impatience. In a corner of her mind, Macy was slightly disturbed to realize she knew the man well enough to read him so well. But his emotion mirrored her own. "Let's get to those interviews then," she said. "Starting with Mulder's security team." There didn't appear to be any way to get onto the estate without security knowing about it.

Which meant one of the members of the team may have been involved in Ellie's kidnapping.

"You've got people out there looking, right?" Chief of Security Ben Cramer folded his arms across his massive chest, his midnight gaze unwavering. "While you're wasting your time on us, the trail's going to shit. Whoever snatched the kid could have her out of the state while you sit here with your thumbs up your asses. We're paid damn well to keep the family safe. My team's the last place you ought to be looking."

"You're head of Mulder's security." CBI Agent in Charge Dan Travis ignored the man's question, and his insult. "You know the specifications better than anyone else. What's the weakness in the system?"

"There isn't one." Cramer's response was immediate. "With all the checks and balances in place, there's no way an unauthorized individual can come on the grounds, waltz in the house, grab the kid, and get out again. I have a team of six rotating through twenty-four-hour security; two-man shifts of twelve hours each, three days a week."

Travis looked ponderous as he did some mental math. "That leaves you with a couple men two days short for their full week."

"Which gives us extra hands to deal with vacations and for those times Mr. Mulder requires personal protection. You think we're a bunch of novices here? I provided security for every major U.S. diplomat to visit Iraq during the first couple years of the war. I earned my chops dodging roadside bombs, not pushing papers."

"No system is flawless," Macy put in crisply. Cramer's attitude wasn't totally unexpected, since it reflected that of the other men they'd interviewed from his team. "The girl is gone. Either an intruder entered the estate—"

"Impossible," the man interjected.

"—or someone known to her carried her away. Either way, there should be video of it."

Cramer's gaze traveled from one of them to the other. "I'm guessing if you'd found it, you wouldn't be wasting time talking to me."

"The fact that we haven't discovered anything on the cameras should worry you, Cramer." Travis leaned forward, his square jaw tight. "Either there's a major flaw in the system—which, as head of security, you should have discovered—or the video feed was disrupted in some way, which again, should have been foreseen."

Cramer gave a short caustic laugh. "If you think every possible turn of events can be anticipated, you've been in your ivory tower too long."

"That's exactly what we're talking about." Macy eyed the two men cautiously. They looked like a couple strange dogs, snarling and snapping at each other, readying to lunge. "She didn't just vanish into thin air. Whether you want to admit it or not, there was some sort of security breakdown. Your team is obviously best acquainted with the specs of the system. Either one of them is involved, or there was a huge failure of some sort. Convince us of which it was."

The other man hesitated, as if seeing the trap in her words. Finally he ran a hand over his graying buzzed hair and said guardedly, "There are always improvements that can be made."

"Such as?"

He flicked a look at the CBI agent, but Travis remained silent, apparently willing for Macy to take the lead for the moment. "I suggested several times to Mr. Mulder that there should be cameras inside the house. A couple men posted in here. He always refused. Said he wanted to keep his daughter safe but didn't want her to feel like she was a prisoner anymore."

Macy's skin prickled. Of course, Cooper would have had some sort of surveillance monitoring the girl while he'd kept her captive. He'd continued to work and socialize, to volunteer at a local soup kitchen, and to serve as a lector in his church. Although she didn't know all the details of that case, she imagined he'd kept the child locked up. Maybe used a computer and webcam to keep track of her throughout the day.

It was understandable that her father wouldn't have wanted any reminders of that surveillance for his daughter when she was returned home.

"What else?"

Cramer lifted a shoulder. "Isn't it enough? I pointed out that if we allowed people access—repairmen, caterers—maybe one stays behind. Hides in the house. Place is big as a fortress. He bides his time, maybe fills his pockets. Maybe plans an assault. So Mr. Mulder took other precautions. They never entertain here, always in their penthouse in the city without the kid around. And anyone let in from the outside like that, a couple of my men are allowed to accompany them inside. Stay with them the entire time and then escort them back out to their vehicle again."

"The log doesn't show any outside access for the last nine weeks," Agent Travis pointed out.

Cramer shrugged again. With his yard-wide shoulders, he could have doubled as a linebacker. "There isn't much traffic through here. Mr. Mulder, he's careful about bringing anyone new on the property. Takes months just to get security clearance on new employees."

Prisons could have different walls. It occurred to Macy that Ellie Mulder had been just as much a captive here as she'd been with Cooper. Raiker had mentioned a teacher living on the premises. Apparently the child wasn't even allowed to attend school, for fear of risking her safety.

"Anything like that, the exterior cameras still would have picked up the guy exiting the house," the agent put in.

"It's my job to point out weaknesses to the boss." Cramer shrugged. "I was satisfied with the alternate precautions we put in place. But you asked about flaws. That's the only one I came across when we went over the specs before putting the system in place."

"Who has access to the security cameras and codes?"

"My men work the front gate or monitor the cameras. I'm the only one on the team with the override code." He immediately corrected himself. "At least the first half of the set. Two code strings are necessary to override the cameras or turn them off. And I wasn't on the property at all yesterday."

"Who has both sets of codes?"

"Mulder. And the company that designed the system."

Travis gave a humorless smile. "Smart guy like you, you could probably figure out a way around that second set of codes and circumvent the system at a time of your choosing."

The two men exchanged hard stares. "You need to talk to the security company," Cramer snapped. "It can't be done. That's why it's cutting-edge. That's why it cost nearly a half a million bucks."

"You realize you've just indicated Stephen Mulder is the only person who could have gotten his daughter off this estate without any video recording of it."

"The hell I did." Macy thought for a moment the security chief was going to come across the table at the agent's suggestion. "That was your scenario, remember? There's no way in hell Mulder arranged to have his own daughter snatched. You see the lengths the man went to in order to protect her?"

"Yeah, everything's impossible, according to you." Temper was leaking through Travis's formally professional tone. "Except the girl's *gone*. And you're sitting here trying to convince us it couldn't happen. Not with you at the security helm. Well, if that's true, how the hell did she get off the property?"

"Maybe she didn't."

Macy's gaze flew up, distracted momentarily from the notes she was scribbling about the interview. "What do you mean?"

Cramer jerked his head toward the CBI agent. "His outfit couldn't find their asses with an extra set of hands. Since me and my men weren't allowed to help search, I'm not convinced she isn't still in the house somewhere."

"You have some spots you suggest we check out?" The agent's tone was silky.

Cramer didn't take the bait. "Oh, you probably looked real hard at the places a kid's body could be stashed. We've got two feet of snow outside. She could be anywhere on the grounds. Or in the house. Trouble with you guys is you don't look for the unexpected."

"Maybe you'd like to—"

Fed up with the two men, Macy interrupted Travis. "What aren't we looking for?"

For a minute she thought the security chief wouldn't answer. He seemed to be having a difficult time contemplating whether it was worth it to take a swing at the CBI agent. Then after several long moments he broke eye contact with the other man to look at her.

"Like I say, they're looking for a spot big enough to hide a kid." The man's expression didn't change, but his eyes went bleak. "Maybe you ought to be searching smaller spots. Just big enough to hide pieces of her."

Chapter 2

"You think Cramer's involved?"

Whitman was alone in the conference room. But Macy didn't have more than a moment to wonder at Raiker's whereabouts. Travis didn't so much as hesitate before responding to the question.

"I think it's a possibility." He ran his hand over his short-cropped dark hair. "I'd bet money he did a lot more in Iraq than drive diplomats around."

The assistant director looked at Macy. "You were there. What was your impression?"

"Cramer's understandably defensive," she said. "Ellie disappeared on his watch. He may not have been here yesterday, but he's in charge, so the failure's his. I found his demeanor to be in keeping with that feeling of responsibility, not necessarily as a sign of personal involvement."

Whitman's gaze shifted to settle on Kell. "What about the other interviews?"

He lifted a shoulder. "All the guards claim Cramer doesn't have both sets of codes necessary to override the system, and

Mulder verifies that. It doesn't sound as though any on the security team had open access to the house. Personal protection wasn't part of their duties while on the property. If it's someone known to the girl, I'd bet on a person who's regularly inside the home."

"I say we need to dig deeper into Cramer's background," Travis insisted stubbornly. "He kept referring to his experience. I'd be interested in exactly what all he was involved in while in Iraq."

"We're looking at everyone's backgrounds," Whitman said. "Should have some preliminary data soon. Dobson is handling that end." He inclined his head toward the thin balding agent sitting at the end of the table with his head bent over a computer. "What's the feel from the rest of the security team you've interviewed?"

"We've talked to all but one. A"—Travis checked his notes—"Nicholas Hubbard. He hasn't shown up yet."

"Everyone says the same thing." Kell drummed his fingers on the table. "Nothing out of the ordinary has occurred in over two months, and that was just a visit from the satellite TV company. The team seems tight. They accept Cramer as the leader. Seem to respect him. He and this Hubbard sound like they're the brains as far as the cameras go. A couple others have some extra training with alarm systems."

Whitman's interest sharpened. "Enough training to allow them to circumvent the system?"

Kell looked dubious. "Anything's possible. But the security company rep I called maintains it would be unlikely. They claim they don't even have anyone on their staff capable of it, and they install the things."

Travis snorted. "Like they'd admit their product was easily manipulated."

Whitman's chair creaked as he redistributed his bulk. "So Hubbard's your last interview for the security members? When's he expected in?"

"I called him. Twice. Said he'd be right here. Gave me the exact same line both times, verbatim," Travis informed them. "Probably should contact him again to see if he's left this time. He only lives twenty-five minutes away. I can't believe it takes an hour, even in this weather."

As usual, Macy found herself sidetracked by words. "Verbatim? Or close to it?"

Travis frowned, his blue eyes narrowing. "Verbatim. Answers the phone by saying 'Hubbard.' Listens a couple seconds then says, 'Be right there.' But he was still home the second time I called, so he obviously wasn't in a . . ."

Kell and Macy's chairs scraped as they pushed them back and rose as one. Travis seemed to catch on a moment later and jumped to his feet.

"It was a recording," Whitman said in disgust. He was already reaching for his cell phone as the three of them headed for the door. "I'll get the DPD over to his address right away and have them sit on the place until you get there."

Macy shrugged into her coat and pulled her hat out of her pocket, pulling it on as she strode through the office door. The man didn't have to voice the rest of the remark. It was highly unlikely that Hubbard was still at his house. He'd had plenty of time to run.

Very possibly with Ellie Mulder in tow.

———

Settled in the backseat with Agent Travis at the wheel, Macy dialed the number the agent had given her for Hubbard. After three rings it was picked up. In an eerie replay of the agent's recital, the disembodied low voice growled, "Hubbard." Remaining silent, she waited for the rest of it. Several moments later that same voice said, "Be right there," and the call was disconnected.

Thoughtfully, Macy redialed. Listened again. There was nothing of note in the words themselves, or in their tone.

"Does Hubbard live in a house or a flat?"

"Flat?" Kell slid a glance at the silent agent driving beside him. "This Hubbard live in London by any chance?"

"Denver," the agent said shortly. He was plainly still annoyed that he'd bungled on Hubbard's call.

Annoyed, she corrected herself. "Apartment, then." Trust

Burke to catch her slip and make a big deal out of it. "Do we know if he lives alone?"

"Her accent tends to be more pronounced when she's heated up over something," Burke said in an aside to the agent. "Friendly word of warning, she can get real haughty, too. She's got this whole duchess-to-serf attitude that she slaps you alongside the head with when you piss her off."

"I most certainly do not have an accent." Hearing the crisp clip to her words, Macy silently damned her British boarding schools. "And I've never seen anyone more in need of a slap alongside the head." She almost delivered it, too, when she caught his meaningful glance at Travis, and the agent's small grin.

Fuming, she sat back in the seat and stared out the window, which was already decorated with a thick collection of fat flakes since it'd been cleaned off at the estate. The snow wasn't heavy enough for visibility to be a problem, but there was still plenty on the road, which didn't look as though it had seen a snowplow recently. It was entirely possible that the missing security agent, Hubbard, had run his car into the ditch on the way there.

She'd almost believe it, if not for the voice mail recording.

It had served its purpose well enough. Everyone else on the security team had expressed shock, bravado, or anger at the girl's disappearance. Hubbard should have been there, doing everything in his power to convince them, as his fellow team members had, that he wasn't involved. That *none* of them could be involved.

His absence pointed a neon *guilty* arrow in his direction. The prerecorded phone message bought him time. But time to do what?

She didn't know the answer but was fairly certain his place would be empty by the time the patrol officers got there.

"According to the records Mulder keeps, Hubbard has a house," the agent answered belatedly. "The team all rotates four days on and three off. Hubbard worked until four yesterday afternoon."

"And do the cameras have him on tape leaving the estate after his shift?"

There was silence in the vehicle in response to Burke's question. What had or hadn't been captured on tape was still a mystery. But it wouldn't hurt to ask Raiker. He'd still been nowhere in sight when they'd left the estate, and she needed to update him anyway.

Macy pressed the speed dial number for him on her cell phone and was rewarded a moment later with his familiar brusque tone. "You took off fast."

"We're chasing down the last of the security guards. The only one who didn't show up for an interview."

"Hubbard. Whitman and I are in the camera room right now. We've got enough to get a warrant for his house."

For the benefit of the two men in the car, she repeated, "You're getting a warrant for Hubbard's place?"

Burke jerked around in his seat as far as his seat belt would allow, staring hard at her.

To forestall the litany of questions sure to tumble off his lips, she switched the settings on the cell to speakerphone. "I assume you're looking at yesterday's feed." Adrenaline was doing a fast sprint up her spine. "Do you have footage of the girl's disappearance?"

"The techs are still working on that. But we have footage of Hubbard coming to work yesterday. We just don't have anything showing him leaving."

"Son of a bitch," Kell muttered.

"Then his vehicle could still be on the property somewhere?" Macy's mind was working furiously.

"One would think." Raiker's voice was dry. "But who knows? If we don't have feed of anyone leaving with the girl, why should we be surprised that there's no video record of Hubbard's car leaving?" His voice went muffled then, and she could hear conversation in the background.

"What's going on?" Kell demanded impatiently. "Who's he talking to?"

Macy ignored him. It was frequently the best solution. And one she'd often wished she'd chosen six months ago.

Travis said, "There's a large garage at the west end of the property for employee use. One of the agents would have been dispatched to take license and model information of all those vehicles right away this morning."

"But have they been matched with the owners?" Since none of them had an answer to her question, it remained largely rhetorical. Macy could feel her own impatience rising until Raiker finally came back on the line.

"Hubbard's car is still in the employee garage," Raiker said. "It's doubtful you'll find anyone at his place, but wait for an officer to show up with the warrant. I've been assured it'll be expedited."

"When can we expect . . ." The line went dead. Experience had her certain it was her boss's usual abruptness to blame rather than phone malfunction.

"Great." Movements jerky with frustration, Kell exchanged his glasses for prescription sunglasses. "Looks like Hubbard is in this up to his neck. And we'll be freezing our respective asses off waiting hours for a warrant before we can get inside his place for a look. Hope this heap has a good heater."

"CBI isn't exactly the neighborhood watch." The tail end of the car fishtailed then, and expertly Travis counter-steered out of the one-hundred-eighty-degree spin. "Whitman will get the warrant, and it won't take all day, either. Look at it this way—we could be stuck at the estate, typing up interviews. Whitman's making noises about sticking someone with those duties, at least until he can get a secretary out there."

Macy caught his eye on her in the rearview mirror and lied blandly, "I don't type." Although she shared Burke's frustration with the situation, she thought she was more adept at controlling her emotions than he was.

Of course, a ten-year-old would be better than Burke was in that area.

The vehicle swerved again, and the agent slowed down even more. Peering out the window, she spied the patchy areas of ice glinting through the tire tracks on the road in front of them. No telling how long it was going to take them to cover the usual thirty-minute trip. At this rate, the warrant could beat them to Hubbard's house.

"Is that employee garage heated?"

Travis lifted a shoulder. "Don't know for sure, but I'd guess yes. The Mulder estate doesn't seem to lack any of the amenities."

Kell seemed to know where she was heading. It was one of the few advantages to working with him. His quick wits were useful for more than coming up with smart-ass quips. "So we have to wonder if there was also surveillance in the garages and outbuildings. If it were me trying to protect my family, I'd have security there. Just another measure in place in case someone somehow bypassed the system at the gate."

She gave a satisfied nod. "So if he hid in the garage or car, those cameras were manipulated as well." Because it was almost certain some of the others had been. "Otherwise someone would have noted it or the fact that Hubbard never returned to the vehicle at all."

Kell turned to look at her. "Which makes you wonder where the hell the bastard stashed himself from four o'clock until sometime after eleven."

"And how he got off the estate on foot, carrying the girl."

"The least the son of a bitch could have done was leave his garbage out." The vents under the dash were blasting out heat, so Kell moved his feet farther away. Already they were sweating inside the insulated boots he wore. It was either freeze or sweat to death while they waited in the SUV. There was no middle ground. "We could at least legally go through that while we wait."

Despite Travis's assurances to the contrary, they'd been sitting nearly two hours since their arrival, after it had taken them twice the usual time to cover the distance to Hubbard's house from Mulder's. Once the agent had badged the officers watching the house, they'd told them all they knew about the property, which had been exactly zilch. No one had been in or out of it since they'd been dispatched to the scene. The snow on the driveway was pristine. The partially filled-in boot prints up to and around the house belonged to the officers, according to them. Kell didn't need the absence of tracks to be able to figure that Hubbard hadn't returned here recently.

They'd spent the intervening time door-knocking and talking to the neighbors they could find at home, largely in vain. Most claimed they hadn't noticed anything out of the ordinary around the Hubbard house for the last few days. Macy had elicited the only useful information.

He glanced in the backseat to note her bent over her PDA. In deference to the warmth in the vehicle, she'd pulled off the butt-ugly hat she'd been wearing to allow her dark hair to curl around her face and shoulders. He remembered vividly that it was as fine and soft as a child's. With those startling pale blue eyes fringed with absurdly long lashes, she looked about as intimidating as a kitten. No wonder Hubbard's neighbor across the street had opened up to her.

According to the lady, Paula Graves, the last time lights had been seen in the man's house was the night before the kidnapping. She'd worked second shift and had seen one inside light on before she'd gone to bed, which had been nearly one. She'd remembered it, she said, because Nick wasn't a night owl like she was. If he was home, his lights were always off by eleven.

And that, Kell considered as he unzipped his coat, meant exactly nothing. Which matched what they had so far on this case.

"So what's a place in this neighborhood cost in Denver?" he asked conversationally.

Travis reached over to turn down the heat. "How should I know?" His voice was irritated. "I'm not a real estate agent. Besides, I live in a condo."

"Fine choice," Kell said approvingly. "Houses are just a pain in the ass, right? Lawn care, snow removal . . . who the hell needs that?"

"People who prefer some character in their homes?" murmured Macy, without looking up.

Ignoring her, he continued. "According to the info Dobson gave us, Hubbard lives alone." The agent was regularly updating them as more details came to light. "What makes a single guy buy a house instead of renting an apartment? Especially if he's planning to stage a high-profile kidnapping in the state?"

"Maybe he wasn't planning it that long." Travis seemed inclined to play devil's advocate. "He's only worked for Mulder for eighteen months. Could be he worked the job day in and day out and thoughts started to form. Maybe harmless at first. If it could be done and how. Then he starts thinking about the money."

"There's been no ransom demand."

This time they both ignored the voice in the backseat. "Or maybe someone approaches him. Says, hey, you can get in, why don't you grab up the kid and I'll cut you in for a slice?"

"Almost has to be more than one involved," Travis stated and Kell nodded. This operation was too big, too complex for a solitary person. The kid wasn't snatched at a low-supervision birthday party this time. She'd been abducted from a property equipped with the most high-tech security measures he'd ever seen at a private residence. That took someone with technical knowledge. The guard might have had the expertise with cameras and live feed, but there had also been the motion detectors to contend with. Not to mention getting into the house itself. All required highly specialized knowledge. But would the same guy also have the experience on grabbing and keeping a hostage?

Because for the life of him, despite Ellie Mulder's background, he didn't see this being the work of a common lowlife pedophile. They usually chose easier pickings. Kids walking home from school or unsupervised at a mall. A playground. Sure, there were instances of them being snatched from their homes, but not off properties as well-protected as this one.

He was willing to bet they'd discover the girl wasn't the target this time, her father was. Was it money? Revenge? He cocked his head, considering the question. They wouldn't know the answer until—and if—a ransom demand was made.

"If money's the motive, there's got to be a cash guy, too.

Someone who will deal with the demand and direct the pay-off or pickup. What's the likelihood security guy has the experience with that?" He tried to remember the update on Hubbard's background that had arrived via Dobson. "He'd worked at a prison, right? Manned their cameras and live feed for fifteen years. Yeah, might have had access to some criminal talent on the job, but I doubt they had support groups on the how-tos of child abductions."

"Raiker looked into the inmates housed at Florence during Hubbard's tenure there. Only three were serving time for kidnapping."

He didn't need Macy's reminder. He'd heard the boss's terse phone report himself.

"He's wasting his time there," Travis said surely. "The man worked in security, not in inmate control. He wouldn't even have had contact with the population."

"Hubbard's property was purchased for three hundred and ninety-five thousand dollars over a year ago." Macy looked up from her PDA when he glanced back at her. "What kind of money was he making with Mulder?"

"Almost a third of that," Travis responded. "The man re-cruits the best and doesn't mind paying them."

"So the place isn't out of the ballpark, given his salary." Kell checked his watch. The exchange was merely a way to pass the time. There wasn't a damn thing they could be sure of until they got inside. He watched Hubbard's next-door neighbor power up a snowblower and begin the torturous job of clearing the walk in front of his house, inwardly shaking his head. If that was part of the *character* of home owning, he'd take his town house, any day.

"We've got company." Macy's words had his attention jerking back to the street. The squad car rolling to a stop be-side them hopefully meant that their forced idleness was over. He got out of the car and waited impatiently for Travis to accept the paperwork that had taken—he checked his watch again—a little over three and a half hours to process. Light-ninglike speed to get a judge to sign a warrant, but he'd never been a fan of stakeouts.

When Travis had finished with the officer, he tucked the warrant inside his coat before circling to the back of the vehicle and popping the trunk. Macy joined them and they grabbed their evidence kits before heading for the nondescript stucco house.

"Where do you want to enter?"

"Less noticeable if we go in the back."

Snow-blowing guy already seemed more interested in them than he was in his task. Kell led the way around the attached garage, where they'd be out of sight of nosy neighbors. The most recent footprints in the deep snow were theirs. They'd taken a look through the windows and knocked on doors when they'd first arrived, with no more success than the officers had had.

"Is there an alarm system?" Macy asked as they headed up the stone steps.

"It doesn't matter . . ." Travis started.

"Give me a few minutes. I think I can circumvent." Kell opened his kit and withdrew his picks before shoving the bag in Macy's arms.

"Circumvent?" Doubt dropped from her word.

"There's no need for that, Burke." Travis was stamping the snow off his boots. "We'll set the alarm off once we're in anyway. Just kick the damn door in."

"That's one solution. But it lacks finesse." He pulled off his gloves and stuffed them in his pockets. Flexing his fingers, he squatted to peer into the state-of-the-art dead bolt. "Ah, six-pin double cylinder. An expensive one, too. Bet they told you it was pickproof, didn't they? Idiots." Pulling on a pair of rubber gloves from the kit, he selected the torque and rake tools and went to work.

"You believe this?" the agent muttered to Macy.

"Oddly . . . yes."

He barely heard them. He was in that familiar zone, listening for pins to release as he delicately manipulated the picks.

"You'll trip the alarm anyway, so what's the use of us

standing out here freezing our asses . . ." Travis's words trailed off as Kell withdrew the tools and rose, turning the knob and pushing the door open. The agent looked at him, then at the door.

"What was that? Under thirty seconds, right?" Kell had forgotten to look at his watch before starting. "Did anyone time me?"

"What are you, six?" Macy jammed his kit against his chest with a bit more force than he thought necessary before stepping carefully over the threshold to the rug spread on the floor in front of the door. She glanced at the keypad mounted next to the doorjamb. The officer stationed out front could deal with the security company rep sent over to check on the silent alarm their entry would set off.

Travis muttered, "A drill would have been faster."

"As it happens, I'm equally adept with a snap gun, but it doesn't hold the same challenge." He gestured for the agent to proceed through the door ahead of him while he tucked the picks inside his coat. Macy already had her boots off and shoe covers on her stocking feet. He followed suit, watching carefully to be sure the agent pulled on gloves and shoe covers. Raiker would have his ass if every effort wasn't made to preserve evidence.

He swung the door shut behind him and just stood still for a moment, absorbing impressions. They were standing in a kitchen that hadn't been modernized for a couple decades. There was an automatic coffeemaker tucked in the corner of the counter, the pot still a quarter full. A cell phone charger was plugged in next to it, minus the cell phone. A thermal stainless steel coffee tumbler sat next to the sink, along with a small insulated lunch cooler. Kell eyed the items but didn't move toward them. Not then. Time enough to collect evidence, and he was willing to bet the coffee tumbler would be a prime depository for Hubbard's DNA. First though, he wanted a thorough look around.

There was nothing else out of place in the area. "Does the security team take lunch to work?"

Travis was moving through the kitchen into the adjoining room. "The cooks I interviewed say they feed the indoor help. Everyone else is on their own."

They stepped into a large family room, and it was immediately easy to guess the room was Hubbard's priority. A huge-screen TV and bookcase took up most of one wall, with two leather recliners and a couple matching couches arranged around it. The kitchen had been nondescript, but there'd be something of the security guard's personality here. This is where he'd relaxed after working all day. Entertained here, too, probably, if that was his thing.

The CBI agent was studying the TV. "I've got one almost like this, except a couple years older."

"Yeah?" Kell picked up the remote and turned the power on. "A Sony? Samsung's the brand to go with these days. The picture can't be beat, even without HD."

"Samsung, huh? I'd heard . . ."

"TVs? Really?"

Kell lifted a shoulder at Macy's pointed comment and watched while the picture formed on the screen. "Just getting a feel for the place, Duchess. Taking our time. Being careful." She was much too proper to snort, but the sound she made came suspiciously close. He checked the channel on the screen when it came on. ESPN. And the program menu showed the DVR set for times and channels featuring pro football. So the guy had a thing for high-tech TVs and football. Didn't exactly make Hubbard unique. But it began to paint of picture of the absent guard that had so far been largely blank.

The other two had fanned out. Kell clicked off the TV and went toward the desk tucked in the corner with a computer sitting on it. "What's the scope of the warrant?"

Travis pulled out the paperwork and surveyed it for a minute before giving a low whistle. "Rooms, contents, drawers, safes, electronic devices . . . anything deemed possible to hide a body or plans of the crime."

"Nice." Impressed, he booted up the computer. There was no such thing as a limitless warrant, but this one was exceedingly generous in its scope. Whether that was due to the CBI's influence or Mulder's wasn't worth speculating. The computer's welcome screen blinked at him, inviting him to enter a password. He muttered an obscenity. His magic with locks definitely didn't extend to computers. "I don't suppose you have some decent hacking skills?" he called to the agent, without much hope.

"We'll take it in." The man was squatted in front of the fireplace, looking inside it. Kell could have told him he was wasting his time. It was outfitted with a cheap gas insert, and Hubbard would have had to be a moron to consider trying to burn something in it. Given the crime the man was suspected of, stupid probably wasn't an accurate adjective.

He riffled through the papers on the surface of the desk. Household bills. Fantasy football picks and strategy tips. His brows rose as he skimmed that sheet. With those selections, Hubbard would need all the tips he could get.

Macy returned from the adjoining dining room and went to the hallway closet. The phone on the desk had the message light blinking. Kell stabbed at the replay button, but there were just a handful of hang-ups.

"Must have just recorded his message and set the phone to go straight to voice mail after a couple rings," he mused.

"It didn't sound like voice mail," Travis muttered. He was looking under the couch cushions and checking the pockets along the side.

Kell set the phone aside to be collected later and began pulling open the drawers on the desk, pulling out a few old receipts and some fast-food menus. Hubbard's taste seemed to run to pizza and Malaysian. There were a couple bank account passbooks, one for checking and the other for savings. The guard had a balance of eighteen hundred and change in checking and nearly ten thousand in savings. He opened the next drawer and found a notepad, flipped through it. He looked up when Macy reentered the room. "Find anything?"

"No. Except that the man is exceptionally neat. The carpet's been freshly vacuumed. I'm heading upstairs."

The CBI agent veered in her direction so Kell trailed after

them up the staircase. There were three bedrooms and a bath on the second floor. Two of the bedrooms were furnished but looked unused and as generic as the kitchen. The remaining bedroom had an unmade king-sized bed. Drawers were hanging out of the dresser. He strolled over to take a look. "So much for being a neat freak. Someone was in a hurry." The remaining contents didn't even leave the drawers half-full.

"Here, too." Macy opened the closet doors wider and he saw the empty hangers inside. She crouched down to dig in the corners of the space, and her coat pulled up, revealing a very fine ass rounding out her black pants. Which was a purely objective observation, and not the reason he headed in her direction.

"A duffel bag is in here, but the marks on the carpet look like something heavier had sat next to it. A bigger suitcase maybe?" She rose and put her hands on her hips, eyeing the overhead shelf. It was filled with some cardboard boxes, but it was the mini filing cabinet in the opposite corner of the closet floor that caught his attention.

Kell squatted before it and tugged on the top drawer. Locked, but these things wouldn't challenge an eight-year-old. He amused himself by pulling out the tools he'd placed in his coat pocket and picking it with his left hand before looking up to check on Macy's progress. She was on tiptoe, stretching as far as her five-foot-five or so height would allow, which had her sweater under her unfastened coat creeping up to show a band of creamy skin on her abdomen. Because he was male, he sat back on his heels and watched, mentally calculating how much farther she'd have to stretch to show anything even more interesting.

Her gaze dropped, caught him staring. He grinned, unabashed. She settled back on her feet and glared at him, yanking at the hem of her sweater. "You ass."

It wasn't the first time she'd leveled the words at him, he recalled. And he had to admit, he got a kick out of the way she said them, all clipped and prissy, with that faint British accent she always denied. "Need some help there, Duchess?"

Ignoring him, she turned to the CBI agent, who was lifting the bed's mattress for a look under it. "Dan. Can you reach this?"

Dan? Kell searched his memory, tried to recall if he'd heard the agent's first name before. When had she? Mentally shrugging, he pulled open the cabinet drawers as the agent came over like a well-trained lapdog and fetched the boxes off the top shelf for her.

Both drawers of the file cabinet were stuffed full of the sort of things people put away for safekeeping and then promptly forgot about. Old bills and receipts, the warranty on the TV, which had run out several months earlier. The deed to the house, property tax stubs, and—his brows skimmed upward when he pulled out the next folder—a birth certificate.

"So where's our guy plan to go after this if he leaves his birth certificate behind?"

Travis—*Dan*—was pawing through one of the boxes he'd retrieved. "Maybe somewhere he plans to use a new identity."

"You have some known talent in the vicinity that dabble in that? New IDs?" He went back to the drawers. "'Cuz that'd give us an avenue to explore." If they leaned on the lowlife hard enough, maybe they'd discover he had an idea where Hubbard was heading. But more important, they'd find out whether he'd supplied the man with a single set of false identification or two. One for a girl, too.

"Local cops will probably know better. We can check." Travis started replacing items in the box he'd emptied. "This just looks like junk from high school. Yearbooks and stuff." He shifted his attention to Macy. "What do you have?"

"Photo albums. Some loose old pictures." She held up a handful. They'd seen the man's photo in the employee file Mulder kept. A much more youthful Nick Hubbard grinned from a photo with an older woman, whom he had his arm around. "Some look like they date back to his childhood, others are more recent."

He switched his attention to the bottom drawer. It appeared to be old tax information. Randomly drawing out a folder, he flipped through several years of Hubbard's old returns without finding anything remarkable. Like a good

American, the man filed regularly, reporting income that seemed in keeping with his current job and the one he'd held earlier for the prison. The thought abruptly dissipated when he found a record that differed significantly from the others.

Looking up, he asked, "You run across any old wedding pictures in there?"

Macy glanced over at him. "Hubbard was married? When? Is he still?"

"Not according to these files. The last time he filed jointly was eight years ago. His wife's name was"—he squinted slightly at the man's cramped writing—"Sophie Hubbard."

Several moments went by as Macy flipped rapidly through the photos remaining in the box. She shook her head. "Nothing in here. Maybe there's a wedding album in the stack Dan's looking at."

The agent made an amused sound. "Doubtful. What guy is going to hang on to old pictures of the woman who dumped him and probably took half of his belongings with her?"

"A sentimental one," Macy suggested.

Kell's mind was heading in a completely different direction. "We need to track her down. Where does she live? Maybe she's heard from her ex lately. Could be he felt her out about the care and feeding of an eleven-year-old."

"Or maybe she's in on this thing with him somehow." Travis looked quickly through the remaining albums before shaking his head. "No wedding pictures in here. Nothing of him with any woman except one who might be his mother."

Kell went through the rest of the tax reports before going on to the next set of folders in the file. No doubt Raiker already knew about the man's marital history. It would have been in the dossier Mulder collected on all prospective employees. He wondered then if the man kept the records of those prospective candidates he turned down for jobs. He made a mental note to mention it to Raiker. They'd naturally look at anyone Mulder had fired in the last few years, but they should look as carefully at the ones he'd never offered a job to in the first place. If Mulder was the target, rather than the girl herself, revenge might be a primary motivation for hatching this plot.

"That's it for the boxes." Travis eyed Kell. "You about done with the files?"

"Almost." The last few folders contained the survey and property assessment for the house and meticulous records of maintenance on the man's vehicle. The final one was thick and contained records of investments Hubbard had with a well-known company. Kell skimmed it quickly, finding little to quibble about in the man's holdings. There was a fair balance between assets, if a little on the conservative side. His own investment counselor would approve. The most current record showed Hubbard's portfolio worth around eighty thousand. He shoved them back inside the drawer and did a perfunctory search beneath and behind it. His fingers slowed when they came in contact with what felt like a plastic bag attached behind the metal backing of the drawer.

He wrestled it out of its tracks and eased it out of the cabinet so he could see what was secreted there. A clear ziplock bag was duct taped to the back metal plate. "I've got something here." He was aware of the immediate interest his words elicited from his companions even as he gently worked the bag free of its attachment.

Macy and Travis crowded closer as he opened the bag and extracted the large folded paper inside it. He handed the bag to Macy and unfolded the pages. The three of them stared at what appeared to be a blueprint of the security schematics of the Mulder estate.

"Jackpot," muttered Kell. There was no legal way for Hubbard to have acquired copies of the specs of Mulder's security. Either he'd somehow gotten them from the security company that had sold the billionaire the system or he'd stolen them from Mulder. Either way, their presence was incriminating.

"Let's start bagging and tagging evidence," suggested Travis. "We're about done here, aren't we?"

"Why don't you check out the garage first?" Kell rose, folding the sheets and handing them to Macy to be replaced in the bag. "That's listed on the warrant, right? This place should have a basement. I'll look through that. Macy, get pictures of every room, and especially on every piece of evidence we're going to be collecting. Oh, go through the garbage first. We need to . . . what?" Belatedly, he noted the looks he was getting from the other two.

"Nothing," she said with that snippy little tone that dripped with the King's English. "Perhaps we could run out and get you coffee, too."

The suggestion had him trying, and failing, to recall when he'd last eaten. "Not a bad idea, but we really don't have time. We can grab a sandwich on our way back, though."

"You're not running this op, Burke." Travis's dry tone succeeded in distracting him from his stomach. "I think that's what your partner's trying to point out, with more subtlety than I'd use."

"Well, Jesus." Mystified, he put his hands up in surrender. "You want to check for a basement while I go outside, I'm fine with that. And you"—he shot Macy a look—"go ahead and do whatever the hell it is that you want to."

"If I did," she informed him as she swept by, "you'd be bleeding."

He made a what'd-I-do gesture to the agent, who just gave him a smug smile as he followed her into the hallway.

"I'll take the garage."

"Good idea," he muttered, wondering what the hell that had been about. Okay, so he'd been accused of being less than diplomatic before, but someone had to take the lead. Sitting down and negotiating who does what just wasted time, and he hadn't been kidding about being hungry. He hadn't eaten since grabbing something from an all-night drive-through on the way to Manassas this morning.

Mood slightly soured, he went to the drawers of the dresser to check them more thoroughly before heading downstairs. Pretty unlikely there'd be any more secret info taped behind or under drawers, but it bore checking out. He'd learned the value of thoroughness through his long years with Raiker.

Diplomacy was a lesson he'd failed to learn from his boss,

since Raiker was frequently devoid of the quality himself.

He pulled the dresser out a bit from the wall to peer behind it, found nothing. Certain it was a waste of time, he did the same thing to the bed so he could look behind the headboard.

"Burke."

The voice was Macy's, sounding closer than he'd expected. She was still somewhere upstairs. "Yeah."

"Come look at this."

"I will." He moved toward the door and into the hallway. "Without complaint, and without getting all bent out of shape about being told what to do, I'll willingly follow your order. 'Cuz that's the kind of guy I am. That's what teamwork is all about."

There was no response to his gibe, which should have warned him. But Macy was frequently silent in the face of his remarks because, he figured, she was more used to dull lifeless guys who talked only about stocks and the weather. Her response was often easy to read, though, and he'd be lying if he denied taking a twisted pleasure in making the color flare in her creamy cheeks.

But the expression on her face when he found her, crouched on the bathroom floor, had all thoughts of teasing wiped from his mind.

"I saw this first," she said without preamble and shifted slightly so he could crouch beside her. Not much bigger than a pinhead, it would be tough to identify the stain on the tile without the magnifying glass she'd taken out of her evidence kit.

"Blood?"

"I thought it could be. But I didn't see any more spots on the floor. So I started looking inside the tub. Check out the hem of the shower curtain. That's how I found it. Shut like that."

Interest sharpening, he pulled the curtain partly open and looked first at the tub. It was clean. Far cleaner than it would have been at his place if he didn't have a twice-monthly cleaning service, because—although he was handy enough with a vacuum and dust cloth—bathrooms grossed him out. Even his own.

Turning his attention to the inside of the shower curtain, he opened it wider and stepped inside the tub wearing the shoe covers he'd donned after taking off his boots inside the door. With a sweep of his arm he closed the curtain again and began inspecting it. He saw what she'd discovered at its hem, although if he hadn't known what he was looking for, it would have taken him longer.

Again, it would require testing to be sure, but it looked like blood. Flecks of it on the bottom seam. None on the face of the curtain itself. None on the tile along the three interior walls. Maybe because someone had done some deliberate cleaning. But to get to the hem, they would have had to turn up the bottom edge, and they'd been too careless or in too much of a hurry to bother.

Her earlier mention of the neatness of the place took on new meaning. Dread pooled in his gut. Pulling the curtain open again, he looked at her and saw the trepidation he was feeling mirrored on her face. "We'd better get a call in to Raiker. Tell him to have Whitman send the crime scene evidence recovery unit over here when they're done at Mulder's."

Chapter 3

Macy clicked through the digital pictures she'd taken at Hubbard's and downloaded onto her laptop once they'd returned to the estate. It was well after midnight and exhaustion was creeping through her system. She wanted to think she was successful at hiding it but wasn't certain how long she'd remain coherent. Because she knew which ones the men would be most interested in, she started with the photos taken in the bathroom.

"Damn small," muttered Whitman, squinting at the screen. She flipped to the ones taken of the shower curtain when Kell had turned up the edge for her. "If it does turn out to be blood, we'll be lucky to have enough for ABO blood typing and a DNA analysis."

"You might get more after the crime techs get done with the shower drain and trap," she said, her voice tight. There was still the possibility that the spots might not be blood at all. That they would end up belonging to the owner of the house. Or even a woman friend, who'd cut herself shaving and left behind evidence of the wound. But that wasn't the scenario that was playing out in her head, and she knew it wasn't the one any of the others in the room were worrying about either.

"We found a smear of blood on a bedsheet in the girl's room, too," Whitman announced tersely. Macy's gaze met Raiker's and he gave a small nod. So he'd known about it. Hopefully he'd been kept fully in the loop in their absence. The knot in her stomach drew tighter.

As if recognizing that, Raiker said, "Ellie keeps a pair of scissors on her nightstand. She's been doing a lot of paper cutting and folding artwork. Her mother said she found it calming. The scissors are the only item her parents can determine that are missing from her room. She may have wounded her assailant, which would be a break for us. Techs didn't find any other blood, but if the scissors were dropped afterward, before being collected and taken away with her, that would account for the stain on the sheet."

"Or he might have used them to subdue her." Agent Travis spoke the words that everyone else was thinking.

"As well as this was planned out, no way he intended to attack her in her own bed," Kell stated. The stubble that was beginning to shadow his jaw was a shade darker than his hair. The seemingly random observation had Macy giving herself a mental shake. She was more tired than she'd thought if she was noticing anything about Kellan Burke other than his annoying habits, which were legion. "He'd have come prepared, maybe with tape or a gag, some way to bind her, but he had a specific method in mind to get her out of here quickly and silently. If he was smart—and so far we have no reason to believe otherwise—he'd have drugged her. Instant submission, no battle. He wouldn't have needed the scissors. Likely he took them away from her."

But not, Macy thought darkly, before blood had been drawn. From Ellie or her attacker?

"That's how we figure it, too." Whitman loosened his tie. The top button of his shirt had already been unfastened.

She clicked through the pictures until she came to the thermal coffee mug on the counter in Hubbard's kitchen. "We bagged this to get a sample of Hubbard's DNA. We also brought the toothbrush from his bathroom. Seminal stains showed up on the bed in the master bedroom in the house." And she refused to read too much into that. Would Hubbard really have brought the girl back to a familiar location to rape her when there was an imminent threat of exposure?

The neighbors had seen nothing. But pedophiliac offenders often exhibited poor impulse control, taking chances that seemed too risky to contemplate. The danger increased their pleasure. She forced herself to calculate the timeline, pushing aside assumptions and dread to concentrate on possibilities. He would have had plenty of time to get the girl off the estate, back to his house, attack, and kill her, she realized sickly. If that had been his intention.

But it begged the still unanswered question of who the real target of this crime was—Ellie or her father.

She was wandering too far abroad from the evidence at hand, always a shaky proposition. It led to erroneous assumptions. How many times had she heard Raiker preach that?

"Mr. Mulder has complete files on all his employees. Background checks, DNA profiles, and fingerprints," Whitman put in tersely.

Concentrating on the pictures, she flipped through to ones showing Hubbard's living room. "You can see from the floor that the carpet had been recently vacuumed. But the bag in the vacuum cleaner was new. The garbage cans were all empty."

"Someone took pains to clean up. Or cover something up." Kell worked his shoulders tiredly. "We bagged his bankbooks and investment information. No record in either of a sudden infusion of cash."

"That would be too easy," Travis muttered.

"Any keys that might lead us to a safe-deposit box?"

"Nothing like that," Agent Travis said. "I figure he'd have taken that with him when he took off. Looked like he packed and left in a hurry."

"Leaving his birth certificate and account information be-hind." She looked at her boss, who showed no signs of weariness. She'd often wondered if the man slept at all. "How long will it take to access his phone records and financial accounts?"

"We should have the warrants for the banks and for cell phone and landline LUDs by noon tomorrow."

"What about triangulation?" she asked.

"Tried it but struck out. His cell phone is shut off, so there's no way of pinpointing his location that way."

"We found his car in the employee's garage, locked. He only has the one vehicle registered to him, so he found another way off the estate. Has his cell, which he isn't answering, and according to you, took about half his clothes, but not his bankbooks. He could still transfer his money, I suppose, if he has online banking, but he'd have to figure either way leaves a trail for us to follow." Raiker toyed with the polished mahogany knob of his cane. "If he'd planned on ransom, leaving the money behind makes more sense. What's a hundred grand if you plan to ask for ten or twenty times that?"

"But there's still been no demand?"

Raiker shook his head at Agent Travis's question. "No. But the techs finally discovered how the security system was circumvented."

Macy straightened, the news erasing her exhaustion. "How?"

"By checking the computer's download history." There was impatience in his expression, in his tone, and she knew intuitively that he thought his own computer techs would have made the discovery hours earlier. "The suspect—presumably Hubbard—covered his tracks, but there was evidence of a software patch downloaded during his shift that caused certain cameras to loop the same scene only between midnight and two A.M. this morning."

"Shit," muttered Travis. The agent's deep-set eyes were shadowed by fatigue. "So much for being foolproof like Cramer claimed."

"It's not exactly something your average burglar could pull off," Raiker said dryly. "Very high-tech. And detailed exactly to match the specifications of this system. Our guy went to considerable expense to acquire the design for the patch, because there's nothing in Hubbard's background to indicate he had this sort of expertise."

Dan Travis wasn't buying it. "He and Cramer were camera experts."

"Capable of troubleshooting problems with the cameras and computer feed. But this . . ." Raiker shook his head. "I talked to Gavin Pounds, one of my employees, and described the setup here. He's a cyber genius. He claims there are only a handful of people in the country capable of designing something so detail-specific, so we can also figure it was expensive. Someone went to a great deal of cost to set this job up."

"Cost is no object when you're pulling down billions a year," Whitman muttered. His reference to the Mulders was clear.

"Or when you hope to recoup that expense and millions more with a ransom demand." Raiker held up a hand to stem any comments. "Assuming one comes."

Kell folded his arms behind his head and leaned back in his chair, face tilted toward the ceiling as he mused aloud. "So a few of the cameras are circumvented. Not turned off—there would have been a record of that. But by replaying a different scene, there'd be no pixel change. One of the criteria to trip the alarm isn't met, allowing the kidnapper to move about the area freely."

"And knowing the specific cameras he disabled points to both entry and exit points for the house?"

"That's right." Whitman worked his shoulders tiredly as he answered Macy's question. "The affected cameras included the one in the employee garage, so maybe he hid in the vehicle until making his move on the house. The camera that would have picked up his movements from that garage to the east side of the home were decommissioned. He probably entered the home through one of the sets of French doors on the east side of the sunroom. Could have left the same way. They can be locked behind a person as they exit."

Having not had a chance to look through the home, Macy had no idea what the layout was. "How far from there to Ellie's bedroom?"

"Across the house," Agent Travis put in. He was frowning, as if troubled by the realization. "Once inside, Hubbard would have had to go through about eight rooms and hallways before getting to the girl's bedroom. And it's only a hundred yards or so from there to the parents' master suite."

"Ballsy," muttered Kell. "So he didn't get in and wait for hours, hidden from sight. Gave himself a total time period of two hours to get in, make his way to the bedroom, snatch the kid, and get out again. With no way of being sure of the parents' schedule, he couldn't be certain how long he'd have to wait until he could make his move." He gave a mournful shake of his head. "This is no amateur we're dealing with. He's done this sort of thing before."

"Hubbard's record is clean." Whitman thumped a heavy index finger against the surprisingly thick file folder in front of him before sending it sliding across the table toward Kell. "Giving Mulder the benefit of the doubt—"

"Yes, let's try that, shall we?" murmured Raiker.

"—he wouldn't have hired the guy for his security team otherwise." If the agent had heard Raiker's comment, he chose to ignore it. "And Dobson hasn't been able to dig up anything else that would make me suspect his employment dossier has been altered. He was honorably discharged from the army, put in fifteen years working for the penal system, and my phone calls elicited nothing but praise for the man. Worked a ton of overtime for them, too. You'd wonder where he found the time to get experience in something like this."

"He didn't need to get experience," Macy said with certainty. The fog of exhaustion had lifted at the onset of this discussion, and her mind was racing now. "He just needed to be approached by someone who had it. Hubbard may have been nothing more than the ticket inside. Whoever the accomplice is could be the one with the planning, the experience, and the expertise."

"That would make Hubbard little more than a lackey." Kell's voice sounded doubtful. "Hard to believe a professional leaving the implementation to an inexperienced rookie."

"We already agreed that Hubbard isn't in this alone,"

Travis pointed out. "Makes sense to me that the pro would bring in whoever he needs to get the job done. Like partners. Each brings something to the table."

"And since Hubbard can get inside the gates of the estate, that makes him pretty indispensable," Macy finished.

"Okay." Kell scrubbed both hands over his face before addressing Whitman. "I assume you got a warrant for the car and checked it out while we were gone."

"We did. Got some random prints, with no matches on the Automated Fingerprint Identification System. Most of them matched the ones Mulder had on file for Hubbard. Found a couple of Cramer's." Whitman's dour tone was reflected in his expression. "He claims he rode to work with Hubbard the day before the kidnapping while his car was in the shop. Checked the hard drive of the security computers for the dates he mentioned and found footage supporting his claim. Other than that, there were a few hairs and fibers found. They'll be checked out."

Raiker checked his watch. "I'm leaving shortly to begin those prison interviews. Agent Whitman and I have discussed division of duties." Nothing in his expression relayed his feelings regarding that particular conversation. "I've offered the services of a mobile lab that could be set up on the property for quicker results. CBI prefers to use the state lab for the time being."

He sent a quelling look Kell's way when the man gave a barely muffled snort. But his reaction was picked up by Whitman.

"We play this strictly by the books until the Mulders are cleared." His tone was testy. "CBI Director Lanscombe has made this case highest priority, and we should get quick lab results. Once we're certain the family isn't involved, Lanscombe might change his mind about the mobile lab."

"You've got some other high-priority cases in the state, according to my sources," Raiker put in. "Suspected serial killer in Boulder. A rash of bank robberies in central Colorado."

"Let us worry about that. Our agency has top-notch resources." Whitman's tone held a note of finality.

Macy remained silent, but Raiker's words had doubt spiking. Evidence was known to languish in state labs for weeks or longer. It remained to be seen just how expedited the test results for this case would be.

And as for the man's reference to their resources . . . Raiker's labs rivaled the best in the nation and came complete with some of the top forensic scientists in the country, all who'd been vigorously cross-trained. He'd recently begun expanding his mobile lab system by establishing satellite offices across the United States. It would take a great deal to rival the experts and resources within his organization.

But it was what the assistant director didn't say that bothered her most. He couldn't have made it clearer that he still didn't trust them not to alter evidence to exonerate their client. She took a moment to be thankful she hadn't been present for the conversation between her boss and Whitman on the subject.

"I want to follow up on Hubbard." Kell's statement jerked her attention back to the matter at hand. "We need to check his ex. See if his mother is still alive. Other family members. Figure out who his friends were. Go at his coworkers again. He's wrapped up in this case. We need to figure out how."

"I agree." She faced her boss and Whitman with equanimity. With Raiker gone for the next few days, the last thing she wanted was to be shunted aside by the CBI, given menial tasks while they followed up on the leads she, Burke, and Travis had unearthed today.

"Good." Given the glint in Raiker's eye, their united front amused him. "Because we've decided that the three of you will do exactly that while the rest of Whitman's team look into Mulder's finances and business associates. Hubbard doesn't have any close relatives living. So after interviewing the ex, check out his old coworkers and track down his closest acquaintances."

"Does Mulder keep a list of people who applied for a job and got turned down?" Kell asked. "Because if this was motivated by revenge, rather than ransom, we need to look at anyone who had a hard-on against the guy."

"I assure you, we've considered all avenues." It was hard to say whether Whitman's irascible tone was due to Burke's suggestion or from lack of sleep. Macy assumed it was the former. He probably expected them to stay silent and await their orders, much as Agent Travis was doing.

"Get some sleep," Raiker advised them brusquely. "You can all start first thing in the morning. You'll keep both me and Special Agent Whitman updated regarding your findings. Agent Travis can show you to your rooms."

Sleep sounded pretty appealing. But even as Macy rose, her gaze sought Whitman's. "I'd like a look at the girl's room before I turn in for the night. Is the crime scene unit done with it?"

The man gave a curt nod. "I have two agents posted at the door. I'll direct them to allow you in."

Kell and Dan Travis trailed her from the room. After closing the door behind them, the agent said, "Our rooms are well away from the family's quarters. Can't you wait until tomorrow morning to look at the kid's room?"

Macy hesitated. The man's weariness was visible in his expression. But she knew her compulsive tendencies would make it impossible to sleep without at least a walk-through of the space.

Kell took the decision out of her hands, a fact that would have annoyed her under different circumstances. "Just walk us by the room and then show us to ours. We can find our way back on our own."

The agent shrugged and turned on his heel. "Fine." He led them down endless corridors past a blur of darkened rooms. Macy observed her surroundings closely as she followed, making a mental note of her location. Right turn by the Grecian urn that looked to be a couple thousand years old. A hundred yards past what was likely an authentic pencil sketch by Picasso. To the left and another dozen feet to the lighted glassed-in collection of Fabergé eggs. Up a set of three steps to a wider hallway, this one decorated in designer hand-painted wallpaper. The dark-suited duo standing outside a door ahead pinpointed the location of Ellie Mulder's room.

Travis halted. "There's the scene up ahead. Down that left hall"—he jerked a thumb to indicate—"will be her parents' suite. Our rooms are this way." He turned around and lost no time heading down the steps and around a corner.

"Paying attention?" murmured Burke as she hurried to keep up with the agent's long strides. He strolled behind her, seeming to have no such problem.

"I can find my way back," she answered shortly. He was much too close behind her, his shoulder occasionally bumping hers. She could have told him she'd made her way around places as grand as this one from the time she could walk but knew instinctively that would be a bad idea. The last thing Burke needed was more ammunition to use for the incessant wisecracks he threw her way.

"You should take precautions, just in case. You probably don't have any bread crumbs on you, but you could always leave a trail of clothing behind, marking the trail." As if on cue, heat flooded her cheeks at the suggestion, and she hurried her steps even more. But she couldn't outpace the rest of his remarks. "Drop a glove here. Another glove there. Get rid of that god-awful hat at the corner ahead."

Momentarily distracted, she asked, "What's wrong with my hat?"

"Did you steal it from a ten-year-old boy?"

Her earlier embarrassment was elbowed aside by annoyance. An all too common occurrence around him. "Hard to take advice seriously from someone whose idea of high fashion is a new pair of jeans."

"Just making an observation." They were rounding the corner he'd pointed out earlier. "Ahead you could leave the coat. Maybe the boots after that. And then things should get a bit more interesting before we get to our rooms. Sort of a Hansel and Gretel–type striptease."

"You have a one-track mind." Which made it even more incomprehensible that she'd spent one very vivid night wrapped around him. A memory that had proven much harder to extricate than she'd like.

"Not at all." His voice dropped even lower. She avoided,

barely, sending a look at him over her shoulder. "I'm perfectly capable of thinking of you stripping—perfect place to leave your sweater here," he inserted, without missing a beat as they passed a dizzying number of closed doors, "while also wondering if the agents left on point at the girl's room were for our benefit or the family's."

She wished she didn't know what he was getting at. But it would be a precautionary measure to post guards outside a crime scene. Especially with parents still in the home who couldn't yet be cleared as suspects in the case.

It was just as likely the agents were there to be sure they didn't tamper with the scene themselves, and the knowledge burned. Regardless of Whitman's talk about teamwork, it was clear that he didn't trust Raiker or his operatives at this point. Travis's assignment with them tomorrow was probably as much a reflection of that distrust as anything.

"Things will change once they clear the parents," she said, her voice as low as his. Travis had disappeared around another turn.

"You're assuming they *will* clear the parents. Good place to leave your pants—and an excellent choice they were—at this corner," he added in a non sequiter.

She did look at him then and found his face as close as she'd feared. "Stop crowding me." The elbow she aimed at him found its mark in his hard belly, although probably to little effect. But he did slow a step, if at least to move out of striking distance. "You can't think the Mulders are in on this."

"If Raiker thought there was a chance of that, he'd have never taken this case. That's good enough for me. I'm just saying it might be a long time before Whitman reaches the same conclusion. In the meantime, he yanks us around, pretends to accept our help as long as it comes with our babysitter, Travis."

She could hardly argue with his logic, since she'd had similar thoughts herself. "Raiker will make sure we don't get shoved out of the investigative side." Travis was in sight again, but there was another intersecting hallway up ahead. How many rooms were in this place?

"Sculpture up ahead."

"I see it," she said irritably. His line of thought had as many twists and turns as this home. The work he was referring to was an abstract metal piece, and she didn't even try to identify the artist. Her stepfather's taste didn't run to anything more recent than the nineteenth century, and most of her artistic experience came from his holdings.

"Just thinking it'd be a good place to leave your bra."

She jerked around, and he raised his hands in false placation. "So we can find our way back to the girl's room. And don't think I don't appreciate your offer to sacrifice this way, leaving a trail for us."

"I didn't offer, I'm not stripping, and you are not coming with me when I go back," she informed him, fuming. This was always what came of too much time spent in Burke's presence. Well, all but that one notable time. No one could tie her up in knots the way he could, and the recognition made her furious.

"Don't blame me then if we get lost."

Her fists clenched in frustration. Certain he'd find it amusing, she mentally counted to ten while she quickened her step. While he displayed his famous charm whenever there was a female in the vicinity, he'd always seemed to reserve his most outrageous remarks for her, and that hadn't changed since their one disastrous night together six months ago. She was determined that her reaction wouldn't fuel his need for entertainment at her expense.

So she studiedly ignored him until Travis finally paused. "These three rooms have been set aside for your use," he informed them. "We're around the corner and down the hall."

Macy eyed the closed doors of each. Two on one side and one on the other. No way did she want to sleep with Burke next to her. "I'll take the one over here."

Travis shrugged. "Better check which one has your stuff in it. How about we meet at seven A.M. in the front foyer?"

"Sounds good." Burke opened the door closest to him and looked at her. "Your things are in here."

With a feeling of trepidation, she watched as he swung

open the next door. "And here's mine." The smart-ass grin on his face told her better than words that he'd figured she wanted to put as much distance as possible between them. "But maybe Raiker wouldn't mind if you wanted to ask him to switch."

"This is fine," she said stiffly. Whatever excuse she was able to fashion for changing rooms, her boss would recognize her true motive. He had an uncanny gift for spotting dishonesty, sort of like a human lie detector. Of course, she wasn't particularly adept in the art of prevarication. Burke didn't need to know how uneasy she was in his presence. She knew him well enough to realize he'd exploit even the smallest show of weakness.

Travis had already disappeared around the corner, so she stepped inside the first room and snapped on the light. The space was roomy, with a king-sized bed and excellent replicas of eighteenth-century antique furniture. She deposited her coat on a chaise lounge and turned back to head across the mansion again.

And tried to ignore, as best she could, Burke dogging her steps the entire way.

———

"Macy Reid," she said crisply to the one of the men blocking her entrance into the girl's room. She held up her Raiker Forensics identification badge, which hung from a lanyard around her neck.

The CBI agent, identified as Agent Dirk Pelton by the ID clipped to his lapel, looked past her to Kell. "Is that Burke?"

She slipped by him into the room. "I have no idea who that is."

"I'm Burke. She's kidding. Macy, tell them you're kidding."

"Let's see some ID," she heard one of the agents say, and allowed herself a small smile as she moved to the center of the room. The space seemed decorated for a younger child. That was the first thought to strike her. As if it was held in suspended animation since the girl had been six or seven.

And since Ellie had been seven when Art Cooper had snatched her, perhaps it had. Macy's gaze traveled over the dolls and stuffed animals peering down from a shelf running the length of one wall. There were Barbies and other toys neatly stacked on a bookcase next to the bed alongside picture books much too young for an eleven-year-old. The bedspread and curtains featured scenes of horses. Girls loved horses, didn't they? That, the computer, and aquarium were the only things that seemed to be even remotely of interest to a girl Ellie's age.

Tuning out the sounds of the argument behind her, she pulled on a pair of plastic gloves she'd brought with her and strolled through the room, steeping herself in impressions. Two bedside tables sat on either side of the denuded mattress. Which had held the scissors? Until they got updated reports of all the case details, she only knew answers to the questions she'd had a chance to ask. Or the information she discovered herself.

Macy measured the distance between the bed and desk visually. Too far to get out of bed to go in search of paper if the child couldn't sleep. She went to the drawer of one table and pulled it out. A tidy stack of construction paper sat inside. Something to calm the girl's nerves if sleep proved elusive.

Or a reason for her to keep a pair of sharp scissors at her bedside.

"Thanks. You were very helpful."

Burke's voice brought a small smile to her face for once. "Oh, were you behind me?" She turned, shot him an innocent look. "I didn't notice."

"Right. Whatever else I could say about you, there's not much that gets by you." Shoving a hand in his jeans pocket, he withdrew a pair of gloves and drew them on. "So what are you thinking?"

Her gaze went past him to the light switch. Although off, the room was still suffused with a soft glow. "It's never really dark in here. Even at night." She pointed from the computer to the aquarium. "Better than a night light, especially if you

don't want anyone to realize you're still scared of the dark."
That observation arrowed a little too deep, so she hurried
past it. "He left himself a narrow window for getting in the
house and back out with the girl, but he'd need a place to
duck into, wouldn't he? Just to be sure everything was quiet
in this wing and that the parents were in their beds?"

"The room next door is another bedroom, although it's
been empty since the family moved here." She turned at Pelton's voice. The man switched on the light and moved just
inside the doorway. "We searched it as thoroughly as we did
this one."

Macy went to the closet and opened the door then, flicking on the light. Rows and rows of clothes hung neatly from
the endless racks. The space, like the bedroom, was eerily
neat. Did the help pick up daily? Where was the jumble of
clothes, worn for an hour or so and then discarded?

Shoes and boots were lined up on shelves that lined one
end of the space. Another set of shelves held folded jeans,
khakis, shirts, and sweaters. The four of them could hide inside it and be undetectable from a cursory observer.

"Plenty of room in here, but he likely hid next door."

"According to the mother's statement, the girl would have
been in bed long before the unknown subject entered the
home," Kell agreed. "Probably slipped into the next room
and got his bearings, made sure all in the wing was quiet
before he headed in here."

"Whoever this guy is, he took precautions." Pelton's voice
was disgusted. "There's a ton of prints, of course. State lab
will go through them, matching them to the people living
or working in the house to see if there's any that don't belong
here. Same thing with the hairs and fibers they found."

"Where was the bloodstain found?"

The agent came in to stand beside the stripped bed. "Right
about here"—he pointed midway down the bed—"below a
jumble of covers. Actually pretty cool, thinking to grab up
the scissors and take them along. Probably never noticed the
stain. It's still pretty dark in here, even with the glow from
the computer sleep screen and the aquarium light. Or maybe

it's the kid's blood, in which case it didn't matter that it was left behind."

Macy's stomach did a quick twist, and she ordered her emotions under control. They had two possible places where Ellie's blood may have been spilled, including Hubbard's house. Tiny amounts, in the grand scheme of things.

Unless they found her quickly, there was likely to be a great deal more bloodshed.

"It seems so empty. Almost like she was never returned to us at all. Like the last two years never really happened."

The whispered words had Macy jerking around to see the woman standing in the doorway. Under different circumstances, the slim blonde would have fit in with the sophisticated crowd that used to attend her stepfather's parties, with her elegant well-cut clothes and air of breeding. But Althea Mulder's patrician face was drawn, and her eyes were shadowed with fatigue. Her lips quivered as she stared in the direction of the bed.

With a stab of remorse, Macy wondered if the woman had overheard the last part of the exchange between her and the CBI agent. After studying the woman carefully, she revised her opinion. Ellie's mother wasn't focused on the scene before her. She'd been sucked in by the past. Back to the first time her daughter disappeared.

Compassion propelled Macy across the room, tugging off her gloves as she moved. "Mrs. Mulder," she said softly, extending her hand. "I'm Macy Reid. My associate and I are with Raiker Forensics."

The woman blinked once as Macy took her hand. "Adam Raiker brought our baby home once." Her hand was cold as ice in Macy's. "When everyone else had given up hope, he brought our Ellie home."

"Yes, ma'am." Gently, Macy took the woman's arm and steered her toward the hallway. CBI wouldn't want Ellie's parents in the room, even if it had been cleared by the crime scene unit. Not until Whitman had cleared *them*. "And we're going to do our best to make sure that happens again."

She was unsure whether the woman had heard her. Her

gaze had turned inward. "We could never have any more children. We'd thought about adoption, but after Ellie was taken, we couldn't bear the thought. Adam Raiker was the answer to our prayers." She seemed to subtly shift then, as if moving back to the present. "She was happy again. Ellie. She was finally starting to smile more. To laugh. How could this . . ." She fought a short battle against tears, before succumbing. "We took every precaution. How could this happen *again*?"

"Let me take you back to your room, Mrs. Mulder." Chest tight, Macy walked the woman down the hallway to the master suite. "Rest will help you keep up your strength. And you'll need that in the next few days. For Ellie."

Stephen Mulder appeared around the corner then, and his step faltered for a moment when he took in the scene before him. Then he strode swiftly in their direction. "Althea."

Macy moved away as the man drew closer. He slipped his arm around his wife's narrow waist, and she seemed to collapse against him, sobs racking her body. "Are we being punished, Stephen? Is this God's way of balancing the scales because we have so much?"

"Come to bed now." The man's voice was soothing. The raw emotion evident in the scene had Macy turning away. "I want you to take one of the sedatives the doctor left." The low murmur of his tone was lost as they turned the corner.

Macy drew in a breath to still the racing of her heart. The past never seemed so vivid as when she was dealing with the family of a crime victim. But it wasn't the past that was important here. Not hers. Not the girl's.

It was the future. Ellie Mulder's future.

Ellie shivered uncontrollably. It was cold wherever he'd brought her, but they were inside some sort of building. If she bent her knees a tiny bit more, they hit something solid. A wall. And she was lying on a hard, cold floor.

For a long time she'd been sort of floating in and out of awareness. He'd stuck her with a needle before he'd taken her. She hadn't fought the darkness whenever it pulled her under again. It'd be better if she could stay out of it and be unaware the whole time. Because she already knew what he wanted.

Her stomach cramped then, and she felt like she'd puke inside the hood still covering her head. Maybe she was sick from the drugs, or maybe it was the waiting for what she already knew was going to happen. The thought of it made her want to scream. To scream and cry and beg.

But that had never helped before.

To take her mind off the roiling of her stomach, she strained to hear . . . anything. She knew she wasn't alone in the place. There had been footsteps earlier. Some banging and then swearing in a voice she didn't recognize.

At least she hoped she didn't.

But no matter how hard she tried, Ellie couldn't hear anything now other than the wind. Was it still blizzarding? Would that make it harder for anyone to find her?

The thought brought her up short. She couldn't expect someone to come after her. She'd learned that from before. And she wasn't a kid anymore, expecting tears and prayers to rescue her. She might be just eleven, but it was an older eleven than any of her friends back in DC. She was different in a way they couldn't understand.

Different enough to know that she only had herself to rely on.

The despair that swept over her at the thought was almost comforting in its familiarity. It was hope that was the enemy. Knowing the worst—expecting it—at least meant she was prepared.

But she wasn't a baby anymore, to lie there and take it either. She'd hurt him—whoever he was—with the scissors in her room. She could hurt him again.

Trying to move her fingers, she almost cried out at the needlelike pain of feeling returning to them. Her hands were tied. Tight. In back of her. Her feet, too. Gritting her teeth, she kept moving them. Tiny little wiggles that shot pain up her arms and legs. But whatever he'd tied her with held fast. She wouldn't be slipping out of the binds.

Ellie lay still for a moment, thinking. Her brain was still a little fuzzy from whatever he'd given her, so she had to concentrate hard. *With knowledge comes control.* That's what Dr. Givens, her psychologist, always said. Of course, he was talking about knowing herself and admitting to what she was feeling. But it could also mean knowing whoever had done this to her, couldn't it? Maybe that would help her make a plan to get away.

She stopped moving her fingers and toes then and experimentally rubbed her cheek against the floor. The hood moved, too. She could feel that the tape was still over her mouth, but whatever was covering her head was looser. Maybe she could get it off.

Concentrating fiercely, she worked her head in a rhythmic motion. Drag it along the floor. Lift slightly to return to the original position and try again. Each time brought the hood up an inch or so.

It was hard to know how long she went on like that. Each time she was rewarded with a slight movement of the hood, she redoubled her efforts. Her progress wasn't much faster than a snail's. But when she saw the first glint of light beneath the hood's edge, there was a fierce leap of satisfaction in her chest.

Long minutes later, the hood was worked up to her forehead. Ellie lay there, blinking. The darkness under the hood had been complete. But there was some light in the room, although the window above her was dark.

Slowly, she craned her neck to look over her shoulder. The room actually looked like a little cabin. There was a small wood-burning stove with a fire in it on one wall. Either the fire hadn't been going long, or it didn't do a good job heating the place. A folding table and two stools were in one corner. But as hard as she tried, she couldn't angle her head to see any farther behind her.

Made bolder by her success, Ellie rolled to her other side

to complete her inspection of the room. A chaise lawn chair was next to the table.

And on it sat a man.

Her heart hammered in her chest like a spooked horse in full gallop. It wasn't Art Cooper. Her stomach jittered and she felt dizzy. She'd known it couldn't be. But she'd still been afraid it would be him.

He just sat there, looking at her in the dim light. Not speaking. Just staring, the way people did at the zoo, while they waited for the animals to do something entertaining.

Dragging in a deep breath, she battled back the fear that was creeping its way up her spine. He had one of those faces that looked sort of familiar, but she didn't know him. He just looked like a guy you'd see on the street. In the mall. Someone you passed and then forgot in the next moment.

"Guess you had to wake up sooner or later."

He sounded kind of impatient, the way her mother did when the hairdresser was late. And thoughts of her mother had tears stinging her eyes, making her angry with herself. *Don't think about her. Don't feel anything. Nothing hurts when you don't let yourself feel.* That mental chant had helped her get through two years with Art Cooper. It'd help her get through this, too.

That thought shattered when the man finally moved. One hand reached inside his flannel shirt and he took out a knife. Ellie shrank away, panic doing a fast sprint up her spine. The blade was long and thin. As she stared, he ran it lightly across the pad of his thumb. Blood immediately welled in its path. He wiped the blood across his lips and smiled at her. A bloody, horrible smile.

"Tell me what you're feeling right now."

Chapter 4

"You're wrong if you think Nick had anything to do with that poor girl's disappearance."

Sophie Brownley stared at each of them in turn from anxious brown eyes. They were seated in the small living area of her Florence ranch-style home. Toys littered the floor. A pile of dolls and stuffed animals were heaped on the opposite side of the couch she was seated on. Her daughter was napping, she'd informed them in hushed tones when she'd let them in. They'd have to be quiet.

"Why do you say that, Ms. Brownley?" Travis took the lead while Kell sat back, his gaze traveling around the small space. Unlike her ex-husband's place, everything about the woman's home shouted family. Assorted pictures cluttered shelves and tabletops. The small kitchen opened onto this room, and there were freshly baked cookies cooling on racks on the counter. The refrigerator was covered with magnetic plastic letters and farm animals and a large sheet of paper covered with indecipherable crayon scribbles. Squinting hard at it, he decided the image most resembled a mutated walrus. In rainbow colors.

"Because he'd never do anything illegal, much less something so terrible." She threaded her fingers together nervously. "He might not work for the correctional system anymore, but he's a law-and-order kind of guy. A crime like this . . ." She shook her head, her glossy blond hair swaying at the movement. "It would never even occur to him."

"Maybe it occurred to someone else," Travis suggested tersely. "Someone who had the idea and tapped him to get in and out with the kid."

She pressed her lips together and shook her head again. "No. I'll never believe that."

"How long have the two of you been divorced?" Macy asked.

Kell slanted her an approving look. Her voice was gentle as a mother's kiss. Well, not *his* mother. But it had a soothing quality. Damned effective at getting people to open up to her. Until last night, the only time he heard that tone from her was in an interview. She'd used it to calm Althea Mulder, at least as much as she was able. He didn't recall it ever being directed at him.

But then, they hadn't spent a lot of time talking the one night they'd spent together.

"Eight—almost nine years. But ours wasn't a bitter divorce. We just had . . . differences."

She gave the woman an encouraging smile. "That's the way it usually goes."

"When's the last time you talked to your ex?"

Travis's insertion shattered the tenuous bond Macy had been building. Kell watched Brownley draw up her shoulders, her hand going to her hugely pregnant belly. The guy was about as subtle as ton of falling bricks.

"We haven't . . . We don't keep in touch. It's been years. Since shortly after our divorce."

"That's a long time. So you wouldn't know whether or not he's changed."

The woman's jaw set in stubborn lines. "No one changes that much."

"What caused the divorce?" Macy asked smoothly. Her

expression was guileless. But then it was most of the time. Except when she talked to him, when it went closed and guarded. Or pink and flaming.

Brownley heaved a sigh and settled more deeply into the sofa cushions. "I wanted a family. He didn't. I knew that going in, but I thought . . ." Her voice trailed away.

"That you could change his mind?"

She gave a jerky nod at Macy's gentle question and Kell shot Travis a warning look. But the agent seemed content to let the two women talk. For now.

"Men do, you know," Sophie said defensively. "After a while sometimes they come around to the idea. But I'm ten years younger than him, and he told me up front he didn't want kids. After about five years, it started getting more urgent for me, and we'd fight about it." She shrugged, a flicker of guilt skating over her face. "My fault, really. I knew how he felt going in."

"As you said, sometimes men change their minds."

Sophie shot Macy a grateful look. "I hoped he would. But he didn't. And I finally felt bad about ragging him about it, when he'd been honest all along."

"Did he ever mention his reason for not wanting a family?"

It was like watching a master fisherman, Kell decided. Macy cast the line, played the lure a bit, then slowly reeled the woman in. Nice technique when the situation called for it. And this situation did.

"No-o-o," Sophie said slowly, her brows drawing together. "Just that he wasn't that into kids. His father ran off and left him and his mother when he was young. They struggled. I think that made an impression on him."

"Maybe it was the cost," Kell interjected, his voice light. When the woman looked at him, he gave her a smile. "They aren't cheap to raise, are they? Was his a financial decision, do you think?"

"I never got that impression." Brownley shrugged helplessly. "Nick was careful with money, but he wasn't cheap. I think it was like he said. He just didn't care for kids much."

Would a man careful with money be motivated by the chance to earn a large wad of it? Kell wondered. Especially if he didn't especially like kids in the first place? He caught Travis's gaze on him and knew they were on the same page. Whatever Sophie Brownley might believe about her ex, Kell remained convinced that Hubbard was involved up to his neck in the disappearance of Ellie Mulder.

"We can be fairly certain that whatever Hubbard is involved in, his ex-wife doesn't know anything about it."

"Assistant Director Whitman will have his LUDs in a few hours." Travis pulled away from the curb in front of the house. The low gray clouds were spitting out a frozen substance that wasn't really snow, yet not quite sleet. It looked, Kell decided, like someone was sprinkling soap detergent crystals out of the sky. "But yeah, I doubt we're going to discover from his phone records that he reached out to her. What she said about their differences . . . that rang true. It also made me think that maybe his thing about kids ran a little deeper than daddy running off and leaving him. Maybe he's got a real dislike for them. That would explain his motive."

"Or maybe he likes them too much."

Kell's head swiveled at Macy's comment. She raised her brows at him. "Well, there's no ransom demand yet. Given Ellie's history, we can't ignore the possibility that Hubbard is just a garden-variety scumbag that preys on children."

"Absolutely nothing in his background suggests it. I imagine that Mulder's background check is extensive." Besides, what were the chances that the girl would be snatched twice for the same reason? They had to be even more astronomical than her being kidnapped twice, at all.

Travis leaned forward to flip on the wipers. "Whitman looked through them and said the background checks were as thorough as those for classified government jobs."

"Then it also would have discovered known associates." Kell was thinking out loud.

"But that doesn't exclude someone contacting Hubbard and pulling him in on the scheme," the agent added.

"Which brings us full circle," Macy murmured from the backseat.

Kell looked out the window pensively. The wind had kicked up, making flurries out of the soap detergent snow that still fell. "Yeah. But that circle closes solidly around Hubbard."

———————

Adam Raiker studied the man sitting across the scarred table from him. Art Cooper wasn't faring well in prison. The blues hung on his frame, as if he'd lost weight since they'd been issued to him. His hair was thinner, his face haggard. But the bitterness in his voice when he spoke was all too familiar.

"What the hell do you want with me now?"

"Just have a few questions," Adam answered mildly.

The man gave a snort. "You ruined my life. What makes you think I'd help you?"

"I'd say you ruined your own life. And after what you did to Ellie Mulder, you got exactly what was coming to you." Some would claim that prison was too good for the likes of Cooper. But this represented justice in America, and Adam had spent most of his life in search of justice.

Reaching for the folder in front of him, he turned it around, flipped it open, and pushed it over to the other man. "Even so, if you give me anything useful, I might be able to help you." He waited while the man looked at the sheets inside, until a flicker of recognition lit his eyes. The papers were copies of the complaints Cooper had filed since he'd gotten to Sussex. And the folder was thick.

"This place is a hellhole," Cooper muttered. His gaze raised to Adam's. "And you're the reason I'm here. So go fuck yourself." His chair scraped the floor as he pushed back to rise.

Leaning forward, Adam hooked his cane behind one chair leg to pull it forcibly against the back of the man's knees, sending him off balance. "Sit down," he ordered. "Or would you have me believe you're really not that unhappy about having Robert Salvoy as a cell mate?"

Swallowing hard, Cooper sat, but his expression didn't alter. "The man's a savage. And the warden won't do a damn thing about it. I'm in constant danger." A whine had entered his voice.

There were some who would consider Salvoy's alleged rapes of Cooper to be the most fitting of endings. The follow-up investigations of the complaints showed inconclusive findings. Hard to tell if Cooper was lying to get a single cell or if the man was truly being assaulted by his cell mate.

Harder yet to care.

"The warden's a friend. If you give me useful information, I might be able to get you a different cell assignment."

Cooper watched him distrustfully. "What sort of information?"

"About that kiddie auction you were attending, for starters. I want you to write down all the names of people you expected to be there who weren't. Names of every single contact from that man-girl love association that you shared photos of Ellie Mulder with." He caught the flicker in the man's eyes. "Yeah, we know you were video-streaming some of your times with the girl to other NAMGLA pervs. We seized your computer, remember? I want to know who else you might have shared photos or videos with, in person or through the mail. I'm looking for names you didn't include in the interviews after your arrest."

"I included every name I could think of."

Adam leaned forward, shooting the man a grim smile. "You'd better hope that isn't true, Cooper. Because if you don't come up with more names for me . . . names that actually pan out . . . you can just count on spending the next twenty-seven years as Salvoy's bunk buddy." He watched the man gray without a flicker of sympathy. "That's longer than some people are married. Stick with a guy that long and it's sort of like a marriage, isn't it?"

Cooper looked past Adam's shoulder to the armed guard at the door of the room. Then he wet his lips. "Yeah, maybe there were a couple pals that I swapped photos with. Old history, right? Doubt they even still have them."

"A pedophile who culls his photo library? Yeah, right." Adam pushed a yellow tablet over to the man and pulled a pen out of his inside suit jacket pocket to lay atop it. "Make it good, Cooper. Search your memory like your future depends on it."

With a hand that shook slightly, the man picked up the pen, and after a brief hesitation, began to write.

Watching him, Adam had a brief flash of déjà vu. There had been too many men just like this one. All guilty of horrific crimes. Hunting them for so many years had immersed him in a darkness that couldn't help but cling to him, tingeing everything else in his world.

That darkness had ruined him for doing anything else.

———

Their footsteps rang hollowly on the nondescript beige scarred tile floor as the prison guard accompanied Adam back to the public waiting area.

"Adam."

Turning, he saw Warden Joe Landry approaching. A genuine smile breaking out, he switched his cane to his left hand to take the man's hand with his right. "Joe." He returned the man's enthusiastic handshake. "Thought you were tied up in a meeting."

At the warden's short nod, the guard fell back a discreet distance as they resumed walking. "Offered the suits prison food and the meeting broke up sooner than expected." He gave a wink. "Works like a charm every time."

"I'll bet." Landry had been his senior partner in the bureau, on his first assignment to the Baltimore field office. They hadn't been together more than two years before Adam was handpicked for special training at Quantico's Behavioral Science unit. The older man had retired early from the FBI over a decade ago but made a point to keep in touch with friends in the agency.

They halted at the first set of heavy automated doors. Landry punched in a code, and they walked through as they swung open.

"Damn shame about that little girl. After you called I did some research to refresh my memory. I recall the Mulder case from a couple years ago now. You finding the girl gave the feds working the investigation something of a black eye."

Adam lifted a shoulder. He'd never cared much for the politics that came with his time in the bureau, which was only one of the reasons for leaving it. "I knew the lead agent. Tom Shepherd. He seemed grateful for the break."

Joe tugged on his earlobe. "Grateful? Maybe. But the way I hear it, after the bad press from the trial, he got banished from his DC post and sent to Bismarck. His 'gratitude' is probably frozen solid by now. Along with everything else."

Frowning slightly, Adam mentally sifted through the gossip for a germ of truth. Shepherd had been a good agent when he'd known him in DC. His rise in the ranks of the agency had been impressive. But the investigation of the first kidnapping of Ellie Mulder had been plagued by bad luck. The birthday party she'd been snatched from had been held at one of those playgrounds at a fast-food restaurant during the noon rush. Witness accounts had conflicted. And Cooper had shown rare shrewdness in choosing a child in a different state from his hometown. "Bismarck, huh? Maybe I'll give him a call." He just might think of someone or something associated with that first investigation that wasn't in Adam's own case file.

Pausing before a second set of automated doors, Landry asked, "Did you get anything useful out of Cooper? And if you did, what's it going to cost me?"

"He seems disenchanted with his cell mate."

The man nodded. "There was physical evidence supporting his claims of sexual assaults. Just nothing that points to the perpetrator. We've got him under a watch, but a place like this . . ." His mouth formed a thin hard line. "As fast as we put out fires, there's something else flaring up."

"I'll let you know if his information pans out. He gave up some names he'd neglected to mention during the course of his arrest, people he swapped pictures of the Mulder girl with. Hard to tell if it will lead anywhere."

Landry's craggy face looked dubious. "These guys trade pics like baseball cards. It's a needle in a haystack. But you're going to shake that haystack, aren't you?"

The doors opened as Adam gave him a quick feral smile. "I'm going to dismantle it, straw by straw."

"Any results on the stains found in Hubbard's bathroom yet?"

Whitman looked irritated at Kell's question. His brown suit was either the same he'd worn yesterday, or its twin. It looked equally rumpled, its creases matching those in his face. "This isn't Hollywood, Burke. In real life, lab results actually take time."

Kell looked unruffled at the man's withering tone. "I guess we have different definitions of expedited." The man had claimed the priority of the case would ensure faster results from the state lab just yesterday. "If you'd agreed to a mobile lab, we'd already have the results. I'll bet your lab hasn't even started running the tests yet."

Ignoring him, Whitman focused on CBI Agent Travis. "So who did you interview today?"

"Hubbard's ex-wife and three of his former coworkers at the prison. The warden. Some friends the ex said he spent time with when he lived there. All speak highly of him. Claim he's an up-front sort."

Giving a grunt, Whitman said, "We probably need to focus on people he associated with since his move to Denver. You'll find the list of phone numbers and their owners in the updated case file." He skidded a green expandable folder across to each of them. "Type up the day's notes and send them as an attachment to the secretary. Her e-mail is at the top of the folder."

Macy observed the crestfallen expression on the agent's face and recalled his dislike for typing.

"What about Hubbard's bank records? Have you gotten the warrant for them yet?"

"Everything we know is in the file, Burke." The assistant director was as snappish as she'd seen him. "Familiarize yourself with it and we'll talk about assignments tomorrow. Now get out of here. Not all of our people are working the case on-site. I'm coordinating input from ten CBI agents and two other law enforcement agencies. I'd like to get to bed before midnight tonight." He stopped then, his fierce glare encompassing both her and Kell. "Did you hear from Raiker today?"

"No."

Her answer only turned his expression more dour. He waved them away dismissively. "Mrs. Mulder has arranged for a cook to be on duty around the clock. If you haven't eaten, find the kitchen."

At Kell's insistence, they'd hit a drive-through on the way home, which was largely responsible for the queasiness Macy was feeling now. Still, she'd make a detour to the kitchen, if only to see if there was any fresh fruit. She wasn't going to be able to exist for long on Burke's penchant for greasy empty calories.

Outside the door, which Whitman called out for them to close behind them, Kell paused and looked at her. "You going to your room?"

"I'm going to check out the kitchen." Without waiting for his response, she brushed by him and headed in what she hoped was the right direction. It was only nine P.M. Plenty of time to read through the file when she got back to her room. And she wasn't even going to pretend not to be relieved at the thought of several uninterrupted hours without Kellan Burke attached to her side.

————

Balancing the bowl of fruit, her purse, and the file folder Whitman had given her, Macy paused outside her room and readjusted things to free up a few fingers. Managing to turn the knob, she nudged the door open with the toe of her shoe and sidled inside. Only to drop everything in shock when she saw the figure stretched out on her bed.

"Bloody hell!" Reflex had her reaching for the weapon she wore in a shoulder harness.

Kell looked up from the file he was reading, taking in the things strewn on the floor, and then observed, "You need some help there?"

She slapped a hand to her chest and waited for her heart to resume a normal beat. Bending over, she began picking up the fruit that had scattered. "What in God's name are you doing in here?"

Despite the lack of an invitation, he got up and padded over, stocking-footed, to crouch down to help her. "Lower your voice," he admonished, handing her an orange. "Travis isn't *that* far away."

The fruit safely replaced in the bowl, she grabbed at the other items she'd dropped. Rising, she snatched the purse that he'd picked up for her. "Get. Out. Of. My. Room." The words were measured. "Now."

Kell managed to look surprised. "But I have something to show you."

Her smile was tight at the transparent euphemism. "I've seen it, thanks."

Giving him a wide berth, she deposited the file on the dresser and set the bowl of fruit on the small table next to the Queen Anne's wingback. Crossing to the closet, she yanked the door open with barely restrained force, slipped off her coat, and hung it up.

"A place for everything, and everything in its place," he murmured, his tone amused.

"Exactly." Whirling to face him, she went on caustically, "Except, that is, for you. I'm in no mood for your version of show and tell. Go find someone else to play with." As soon as she saw the stunned expression on his face, Macy realized her mistake.

"You think I came in for a repeat of our one time together?" he said incredulously. "Don't get me wrong, it's not like the thought hasn't occurred, but we're working here."

She could feel the heat firing up her throat, spreading across her cheeks. Even her earlobes burned. The curse of fair skin.

Time to beat a fast retreat and salvage what she could of her dignity. "I think you came in to badger me some more, and I'm not in the mood. I have work to do."

His pale green eyes were alight with amusement behind his glasses. "You did. You thought I came in to play a little naked duchess and serf. I have to admit, the thought holds some appeal. You silhouetted against a thin sheet suspended before a fireplace. Me, lugging in hot water for m'lady's bath. And then the sheet falls. You clutch the towel to your naked breasts . . ."

"And then I kneecap you for staring."

Kell's mouth quirked. "You have an effective way of shattering a man's fantasy. Although you're the one who started it this time. C'mon." He dropped heavily down on the bed beside the papers strewn over it. "Bring your copy of the file over here."

She stared at him silently for a minute. There was no way in hell she was going to sit next to the man on that bed. Probably no way she was going to get any sleep in it after he left either, damn him. "What's this all about? My copy of the file is exactly the same as yours."

He didn't shift his attention from shuffling papers. "I have no doubt of that."

"Then why . . ."

"It's not my file I want to compare yours to," he said, raising his head to glance at her. "It's Travis's."

It took a moment for comprehension to filter in. With it, came disbelief. "You stole Travis's file?"

His expression went pained. "'Stole' sounds so judgmental. It was more sleight of hand."

"But how . . ." She pressed her fingertips to her forehead, where a headache was beginning to drill behind her eyes. "Why would you take a chance like that?"

He shrugged and went back to the papers in his lap. "What chance? If the files are identical, he'll never know. If they're not, he still probably won't realize it right away. And what's Whitman going to do, admit he had two different sets of files prepared? There's no risk, and if I'm right, we access valuable details they're trying to keep from us. Now will you bring that file over here?"

Woodenly, she retrieved it from the dresser. Then paused. Damned if she was climbing on that bed with him. Let him think what he wanted. She crossed to the chair and dragged it over to the bedside. It was heavy. Not surprisingly, he didn't offer to help.

Sitting down, she opened the expandable file and withdrew a set of folders. Flipping through them quickly, she noted that they were in some semblance of order. "We've got interviews of employees in folder one." Closing it, she opened the next. "More of the family members and business associates in two." She shifted those to the bottom of the pile before looking at the third and scanning the pages inside. "Inventory of the girl's bedroom; evidence bagged by the crime scene evidence recovery unit." His silence was starting to get on her nerves. "The fifth deals with our discoveries at Hubbard's home." She flipped through the remaining files without a clear idea of what she should be searching for, then looked at him.

"Now let's switch." He handed her a bundle of files that—thanks to his rummaging—were much less organized than the stack she exchanged with him. But as soon as she took it from him, she recognized a difference.

"These are heavier."

"No shit. That's because the files are thicker." He looked up long enough to give her a tight smile. "The files are thicker because . . ."

"Travis was given information that we weren't." Disbelief gave away quickly to a burn of anger. "This is exactly what Raiker warned Whitman about."

"And so did Mulder," he reminded her.

She shouldn't be shocked, but the realization infuriated her nonetheless. This sort of behavior was all too familiar. She'd had detectives try to cut her out of the loop on an investigation before. They usually came around once they saw what she brought to the case.

But they didn't have time wait for Whitman to start making nice. Ellie Mulder had been missing nearly forty-eight hours. They had nothing of substance to go on yet. And the CBI assistant director wanted to play turf games. "Bugger him," she muttered.

"What was that?"

"You're making a mess of things." Macy got up and went to her laptop case and unzipped the side pocket for some highlighted tabs and colored pens. "Let's use the floor. Two separate arrays for the files. We'll go through them page by page and flag those that are different."

Walking swiftly back to the chair, she grabbed the file he'd handed her earlier and headed to an expanse of carpet beyond the footboard of the bed.

"I like a woman who takes charge."

His quip didn't lighten her dark mood. "Then you're going to love the next few hours."

"My back is killing me," Kell complained, working his shoulders. "I'm going to need a massage. And since it was your idea to sit on the floor . . ."

"Quit being a baby." Macy didn't bother to look up from the notes she was scribbling. She'd started a list of the information that had been included in Travis's file and absent from her own. "Whitman's a piece of work. Why would he even bother keeping this from us? It's not like he's got any major breaks here." The sheets that had been marked CONFIDENTIAL across the top had been found only in Travis's file.

"Which means he's just being a dick." Kell stretched hugely, one arm nearly smacking her. "He's doing it because he can, and maybe to jab at Raiker some."

"Well, we can't be sure he won't give Adam a modified file, too, so I'm going to make copies of the pages when I'm done here." Besides her laptop, she'd brought a combination scanner/copier. She'd need it when—if—a ransom note arrived.

"What's the point? We have Travis's copy of the file. All modesty aside—"

"As if you had any," she muttered.

"—I'll have no problem getting my hands on his copy each time we're updated. No use making extra work for yourself."

"The point," she informed him, finally raising her gaze to fix it on him, "is that you're going to switch the files back tomorrow morning."

He stopped rubbing his neck to stare at her. "Why would I do that?"

Macy set the pen down to enumerate on her fingers. "Because number one, you can't be sure Whitman won't have some private communications with Travis, in which he refers to information that will not be included in the file you left with him. And two, there's no reason to raise suspicions if you don't have to. We hold the upper hand as long as Whitman doesn't suspect we know what he's pulling. And three, if we get caught with the wrong file in our possession, CBI will just guard the case details even more closely."

"Double the chances of getting caught if you're intent on switching the files back every morning," he muttered. But she could tell from his expression that he hadn't rejected her logic outright.

"We have the advantage as long as Whitman doesn't realize that we know what he's up to." She shifted her attention back to her notes. "That might come in handy later."

"Very devious." She could feel him studying her. "And surprising, coming from you."

"Devious was switching the files in the first place." She shot him a glance then. "How did you know Travis's file had more information in it just by sight? The number of file folders is the same as mine. It's just the number of pages that differ."

"Superior observation skills." When her eyes narrowed, he shrugged. "And years of experience. I was making a pretty good living at sixteen targeting corporate types to follow into coffee shops and swiping their bags or briefcases." He got up and wandered over to the bowl she'd placed on the table, helping himself to an apple.

Gaping at him, Macy was at loss for words. "You . . . stole things? For a living?"

He took a big bite, then chewed, plainly unconcerned with his admission. "Technically, I made my living selling the bags back. So that's not actually stealing at all."

"No, it's extortion." Mind still reeling, she studied him. At sixteen she'd been enrolled in an all-girls school in London. And he'd been well on his way to a life of crime. She wondered if he'd acquired his affinity for locks in that same period.

His eyes glinted. "We can't all be raised in castles, Duchess."

"I wasn't . . ." She stopped. Her homes may not have been castles, but it was safe to guess that they had far more in common with the Mulder estate than Kell's childhood home. "With that kind of background, how'd you end up working for Adam?"

He finished the apple and three-pointed it into the trash can by the dresser. "He recruited me. We go way back."

"Way . . ." Her eyes widened. "You *stole* from Adam Raiker?" The thought positively boggled the mind. Trying to do the mental math, she guessed, "When he was in the bureau?" He would have been dangerous, even a decade and a half earlier. "You didn't have very good instincts, did you?"

Kell's grin was lopsided. "I was usually pretty good at pegging cops, but Raiker didn't look like one. More like a ruthless corporate raider type. I think it was the clothes that threw me."

She nodded. Raiker was a clotheshorse. The suit Mulder had been dressed in when they'd met probably hadn't been pricier than any of the ones her boss normally wore.

"Anyway, I picked out him and another suit and followed them inside. I cultivated a real clean look. Sort of preppie, though I hated the type. But fewer people suspected someone who looked the part. I'd targeted Raiker's buddy, but the way things were positioned, couldn't get to his bag. So I decided to grab up Adam's." Amazingly, from the expression on his face, the memory was a good one. "The boss is fast as a snake. Nearly broke my arm."

She was trying and failing to imagine the scene. Fascinated, she gave up all pretense of working. "So you failed."

"Nope. The companion—who I later discovered was a

lawyer—finally figured out what was going on and tried to help. Just balled things up. I was able to shove Adam into the other guy and they got tangled up and went down. I skipped with the briefcase."

"And then you tried to blackmail him?"

He winced imperceptibly. "You have such an ugly view of the world, Macy. Using the information inside the case, I contacted him and offered to negotiate its return. He had a few choice words for me but refused to give me any money. I hung up, figured I'd let him stew a while, and in the meantime, I started going through the contents. And was blown away. It was a case file on a string of murders in DC. I recognized a few names . . ." He broke off when her expression grew incredulous. "I knew people, okay? On the street. Some of the 'businessmen' on the street corners. We worked the same neighborhood."

She stared at the man as if she'd never seen him before. And she hadn't. Not like this. The rare glimpse into his background was the last thing she would have imagined for him.

He padded back across the room toward her and sat down again, this time using the foot of the bed as a backrest. "So anyway, the next time I called him, I was more careful. It had occurred to me that pissing off an FBI agent could do serious damage to my ability to conduct business, so I struck a deal. I offered to help put them in touch with some of the people they were looking for."

"For free."

He looked pained at the suggestion. "Please. I was a businessman. My fee would be for my assistance, rather than for the return of the file. Raiker agreed, and with my help, he was eventually able to solve twelve homicides in the area. He also saw to it that I served six months in juvie." His expression went wry. "He was never the forgiving sort, even back then."

Macy leaned forward on her desk. She'd figure he fabricated the entire thing—he wasn't above it—if it didn't have a ring of truth. "So years later when he started his own company, he thought of the young thief—*excuse* me," she corrected, at his swift look, "*businessman*, and thought his company wouldn't be complete without you, so he tracked you down again."

"Didn't need to track me down. Adam's been in my life, one way or another, since I was sixteen. Before I joined Raiker Forensics, I put several years in on the Baltimore PD, the last few as detective."

She turned back to her work, although her mind was still full of the revelations he'd made. There was more to the story than what he'd told her. A lot more. And she was slightly bothered by the degree of fascination it elicited. She didn't want to know any more about Kellan Burke.

The little she did know—intimately—still haunted her.

Reaching for another tagged sheet, she began skimming it.

"Where'd you work before joining Raiker's agency?"

Her attention splintered when she realized what she was reading. Lab reports. And Whitman hadn't mentioned a word about them.

Distracted, she managed, "BII." Apparently at least one task had been expedited by the state crime lab.

"Bureau of Intelligence and Investigation? Funny. I wouldn't have pegged you for a California girl."

She jammed the sheet in his hands. "Look at this."

Obediently he took the sheet and scanned it. "Son of a bitch. They identified the latents left in the girl's room and the one next door."

"I suppose all they really did was match the fingerprint records Mulder had on file for his employees, and those for the family themselves." There were still unidentified prints on the sheet that hadn't yet been run through AFIS. "But look here." She leaned over to point to the section in question.

A partial thumbprint found inside the closet in the room next to the girl's had been positively matched to Nick Hubbard.

Chapter 5

"I don't get it." Macy looked both excited and puzzled. "Why would Whitman want to hide the fact that Hubbard has been positively linked to the kidnapping?"

"Because he doesn't want Mulder to know yet. Hubbard is Mulder's employee. His involvement in the girl's disappearance doesn't exonerate the family. Just the opposite. And Whitman thinks we're a direct line to Mulder. Or at least he isn't taking any chances that we might be."

Kell pushed away from the bed to crowd closer to her. "What else do you have there?"

She shrugged him away irritably. "You've seen what I have. The bank account records were in Travis's file but not ours. So were the LUDs from Hubbard's cell and landline phones. These lab results. And what looks like the beginning of a comprehensive background check on Stephen and Althea Mulder." She leaned forward to snatch up the report in question. And to her chagrin, he didn't move away, as ordered. Instead he chose to read over her shoulder.

That was a habit she invariably found annoying. It was

doubly so with Kell. At least she told herself that's what she was feeling. Her galloping pulse and jittery stomach made it impossible to concentrate.

She scooted away. "You have personal-space issues."

His smile was slow and wicked. "Do I make you nervous?"

Because she had no response—an all too frequent problem in his presence—she chose to ignore his remark. Scanning the page quickly, she flipped the page. "Mulder has opened up his financials to them. It would take a handful of forensic accountants to work that lead alone. But from the looks of things, he could buy a couple third-world countries without making a dent in his money."

Falling into silence, she looked through a few more pages. After a couple minutes, she said, "There are also the beginnings of reports on the lawyer—Alden. And it looks like they've made a good start digging on every employee on this estate."

"Alden was here the day she was taken," he recalled. "So were Lance Spencer and Tessa Amundson. They'd have to find some link between any of them and Hubbard." He fell silent, but she could tell his mind was racing. "Whitman probably has an ulterior motive in putting us onto him. Hubbard's a direct line to the girl. Hard to believe he doesn't want a whole CBI team following up on him."

"He's trying to keep us away from the Mulders as much as possible." Macy was surprised the realization hadn't hit her before. "Probably afraid we'll collude with them. Pass along information." The agent's doubt of their integrity burned anew.

Kell nodded. "His distrust of us actually puts us in a better position on this case. Hubbard is key to solving it."

"We're in a better position because of the switch you made with Travis," she admitted.

He cocked a brow. "Glad to hear you approve." He got up lazily and stretched before ambling over to put his shoes on. "'Cuz you're going to switch the files back in the morning."

Her head snapped up. "What? No. I can't."

"Sure you can." To listen to his encouraging tone, one would think he was giving a pep talk to a Little Leaguer. "He's going to get suspicious if I'm always arranging ways to get him to put his folder down. You're a female. You can bring a whole different aspect to things."

Her mind had gone blank. Scrambling to her feet, she hurried after him as he headed for the door. "I'm not good at things like that."

"You'll think of something."

"No!" Panicked, she lowered her voice. "Wait." He turned, one hand on the knob, his expression quizzical. "Um . . . let's talk about this. Maybe I could help you. I could . . . distract him somehow and you could make the switch."

"That's what I'm saying. Wear something low-cut. Bat your lashes at him. You know." He fluttered his hands in a feminine gesture that under other circumstances would have amused her. "Use your wiles."

When he would have pulled open the door, she grabbed for his shirt to yank him to a halt. "Burke," she hissed desperately, all sense of self-preservation gone. "I don't have wiles."

He looked at her then, really looked at her. And she could tell he was about to say something she'd have to make him regret. But then the expression on his face changed. His pale green eyes glinted with something very different than humor.

Macy swallowed. For the first time she realized how close they were standing. But for the life of her, she couldn't move away. His gaze was arrowed on her mouth. Nervously, she moistened her lips, then caught her breath when she saw the muscle jump in his clenched jaw. She couldn't begin to count the number of times she'd wanted to see him regard her with any expression other than amusement.

Heat flared in her belly when she read what was on his face. Desire. An emotion she couldn't—wouldn't—return.

His lips looked firm. And somehow closer than before. Tiny tendrils of fire zinged through her veins. The breath strangled in her throat. His headed dipped imperceptibly.

Then he stopped, as if pulled back by an invisible wire. His jaw clenched. It seemed to take him a moment to fight for control. "Oh, yeah," he muttered. "Take it from me. You've got wiles."

He yanked open the door with barely restrained force. And this time she knew better than to try to stop him. Couldn't have if she'd wanted to. It was all Macy could do to remember to haul in a shuddering breath. And then another. She shut the door after him. Locked it. Then checked the lock three times before turning and forcing herself to move across the floor.

Well. With effort, she reached for her scattered senses and tried to force them in some semblance of order. Heading for the bathroom, she scrubbed her face with a washcloth that felt cold against her heated skin. It gave her something to concentrate on besides that moment of suspended animation with Kell.

Carefully she spread the cloth out to dry and turned her attention to brushing her teeth. For an instant or two she'd been convinced he'd been about to kiss her. And history told her just how big a mistake *that* would have been.

She'd known getting involved with him, however briefly, would complicate their teaming together in future cases.

But recognizing that hadn't stopped one night of madness after they'd shared a ride home from a colleague's wedding. He'd suggested stopping somewhere for one more drink. She closed her eyes painfully. There had been dancing. Burke was as smooth at that as he was everything else.

As she'd found out firsthand a few hours later.

Unconsciously, she spread toothpaste on the brush a second time and began brushing again. Maybe she'd interpreted the recent interlude incorrectly. After all, earlier tonight she'd been half persuaded he'd shown up in her room for a very different reason than the one he'd had, and she'd been proved wrong about that. She was usually a far better judge of people, but Burke screwed with her normally reliable instincts.

And that had been just one in a list of very solid reasons

to not see him again outside of work. Another was that he didn't fit in her carefully constructed life. There was nothing wrong with wanting order in it. Control. Burke created chaos. Uncertainty.

She began brushing her teeth for a third time. If he'd kissed her, she would have pushed him away. An inner voice jeered as she had the thought, but she clung to it stoutly. This case was as serious as it could get, and none of them could afford diversions.

Breathing a bit easier, she carefully replaced the cap on the toothpaste and turned to return to the bedroom, flicking the light off. On. Then off. On again. Off. Crossing to the dresser, she swiftly changed into pajamas and folded her clothes, placing them in drawers. Gathering up the file, she laid it on the top of the bed, firmly pushing away the image of Kell sprawled on top of it. She switched on the bedside lamp and then moved to the overhead switch and turned it off.

There was really nothing to worry about. Burke wasn't the type to moon over a woman who'd been quite clear about not wanting a repeat performance. There were too many other willing women eager to take her place.

The thought did nothing to lighten her mood. She moved to the bed, carefully folded down the bedcovers, and smoothed them lightly. Once. Twice. Again. It was probably nothing more than habit for him, and she'd just happened to be there. If he hadn't returned to his senses, well, she'd never taken leave of hers. Nothing would have happened.

She fluffed the pillow. Once. Twice. Before she caught herself and went still.

Oh, God.

She replayed the last few minutes in her mind. How many times had she brushed her teeth? Turned out the lights? Her gaze fell to the covers that she'd smoothed repetitively.

Deliberately she tossed the pillow on the bed and refused to allow her mind to linger on the way it sat askew against the others, the arrangement a bit off kilter. Anxiety sometimes still brought out her strange compulsion to do things in threes.

And there was plenty to be anxious about in the last few days. The few moments with Kell were the very least of them.

A girl was still missing. Terrified. Probably waiting for a replay of the horror she'd endured only a few years earlier.

With grim resolve, she slid into bed and reached for the case file. Macy was going to go through it again. Commit as much of it as she could to memory.

And the only compulsion at work this time was the need to bring Ellie Mulder home.

Alive.

"No. I'm going to kill her now." It was freezing on that damn mountain, the sort of deep bone-numbing cold that would take hours near the stove to dispel. There had been no reason to have this conversation outside. It wasn't like it mattered what the girl overheard.

"You'll follow my instructions exactly." The voice was robotic. A distorter was used whenever they had phone contact. "The girl has to stay alive until I give the word."

"I'm not a fucking babysitter." Emotion flared, and he stopped to identify it. Frustration. Feeling anything at all was rare enough that the experience distracted him. The wind whipped icy pellets of sleet to sting his cheeks, bringing him back to the matter at hand. "I'm not going to sit on this damn mountain playing nursemaid to a kid."

"You have a gift for revisionist history, my friend." Even with the distortion, the mockery in the caller's voice was evident. "You agreed to the kidnapping for an additional fee. This is part of that sum. The second half of your very generous payment is only forthcoming if you can follow directions."

He took the phone away from his ear and considered it for a minute. The person on the other end of the line was wrong. The money had been only part of it. There weren't many in his line of work who would take a job with a kid involved.

But that had actually been his primary reason for taking the hit. He'd never killed a kid before. But he was convinced it was exactly what he needed to be normal again. To *feel* again. He'd been numb for a very long time.

Resuming the conversation, he shrugged. "Just don't take too long. I'm about to go crazy on this damn mountain. It snows all the fucking time. And there's no reception for the TV.

"Read a book." The voice was unsympathetic. "I just need to be sure you're going to be able to end things when I give the word. Are a few more days with the kid going to make you go soft toward her?"

He gave a grim smile. "Hardly. You could say I'm looking forward to it."

"Just don't get in a hurry. Things have to go exactly according to plan."

He snorted. Reaching up, he broke off the enormous icicle hanging from the branch of a nearby fir. It was thick and sharp. He imagined drilling it through the caller's eye, into the brain. He might not know his employer's identity, but he could imagine the type easily enough. Just another corporate asshole, used to calling the shots from his cushy corner office, while feeling safely anonymous.

"Nothing goes exactly according to plan. Things come up, I adapt and move on."

"Well, don't try any 'adapting' before speaking with me first." The voice was sharp. "We've come too far for any screwups now."

The call abruptly ended. Tucking the satellite phone back inside his pocket, he blew out a breath just to watch it steam and then climbed back up the steps and into the shelter. A welcome blast of heat enveloped him at the door. Slipping out of his coat, he threw it and his gloves and hat in a pile on the floor and pulled off the boots before walking further inside. It was going to be hard to wait. Give him more time to plan, sure. He was adept with a gun, but the knife had always been his favorite. He could always get started early. Take a piece of her at a time. Make it last.

Once he'd lost the thrill of his work, he'd taken to using the gun more and more often. Quick and over then back home again. But this time had to be perfect. It might be his one chance to get that joy back. To get *any* feeling back.

Yeah, he could wait. And while he waited, he'd plan every second of how he'd do it.

A fraction of movement caught his eye. He looked hard at the kid, sitting on one of the camp stools at the table. She went still, looking at him with those big doe eyes.

Then she shifted again. "I can't get comfortable."

Swiftly, he strode around to the back of the stool and checked the length of tape securing her other wrist to the table leg. "Jesus." The spoon was nearly hidden up the long sleeve of her pajama top. He reached for it and threw it on the floor. "Give it up, kid. Think you're going to saw through duct tape with a plastic spoon?" So much for freeing one of her hands so she could eat. But damned if he was going to hand-feed her. He headed for the battery-operated TV. Reception up here was a joke. But even a channel that was little more than static was better than nothing.

"Who were you talking to out there?"

Stilling, he slowly turned his head to look at her. A quick flash of fear crossed her expression. But she persisted. "You took that phone outside. Who was it?"

"No one you know."

She didn't look convinced, but that wasn't his problem. He picked up the remote and started hunting through the channels for one that wasn't totally fuzzy.

"Is someone else coming up here?"

Why in hell she'd sound scared now when she hadn't really showed much fear since that first night, he couldn't say. And didn't care. "No one's coming for you. Now shut the fuck up."

She shut up. The kid was polite, he'd give her that. If he'd been stuck up here with a whiny brat, he'd have done her that first day, without waiting for the order.

If this thing dragged out too long, he still might.

Whistling tunelessly, Kell headed toward his bedroom door. As little sleep as he'd gotten last night, it'd almost been a relief when morning had hit. He blamed his restlessness on the case details that had replayed in his head all night long.

That excuse would play a lot better if images of Macy Reid hadn't been stuck there, too.

Scowling, he reached for the knob. He'd almost made a dumb decision last night. Very dumb. She'd made it abundantly clear months ago—in a crisp matter-of-fact tone that still rankled to remember—that the two of them weren't going to happen again. Hell, he'd even agreed with her assessment. They were colleagues. Occasionally paired together on a case. It was just asking for trouble to muddy that up.

And the fact that it had only happened once—and wasn't likely to recur—was undoubtedly the reason he hadn't been able to get their encounter out of his head in the time since.

Kell stopped short, mentally slapping his forehead when that thought elicited another. He owed a phone call to the woman whose bed he'd hurriedly left when he'd received Adam's callout the other night. By his calculations, the call was a couple days overdue.

Shit. It took a glance at his watch and some mental gymnastics to recall the time difference. Nearly nine back East. With any luck, she'd already be at work with her cell turned off. He could leave a message and hang up, having done his duty.

Quickly he dialed her number and headed out the door. After it'd rung a few times, a familiar voice picked up. The message he'd formulated in his mind died a quick death. "Celia." Trying to inject a note of pleasure in his voice, he walked past Macy's door. "I was afraid you'd already be at work."

Intent on passing by, he stopped dead in front of Macy's open door. She was on her hands and knees, scrabbling for the fruit that had mysteriously fallen to the floor again. And Agent Travis, *Dan*, was down there with her.

"Of course I didn't forget." He delivered the lie mechanically as a vicious stab of jealousy seared through him. What the hell was the agent doing in Macy's room? "This is the first moment I've had free. Had to catch up on the case. How's your mom doing?"

"I'm so sorry." Damned if Macy's voice didn't sound breathless. And her cheeks were flushed. Could she call the color at will? "I'm not usually such a klutz."

"First thing in the morning, I'm lucky to put one foot in front of the other," Travis assured her as he handed her two apples he'd rescued.

Kell's lip curled. Apparently gallantry wasn't dead. Just—in the case of the agent—very very rusty. Dimly aware of a lull in the conversation with Celia, he interjected, "I'm glad to hear that."

Macy was rising. Sir Galahad did, too. "I guess you should be grateful I didn't offer you coffee."

The rise in Celia's tone yanked his attention back. "No, I'm not glad she's in the hospital again. I'm sure gout is very painful. I meant I'm glad to hear you can be with her."

"I'd take whatever you offered."

Kell's brows skated up and he threw a narrowed glance at Travis, who seemed to recognize belatedly how the words sounded. "I mean, this time of day, I'm ready to eat or drink anything. Matter of fact, I was on my way to the kitchen to grab a quick bite before starting the day. Join me?"

Macy took the bowl of battered fruit he held and handed him a green expandable file folder. And comprehension hit Kell like a ton of bricks.

She'd staged the whole thing to switch the folders back. He wanted to believe the flare of relief he felt had nothing to do with the fact that he'd bought her act. Hook, line, and sinker. "I'd like that." Her baby blues were guileless as she gazed up at the much taller agent, who wore the sappiest grin Kell had ever seen outside his grandpa's old hound at biscuit time.

"Hope things continue to improve," he said rapidly, as Macy and Travis walked by him. The look she shot him would have skewered a lesser man. "I don't know when I'll get a chance to call again, but I'll be thinking about you."

That brought a giggle and a very unladylike suggestion that he hoped Celia wasn't making in her mother's presence. "Let's rain check that. But I like the way you think." He clicked the phone shut and slid it in his pocket, the conversation already forgotten. "So. You guys going down for breakfast? I could eat."

Neither bothered to answer. "I hear the cooks here studied in Paris," Agent Travis told Macy as they moved down the hall ahead of Kell. "Maybe I can talk them into making some crepes."

"I like those, too. Especially the ones with fruit in them." Kell may as well have been invisible for all the attention the other two paid him.

"I'm more of a fruit or cereal person in the morning," Macy confessed.

"I saw that earlier."

They both laughed, and Kell shoved his free hand in his pocket, disgusted. Travis was about as funny as a train wreck. Macy was sort of overdoing things. Switching the folders was one thing. If she kept this up, she'd have the guy following her around like a trained poodle by the end of the day.

Hell, for all he knew, Dan Travis was exactly the sort of guy she normally went for. No personality. No sense of humor. No threat.

Yeah. He ambled along behind them, shamelessly eavesdropping on their innocuous conversation. He'd lay odds that Macy went for the vanilla straightlaced guys. Safe and boring. Which just meant they'd both made the right decision about going their separate ways months ago. He couldn't guarantee her safe. And he'd never been described as boring.

They were walking by the conference room where Assistant Director Whitman was framed in the doorway, his face grim. "Reid. Can you come in here?"

Macy immediately veered toward him. Travis would have kept on moving toward the kitchen but must have noticed that Kell was following Macy into the room. He paused and changed direction to trail behind him. When Kell saw everyone collected in the room, his gut took a quick vicious twist. He didn't need Whitman's terse explanation to guess the reason for the invitation.

"There's been a ransom demand."

Macy went to stand beside Stephen Mulder, who was staring blindly at the screen of his laptop. His wife sat next to him, her perfect profile ravaged by tears, one fist pressed to her lips. Swallowing hard, Mulder pushed the computer around so she could read the message.

A GUY LIKE YOU IS USED TO BUYING WHATEVER YOU WANT. IS GETTING YOUR DAUGHTER BACK WORTH $10,000,000? YOU'VE GOT FIVE DAYS TO GET THE MONEY TOGETHER AND AWAIT FURTHER ORDERS. THERE'LL BE NO EXTENSIONS. SHOULD YOU DECIDE NOT TO COOPERATE, SHE GOES ON SALE TO THE HIGHEST BIDDER. THE MIDEASTERN MARKET FOR WHITE PRE-TEEN FEMALES IS VERY LUCRATIVE.

"Is this your personal e-mail account?" she asked the man quietly.

"No." A muscle clenched in his jaw. "It's the one I use for work."

"How do we know she's still alive?" It was difficult to make out Althea Mulder's words, choked as they were by sobs. "I need to talk to her. I have to hear my baby's voice . . ." Her husband slid an arm around her shoulders then, and she collapsed to weep against his shoulder. He pressed his lips against her blond hair, seeming to struggle with his own composure.

"The message was in Mr. Mulder's in-box this morning," Whitman explained, looking grim. "As you can see, it's time-stamped four thirty-seven A.M., but that doesn't necessarily mean anything. There are ways to change the time on e-mails sent, just like . . ."

". . . There are ways to change the address it appears to be sent from," Macy finished quietly. The sender's name was listed in the lengthy header as nkelliott@aibs.com. She shot the agent a look. "I assume you already have computer techs following up on the IP address."

"Of course. We'll have a warrant in a matter of hours." He switched his attention to the Mulders, and his voice went gruff with what might have been sympathy. "I know this is difficult. But hearing from the kidnapper is actually a good thing. It keeps the lines of communication open. And the time frame cited in the e-mail gives us several more days to track him."

"What communication?" Althea Mulder's face was splotchy when she raised it to stare tremulously at the agent. "You said you didn't think this was his real return e-mail address. We can't respond, we can't ask for proof that Ellie is alive. And that's why he chose this way, isn't it?" Her voice went shriller, even as her husband hugged her closer and murmured in her ear. "He's in control. We have no way of making any demands of our own."

"That could change." Ignoring the narrowed look Whitman threw at her, Macy went on calmly. "He leaves the message open-ended. You know he'll be contacting you again. And it's chancy for him to rely on one-sided communications throughout this process. At some point, he needs to be sure that you have the money ready. That you understand the directions he'll be giving."

Hope lit up Althea's watery eyes as she turned her attention on Macy. "Do you think at that point he'll call? Let us talk to our daughter?"

Whitman answered before she could. "Reid's specialty is forensic linguistics. Examining this message and any others that might be forthcoming could give us valuable information about the identity of the person we're dealing with."

"You mean Nick Hubbard?"

Whitman's eyes flickered at Stephen Mulder's terse question. "Right now it looks like he's involved. Although it's entirely possible he isn't acting alone."

Mulder gave a jerky nod, and the expression on his face was terrible to see. "And he was here because of me. I gave him a job." It was his wife's turn to comfort him, as she took his hand and laced their fingers together. "I brought him into our lives." His voice cracked on that, and he dropped his head, battling for composure.

The sight of her husband's grief seemed to strengthen something in Althea. She lifted their linked hands and pressed a kiss against his, the gesture filled with tenderness. Her face was still streaked with tears, but her voice was steady as she stood, tugging at her husband's hand so he'd join her. Her words were directed at Macy. "Do what you're trained for, Ms. Reid. Help lead them to the bastard who took my baby. And we'll do the only thing left to us right now." Gently she turned her husband toward the door. "Pray."

The room was silent behind them as the couple exited the room. Macy concentrated fiercely on the message on the computer screen, willing away the tight knot in her throat.

"I'm assuming Mulder is willing to pay the amount and won't have trouble getting the cash together." Kell's voice was the first to break the quiet.

Whitman scowled and glanced at Agent Pelton, who was seated beside him. "He indicated he was willing. But I don't know that that will be the process I'll be suggesting. It depends on what the demands are regarding the payment."

"His finances appear to be in order," Pelton said matter-of-factly. The whipcord-lean man tapped a sheaf of papers on the table before him. "At least there's nothing that the forensic accountants have found that would indicate a sudden shortage of money. The fact that such a sizable amount was demanded might mean the kidnapper had some insight into the Mulders' holdings."

She was surprised when Whitman leveled a look at her. "What do you think?"

"It's possible," she said honestly, staring at the computer screen again. "Certainly someone close to the family or affiliated with the store empire would realize their worth. But Mulder is listed in the Forbes ranking of top twenty wealthiest Americans every year. Ten million isn't an unreasonable demand for someone who has researched the family, even a stranger."

Whitman gestured toward the computer. "What can you tell us from that message?"

"It's brilliant," she said with a tinge of bitterness. "The threat included is more devastating than death. It plays on these parents' worst fear. That was deliberate."

Agent Travis crossed the room to read the screen over her

shoulder. "The message contains two contractions. That suggests a native English speaker, right?"

"And the wording used." Pelton scribbled in the margin of a page in front of him. "Extension. Lucrative. Sounds like someone educated."

It took effort—a great deal of it—for Macy to restrain a wince. "Not necessarily. Vocabulary can be consciously chosen to create a certain impression. So can the use or absence of contractions. I'm going to be looking for patterns in the syntax, which is much more unconscious, and therefore less easily disguised."

Agent Pelton frowned. "I was involved in a trial just last year where a forensic linguist was called in. His testimony focused on the wording of the defendant's alleged confession. He didn't say anything about syntax."

She sent him a small smile, even as her jaw clenched. Now was not the time to get into a lecture on stylistics vs. research-based forensic linguistics. "I rely on a scientifically researched author-identification database formed from hundreds of ransom and suicide notes."

His expression still doubtful, Pelton sent a sideways glance toward Whitman. "Still . . ."

"It has a five to six percent error rate," she responded crisply. "I've been qualified as an expert witness in thirty trials to date. As a matter of fact, I've got another trial appearance in two days in Chicago." The agent shut up at that. She met Whitman's gaze squarely. "I can also do a threat assessment on the note, although the error rate for that is greater. More like fifteen percent."

"To determine whether the author intends to follow through on the selling the girl if the ransom doesn't come through?"

She nodded, her attention returning to the screen consideringly. "Like I say, the inclusion of that particular phrasing is calculated. But that doesn't mean the threat isn't real."

"It might also be included to throw us off track."

Like everyone else in the room, her attention switched to Kell. He wore a thick navy sweater with jeans today, the informality of his dress a stark contrast in the room full of suit-clad men. He gave a nod toward the computer. "That threat strikes fear into the Mulders' hearts, yeah. But it also makes us think immediately of pedophiles. It might have been deliberately included to lead us astray. Make us think of the last kidnapping and focus our energies there. Nothing in Hubbard's background suggests he's a girl lover."

"Doesn't have to be," Pelton shot back. "He just has to have connections to a human-trafficking ring."

"Why don't we give Macy a chance to work her magic and we might have a better idea of what we're looking at," suggested Travis.

To her chagrin he gave her a surreptitious pat on the shoulder before moving away. From the angle of Burke's brow, the gesture hadn't been lost on him. The agent's attitude was slightly alarming. Maybe she'd overdone the helpless female this morning when she'd switched folders. Mentally, she kicked herself for letting Kell talk her into concocting that episode with Travis earlier this morning.

"I'll need samples of written communication from everyone you want to check as a match for the author of this note." She nodded toward the computer. "Have your techs gotten into Hubbard's computer yet? If I had access to his sent e-mails, I could compare them to this note."

"I'll get someone on it right away. How long does it take to run each of these tests?"

She lifted a shoulder. "After I diagram the samples, the author identification will require about ten minutes for each. Just the time it takes to scan the written communication into the database and run the match. The threat assessment will take longer. About two hours."

The assistant director looked thoughtful. He'd gotten rid of the dreadful brown suit, but the navy one he wore now was just as ill fitting. "And it needs to be written communication? Transcribed notes of the interviews we conducted, for example, wouldn't be appropriate?"

"They wouldn't be as valid. The notes wouldn't be a verbatim duplication of what was said, and the rhythm and patterns of people's written speech often differs from their oral speech."

Whitman gave a short nod. "We'll start with written communications from Hubbard and the Mulders. Then we'll see about getting samples from the rest of the employees. The lawyer, Alden, was here that evening. The accountant, Lance Spencer. Mulder's executive secretary, Tess Amundson. We should be able to get samples from them from Mulder's computer, as well. We'll have enough for you to start with when you return this evening."

He riffled through the stack of pages on the table before him. His face looked flushed, although it wasn't particularly warm in the room. Macy had been chilled since she first stepped off the jet. Although Virginia had its share of cold weather, there was something about the difference in altitude that made the Colorado temperature seem even more frigid. "Here's a list of the owners of each of the phone numbers listed on Hubbard's cell and landline LUDs." She got up to take her copy from him. "We've identified all of the numbers except for one, and that just might turn out to be the one belonging to a partner or accomplice."

"Trac phone?" Kell suggested. "Or satellite?"

"Not a SAT phone." Whitman dropped heavily back into his seat, as if the act of leaning across the table to hand out the sheets had exhausted him. "More likely it's some kind of disposable. We're still digging. The last call that came from it was logged on Hubbard's cell phone at twelve oh two A.M. the morning the girl was kidnapped. From the time logged, it's doubtful the call was answered."

"Could have been some sort of signal," Agent Travis suggested.

Whitman gave a slight nod. "Whoever the number belongs to, there are frequent calls, beginning about three months prior to the kidnapping."

A flicker of interest sparked inside her. An operation of this scope would take plenty of advance planning. "Is there a pattern to those calls?" At Whitman's look, she went on, "Do they all come late at night, like the last one, or different times during the day? How long do they usually last? Are they logged on both phones, or just the cell?"

He consulted the pages again before answering. "There's one call from that number on the landline January fifth, ten minutes after a call had been logged on Hubbard's cell. The rest all went to the cell." He went silent for a moment as he skimmed the pages. "Looks like they range in length from a few minutes to over a half hour. And all but two of them occur after seven o'clock P.M. There are fifteen in all. And Hubbard called that number, from his landline and cell, a total of twenty-one times." There was a slight rustle of papers as he shuffled them together and looked up.

"I assume you've tried calling the number."

Whitman looked testy at Kell's suggestion. "Of course. But it hasn't been answered. At any rate, we'll keep with it. You, Reid, and Travis take this list of contacts and track down every person and place Hubbard called in the last couple months. And swing by his house again to get his tax returns. I want to match some figures to his bank account records. Let's see results today. We've been given a timeline, people."

His impassive façade cracked, for just a moment, and Macy saw a hint of bleakness in his eyes. "We've got five days."

Chapter 6

She watched the man from beneath her lids. And to think at first she'd thought he looked so ordinary. He was spooky, and not just because of the knife. He reminded her of a dead rat one of the stable cats had killed. The teeth on the rodent had been bared, and it had still looked vicious, but its eyes had looked shiny and dead.

The man's eyes looked like that, too. Like he was dead, but his body didn't know it.

They settled on her now, and a chill broke out over her skin. She was still wearing the pajamas he'd taken her in, and a thick blanket. But it wasn't the cold that gave her goose bumps whenever he looked at her. It was those eyes. Pale brown. Almost tan, really. Light like his hair and skin.

Cooper had been a disgusting nasty man. But he had *looked* nice. Normal, even. This guy didn't look normal. And even a little kid half her age would realize just by looking at him that he wasn't *nice*.

"Anyone ever tell you it's rude to stare?"

"Anyone ever tell *you* it's rude to kidnap people?" The

words came without her thinking about them. Horrified, she stopped, barely breathing, waiting for his reaction.

He smiled, and that just made him look creepier. Like a dried-up fish on the beach, eyes flat and staring and lips stretched out in a wide grin. "I liked you better when you were scared. You should be scared, kid. You and me, we got business to conduct up here."

Her skin prickled, and her stomach cramped. She could feel her palms going damp and the familiar dread sliding over her like a wet dark curtain. *Oh please, oh please, oh please . . .*

"Are you going to fuck me?" It was as if someone else had taken over her speech. Over her brain. It had been like that after a while before. When Cooper had stolen her away. And every time he'd touched her like that, there had been less of her left. And more of the girl she heard now. The one who was too numb to care about anything.

The one who had learned to stop feeling at all.

His gaze flicked over her once. Twice. Then, as if bored, he looked away. "You got no tits."

The relief streamed out her in a long loud sigh, and he looked back at her, the boredom gone now. In its place was that expression he'd worn when he'd first shown her the knife. "What are you feeling now? Right now?" he demanded. When she didn't answer, he pulled out the knife and sprang from the lawn chair, striding across the cramped space to yank her up by the shoulder. "Tell me or I'll gut you like a rabbit. Right now!"

She shrank away from him. He was so freaky! And then he let go of her so suddenly she got tangled in the blanket and fell to the floor. But then she wasn't scared anymore. Not at that moment. Because all of a sudden she realized exactly what he meant. What he wanted.

"You don't feel anything, do you?" He stilled, staring at her with those creepy eyes. "That's why you keep asking me those questions. But my answers don't matter. You can't feel someone else's feelings just by hearing about them."

"Shut the fuck up." He went back to the chair and dropped

down on it. Picking up the remote, he clicked on the TV that sat on the cot he slept in.

"I thought my feelings were gone once, too," she whispered. Wiggling under the blanket was a struggle with her hands tied but all of a sudden she was cold again. So cold. Slowly she scooted the stool back until her shoulders pressed against the wall. "I wanted them to be. After a while, when things are so bad that you'd rather be dead . . . you get sort of numb."

She knew he was listening. He was staring at the staticky TV. But he didn't turn up the volume. "I thought I'd be numb forever. And I wouldn't have cared." It had been so much easier when she hadn't felt anything. Not when she saw her parents again. Not when they'd moved across the country to the big house with the tall walls that hadn't kept this man out.

She drew a deep shuddering breath and drew up her knees, dropping her forehead to rest upon them. "I wish I could be like that again."

———

"Adam?"

Macy's attention snapped to Kell. He was frowning as he pressed the phone closer to his ear. "The connection sucks. It sounds like you're in a tunnel." He paused for a moment and then chuckled. "That'd explain it, then. You got my e-mail last night?"

Sending a glance in Travis's direction, she realized he was listening, too, although he pretended not to be. To distract him, she said, "If you ever get tired of doing all the driving, you just have to mention it. I wouldn't mind switching off. I'm sure Kell wouldn't either."

He lifted a shoulder, meeting her gaze in the rearview mirror. "Thanks, but I'm familiar with the area. Neither of you are. Probably not used to these driving conditions either."

Kell's voice had dropped. It was too bad, she reflected, that Adam had chosen a time to call when they had no privacy. Although Kell had mentioned e-mailing him last night. Hopefully he'd been able to share any information then that he wouldn't be able to with Travis in the car. Like the way Whitman was trying to keep them out of the investigation.

"We have snow in DC," she responded belatedly. "Of course, it's not like here. No one out there seems to know how to drive in it. It shuts down traffic."

"You have to have experience with these road conditions," Dan said earnestly. "The most common mistake people make is to use too much brake." To illustrate his words he braked suddenly, and the car fishtailed. Macy clamped the armrest and strove to coax her stomach back down out of her throat. "That and they don't know how to counter steer." He palmed the wheel expertly and straightened the car to the middle of the lane again. "Helps, too, to have studded tires."

"Good to know," she managed weakly.

Kell slipped his phone back in his coat pocket and looked over the backseat at her. "Getting a driving lesson?"

"Might come in handy." She raised her brows at him quizzically.

"Raiker is finishing up the prison interviews. He left Terre Haute for last."

Her stomach gave a quick vicious twist. It took effort to make sure her reaction didn't show in her expression.

He was continuing. "He's got Abbie and Ryne combing Charleston following up on the lead Cooper gave Raiker. They've focused on the friend he claimed he shared Ellie's photos with. The guy's a known kiddie lover. Just served a warrant at his place. The Robels will keep us posted with the results of that search."

"Robels?"

She responded to Travis's question automatically. "Abbie and Ryne are two of Raiker's operatives." Although Ryne was a relative newcomer. A former detective for the Savannah-Chatham Metropolitan PD, he and Abbie had met over a case they'd shared down there. Afterward, Ryne had left the department to be closer to the woman he'd fallen for. Although Raiker wasn't a big believer in love, he knew talent when he saw it. He'd offered Ryne a job the first time he'd met him. Five offers later and Ryne had finally taken him up on it.

"They're married? Don't see that a lot."

"There are about sixty million couples in the U.S., give or take. Seems common enough to me."

Sounding sheepish, the agent said, "No, I mean law enforcement types. I don't know any couples working for CBI. At least, not as agents."

"Probably because they know the odds of a marriage lasting and decide to forgo the inevitable." Slouching as far down in his seat as the seat belt would allow, Kell opened the file Whitman had given them with Hubbard's phone records.

"A marriage cynic? What a surprise. Does the woman you were talking on the phone with this morning know your opinion on the subject?"

He didn't bother to turn around at her question. "The topic hasn't come up. And I'll be long gone before it gets to that point."

Figured. Burke was the type who breezed through females without getting entangled in any of the stickier emotions. Hardly surprising, given what she knew of his ease with women. That only made her decision about not getting involved with him months ago seem wiser.

And the next time she was tempted to lower her guard, his words should serve as a warning. As if in defense, she reached up and pulled the hat he detested so much more snugly over her ears. Her stepfather often teased her about her cautious nature.

It was a nature that would serve her well when it came to Kellan Burke.

"I know a lot of guys that think like you," Travis was saying. The Denver city limits were coming into view. And traffic on the interstate was brisk, regardless of the patches of black ice that liberally dotted the lanes. "But I liked being married. Liked the stability. Liked having someone to go home to."

"You could get a dog," Kell suggested, not looking up from the sheets in his lap.

Because the agent seemed to expect it, Macy asked, "What happened to your marriage?"

"My wife died four years ago. Aneurism." He looked up to catch her gaze in the mirror. "It was a tough time. But I'm ready to move on. Wouldn't rule out getting married again sometime, that's for sure."

This time Kell did turn around and the smirk on his face did nothing to ease the discomfort she was feeling. She'd have to be dead to miss the look in Travis's expression, and for the first time in her memory, she was grateful for Kell's presence. "I hope you find someone," she said inanely and then seized the opportunity to change the subject. "How do you want to organize the interviews today?"

"Makes most sense to start with numbers most frequently called."

"I think we should do it geographically." Travis objected to Kell's suggestion. "Saves us time and we can cover more ground if we're not constantly backtracking."

"Okay, we'll give Macy the tie-breaking vote," Kell said easily. And she would have dearly loved to smack that wicked grin off his face. "Which will it be, Duchess?"

"Don't call me that," she snapped. Feeling Travis's gaze on her in the mirror again, she mentally searched for a way out and failed to find one. "As much as it pains me to agree with Burke, I think he may be right this time. There's no way we're going to get to everyone on that list today. With the timeline hanging over our head, we need to contact the people who knew him best. Those are probably the ones he had the most phone contact with."

"Okay, your call." The agent's tone was entirely too cheerful. She knew it wasn't her imagination that his easy capitulation was a result of a newfound interest in her. Looking out the window at the cars whizzing by them, it suited her to blame that on Kellan Burke.

With a feeling of déjà vu, Adam Raiker approached the interview room. He'd deliberately left Castillo for last and didn't expect much to come of the conversation. As the mastermind in the child-swap ring, the man had had the most to lose in the trial. He'd gotten the longest sentence and was unlikely to ever see parole.

And he still hadn't gotten half what he deserved.

"I'll stay here. Signal me when you're done."

Adam gave a curt nod at the guard's words and walked through the door the man opened for him.

As soon as he stepped into the room, he heard the door close and lock behind him.

He crossed the worn beige institutional tile floor to sit at a battered folding table with government-issued metal chairs. He'd visited identical rooms in a dozen prisons dotting the map in the last few days. The only thing that changed was the location. Same security. Similar drab interiors. Same sort of men facing him across the tables.

But Enrique Castillo was different in one respect. He'd been the brains behind the child auction where Ellie Mulder had surfaced after her first disappearance.

A door at the side of the room opened, and Castillo entered, doing the prison shuffle. He wore leg and wrist shackles, a telling reminder that the man's time inside so far had not been spent as a model prisoner. Adam waited for him to sit down in the chair opposite before nodding at the guard, who then withdrew, turned the lock.

"I hear you haven't been playing nice inside, Enrique. That saddens me. Makes me wonder about your commitment to rehabilitation."

The man grinned, revealing a gold-backed front tooth. "I have wondered about you, too, my friend. Wondered if my prayers had been answered and an unfortunate accident befell you. Or perhaps if someone had the good judgment to gouge out your remaining eye and shove it up your ass." His chains clanked as he clasped his hands on the table in front of him.

"Your concern is touching," Adam drawled. Studying the man intently, he decided that he was weathering prison much better than Cooper and some of the others he'd visited in the last few days. But then, Castillo was an adaptive son of a bitch. Which was how he'd managed to evade authorities in at least three countries for more than two decades. "Prison seems to agree with you."

There was a flash of something in the other man's eyes. "I have you to thank for my stay here. I have not forgotten."

Adam leaned back in the seat nonchalantly. "If I were you, I'd be mad as hell. It must really suck to be in here, knowing you have friends on the outside who deserve to be serving time along beside you." He paused for a moment before going on. "Maybe someone who's just as guilty as you. More so. Still walking around outside. Eating in restaurants. Taking vacations. Spending time with family. All the things you'll never do again."

Castillo scratched one pockmarked cheek. "That is assuming that I am guilty in the first place, my friend. If you will recall, I pled innocent to those phony charges."

Deliberately baiting the man, Adam grinned humorlessly. "And look where that got you. Locked up for the rest of your life while others continue the very activities that landed you here. That must be very hard to contemplate. And you do have a lot of time in here to contemplate."

The inmate's hands clenched for a moment before he deliberately relaxed them. "It is as you say. Much time. Especially in solitary."

"Maybe you could win some concessions. You provide me with what I want, and I speak to the warden on your behalf."

The gold tooth glinted again as the man grinned. "You would do that for me? Grant my wishes? Because you know there is one thing I wish very much." He leaned forward and lowered his voice conspiratorially. "The lovely Macy Reid. You could send her here to see me, could you not? I would like very much to talk to her once again."

An alarm bell triggered in Adam's mind. Deliberately, he silenced it. "It depends on what you have to trade in return."

"Ah." Castillo shook a finger at him playfully. "You are a wily man, Adam Raiker. You do not pretend that you cannot arrange such a thing. That is wise of you. I have followed Senorita Reid on the Internet. I know she works for you now.

That is a—what is the word—irony, is it not? You could say I brought the two of you together."

"You could say that." Certainly Macy's testimony in Castillo's case had brought her to Adam's attention. And had effectively shattered any hopes Castillo had had of an acquittal. "But let's talk about who deserves to be in a place like this even more than you. Maybe we were shortsighted when we rounded people up at the auction. Your lawyer suggested someone else was at the helm of the child slavery ring. Let's talk about who that was."

But the other man merely smiled at him. "Ah, lawyers. They say what they are paid to, *es verdad*?"

Adam pressed on. "I hear the ring is up and running again. New person in charge but using all your contacts. Even using the same hunting grounds you used to: Colombia, El Salvador, Mexico, Southern California, and Arizona." He was outright lying now. As far as he knew, that particular pipeline of kidnapped children for the sex trade had been cut off with the arrest of this man. "That makes you look like a chump, doesn't it, Enrique?" The other man abruptly sat back, the smile leaving his face. "All your hard work and someone just waits for the law to grab you and steps in and reaps all the profit."

"I think you are doing the fishing game. If it is true what you say, then that is your problem. If you know this, then you must do your police work and bring those bad people to justice."

"See, I knew we had something in common." Adam shifted to stretch out his leg when a cramp seized it. The pain was too familiar to register with him. "Justice. I'm interested in that, too. I'm willing to bet our definitions of the term differ somewhat. Who do you want to bring to justice?" Before coming he'd had Paulie Samuels, his right arm at headquarters, comb through Castillo's background again. He'd come up with nothing they hadn't found before the trial. And what Paulie couldn't find usually didn't exist.

But it was probable that Castillo was harboring a huge

grudge against him, and possibly against Stephen Mulder. The man's high profile had brought increased scrutiny in the trial.

"What am I interested in? I have shared my hopes regarding your future, my friend." The smile the man flashed was anything but friendly. "You know about suffering perhaps." He gestured toward the scars on Adam's hands. "I can only wish more for you. Far more."

"Of course," Adam agreed politely. "Anyone else?"

Castillo leaned back in his chair, folding his arms across his chest with a faint jangle of chains. "I am not a vindictive man. I seek only to right old wrongs. But you are correct about one thing. I have something to say that would interest you very much. Something I'm sure you do not know." His smile grew sly. "But I will tell it only to Macy Reid."

The man was lying. Adam settled into the back of the rental after giving the driver instructions and considered the scene with Castillo. He hadn't expected to get much from him, so in that vein he hadn't been disappointed. Castillo was far wilier than most they had scooped up when they'd broken up the kiddie sex ring. If he knew anything about Ellie Mulder's recent disappearance, he hadn't let on. And try as he might, Adam hadn't been able to discover any way to connect the man to it.

Castillo had been running a pipeline of kidnapped girls from Colombia, El Salvador, and Mexico into the United States and selling them at auction to pedophiles. Allowing scum like Art Cooper to swap the children who had grown too old for their taste, he plucked the ones that caught his eye and reversed the supply line, selling them to wealthy buyers in Latin America. He didn't run the risk of kidnapping U.S. children that way. Which was quite possibly how he managed to stay free as long as he had.

His cell beeped, and he drew it out of the pocket of his cashmere overcoat to check the caller ID. It was Paulie. Knowing the man detested talking on phones as much as he did himself, Adam withdrew his laptop from his zippered briefcase and logged on to his video conferencing software. He typed in the necessary commands to reach Samuels while mentally replaying the scene with Castillo.

He decided it was doubtful the man had anything of importance about this case to share. But he'd use Adam's interest as leverage to get something he desired—a face-to-face meeting with Macy.

Adam was going to make damn sure the man didn't get what he wanted.

He leaned forward to punch the button that would close the privacy window between him and the driver as Samuels's face came on the screen. "Paulie. What do you have for me?"

The man's round face wore its usual smile. It was rare to see it otherwise. "I've got a sure thing on a sweet little filly in Louisville. An intriguing offer to join a high-stakes and extremely illegal poker club in Old Alexandria. And a pocketful of winnings due to my uncanny trifecta pick at the dog track yesterday." His pudgy hand reached up to smooth his tie, which bore aces of every suit. "As usual, should you be interested, I'd be happy to supply you with tips."

"As usual, I'll pass," Adam said dryly. The man's interest in gambling was nearly as legendary as his prowess with finances. When they'd been in the bureau together, Paulie had been the agency's top forensic accountant. Since coming to work for Adam, his talents were mostly put to use as chief financial officer and information broker. He was the one person in the world Adam trusted with his life. For very good reason. "Do you happen to have anything for me that has to do with the case?"

Paulie's smile dimmed. "Not on Castillo. Didn't hit any walls there. I just don't think there's more to find."

Adam pondered the news. It was no more than he'd expected. Which meant the convict had been blowing smoke about having information he'd share with only Macy.

Again, as expected.

"You found no threads that connect Castillo with Mulder at all?"

The other man shook his head vehemently, then reached up to smooth the thinning hair his gesture had dislodged. "I don't see where Castillo has the network in place in this country to pull off anything like the abduction, even if he wanted to. In Mexico or Latin America, sure. But not here. Those he dealt with in this country would have been pedophiles. High-roller child lovers with deep pockets. I also managed to take a peek at his financials—online bank security in Latin America is a joke—and he doesn't have a handy reserve of cash at his disposal. His business was lucrative, but he lived pretty high. He wasn't much for saving."

"Probably because he figured there was always more where that had come from," Adam muttered. "Well, Castillo was the last of them. I'll probably head to West Virginia from here to see what Abbie and Ryne turned up and then back to Denver."

"There is one other thing you should know."

Paulie's sober tone had Adam's interest sharpening. "We've got someone poking around in your history, especially your financials."

"How deep did they get?"

"Second level. Before he could try for the third, I threw up another firewall and sent a dandy little virus back his way. Should've fried the bastard's computer if it did its job." The thought brought a note of merriment to Paulie's voice. "And I'm sure it did."

"Did you trace the probe?"

Samuels shook his head woefully. Adam knew him well enough to realize the man would consider it a personal failure. "Used unregistered machines and accessed various Internet cafés across the country." He looked down as if consulting notes. "Houston, Minneapolis, Tampa. Or more likely, the son of a bitch is good enough to make it look that way. He covered his cyber tracks, bounced me around. You want me to bring Gavin in on this, just to make sure I didn't miss anything?"

Gavin Pounds, their resident cyber genius, was brilliant with computers. But Paulie was brilliant, too. "No. Not yet."

The other man nodded, as if Adam's answer was no more than he'd expected. "Keep your eye on it and let me know if there's another attempt."

Paulie's high forehead glistened with perspiration beneath its receding hairline. "No one's getting through the security layers I constructed, Adam." For once his expression was completely sober. "You can trust me on that."

"I always have." He looked at the man who was closer to him than any brother could be. Their bond was forged in blood, if not the biological kind. "Give your wallet a rest and stay away from the casinos tonight."

"Sure." The smile was back, and with it, Paulie's usual irreverence. "Stay away from guys who want to hold a knife to your eye."

Dark humor flickered. "Too late for that."

"Back atcha."

With a chuckle, Adam disconnected and the screen went blank. The day Samuels gave up gambling would be the day he stopped breathing. The gamble he'd taken seven and a half years ago had bound them together for life. Adam had long since stopped wondering if that was a good thing.

He used his mobile Internet to access his e-mail and settled in to catch up on his messages. But first he reread the one Burke had sent him last night. The stab of annoyance it had elicited was still sharp.

So Whitman was playing territorial turf games. It couldn't be said that he hadn't given the man a chance. They could ill-afford this kind of pissing contest now that the ante had been raised with the ransom note. It was time to push back. He sent a quick e-mail to Caitlin Fleming, his main forensic operative in the new western satellite office, instructing her to send a mobile lab to the Mulder estate. His next message was to Ty Corbett, his lab manager, telling him to get an available scientist on the first plane to Denver. Then he picked up his phone and called a number he'd placed in his contacts directory in case a situation like this one arose.

One hand dropped to his thigh, rubbing at the constant pain there in an unconscious gesture. When the call was answered, he cut through the secretary's automatic greeting brusquely. "I'd like to talk to Senator Barnes. Tell him it's Adam Raiker."

———

Kell stopped Agent Travis when his hand went to the car door. "Wait. I think it's time to change our strategy."

Travis sent him a look from beneath his low brows. "Remember, you were the one who called this strategy. You said to start with the people who Hubbard communicated with the most. I was the one who wanted to . . ."

"Actually the tie-breaking vote went to Macy, but why quibble."

"Chivalrous to the end," Macy murmured from the backseat. But she was more than willing to switch approaches. The seven men they'd interviewed so far had been increasingly uncooperative. All had professed friendship with Hubbard and none had been overly forthcoming when it came to answering questions about him.

"I think Macy should take this one by herself."

A quick flare of annoyance surged at Kell's words. If he recommended the low-cut distraction ploy again, she really would smack him. "And why is that?"

"No." Travis's response was swift. "We all go in together. Or I could go alone, if you prefer."

Her annoyance faded as she considered the other man. He was avoiding looking at either her or Kell. And she knew intuitively that Whitman had warned him about letting either of them out of his sight.

Her annoyance with Burke shifted to the Travis. Deliberately, she asked, "What do you have in mind, Kell?"

"We haven't gotten dick from the guys we've interviewed today."

"Not true," the agent said halfheartedly. "We now know Hubbard was a fitness fanatic and that he was seeing a woman for the last several weeks."

"That no one has met." Burke turned to look at her. "Guys close up when they see us coming, but you might have better luck. Chances are this guy"—he jerked his head toward the auto garage across the street—"may already have been tipped off by someone we've talked to. He might be looking for the three of us. One alone stands a better chance of getting information if that's the case."

Travis frowned as he mulled it over. "You mean by talking to him on some pretext."

The patience in Kell's tone was admirable. "That's right. We haven't gotten too far being up front about what we want. Tim Molitor"—he nodded toward the garage—"might be a little more open with Macy."

Travis rubbed his chin contemplatively before sending her a look. "Are you comfortable with that? It would mean you having to think on your feet. We'll come up with a story for you to approach him with, of course."

"I think I can handle it," she said dryly. "I do have some experience in the area."

"Some fairly recent," Kell add wickedly.

Macy grabbed her purse and glared at him. She'd been referring, of course, to her time with BII and Raiker. Trust Burke to reference her episode with Travis this morning.

"I still think we need to brainstorm a cover story . . ." The agent's words were lost as she yanked open the car door and got out. Quick reflexes were the only thing that saved her when she immediately slipped on the slick pavement and nearly landed on her backside.

"Watch that first step," warned Kell blandly.

Sending him her most killing glare, which lacked a little something in light of her ignoble exit, she slammed the door and rounded the hood to march to the corner. She heard the buzz of the window as it lowered behind her. "Word of advice—lose the hat."

Since no fitting rejoinder came to mind, she chose to ignore him. And kept her eyes warily on the pavement as she crossed at the light, heading toward Honest Tim's Auto.

It occurred to her that most honest businessmen didn't feel compelled to advertise that trait, but then her suspicious nature had been acquired early in life. Once she'd crossed the street without incident she stopped to surreptitiously pull out her BlackBerry and do a little belated research. Then she squared her shoulders and headed into Honest Tim's.

Manufacturing a harried smile for the bored twenty-something girl behind the counter, she asked, "I'm looking for Tim."

The girl jerked her head to an adjoining door. "In there."

Macy looked through the door's window and saw that she was referring to the auto bay. Slipping through the door, she approached a pair of legs that were jutting from beneath a minivan. "Is Tim around?"

The creeper rolled out from beneath the vehicle. Its occupant was in his forties, with a porn-star mustache and a thicket of wiry dark hair. He wore insulated coveralls with an embroidered name tag. She'd found Molitor. "Hi," she said with phony enthusiasm. "I'm Sandy Jenkins. Nick recommended I talk to you about my fuel pump."

"Nick?" Wariness flickered across the man's face as he got up.

"Nick Hubbard. He said you had a car place and that you'd treat me right. I got a quote from E-Z Auto, on Greeley and Seventy-sixth. They want over a thousand dollars for a new fuel pump, installed. I was talking to Nick about it at the gym last week. He said they're ripping me off and told me to talk to you." She bumped up the wattage of her smile. "So I'm talking to you. Is that a good price for replacing a fuel pump?"

He grabbed a grease rag from his back pocket and rubbed his hands on it. "You the gal he's been dating?"

"He's dating someone?" She strove for a surprised expression. "He didn't say." She lifted a shoulder. "We just talk at the gym, you know?"

"Yeah. He's nuts about working out." Obviously more at ease now, he made no attempt to hide his once-over. "Looks like you put in plenty of time there, too."

Honest Tim was a lowlife lech, but Macy forced herself to nod enthusiastically. "I do, but I haven't seen Nick there all week. Maybe he's been busy with that woman you mentioned. The one he's been seeing."

"Denise . . . or is it Diane?" Shoving the grease rag back in his pocket, Tom scratched his chin. "No, I think it's Denise. Never met her, you know? And Nick doesn't say much. But I know they've had a thing now for two or three months."

"Well, I'll have to tease him about her next time I see him. He's always giving me a bad time about my reps."

"No one's talked to you yet?"

Feigning ignorance, she asked, "About what?"

The mechanic lowered his voice conspiratorially and took a step closer. "A buddy of mine and Nick's called this morning to warn me. Said some feds are nosing around asking questions about him."

Feds? She nearly rolled her eyes. Difficult to say if the buddy had screwed up their identification that badly or if Honest Tim was trying to impress her. "Why would they have questions about Nick?"

"You ask me, they're trying to hang him with that kid's disappearance. You knew he's a security guard for Stephen Mulder, right? The billionaire whose kid was snatched a few days ago?"

Macy rounded her eyes and considered that the stage could have used her talents. "OhmyGod, I never knew . . . they think he kidnapped that little girl?"

Tom smoothed his thin mustache. "Sounds like it. I got a theory that Nick took off when it looked like they were gonna blame him for it and is lying low until they catch the real kidnapper. You ask me, he's holed up with his girlfriend until this blows over."

"That's smart, I guess," she said slowly, her mind furiously racing. Since no one they'd talked to so far knew the identity of the woman in question, it might be a good place for Hubbard to hide.

Maybe even with the girl.

Chapter 7

"I need to talk to the officer posted in the car out front first. I'll get the key."

"Go ahead." Kell was already getting out of the car. "They've got the security alarm turned off now, right? I can let myself in."

"Burke . . ."

He walked rapidly toward the house. It was dark. He was cold and hungry, never a safe combination. And that duo surely accounted for the annoyance he was beginning to feel every time Travis sent Macy one of those looks via the rearview mirror. Seriously. The guy was about as subtle as a lovesick poodle.

Hubbard's neighbor, Snowblower Guy, was hard at work on the inch of fresh snowfall. The machine actually had a headlight on it. Kell was pretty certain there was no place he could be tempted to live that required frequent use of a snowblower, with or without headlights. Virginia got snow, although nothing like this. But condo living meant he never had to deal with its removal personally. Some things were meant to be delegated.

"Someone's cranky. Miss nap time?"

Macy's voice sounded at his elbow, but he didn't slow to look at her. "No, I missed lunch. And dinner. What is it the two of you have about not eating?"

Amusement sounded in her voice. "Remind me tomorrow to be sure to swing by McDonald's at noon. Something tells me you prefer the ones with the indoor playgrounds."

"I prefer the ones with food." He was already heading around the attached garage to the back before it occurred to him that the front door was probably no more of a challenge. And didn't require wading through a foot of snow. Sure they'd attract more attention out front, but a DPD squad car had been parked out there for days now. They weren't exactly keeping a low profile.

He hunched his shoulders against the frigid blast of air as they turned the corner into the backyard. Brainpower required fuel. Food provided fuel. Tomorrow he'd make damn sure they picked up a sandwich sometime during the day. Or maybe he could grab something in the kitchen to pack for a snack.

"Geez, it's dark out here," he heard Macy mutter. "I thought we left the back porch light on."

"We did. Probably burned out." He reached into his inside coat pocket where he'd tucked the kit of picks and plucked out a pencil flashlight. Switching it on, he handed it to her. "Here. You'll need to hold this anyway so I can get us in."

"Shouldn't we wait for Travis?"

"If you can't stand to be apart from the agent for a few minutes, you know the way back to the car." They'd reached the back steps. He climbed the first one before stomping the snow from his boots, then continued up the rest.

"You are really a child."

Ordinarily her clipped prissy tone would have amused him, but he was too irritated. "Just saying you might want to tone down the dewy-eyed sympathetic ingénue bit." He stopped and pulled out the kit of picks with a bit more force than needed. "I know it was my idea last night, but keep playing it out, and it's just gonna be cruel. The guy is starting to buy it, know what I mean? And unless you have a longing to settle down and become a Colorado cowgirl with . . ."

The penlight rapped smartly across his head. "Ow." He reached a hand up to rub at his temple, glowering at her. "What's your problem?"

"You," she informed him, "are an ass. And you change your mind faster than a three-year-old in a toy store."

The fact that her point had merit didn't mean he had to agree with it. "Shine the light over here." Once she obeyed, he shoved his gloves into his pockets and went to work on the lock. "I'm just saying. Don't blame me if you're fending off Travis's vows of undying devotion before this is over. The guy is already half-smitten."

"Since he might be joining us at any moment, I suggest you drop it." The statement sounded like it had been made from between gritted teeth. "I'm tired of hearing you bang on about it. I had no idea he'd be so . . ."

"Susceptible to those wiles you claimed you don't have?" The tumblers fell in place on the dead bolt, so he turned his attention to the doorknob lock. "Like I told you, they're more potent than you . . . What the hell?"

"What?"

"The lock on the doorknob wasn't secured. So much for Whitman's crime scene techs. They must have neglected to secure it when they left."

She snapped on the lights just inside the kitchen and looked around warily. "Unless someone's been in here since then."

"Yeah, maybe Hubbard came back and picked up a few things he left behind."

"You're impossible." After taking off her boots, she stalked by him, managing to seem somehow regal and miffed at the same time. He wrestled out of his boots and followed in her wake, more than a little shocked at his loss of control.

What the hell did it matter to him if Travis all of a sudden was tripping over his tongue when it came to Macy? They could use his reaction to her, if this morning was any example. Although from the sounds of what the man had revealed today, he'd probably been through some rough times. Which just made Kell feel like a jerk, further souring his mood.

"Don't touch anything," he called to Macy. "I know exactly where those files are." Her silence wasn't much of a surprise. He hadn't met a woman yet who didn't know how to use the silent treatment to good effect. His guilty conscience just made it more effective.

He took the stairs two at a time and caught up with her halfway to Hubbard's bedroom. "Look, I was joking, okay?" It was only a half lie at any rate. He snapped on the light to the bedroom as he followed her into it. "Blame it on lack of food. I have the metabolism of a ten-year-old boy."

"From my observation, the similarities don't stop there."

"Good one." He shook a finger at her admiringly. "You're better than you used to be with the comebacks. Have you been taking lessons?" The flush that flooded her cheeks at the suggestion had him stopping to peer closer at her. "That's it, isn't it? What'd you do, go online for a list of insults? Or ask someone to tutor you?"

"You're being ridiculous." The color was still there, but her voice was cool. "Just get the files Whitman wants." He cast her a long considering look before obeying. He was onto something there. It wasn't just the flush in her cheeks—it was the absence of a denial.

Crossing swiftly to the closet, he knelt in front of the filing cabinet and pulled the bottom drawer open. He hadn't relocked it because the crime scene evidence recovery unit was being called in after their visit last time.

He flipped through the files and withdrew the tax records when a small sound alerted him. Turning to look over his shoulder, Kell was shocked to see Macy holding her weapon. "Okay, I apologized once, okay?" It had been an apology of sorts, hadn't it? Rising, he noted two things at once. The gun wasn't pointed at him. And the imperceptible cock of her head indicated something in the hallway.

He set down the file and withdrew his weapon with one smooth motion, continuing to talk in a slightly louder voice. "It's not your fault you needed lessons for witty replies, you know. I blame too much British television. No one else in the world thinks their humor is funny, so it's no wonder your education is lacking in that area."

Sidling up beside her, he peered in the direction she indicated and saw nothing outside the room but shadows.

"I don't know how many times I have to tell you, I wasn't raised in England."

Her voice sounded normal. Slightly peeved, which was the norm, at least when she spoke to him.

"Couldn't prove it by me, Duchess." He strained to see beyond the hallway into the empty bedroom beyond it. They'd found nothing of interest there the first time they'd searched. According to the report he'd lifted from Travis, neither had the crime scene unit.

He carefully scanned the dim interior of the opposite room. Nothing seemed out of place. "Travis might be different, though." Headlights from a passing car sliced through the darkness of the space. Silhouetting a black shape crowded into the corner of its closet. He sidled closer to Macy. "I was never much a Monty Python fan, myself." He caught her eye and signaled for her to head downstairs. Was rewarded by a vehement shake of her head. Big surprise. "But I can actually see the two of you cozied up on a couch watching *The Holy Grail* together. Or bonding over Benny Hill." With his free hand, he pointed to her and used his fingers to mime her walking down the stairs. Turning off the lights. Closing the door. And watched, relieved, when comprehension dawned on her face.

"Stop babbling and get the file. I'll wait for you in the car." Easing back on the safety, she slipped the weapon in its holster and started for Hubbard's bedroom door.

Kell hoped like hell she was just playing along and not intent on summoning Travis. The last thing he needed right now was for the CBI agent to come charging in here. He'd worked with Macy before. He trusted her instincts.

The same couldn't be said for the other man.

He heard the faint sound of the kitchen door closing. He made no effort to move silently as he retrieved the file and carefully placed his weapon inside it. Not a perfect point from which to draw if he needed to, but it would do. Then he snapped off the light and left the room, jogged down the steps.

Macy had left the house dark, and he bumped into the edge of the hallway table as he took the corner too sharply. He recognized her form, slight and shadowy, yet somehow feminine, standing inside the kitchen door. Drawing closer, he jerked his head toward the outside. She shrugged, indicating that she didn't know where the agent was.

He reached past her, twisted the knob, and pulled the door open, only to shut it again loudly. Then he set the file on the kitchen counter and retrieved his gun from it. Tiptoeing back toward the stairs, he felt Macy right behind him.

Without waiting for his order, she fanned out, moving to crouch behind one leather couch as he stationed himself around the corner of the dining room. They didn't have long to wait. A stair tread creaked lightly.

Someone was heading down the stairs.

Kell eased back the safety on his weapon. The intruder was at a disadvantage because he was staying low. Smart. The window of the front door faced the stairs. No movement in front of the window to alert the cop in the patrol car out front. He waited until the figure was within two feet of his hiding place when he swung around the corner. "Stop right there."

The shadowy figure paused, then rose in one lithe motion and swung a bag in his direction. He sidestepped unharmed, but Macy had already rushed to hem the stranger in. "Drop it. Hands behind your head."

The first thing he realized was that the person almost certainly wasn't Hubbard. The figure was far shorter than the security guard's six-three height. Then when the bag was slowly lowered to drop to the floor with a slight thud, that realization was closely followed by another.

It also wasn't a man.

Reaching out with his free hand, he felt along the wall until he located the switch for the dining room lights. Flipped it on. "She's armed."

"I can see that." Without lowering her weapon, Macy approached the stranger. "Keep your hands where we can see them."

"I know what you're thinking," the woman started. She was a couple inches taller than Macy, long and lithe where the other woman was short and curvy. Her hair was sandy brown and cut almost as short as a man's. Her eyes, alight with resignation and worry, were brown.

"Really, you're psychic? Let's see how good you are," Kell said conversationally. "You broke into the house of the prime suspect in a high-profile kidnapping case. You hid rather than identifying yourself when we came in." Macy lifted the edge of the woman's coat and plucked the sidearm out of its holster. "No camera in sight, so that means you're not paparazzi. So I'm thinking you're an accomplice of Nick Hubbard's, here to fetch something for him. How 'bout it? How close were you?"

Macy started to frisk the woman.

"You're not CBI," the woman countered brazenly. "And you're sure as hell not local law enforcement. Maybe you don't have a right to be here either."

He smiled humorlessly. "Turns out you're not psychic after all. Ah-ah." He wagged the weapon at her as she started to lower her hands. "What'd you find, Macy?" She'd withdrawn a couple items from the woman's coat pockets and was perusing them.

At his question, she held up a picture ID hanging from a lanyard. He squinted to read it then smiled grimly. "Denise Temple. Looks like a two-fer. I think we've found Hubbard's girlfriend. And a Denver police officer."

"Sergeant," snapped the woman. "And I'm lowering my hands."

"Go ahead," Kell invited pleasantly. "Just don't forget you have two weapons trained on you, a DPD officer stationed out front, and a CBI agent coming through that door any minute. So start talking. You can begin by telling us where Hubbard is."

"How would I know?"

"You've been dating him for the last several weeks. You'd probably know better than anyone else where he might be right now."

"I have no idea. Really." The woman's gaze encompassed both him and Macy. "Don't you think I'd have gone to my captain if I knew? I'd much rather be a hero in this thing than sneaking around trying to save my badge."

Macy was rifling through the dark garbage bag at the woman's feet. "When was the last time you spoke with him?"

"Three days ago. I spent the night and we had tentative plans to meet for a late dinner the next day. I phoned him a couple times"—she lifted a shoulder—"but he never answered."

"When did you call?"

"Around five and again at midnight. I was pissed, because he blew off our plans." Her voice was sour. "Now I know why."

"The bag's empty except for a towel and boots," Macy observed, rising again.

"How'd you get in?"

"I have a key Nick gave to me. Another few minutes and I'd have been out of here and no one would have been the wiser." Her expression went dour. "Add poor timing to my lousy judgment of men."

"So you think Hubbard kidnapped the Mulder girl?"

"You tell me. It's what the CBI thinks, isn't it?"

"I'm asking you." Out of the corner of his eye, Kell watched Macy go through the contents of the woman's other coat pocket. "You were sleeping with him." He saw the almost imperceptible wince the woman gave and wondered at it. "What do you think?"

Temple blew out a breath. "Nick's the last person I'd ever expect to do something like this. But DPD has been getting BOLO reports from CBI ever since they came in on this thing. If they want us to be on the lookout for Nick, they must believe he has something to do with this. And like I say, he blew off our plans, hasn't been answering his phone . . . It doesn't exactly look good for him."

"So you're not here to clear his name, I take it."

"Looks like we've discovered the owner of the unidentified caller on his LUDs," Macy murmured, holding up the woman's trac phone.

"A couple weeks ago I was sleeping over. He got a call from work and didn't have any paper upstairs." Temple lifted a shoulder. "I pulled a business card out of my purse and he wrote on the back of it. I got to thinking . . ."

"That we found your card and you were implicated in this thing."

She flushed. "I figured you probably hadn't because no one had contacted me. And I knew it'd be hard to trace my phone. But I got paranoid. No one knew we were involved, but if he had hung on to that card . . . I started thinking maybe I was being watched. It affected my job. So I decided to come check for myself. Like I say, stupid."

He shot a look at Macy. She gave a slight shrug. It appeared neither of them were convinced yet. "Why the untraceable phone?"

But the cop was obviously done cooperating. "I don't even know who you two are. Are you CBI? If so, let's see some ID."

"Not really in the position to be making demands," Kell reminded her. "We're special consultants working with CBI."

Suspicion settled over her face. "I haven't heard about any special consultants being called in."

"DPD isn't exactly in the loop on this thing," Kell reminded her. "My guess is your department is being used strictly for manpower and any info is on a need-to-know basis."

She shot him a look filled with dislike. "Come to think of it, maybe you are CBI. The agents I've met from there are all arrogant."

He grinned in genuine amusement. "Finally we agree on something. And you still haven't answered. Why all the secrecy about dating Hubbard? Why the phone?"

After seeming to weigh her options for a moment, the woman capitulated. "I've got a douche bag ex who has a habit of appearing when I can least afford trouble. This job is going well, and I don't want him showing up and screwing things up with my boss. He's a cop, too, so it gets messy."

There was the sound of footsteps coming up the front exterior steps. Quickly he grabbed Temple and hauled her into the dining room, out of sight. To Macy, he said, "Get rid of him."

"What?"

He jerked his head toward the door, where a key was sounding in the lock. "Travis. Get him back to the car. Buy me fifteen minutes."

"Fifteen . . . I can't . . ."

"Now!"

The look she gave him would have dropped a lesser man in his tracks. He was half-surprised to see her stride toward the door as it squeaked open. "Did you get tired of waiting?"

He slipped his gun in his pocket and pulled out his phone and hit the contact number for Paulie Samuels, Raiker's second-in-command. He sent a short silent text to get him background on Denise Temple of the DPD and have it back to him in ten minutes.

"What's taking so long?" he heard Travis say. "I could have been in and out three times by now."

"You know Kell. He wanted to do another walk-through and then he . . ." The door closed behind them and he could no longer hear their conversation. Given that last look Macy had sent him, he figured that might be a good thing.

It didn't matter what she told the other man, though. As long as she bought him enough time to get a response from Samuels and to decide what to do about Denise Temple.

She couldn't stand the way he looked at her.

Sometimes he'd play with the long wicked blade while he stared, absently running his thumb along the sharp edge. When it broke the skin and left a long thin line of blood, he'd bring his thumb to his mouth and suck the blood away like a vampire. She had a feeling he wanted to use that blade on *her*.

Ellie wondered what was stopping him. What was he waiting for?

Art Cooper hadn't waited. At least not for long.

She'd been coming back from the bathroom at the party when he'd yanked her into the men's room and shoved that stinky cloth in her face. And then she didn't remember anything until he'd opened the trunk of his car and pulled her out and into the backseat on that gravel road. She'd screamed and screamed and screamed, but there hadn't been anyone around to hear.

Cooper hadn't liked it when she screamed. But she had a feeling this man would.

She looked away from him as her stomach cramped up again. There wasn't a real bathroom in the small area. Just a bucket in the corner. He'd let her use it but he always watched her, so she waited as long as she could before asking.

"Are you scared?"

Reluctantly she looked at him again. The only time there was ever expression in his eyes, on his face, is when he asked her a question like that. "I'm not afraid of you," she lied, and he laughed, a low ugly sound.

"You're a liar, little girl. Not a very good one either. If you aren't scared now, you will be. But terror will be just one of the things you'll be feeling."

"How do you know?" His eyes went flat and cold, and she swallowed hard. But something inside her made her continue. "I'll bet it's been a long time since you've felt anything. You probably don't even remember what it's like."

He moved so fast it was like a blur. One moment he was on the lawn chair and the next he had her head yanked back by her hair. "Are you stupid?" The tip of the blade pricked the skin beneath the chin where he held it. She could feel blood running down the side of her throat. Memories flipped through her mind, like a movie on fast-forward. Presents that Cooper would bring her. Special cakes and treats. And she'd known what he wanted. A little girl that smiled and laughed so he could pretend she loved him, loved being with him.

Not giving him that had been her only weapon. He beat her every time she tried to escape until she was kept tied all the time. But she hadn't given him the one thing he wanted more than almost anything else.

And she wouldn't give this man what he wanted either.

Her fear.

That familiar numbness was sliding over her again. She welcomed it like an old friend. Looking straight in his eyes, she whispered, "What are you feeling right now?"

———

"I told you to meet me in my room in ten minutes." The door had barely opened before Macy grabbed a handful of Kell's shirt and pulled him inside.

He grinned. "I like a lady who's eager. Watch the plates."

Glaring at him, she reached to take one of the covered dishes out of his hands. "Seriously? You went to the kitchen before coming up here? You're pathetic."

"Pathetically hungry." He carefully set Travis's copy of the updated files on her bed, then settled himself on it with his plate in his lap. "Hope you like burgers. Travis was waiting for some fancy chicken dish to get out of the oven, but I nabbed the sandwiches and fries and headed up as soon as I could."

She sent a belated look toward the file he had set down. "With Travis's file?"

"Like taking candy from a baby. It's so easy I'm thinking of working left-handed, just to even the odds a bit."

"It's not wise to get cocky. Of course, you seem to be full of unwise decisions today."

"You mean because of Temple?" Knowing an invitation wouldn't come, he made himself comfortable on her bed and uncovered a heaping plate. The two burgers with full fixings looked better than anything he could have hoped to score if he'd had a chance at a drive-through, but his standards tended to lower when he was starving.

"Yes, I mean Temple, and don't you dare eat that on my bed."

He picked up a sandwich and bit into it, his eyes sliding shut in appreciation. Even better than he'd expected. After swallowing, he advised, "You better eat. You're grumpy."

The burger was half gone before his hunger had subsided enough to notice that not only had she not taken his advice, she was looking at him as though she were giving serious consideration to heaving the plate she held at his head. "If you're not going to eat that, bring it over here."

She stalked—there was no other word for it—toward the chair she'd pulled up to the bed yesterday. "You let her go?"

He had a healthy enough sense of self-preservation to know better than to feign ignorance. "I let her go."

"That was a mistake."

"It was a calculated risk," he corrected, and polished off the rest of the burger before continuing. "Samuels did a quick dive into her background, and she checked out, at least on the surface. The story about the ex, the change of jobs . . . that's true. She's filed two restraining orders against a Henry Cole—she took her maiden name back—in the last three years. He's a lieutenant for the Phoenix police department. She's not going anywhere. She's got a mortgage."

"So does Hubbard."

He thought it wiser to ignore her. "She's also up for a promotion. Paulie's been sending me regular updates since he started digging. I don't think she's going to run. And I figure she's telling the truth about not having any idea where Hubbard is."

"You can't possibly know that."

From her tone, he hadn't yet convinced her. "I can be reasonably certain, so I took a calculated risk. I asked Paulie to fill Adam in and get a private investigator over to her house, make sure Hubbard isn't holed up there."

"You took a risk for very little reason," she corrected. But at least she'd lost enough of her ire that she was uncovering her food. "There's nothing to be gained by keeping Temple's secret from the CBI. Whitman was very clear about what his reaction would be if we pulled something like that, not that he's been exactly pure in that area."

"I'll let Adam have the final say tonight when I talk to him." He lifted a shoulder and bit into the second hamburger. And silently acknowledged that his boss's reaction could well reflect Macy's, minus the snootiness. "With what Paulie has given me so far on Temple, I'm comfortable with giving her a little rope. As long as she comes through with what she promised in return."

The look Macy shot him then would have seared stone. "It's so not what you're thinking, and God, you really don't hold me in high esteem, do you?"

"Are we talking about your skills or your morals?" she inquired sweetly.

The verbal jab stung a bit more than it would have coming from someone else. And he didn't want to spend time thinking about the implications of *that*. "Look, Paulie will keep looking, and at the first whiff of something funny, we can always backtrack. But Temple has access to info within the DPD and that might help us. She can give us a heads-up if something comes to light that might relate to our case, information that we have to steal to get from Whitman."

The ire faded from her expression as she chewed reflectively, and he knew intuitively the words had been well chosen. The agent's actions galled her as much as they did him.

"It's not like DPD is being kept in the loop though," she said, after polishing off her hamburger with delicate greed. "I don't see what she can offer."

"Let's see how creative she gets. Temple is pretty desperate to keep her relationship with Hubbard quiet. I get the feeling the messy divorce with her ex jammed up her job with the Phoenix PD, what with him being a cop. She isn't going to want to screw up in Denver, too. She'd wash out of law enforcement completely."

Macy was quiet for a moment. She studied him as he polished off his French fries, which were far better than anything he could have gotten at a fast-food place. There was a quick and agile mind beneath her prim exterior, and it never failed to fascinate him. Of course, there were several aspects of her exterior that fascinated, as well, but it was best not to dwell on them when they were alone in her bedroom. He shifted uncomfortably. Especially with him stretched out on her bed.

He dug into his jeans pocket and pulled out an object, held it up for her to see. She stared, then her lips curved slowly. "You have her trac phone."

Kell didn't answer for a moment. He couldn't. He was still reeling from the punch-in-the-gut smile of hers. It was just a facial expression, for God's sake. The work of a cooperative handful of muscles. No reason for it to have the breath clogging in his lungs. It suited him to blame it on shock. He didn't think he'd ever had Macy smile at him quite like that before.

When the smile faded, and her expression became questioning, he hurriedly answered, "I said I was taking a calculated risk, not a stupid one. Checked it over back at Hubbard's while I was waiting for Paulie to get back to me. There hasn't been a call placed on it to Hubbard since the ones she told us about the night the girl disappeared. Nothing has come in from Hubbard's cell either." No surprise there. They already knew there had been no activity on his phone since he'd disappeared.

Kell looked at his plate, noted with a measure of surprise that he'd finished it off. He turned a considering eye toward hers. Reading his intent, she covered her fries with a protective hand while raising her fork threateningly.

"Don't even think about it."

"Be stingy. Don't blame me if you get fat."

Storm clouds were brewing in her startling blue eyes. He seemed to have a knack for putting them there. "No wonder women fall at your feet. It must be that silver tongue of yours."

He smiled wickedly. "I think I like the mental image of you falling at my feet. You'd be naked, of course. And there might also be Cool Whip and soft handcuffs involved."

Three seconds. That's all it took for the color to flood her face. He knew because he'd been counting.

She opened her mouth. Snapped it shut. Opened it again. "You *ass*."

He grinned. "I think the British pronunciation is *arse*. And that seems to be your standby retort when you can't think of anything else to say. Hope you didn't pay too much for that tutoring. You got robbed."

When she rose, he ducked reflectively. It never paid to underestimate a woman in a snit. But Macy was much too regal to bash him in the head with her plate. Even when he deserved it.

"Get out. I've got work to do."

"Well, yeah. Me, too." He gestured toward Travis's file. "Go ahead and get busy. I'll keep you updated on the discrepancies in the files."

"Send me an e-mail. You don't need to work in here."

"Why would I send you an e-mail when I could just sit here and talk to you?" he asked reasonably.

Her glare was familiar. And infinitely more comfortable to witness than the smile she'd graced him with earlier. "Why does everything have to be an argument with you?"

He was spared the trouble of a response when a knock sounded at the door, followed by Dan Travis's voice. "Macy, I've brought you some dinner."

She froze. When he opened his mouth to make a cynical remark, she shook her head furiously at him and waved him off the bed, pointing to the bathroom.

Just as adamant, he crossed his arms and stayed put. Damned if he was going to cower in the next room just because Travis had stopped by to further his cause with Macy. It'd do the man good to have a little company, in any case. The last thing he needed was more encouragement.

But he hadn't reckoned on Macy's reaction. "Just a minute," she called. "I'm on the phone." Then she strode to the bed and wordlessly ordered him off it again. Amused, he patted the spot on the bed beside him in silent invitation.

His amusement faded in the next instant when she reached across the space and pinched him. Hard.

"Ow!" Her free hand clapped across his mouth to muffle the sound. Damn the woman, she had a grip like a mastiff. And apparently knew the tender underside of the arm was a surefire way to ensure compliance.

Yanking away, he rolled to the side of the bed and rose, going toe-to-toe with her. Silently he mouthed, "You're going to pay for that."

Macy kicked him in the shin with surprising force, considering that she was shoeless. She mouthed back, "I'll aim higher next time." And then shoved him in the direction of the bathroom.

Ticked, he limped the rest of the way out of the room and swung the door partially closed behind him. Who would have thought Macy Reid had such a mean streak? Rubbing at his arm, he strained to hear the conversation in the other room.

". . . is so sweet of you," she was saying.

Kell rolled his eyes. It didn't escape him that he hadn't gotten similar treatment when *he'd* brought her dinner. The observation made him vow to take another swipe at her fries.

"I thought, maybe . . . you know, we could eat and talk. About the case. And . . . other things. If you want."

If he weren't so irritated, Kell would have felt a stab of pity. Listening to Travis stammer around was almost painful. The man was seriously out of practice at this thing, if he'd ever had game to begin with.

The warmth in Macy's tone must be reserved for talking to everyone but him. "I can't tell you how much I appreciate your thoughtfulness. But I have hours of work ahead of me on analyzing those written communications. I'm going to be up half the night as it is."

"Oh, yeah. Me, too." The disappointment in the man's voice was evident, even to Kell's ears. "Got to transcribe today's notes to send to Agent Whitman. Here." There was a faint clatter of silverware. "I'll just put this . . . oh. Looks like you already ate. You should have said."

"I had something sent up. But I have no doubt that before

the night is over I'm going to be hungry again. And when I am, I'll eat this and be thankful to you all over again."

Kell rolled his eyes. She was laying it on a little thick, but she was quick on her feet, he'd give her that. "I like a woman who's not afraid to admit to an appetite," Travis was saying, "instead of just pushing food around her plate and pretending to eat."

Seriously, maybe the CBI agent was the one in need of some tutoring. Kell tuned them out as he unbuttoned his shirt and withdrew his arm, using the mirror to inspect the damage Macy had inflicted. He'd never met a woman yet who would think "having an appetite" constituted a compliment. But then he'd never met a woman like Macy before. She was a mystery in many ways. He'd worked with her on a couple other cases, as well as knowing her at headquarters. Try as he might, he couldn't recall one thing he knew about her personal life. She was remarkably closemouthed. Which left him to draw his own conclusions, most of which infuriated her.

The bathroom door swung open. Quick reflexes had him stepping away before it caught him in the shoulder. Whatever Macy had been about to say went unuttered as she stared at him shrugging back into his shirt.

Her eyes went to the scar over his heart. He wondered if she was remembering how she'd traced her lips and tongue over it that night. Her touch had provided a measure of healing he hadn't even known he'd been in need of.

Meeting his gaze again, she said, "I don't even want to know what you were doing in here." Turning on her heel, she headed back into the bedroom. He trailed in her wake.

"I'm going to bruise," he informed her. "It's the Irish curse of fair skin. And when I do, you'll have to kiss it better."

"When they serve lemon popsicles in hell," she retorted quickly.

The familiarity of the phrase distracted him momentarily. Then he snapped his fingers. "Ramsey Clark."

She stilled. When guilt flickered over her face, he knew he'd nailed it. "You've been taking comeback advice from

Ramsey. That phrase is totally one of hers." Ramsey was another of Raiker's investigators and blessed—or cursed—with the most caustic tongue he'd ever heard on a woman. "You picked a good tutor. Half the staff at headquarters are terrified of her."

"Ramsey isn't terrifying. And it's not Clark anymore. She's on her honeymoon, remember? She and Dev are in Europe." Macy crossed the room and sat down in front of the desk holding her laptop and other equipment she'd unloaded.

"I was at the wedding, wasn't I?" He wasn't likely to forget the surreal ceremony. Of all the women he knew, Ramsey was the last he'd have expected to dive into marriage. He was happy as hell for her, but that didn't mean he didn't wish Stryker luck. Ramsey was a tough nut, but she'd looked all soft and sort of glowing at the ceremony.

Weddings weren't his thing, but he made an exception for those of his colleagues. And maybe there'd been a cloudy, deeply buried hope, that the event would spark a desire in Macy to reconsider her decision about the two of them.

Instead, she'd spent the entire evening staying as far across the room from him as possible, and he'd gotten on particularly good terms with a bottle of Scotch.

He spied his empty plate on the floor next to the bed. She must have placed it there before answering the door. He picked it up and set it on the bedside table before wandering over to peer over her shoulder. "How's this linguistic thing work?" When she merely leveled a look at him, he shrugged. "I know what you said to Whitman. But you've never said how you do it."

She blew out a breath then pushed a strand of hair back from her face. His gaze traced the gesture. "It's sort of like diagramming sentences. Did you ever do that in English class at school?"

"If we did I skipped those days." He'd actually skipped more days than he'd attended and had graduated a step ahead of the truant officer.

She flipped open the file Whitman had given her and took out a copy of the ransom note. The next page was an e-mail communication from Stephen Mulder to his accountant, Lance Spencer. "I'm going to break every sentence down into its parts. Nouns, adjectives, verbs. Gerunds and participles. Then I'll look for particular patterns in the way the different parts of speech are used. How many times does that pattern repeat within the document? Once I have the patterns for the statements, and the ransom note, I'll feed them into the database." She nodded at the computer. "From that point it just takes a couple minutes for each to determine if we have a match."

"After you do all the diagramming first."

"That's right."

"Sounds boring."

She gave a slight smile. "It's fascinating, at least to me. How people communicate and the hidden messages in their speech is like piecing together a verbal puzzle."

"So that's what you did for BII?" He nodded toward the computer. "Threat assessments and comparisons like this?"

Leaning forward to pick up a pen, she gave a slight grimace. "Mostly. I wanted to work as an agent, as well, but BII was more interested in keeping me in the labs. That's one of the reasons I accepted Adam's offer to work with him."

Intrigued, he studied her as she began making marks on the copy of the ransom note. "So you were both on Castillo's trail. You said that once. BII investigates kidnappings across country boundaries, right? I can see how investigators might be called to testify at the trial, but you being there means there was some written communication tying Castillo to the case. How'd that play . . ."

"Burke." It wasn't just the snap in her voice that drew his attention. It was her grip on the pen. The knuckles on her fingers had gone white. "If you're going to stay in here, two words: Shut. Up."

Clearly, he'd hit a nerve. Hell of it was, he hadn't even been trying this time. She revealed things from her past so rarely he'd just taken the opportunity to get a few answers to the questions about her that seemed more and more compelling every day. Her reaction put his instincts on red alert.

He watched her for a few more moments. She'd gone

back to her work but hadn't loosened her grip on the pen. And then he did something he did too rarely, especially with this woman.

Kell backed off. God knew he had things in his past he didn't like to talk about. And before he started to get too sensitive, there was one other thing to focus on.

She hadn't kicked him out again.

More cheerful, he returned to his spot on her bed, detouring to pick up the plate Travis had brought her. It was going to be a long night. And those two burgers hadn't quite made up for missing lunch.

It was a little after midnight when he looked up from the pages he was studying to meet Macy's quizzical gaze. Voices and footsteps could be heard outside her room. If the noise hadn't alerted him, Kell was convinced the CBI agents would have left him completely out of the action. Rat bastards.

As one, they rose and jammed their feet into shoes and ran to open the door. "Pelton!" Kell called out as the last agent rushed by. "What's going on?"

"The warrant came through," the other man called back. "Predawn raid of the residence the ransom note came from."

Chapter 8

The scene outside 16125 Elman Avenue was dark and still. Not surprising for four A.M.

Kell could make out several other vehicles in the vicinity. CBI didn't believe in going in undermanned. Which made Whitman's reluctance to include him all the harder to swallow.

"Remember what Assistant Director Whitman said," Dan Travis reminded him. "DPD's Special Response entry team leads the way. We'll bring up the tail end. You go cowboy on me, and we're both going to end up with our ass in a sling."

The CBI agent sounded worried, and he had some cause. The showdown between Kell and Whitman had been short, loud, and moderately profane. The only real reason for the supervisory agent's capitulation was there was no way the man could have prevented Kell from following in one of Mulder's vehicles, and the man had recognized that.

He just hadn't been happy about it.

Straining his eyes, Kell kept watch on the vehicles on the street for any sign of movement. "Like I told Whitman, I have some experience in these situations." Enough to know when to sit back and follow orders, even when they chafed. "And regardless of what he thinks, so does Macy."

If Kell had been irritated by Whitman's attempt to close them out of the raid, Macy had been incensed. But for once he'd agreed with the man's reasoning. They had plenty of manpower for the raid. Macy was the only one with the knowledge of linguistics. She couldn't be spared from that task.

Which hadn't meant she'd been happy about it.

He gave a quick grin, recalling her succinct remarks about the turn of events before they'd gone out the door, her last words sounding after them. He preferred to believe the "blooming wanker" remark she'd muttered had been directed at Whitman, and not at him.

"This is no situation for a woman," the agent said.

Kell cast a disbelieving look at the other man. He looked as foreign as Kell probably did himself, wearing the tactical headgear and heavy-plated load-bearing vest. "If you're going to say that to Macy's face, I'd advise you to keep your gear on. And protect your balls."

"I'm not being chauvinistic. There are just some circumstances better suited for men."

"You should share your thoughts with her," Kell advised blandly. "I know she'd appreciate hearing them." And he'd enjoy hearing her take the man off at the knees when he did so.

The back of the tactical truck opened then, and his muscles tensed. A swarm of gear-clad men clambered out, and Kell opened the car door.

"Wait," hissed Travis.

"Game's on." He fitted the night vision goggles over his eyes, adrenaline doing a fast sprint up his spine. If the mastermind of Ellie Mulder's kidnapping was sleeping blissfully inside the small clapboard house the team was rushing toward, they might be only minutes away from discovering the girl's whereabouts.

She was almost certain he was asleep.

Ellie strained her ears, but she could hear nothing. He'd

turned the TV off hours ago. In the sudden silence she'd stilled her movements and feigned sleep before the footsteps headed toward her.

She'd had lots of practice pretending to be asleep.

He hadn't spent much time checking on her. The footsteps had stopped beside her cot for less than a minute. But just thinking of those blank tan eyes of his staring down at her had made her stomach twist.

Then he'd moved away. She'd heard him heading across the space to his cot, tucked in a corner. There were no walls or doors inside the area. Which meant she was going to have to be very, very quiet.

She was good at that, too.

The cot she was lying on was just a flat piece of canvas secured to the metal frame by a series of springs. But every time he'd left the place to relieve himself or to talk on the phone, Ellie had scooted her stool over to the cot. She'd brought both feet up and slammed them down on the canvas close to a spring halfway up the frame. Although the cot looked new, it hadn't taken that long for the spring to break away from the fabric.

And the edge of that metal spring was far sharper than that spoon that he'd found and taken away from her would have been.

She'd been maneuvering for hours. Ever since she'd gone to bed. Under the lone blanket she'd worked her bound wrists back and forth over the sharp end of the spring.

Her wrists were slippery with blood. It was taking forever. She had to work by touch alone and had gouged and scraped her bare skin. It was hard to keep the spring in place.

But the tape was shredding, too. And that was enough to have her continuing.

Ellie knew she was going to die in this little room if she didn't do something. No matter how much she'd prayed, no one had found her at Art Cooper's house. No one would find her here, wherever *here* was. It was up to her to get away.

And if she died trying, it couldn't be as bad as waiting for the man to use that knife on her.

She jumped when her movements resulted in a quick flash of pain. It took a moment to figure out the wire was slicing bare skin. The tape had been torn away.

The realization had her going limp for a moment, her eyelids sliding shut. Her heart began to hammer hard in her chest. Easy to plan how she was going to do it while the tape still held tight. But now it was time to act. And for a few moments, courage deserted her.

Maybe someone would come. An inner voice jeered, but she grasped at the hope. Maybe those men her dad hired— the ones she wasn't supposed to know about—would figure this out and follow their trail up here. She wouldn't have to go out in the cold and dark and try to find her way to safety.

And maybe—probably—her kidnapper would use that knife on her before anyone came to the rescue. Or even the gun she'd seen under his shirt, tucked into the waistband of his pants.

To summon her flagging courage, she imagined his eyes again, staring at her. Lifeless and considering. And knew she had no choice.

Rolling from the bed as quietly as possible, she stood, rubbing the circulation back into her wrists. The day the man had gotten a phone call, she'd looked out the back window. So she knew there were no houses nearby. Maybe not even for miles. They were somewhere high. If not exactly in the Rockies, at least in the foothills. But they were surrounded by evergreens. And she knew the only chance she had was if she could hide herself among them as she worked her way toward a road. Any road.

She'd had to have some way to pass the time to avoid going crazy since he'd bought her here. So she'd plotted how she'd get away. Tried to recall everything her dad had taught her on their winter camping trips. She'd hated them at the time. Hated the cold and the snow. But now she tried to remember every detail of them. She tiptoed noiselessly toward the door.

The space wasn't totally dark. There was a faint glimmer coming through the weird windows in the wall. All he'd have to do is open his eyes at that moment to see her highlighted in the light cast by the woodstove as she crossed in front of it.

Holding her breath, she moved as fast as she dared. When she reached the front of the stove, she couldn't help glancing toward his cot. She could see the shadowy shape of it. The outline of his body lying there.

Ellie moved more quickly. She was good at moving quietly. Last year, after Dad had bought Lucky for her, she'd started sneaking out to the stables at night when she couldn't sleep. Thinking of her horse now brought a quick hitch to her chest. Sometimes when she couldn't breathe anymore, when everything seemed too close and heavy, just putting her arms around her horse's neck made it all melt away.

Her dad had found out, of course. The men who watched the cameras, the ones he thought she didn't know about, would have told him. He'd sat her down and explained why she couldn't sneak out alone anymore. He hadn't been mad. He'd even said she could wake him up anytime and he'd go to the stables with her.

She hadn't, of course. What would have been the point? So she had stopped sneaking out at night. But it had been good practice for her escape tonight.

When she reached the front door, she stopped again to listen. It was silent except for the faint crackle of logs in the stove. She picked up the heavy winter coat he'd put on when he'd gone outside to talk on the phone, discovered snow pants beneath it. Ellie hesitated. She had no outdoor clothes to put on. There was only that heavy insulated bag thing wadded up next to the coat that he must have brought her here in. Wrinkling her nose with distaste, she pulled his snow pants on. They were much too big, as were the boots she shoved her feet into. She hesitated when she saw the snowshoes. On the winter camping trips she'd tried snowshoeing with her mom and dad, but she'd never been able to get the hang of the stupid things. These would be worse because they were so big.

There was a slight noise then, and she froze, panic racing up her spine. Slowly, she turned her head, expecting to see him standing there. Watching her. The knife's blade glistening in his hand.

But he was still on his cot. And as hard as she strained her ears, the only sounds she could hear was the hiss and crackle of the wood burning in the stove.

A feeling of urgency filled her. She'd put the snowshoes on outside where he wouldn't see her. They could always be gotten rid of if they slowed her down. She grabbed the coat and jammed her arms into it, encountering a pair of gloves in one sleeve, a face mask in the other. Ellie put those on, too. The too-big clothes would slow her down, but she couldn't leave in only pajamas and a blanket. She'd freeze before she got a mile.

Unless he'd brought more winter clothes with him, taking his things would make it more difficult for him to follow. And she'd planned that, too.

Not daring to zip the oversized coat for fear of the noise, she turned her attention to the door. There was no way to turn the dead bolt silently. The sound it would make opening would be a small one, but she had to figure that it might wake him.

Which meant once she got out on the porch, she was going to have to run like the wind, for as long as she could stand it. And then longer.

She picked up the snowshoes and tucked them under one arm. Then reached out a hand, found the lock. Her fingers were still numb from the binds and didn't want to work right. Ellie pressed the bunched-up fabric of the coat sleeve against the lock, hoping it would muffle the sound a bit as she worked it.

The slight sound it made when she turned it had her heart pounding like Lucky's after a hard gallop. Turning the knob, she eased open the door.

The frigid air kissed her face as she slipped outside and closed the door behind her, as quietly as possible. Clouds blocked out the moon and stars, leaving her shrouded in absolute darkness. She dropped the snowshoes. Guided her feet into them by touch alone and secured the straps before rising again.

For a moment there was a rush to her head, a weakness

to her knees. The sense of freedom was dizzying. Something inside her screamed for her to run, fast, straight down in front of the small house where surely there was a driveway buried beneath the snow. But instead she turned to the left. Toward the trees that crowded together, a dense unwelcoming wall of shadows. And toward whatever might lurk within them.

She ran clumsily in the oversized boots and snowshoes, getting only a few yards before hitting a drift nearly to her chest. Ellie imagined the man coming awake. Going to her cot, finding only the wadded-up blanket. Chasing to the door and discovering his clothes missing.

Fear fueled her escape as she fought through the snow, the icy air like blades in her lungs.

Even the unknown ahead was better than certain death behind.

It had been after three when she went to bed, so Macy hadn't set her alarm. She figured she'd hear Kell and the CBI agents coming back in. But in the end, it was Raiker who woke her.

The insistent ring of her cell had her rolling over, searching for the phone while struggling to drag open her eyelids. "H'lo?"

There was a moment's silence, then her boss's familiar impatient tone. "What the hell's going on out there? Neither Burke nor Whitman are answering their phones. You sound like you're still in bed. Is anyone actually working the damn case?"

With effort, she sat up and peered at the clock. "Adam, it's six A.M."

"And your point is?"

Mentally, she conceded. Sleep was a luxury where her boss was concerned. "I was running data analysis until three. Kell joined the tactical response team Whitman put together. They narrowed down the location the ransom note was e-mailed from and the warrant came through. They left just after midnight."

"The ransom demand came in nearly seven hours earlier."

"Things don't exactly progress at a lightning pace here," she said around a yawn. "Maybe you should come back and work your magic. I thought Kell and Whitman were going to come to blows when he insisted on being part of the raid."

Raiker grunted. "Good for him. Whitman's mood isn't going to improve any time soon. I've got a lab arriving sometime today, and all the trace evidence gathered so far is being transferred from the state crime lab as we speak."

Despite herself, Macy was impressed. Superseding the CBI was a feat, even for Adam. "You had to pull a few strings to accomplish that."

"I had to extend markers it'll take me two lifetimes to repay. But the backlog at the state crime labs there did most of the work for me. What have you come up with on those samples you analyzed?"

The reminder of her night's work quickly deflated her. "None of them matched authorship of the note. I double-checked them twice to be sure."

"Who'd you have samples from?"

"Stephen and Althea Mulder, the lawyer and accountant, Mulder's executive secretary, and Nick Hubbard."

There was silence while Raiker mulled that information over. Then, "Get more. Make sure you check out Cramer, head of Mulder's security. And then start working on getting samples from every employee with access to Mulder's estate."

Although he couldn't see her, she nodded unenthusiastically. She'd already planned on getting each of the employees in for another interview, and this time have them give her a writing sample. It would be time consuming, and she knew intuitively that she wouldn't be actively working the case with Travis and Kell for a while.

"What about the threat assessment?"

Her gaze went to her computer, where it sat on the desk in the corner of the room. "The threat is real," she responded quietly. "The kidnapper means harm to Ellie Mulder." She left the rest of her thoughts unspoken, but they were there between them.

If she hadn't been harmed already.

"All the more reason to get moving on that lab work," Raiker said after a moment. "I expect CBI Director Lanscombe will kick up a fuss, but I also expect the samples to be there by the end of the day. We've got to send this thing into high gear. Let me know what turns up on the raid."

"Okay."

Macy fully expected one of Raiker's signature abrupt disconnects. So she was surprised to hear him say, "There's something else. I met with Castillo yesterday. He was asking about you."

The oxygen leeched from her lungs. For a moment, she fought to breathe. The primitive response had anger flaring. Deliberately, she drew in air, released it. "Not surprising. I assume he was more interested in game playing than in offering anything helpful."

"Oh, he offered. But I'm certain he's blowing smoke. Claimed to have information we'd find interesting but would give it only to you."

Her gaze dropped to her free hand, where the fingers were creasing and smoothing the sheet rhythmically. *One, two, three. One, two, three.* Deliberately, she stilled them. "It wouldn't hurt to find out."

"No." The word had her going limp with relief. "He's just trying to manipulate us. We aren't going to give him the satisfaction with another face-to-face. Paulie is as sure as he can be that Castillo doesn't have the connections in the States to pull off something of this magnitude. Leave it alone, Macy. That's an order."

The heaviness in her chest lightened a bit. "Well, you know how I feel about orders."

"I do." The silence that stretched then was unusual for Raiker, who was more accomplished at giving directives and then hanging up. "If I thought there was even a chance that he had something useful to offer, I wouldn't hesitate to ask you. I wouldn't like it, but I'd ask."

"I know."

"He wants to hurt you. We aren't going to give him the chance."

It took everything she had to force the word past the boulder that had formed in her throat. "Okay."

"Now go to work and solve this thing."

The words, the tone, were so familiar, so at odds with the unfamiliar compassionate one of a moment earlier that she gave a short laugh. And disconnected, because, of course, Raiker had already hung up.

Swinging her legs over the side of the bed, she paused to turn on the bedside lamp before standing. She caught a look at her reflection in the mirror. Pale. Deathly pale but for the two flags of color in her cheeks and eyes that were much too bright. She wasn't going to try to lie to herself that his order was unwelcome. There was little she wouldn't do to avoid ever having to see Enrique Castillo again.

She headed toward the bathroom. Raiker was right. It was past time to get started on the day. Whitman's absence was a perfect opportunity to quiz Althea and Stephen Mulder about any communication samples they might already have from any of the estate employees. That would save her some interviews. It would take her mind off what was transpiring with the raid. And the ire that still burned from being cut out of it.

The fact that Whitman had been right when he'd said they needed the data analysis as soon as possible was only slightly mollifying. Witnessing the near brawl that had met Kell's insistence on joining them was enough to convince her of the truth: if he'd had the power, the assistant director would have kept them both out of the action.

So she was petty enough to relish the man's reaction when he was presented with a fait accompli regarding Raiker's mobile lab.

Hopefully he would soon learn a hard lesson in cooperation.

————

Kell stood in the corner of Nancy Elliott's tidy family room, content for the moment to watch the swarm of activity around him. An agent was sitting a few feet away at the computer—

the only computer they'd found on the premises—doing something that hopefully would verify that the e-mail originated from that particular machine. The family members had been rousted from their beds then taken to separate rooms of the house with a couple CBI agents to get their statements. He'd chosen to stick here, where Whitman was questioning the single mom.

Nancy Elliott was thin and mousy and looked ten hard years older than the age she'd given the agent. Her gaze kept darting toward the back of the house, where her mother's voice could be heard, growing increasingly strident.

"I should be with my mom," she said nervously, drawing the tie of her robe tighter around her waist. "She has dementia, and she's going to find this all very disorienting."

"You can go to her soon." Whitman displayed more skill than Kell ever would have credited him with as he calmed the woman.

But Elliott twisted around from her perch on the edge of the plaid couch to look in back of her. "And my son. What have you done with David?"

"He's fine. He's talking with another agent. I want you to look at some pictures." Whitman took a big manila envelope from inside the overcoat he still wore and shook some photos out. Kell shifted position so he could get a better view. The pictures were of Nick Hubbard.

Elliott glanced at them. "Who is this? I don't know him."

"Take some time." Whitman managed to make the command sound like a suggestion. "Think back. Maybe he came here to fix the cable. Asking for directions. Maybe he's someone you talked to on the street. At a mall."

The woman shook her head more emphatically, even as she picked up the photos to peer more closely at them. "No. I'd remember if a strange guy stopped to talk to me, for any reason." Then she sent a quick glance in Kell's direction and hastened to add, "Not that I don't get my share of attention."

He gave her a slow smile from his stance against the wall. "I don't doubt it." Nodding toward the pictures she still held, he added, "But maybe he's a friend or acquaintance of your boyfriend or ex." She'd already informed them that she'd been divorced for over ten years. "Or could be you met him through one of your coworkers."

She gave him a coy look and flipped her hair over her shoulder. "I'm not seeing anyone right now." Then casting a quick glance back at Whitman, she added, "I've never seen him before. Sorry."

"Have you gotten any phone calls lately? Someone asking you to do a favor for him, perhaps?"

Elliott drew in her bottom lip. "What kind of favor?"

Kell was actually impressed when Whitman didn't seem to lose his patience. Who would have figured it? The assistant director was actually good at this.

"You tell me. Someone wanted to use your computer. Maybe borrowed it for a while." She was already shaking her head in response. "Or asked you to leave your house unlocked overnight."

She looked at him askance. "In this neighborhood? In Denver? Are you kidding? As soon as I can afford it, I'm getting myself one of those home alarm systems. Why, my neighbor down the street got her house broken into just last Tuesday, in broad daylight. It's getting to where a woman isn't safe in her own home, anymore. Not that they care. The streetlight out front has been burned out for a week. I've called the city twice about it, and it hasn't been fixed yet."

The cell in his pocket vibrated. Kell had shut the ringer off when he'd waited with Travis prior to the raid. Checking it surreptitiously, he recognized the number and felt an answering leap of adrenaline. He strode across the room, ignoring Whitman's glower, and let himself out the door before answering it. "What do you have for me?"

"Nothing of interest, I'm sure." Denise Temple's voice was sour. "I told you before, I'm not going to be able to give you any information that CBI isn't getting."

"Humor me," he suggested, pulling on his gloves. Temperatures in this godforsaken city seemed to swing between frigid and cold as hell. But at least it had stopped snowing.

There looked to be well over a foot of the stuff all around.

"Okay, I looked at the district crime blotter for the last few days. And then what I could find on Coplink."

"Coplink." He stamped his feet in an effort to get warm. "What's that?"

"It's a commercially developed software that many of the law enforcement agencies in the area use. We input data about crimes or stops we make, the information links seamlessly to the rest of the data in the system, spits out any commonalities."

Kell's brows raised, impressed. "Nice. What'd it spit out?"

"You got a pen and paper? It's quite a list."

"Give me a rundown."

Temple gave a long-suffering sigh. "Okay, police blotter first. Going back a week ago, we had an armed robbery of a gas station over on Ninetieth Street West. Twelve rapes. Suspected arson on Colfax. Thirty-four B and Es. Fifty-seven stolen vehicle reports . . ."

As Kell listened, he observed the surrounding area. Despite the temperatures, there was a small group of people gathered beyond the barriers some of the officers had put up in the street, all gawking at the house, wondering, no doubt, what the hell was going on here. Apparently they didn't have jobs to go to.

He listened for several more minutes until Temple ran down before speaking again. "I appreciate this, Sergeant. Really. I'd appreciate it more if you e-mailed me that list."

"No." The word was emphatic. "No paper trail. I'm putting nothing in writing."

He sighed, wondering if it was in every woman's makeup to make his life difficult. "Well, don't do it from a work computer. If you don't want to do it from home, go to an Internet café and send it to me." He rattled off his e-mail address. As he did, he watched one of Temple's counterparts direct a particularly curious onlooker back behind the barricade. Crowd control in this weather couldn't be regarded as pleasant. "And keep them coming."

There was a long silence. Then, "I did a little digging on

your outfit." She hadn't been satisfied back at Hubbard's house until Kell had shown her his ID, he recalled, after Macy had waylaid Travis. "With Raiker's rep, how is it that you're not getting this information from CBI? Because I can guarantee you someone from DPD is updating them daily."

"I don't think they know how to play well with others."

She gave a short laugh. "Yeah, I've heard. Guess it wouldn't hurt to send you the blotter reports, seeing as how it's info that is being fed to CBI anyway."

"And the Coplink information. You said surrounding area law enforcement agencies used it, too, right? Is that including the county sheriff's departments?"

The door behind him opened, and he was joined on the small porch by Agent Travis. When the man just stood there, Kell realized he'd been dispatched for the sole purpose of checking up on him. Lost between amusement and irritation, he had to give Whitman credit. Even in the midst of an investigation, he managed to keep his mind on the truly dangerous element of the case, Kell himself.

"A few of them. Jefferson, Adams, Summit . . ."

"Yep, I'd be interested in hearing stories from there." Mindful of Travis's unabashed eavesdropping, he was choosing his words carefully.

She was silent for a moment. "What the hell are you talking about?"

"A threesome. I know you're interested."

"Listen, you son of a bitch . . ."

"Listening. Yep." He sent a broad smile to Travis, who hunched his shoulders and looked away, hands shoved in his pockets. "I like the way your mind works."

"Three . . . There's someone there? Listening?"

"That's right."

"Damn lucky for you that's what you meant," she muttered. "Okay, I'll e-mail you what I've got. But you better hold up your end of this deal, Burke. My name stays out of it, are we clear on that?"

"I remember everything you told me. Snookums."

She gave a snort. "Laying it on a bit thick, aren't you?

Listen, I've heard chatter about a tactical raid on the east side. You wouldn't happen to know anything about that, would you?"

He shot another look at Travis, who was trying hard to appear interested in the scene in the street. "Baby, you know our arrangement doesn't work like that." The suggestion she made then was neither polite nor anatomically possible. "I've always enjoyed your imagination. I look forward to hearing from you."

Sliding the cell phone in his coat pocket, he looked at Travis. "You need something?"

"Jesus, Burke, we're running an op here. I'd think you could keep your mind off your sex life for a few hours."

The tips of the agent's ears were red. Kell wondered if it was from the cold or from embarrassment at what he thought he'd overheard.

"We all have our priorities."

"Look, we can probably head back. This is going to take all day, and they have plenty of agents inside to take care of things."

He looked at the man carefully. It was to Travis's credit that he couldn't meet Kell's eyes. "That ever get old, Dan? Being Whitman's bitch?"

His words had the agent's gaze bouncing to his, temper evident. "Watch it, buddy. I can't quite figure out what sort of outfit Raiker is running, but I haven't been impressed so far. Our agency has a hierarchy, and I'm not going to apologize for taking orders. Or are you going to tell me that your boss gives you free rein?"

Just the thought had amusement rising. "Free rein with Raiker? Hardly. But he lets us do our jobs, and that's a helluva lot more than I can say for the assistant director." But his ire was already fading. He'd spent enough years with the Baltimore PD to recall what it was like following the chain of command. He hadn't once missed it since he'd left either. "C'mon." He was already turning toward the door. "I want to hear what the kid has to say." Teenage boys hung out on the Internet a lot, didn't they? And they needed to check the cell phones in the house. Depending on the provider and package, e-mail could be sent from cells, too.

The hand on his shoulder stopped him. He looked at it. Then at Travis.

"Whitman . . . it wasn't a suggestion, Kell." The man looked discomfited but determined. "I'm to take you back. We've got plenty to concentrate on anyway, right? We still haven't followed up on all of Hubbard's phone contacts."

"You gonna shoot me, Dan?"

"What?" The hand dropped from his shoulder.

"Do you intend to shoot me?" He gestured toward the man's weapon. "Because that's the only way you're getting me to leave here before I'm ready." He didn't wait for a response. He was already reaching for the door and letting himself back inside the house. He caught the look Whitman threw, first at him, then at the agent trailing him. He returned it, in spades. There was a showdown coming between him and the assistant director, that was certain. Kell welcomed it.

But for now, he contented himself with a terse nod toward the beefy agent as he continued through the house in search of David Elliott.

———

"I've contacted all the people you requested," Stephen Mulder was saying. He hadn't sat since they'd entered the room where'd he set up his new office. Whitman was ensconced in his other one. Hands shoved deep in the pockets of his trousers, he paced the length of the room and back again, as if compelled to move. "They ought to be here soon. Cramer, of course is on the property. I'll call him in whenever you're ready."

Althea Mulder sat in the chair next to Macy, her gaze fixed on her husband worriedly. "You must not have come up with a match on those other samples you tested. That's it, isn't it? And now you need more samples, hoping one of them will match the ransom note?"

"I want to be as thorough as possible."

Stephen turned to make a return trip across the room. He

was dressed more informally today than she'd ever seen him, in trousers and a cashmere sweater, with Gucci loafers. But he looked as though he hadn't slept for the duration of this trauma. "You told Whitman the program has a five percent error rate. So we can safely delete any of the authors of the samples you've tested as being involved."

"The odds are against any of them having authored the note," she corrected. "Involvement is something else."

He threw her a look filled with dark humor. "Well, damn. And here Althea and I were hoping this at least proved our innocence."

"Adam never suspected you," she responded, speaking more freely than she would have in Whitman's presence. "His opinion is the one that matters most to me." But having the Mulders cleared on the tests she ran last night didn't hurt. "There's something else I wanted to broach with you. A man in your position gets a lot of threats."

Mulder looked impatient. "Of course. But I gave that information to Whitman the first day. Don't tell me that hasn't been tracked down yet?"

As a matter of fact, if it had, those details had made it into neither their files nor the ones prepared for Travis. Macy vowed to follow up on that fact later. "Do you have a file of those threats? I'd like to run comparison samples on them."

Comprehension lit his expression, with a bit of hope. "Of course. The chief security officer at my company headquarters has copies of all written threats. I'll have them messengered over today." His expression lightened a bit. "There aren't *that* many of them, despite what the press would have you believe. Crackpots, for the most part."

"Stephen and I have been talking." Today Althea's blond hair was arranged in an artful French twist. But her face was drawn with fatigue. "We think we should offer to do polygraph tests, but Mark is advising against it. He says they're unreliable and that the results can be twisted. What do you think?"

"I think you should run it by Adam," Macy said firmly. That was an area she wasn't about to get into.

"I did." Stephen began another turn around the room. "Just this morning, in fact. He wants me to hold off, at least until his return."

"You talked to Adam this morning?"

Stephen gave her a grim smile. "He's good about checking in daily. Hell of a lot better than Whitman about sharing information. He won't be back in time for you to use his jet for your trip to Chicago tomorrow. I assured him I'd place my personal jet at your disposal." He veered toward the desk in the corner and scribbled something on a notepad, before ripping the sheet off and walking over to hand it to her. "My pilot's on standby but you should call him and let him know your timeline. One of my drivers will take you to the airport."

Macy tucked the paper into the file in front of her. "Thank you."

"It's a relief, at any rate, to eliminate some from the list." Althea lifted a hand as if to ward off objections. "I know you said that doesn't mean they aren't involved. But I hate to have our suspicion fall on those closest to us." An unusual flicker of bitterness tinged her expression. "*Again.* Friendship with our family has become something of a burden."

It was telling that the woman didn't mention having suspicion fall on her and her husband twice now when tragedy had struck. "So Alden, Spencer, and Amundson are among your closest friends?"

"Mark, Lance, Stephen, and I went to Harvard together." Something eased in Althea's expression at the memory. "They're closer than brothers, really. They stood up for him at our wedding seventeen years ago."

"That's a long time to be friends," she answered gently.

"The three musketeers, I always called them when we were dating." There was a slight smile on the woman's face, even as she tracked her husband's pacing with her gaze. "I used to complain about never getting enough time alone with Stephen. The other two were usually close by."

"And you all ended up in business together?"

"Not right away." Stephen withdrew his hands from his pockets and flexed them, then seemed not to know what to do with them. "Mark and Lance came from well-to-do families, and they had jobs waiting for them when they graduated."

"Mark's father is former Vice President Richard Alden," Althea put in. "His father was in office when we were in college, so there was also the Secret Service to contend with when he was around. Used to drive him crazy."

Macy's eyes widened a bit. "I didn't realize that."

"Well, he'd never mention it." Althea gave a delicate shrug. "People think that means he had it easy, but he has a fairly significant learning disability that made graduating from college and law school a real triumph. He was with a prestigious East Coast firm for years. And Lance's family are heirs to a digital empire that I've never really understood. But it's Stephen who started out with nothing and built a company from the bottom up." The pride in her voice was obvious. "When he did, Lance and Mark came to work for him."

"With me, not for me," Stephen corrected dryly. "I credit a lot of my success to the two of them."

"So Lance Spencer has his finger on all your finances?" Macy said slowly.

Mulder gave her a tight smile. "We have dozens of people in finance, but yes, it's Lance at the helm. He and Mark are working on liquidating some of my assets so I'll be able to meet the ransom demand by the deadline."

His words brought the worry back to his wife's eyes. Looking at Macy, she said hesitantly, "You haven't said . . . you compared the samples of authorship but you were going to do something else. A threat assessment, you said."

Her stomach plummeted as the parents both fixed their gazes on her. "What did you discover?"

Choosing her words carefully, Macy said, "There's really no way to be sure that the exact threat in the note will be executed. The database really just gives statistical odds regarding intent to harm."

Looking from one of them to the other, she wished she could be anywhere but there. "But the threat assessment is positive. Your daughter is in real danger."

Chapter 9

"So what have you come up with?"

Abbie Robel answered Adam's question first. "Rob Bigelow is a bona fide kiddie perv. And we did find the pictures Art Cooper sent him of Ellie Mulder in his rather extensive collection."

"But we haven't found any evidence that Bigelow ever acted on his fantasies." Ryne draped an arm around Abbie's shoulders. "We're getting good cooperation from local law enforcement. They were grateful for the tip and didn't waste any time getting a warrant. Even let Abbie have a go at Bigelow in interrogation, and she was a sight to behold." He gave his boss a grim smile. "I think Bigelow was ready to piss himself before she was done with him."

Abbie tapped a finger against the table in front of her impatiently. "He was scared. The guy's a weasel. I think I got everything he had. He gave us a list of names of people he swapped photos with. Websites he visited. Kiddie porn live streams he'd subscribed to. He has three computers at his place, and all of them are full of images and movies. But his alibi checks out. He showed up for work every day for the last month, on time. He certainly wasn't in Colorado a few days ago."

"He wouldn't have the brains or the balls to put together the kidnapping of Ellie Mulder," Ryne put in. "Personally, I wouldn't be surprised if something arises once news of his arrest gets out. Maybe a victim will come forward. But I'm not seeing how he impacts your case."

Ruthlessly, Adam tamped down a surge of impatience. "You said you had something I needed to see. So far you've given me nothing."

The look Abbie sent to her husband was telling. "We did discover that Bigelow shared those old photos of Ellie that Cooper had sent. Apparently these guys network widely. There are secret portals on the Internet. They hijack legitimate pages and you click on a letter or corner of a graphic, and bam. You're in pervertville."

"Then they change that up on a regular basis to stay one step ahead of law enforcement," Ryne added.

"I'm familiar with their tactics." Seven and a half years ago, his last case for the bureau had involved one of the most sadistic child predators operating in the country. "You said Bigelow shared Ellie's photos. How widely?"

"The tech has found traces of the images being sent hundreds of times." Ryne shook his head in disgust. "It's like a spiderweb, Adam. You can follow the threads all over the world and still come up with nothing but more threads. There's no telling how many hard drives have her picture on them."

Adam battled back a wave of frustration. It had been a long shot, after all. And the process of following it had removed one more lowlife child porn lover from the street.

But it hadn't brought them any closer to the person responsible for kidnapping Ellie Mulder.

"What's the local LEO's involvement?"

"They're on this in a big way. Multiagency task force. They'll be chasing down all the leads on this thing with a vengeance, going after every e-mail sender and recipient, and every website visited. For as long as the money and interest holds out, I guess."

Adam nodded. "Stay with it awhile longer. Concentrate on getting identities to go with the e-mail names. Check out their backgrounds. Then cross-check them with the file I sent you of disgruntled ex-employees from Mulder enterprises. People he's turned down for jobs. Those that have made threats. See if you can find an intersection."

The two exchanged looks. "Okay."

He stared first at Abbie, then at her husband. "There's nothing quite as annoying as these shared spousal looks, full of secret meaning. Do you practice that? Is there some sort of marriage seminar that teaches it? You should know the rest of the world finds it damn annoying."

"We found something else." Ryne took a thin file folder out of the portfolio on the table in front of him and slid it over to Adam. "Can't see how it applies to this case. But thought you'd be interested."

His mind already on the next leg of his journey, he flipped open the folder and scanned the contents. There were three sheets inside, all dated a decade ago. Each was a copy of an e-mail exchange. Unsurprisingly, one of the names was Bigelow's.

But the other name had memory rising up like a red-hot poker, searing inside him. John LeCroix.

He read the pages more carefully. Bigelow had been at this game for a long time if he'd corresponded with LeCroix. From the gist of the messages, it seemed that Bigelow had received some photos from the other man ten years ago. He'd thanked LeCroix, praised the detail and content of the pictures, and informed him he was a girl lover, asking if he had any other images to share.

Adam's empty eye socket throbbed in phantom pain. "LeCroix liked little boys. We know he showed off his work. But none of the photos would have had him in them. He was a careful bastard."

"What do you want us to do with this?"

Adam considered for a moment. "Send it to Paulie. He keeps a file on LeCroix." Then he grabbed his cane and used it haul himself to his feet. "Stay on the Bigelow lead until I let you know otherwise."

Without another word, he let himself out of the West Virginia motel room. At his appearance, the driver of his rented town car started up the car and did a slow U-turn in the lot and headed toward him. And all the while the name repeated itself in his mind like echoes of clanging metal.

John LeCroix.

The man he'd chased across Florida, Georgia, and into the Louisiana bayou country. The man responsible for the kidnap, rape, torture, and murder of twenty-seven boys under the age of ten. Adam had managed to rescue his latest victim, but LeCroix had captured him shortly after.

And that memory was destined to haunt him for the rest of his life.

John LeCroix had cost him his eye. Very nearly his leg. Unconsciously, he raised his hand to finger the scar across his throat. It'd been three long days before he'd escaped from the makeshift torture chamber in the dark swamp.

The only positive memory about the whole mess was the one where he'd sent the son of a bitch to his grave.

Martin Becker vigorously cleaned his wire-framed glasses with his handkerchief. "This is highly unsettling." There was a hint of Long Island in his voice and a sheen of nerves to his expression. "I've already talked to some CBI agents. Just hours after Ellie was found missing. I gave a statement then. I haven't recalled any other useful information to give you."

"What can you tell me about your observations of Ellie Mulder?" Macy suggested. She had a copy of the man's statement. Of all the statements gathered in the course of the investigation. And although what she was after was a handwritten communication from the man, she couldn't resist the opportunity to gather a few details about the girl they were seeking. *Know the victim, know the crime*. It was Raiker's most oft-repeated mantra.

The request seemed to startle the man. "Ellie? Well, she's an average eleven-year-old girl, I suppose."

When Macy raised her brows, he seemed to flush. "Academically speaking, of course. She's bright enough. I don't believe she received any schooling for two years . . . um, when she was gone before. But under my tutelage, her deficits were remediated. She not only caught up but surpassed other students her age. Not that she always works up to her potential—she can be a bit disengaged at times—but she's an intelligent, if unimaginative student."

The compliment was couched in rather unflattering terms. "Unimaginative. You mean creatively? In her artwork and writing?"

"More in her problem-solving ability. Ellie tends to approach things in a rather pragmatic, concrete way. Functional, certainly, but until she has a better grasp of the abstract, she won't be a truly great thinker."

Stemming a strong urge to remind the tutor that the child was only eleven, Macy asked, "What are her interests? What kind of music and books does she like?"

Martin settled his glasses back on his rather pointed nose. "I don't teach her music. She has a piano instructor for that."

It took a deep breath to summon patience. Macy was beginning to wonder if Becker wasn't the unimaginative one. "I mean, how does she like to spend her free time?"

His brow furrowed. "Well, she spends more time with that horse of hers than she should, but other than that, I really couldn't say. It's not my area."

He'd managed to startle her. "Not your area? You talk to her, don't you? You must spend more time with her daily than even her parents, at least during the week. How can you not know what she likes?"

"Ms. Reid." Becker smoothed his thinning blond hair. "I have three advanced degrees. I was an adjunct professor for an Ivy League college, on the fast track for tenure, when I accepted Mr. Mulder's offer for a position here. My duties were clear. To catch young Ellie up on her studies and ready her for whatever university her parents choose for her. I assure you, I take my obligations seriously. But they don't encompass befriending the child. I'm her teacher, not her counselor. Our conversations focused solely on her academics, as is fitting."

Macy had wanted to get a better picture of the child, but this man was shedding very little light on that question. She was, however, getting a better understanding of the girl's days, and thinking of her spending hours at a time cooped up with this humorless, priggish man was discouraging.

Having spent her life shuttling between one embassy post to another meant that Macy had experienced her share of tutors. Becker bore an unfortunate resemblance to one in particular, a Reginald Fox. The only difference that she could see was that her stepfather had gotten rid of the man when he learned how much Macy disliked him.

She wondered if Ellie had ever complained about Becker to her parents.

Sliding the yellow legal pad across the table, she simply said, "I need a sample of your written communication. Why don't you write me one hundred words on developing imaginative abstract reasoning skills in eleven-year-old students."

"You do a lot of gaming, David?"

The sullen fifteen-year-old barely looked up at Kell's question. He seemed more concerned with the computer that an agent was currently boxing up in the adjoining room. "Some."

"What system do you prefer? The Wii? PlayStation?"

"I've got a Wii. Mom won't get me a PlayStation." It was clear from his tone that the boy found her refusal to be totally unreasonable.

"I'm a pretty good Wii boxer." Kell settled his shoulders more comfortably against the wall and crossed one booted foot over the other. "What about you, Agent Pelton? You look like a *Mario Brothers* man to me."

Pelton looked mystified. "What?"

But he'd managed to capture the kid's attention. David's lip curled. "*Mario Brothers* is stupid. I like *Killer Instinct. Mortal Kombat II. No More Heroes*."

Kell hid his reaction. The kid liked his gore. "Takes a lot

of practice to be good at those games. You spend a lot of time on it?"

The kid shrugged, already losing interest. "When are we going to get our computer back?"

"I don't know. A few weeks, probably."

"How much time do you spend online, David?" Pelton steered the conversation back to the interview.

Lifting a shoulder again, the teenager said, "I don't know. Some."

"Every day?"

"Sure. Facebook and e-mail . . ." He frowned, throwing Kell an anxious look. "Hey, you guys can't hack into my Facebook account, can you? That'd be like an invasion of privacy, right?"

"We served a warrant," Pelton said impatiently. "You have no reasonable expectation of privacy."

Seeing the kid's panicked expression, Kell said mildly, "But we're looking for certain information. Anything else we find doesn't interest us." When the kid's anxiety didn't lessen appreciably, he added, "No reason for us to share any of that information with your mom, unless it's illegal."

Tension eased from the boy's shoulders. "Yeah? It's not illegal. But she would freak. I've got e-mail messages saved from my dad."

"And she doesn't want you communicating with him?"

He shook his head, then hunched his shoulders. "They hate each other, y'know? But I hardly get to see him. He lives in Oregon."

Agent Pelton leaned forward in his chair, his hands clasped between his open knees. "What's his name?"

"Walter Elliott."

"And he hasn't been by to see you recently?" Pelton tried for a friendly smile that came off looking, in Kell's estimation, pretty damn creepy. "Maybe slipped into town and met you on the sly? Without your mom knowing?"

"I wish," David muttered. "He doesn't have any money. Lost his job last year. He had to move back in with my grandparents."

Kell could see where Pelton was going with the questioning, but he was angling a bit far off base. Even if the man were destitute, even given the snowball's chance in hell that he could be involved in this, why would the guy take the chance of implicating his son by sending a ransom note bearing their IP address?

"What time do you get up in the morning, David?" Pelton looked annoyed at his interruption.

"Not until I have to. School starts at eight thirty. Usually seven or so."

"I remember high school. Can't say homework was high on my priority list. Used to have to pull a few all-nighters to get papers done sometimes." He uttered the lie without a flicker of conscience. It had been more his style to pay someone to write the papers for him, but he doubted that was something to be shared with a fifteen-year-old who looked to lack his own work ethic. "You ever do that? Have to stay up late to get something done for school?"

The kid looked at him like he was crazy. "No, I'd rather take the F. But sometimes if I can't sleep, I might use the computer or play Wii all night. I did that a few days ago. Got my highest score on *Mortal Kombat* ever. Wanna see?"

Kell exchanged a look with Pelton. "Okay if we continue this in the boy's room?" In answer, the agent got up and they followed the kid out of the dining room and up the stairs.

It was, Kell figured, a normal enough teenage boy's room. There were clothes strewn on the floor and on the foot of the unmade bed. Glasses and empty plates littered the desktop next to the TV and gaming system on the desk. He was constantly surprised by the gadgets and high-tech equipment kids scored these days. He'd been lucky to have a couch to sleep on when he was young. And when he was David Elliott's age, he'd had to pick the lock on his mother's door to get inside the house at all. Carrie Burke was about as nurturing as a rabid wolverine.

With the most animation he'd shown all day, David crossed to the system and flipped it on. "I've got a buddy who's always bragging that he beat the game, but I did it with a higher score than he got. Look at this." Pelton peered over the kid's shoulder, but Kell's attention was diverted to the window. The bedroom was in the front of the house, directly above the room where the computer was kept downstairs. Blinds covered the window that faced the street, but they were askew, as if the cord had gotten yanked hard and jammed. The result left the blinds halfway up, hanging at a diagonal. "Bet your buddy was impressed."

"Are you kidding? He's pissed. Won't hardly talk to me. The dick."

Kell peered at the time stamp on the screen. Yesterday at three thirty A.M. Adrenaline kick-started inside him. He jerked a thumb to the window. "You see any activity on the street out front when you were playing?"

The kid shook his head furiously. "I was busy concentrating on the game, you know. People don't realize you have to have intense concentration. Good reflexes. Take your eyes off the action for a minute, and you miss your chance of reaching the next level."

Pelton had picked up Kell's train of thought as smoothly as if they'd been working together for years. "But you'd notice if a car went by that time of night. Quiet street like this, you must not get a lot of traffic. Headlights would shine right in your window."

The boy was silent for a long time. Then, "Maybe there was a car out there. Parked across the street in front of Gorley's. But it took off while I was playing."

Kell and the agent exchanged a look. "Can you describe the vehicle?"

The boy started playing a game that resulted in a lot of machine gun fire and obscenities from the characters on the screen. "I'm not that good with cars. But I know it was silver."

"Oh, I'm sorry." Macy stopped in the doorway, nonplussed. "I thought I'd find Stephen in here."

The room was the office Mulder had transformed for his

use when his had been commandeered by Whitman. But neither of the men inside the room were Stephen Mulder.

"Ms. Reid, isn't it?" She recognized Mark Alden, Mulder's lawyer from the first day they'd arrived. "He's supposed to meet us in a few minutes. You're free to hang out in here with us and wait."

"In fact, I think I'll have to insist on it." The second man rose from his chair lazily, aimed a smile in her direction. "I'm Lance Spencer. I don't think I've had the pleasure."

Ah. The accountant. Macy gave them both a quick smile. "I think I will wait, if you don't mind. I just need a minute of Stephen's time."

And she wasn't averse to learning a bit more about two of the people who had been in the house hours before Ellie had been kidnapped.

Lance Spencer had Greek god looks and a slick charm that was the polar opposite of any accountant she'd ever met. He appeared similarly taken aback with her. "So." His bright blue eyes sparkled wickedly at her. "If you don't mind me saying, you don't look much like a cop."

"She's not a cop, Spence." Alden got up and went to a container in the center of the table filled with beverages on ice. "Can I get you something to drink, Ms. Reid?"

"Macy, please. And I'll take a water." He fished one out from the container, and she walked over to take it from his outstretched hand. "Thank you."

"Well, if you're not a cop, Macy Reid, what are you?"

She twisted off the cap of the water, returned Spencer's bland stare. "I'm a consultant with Raiker Forensics."

The accountant shook his head. "Nope. You don't look like a consultant either." He turned away then to address Alden. "I'll take one of those waters, Mark." He reached up a hand and caught the bottle the other man tossed to him, his attention back on her. "If I'd had to guess, I'd peg you as an elementary school teacher." He opened the bottle and took a long swallow. "You have kind eyes and a faintly exasperated air."

"And I'd peg you as a used car salesman." She smiled blandly as both men laughed.

"Maybe that's why I can't get a woman," Spencer joked.

"No, I think that's because you're not looking for *a* woman, you're looking for *every* woman," Alden put in dryly.

"True." The man's eyes were amused and invited Macy to share the joke. "But we can't all meet our true loves in college like Stephen and Mark did." He lowered his voice conspiratorially. "Mark used to pay Dianna to write his papers for him. That's how they met. She never minded that the man has an indecipherable scrawl that would put a doctor's to shame."

If his friend was embarrassing him, there was no sign of it. "Well, I redeemed myself by moving her out here two years ago." To Macy, he said, "My wife is a ski bunny. On the slopes more than she's at home."

Lance slowly twisted the top of the cap on his bottle. "I hope you've got good news to share with Stephen. They're due for some after the last few days."

"The investigation is progressing." And more than that she wouldn't say to anyone outside the case. "Both of you were here that night."

The men nodded in unison. Alden sat down in one of the chairs at the conference table. "We were working on a new project for the philanthropic side of Mulder Stores."

Lance took up the telling. "A mentoring program for troubled teens." His smile was wry. "Mark's making sure I join him as a mentor. Not really my thing, but I'll give it a shot."

"Do you good," Alden told him. "Keep you out of the strip clubs."

"That's what I'm afraid of," the man shot back.

"Did any of you ride together that night?" she asked before tipping the bottle to her lips.

Spencer looked at the lawyer. "You and Tessa came together, didn't you? Because of the weather?"

Alden nodded. "Yeah, she didn't want to drive because it was supposed to turn bad." He looked at her then, his pleasant face serious. "We'd like to help here, Ms. Reid. Stephen is our closest friend. If there's any way we can assist the investigation, please let us know."

"Reid."

Turning, she recognized the chief of Mulder's security, Ben Cramer, standing in the doorway. His glower was all too familiar. "You're supposed to run any company you're expecting through Mr. Mulder, who would let me know."

Rising, she headed toward him. "That's why I came to find him."

"Well, it's too late now. We've got an RV and a car outside the front gate. They say they're with you."

Adrenaline spiked. The mobile lab that Raiker had promised had arrived. She could only hope that the CBI was as quick about sending the lab specimens to be tested. "Do you need me to come down and identify them?"

"Well, I'm sure as hell not letting them in if you don't."

Charming as ever. Rising, she told the two men, "I guess I don't need to see Stephen after all."

"Nice meeting you," Spencer called after her.

She smiled sweetly at Cramer as she brushed by him. "And you can join me in the next room in thirty minutes. I have a few questions for you."

"Zach." Momentarily nonplussed to see the driver of the lab, Macy's steps faltered. "Since when have you been filling in as a driver?"

"Since the satellite lab crew got hit by a flu bug. Both drivers are down, and Cait was looking a bit green herself. The only way I could convince her to go to bed was to promise to deliver it myself." His expression went dour. "I don't plan to make a regular thing of it."

Laughing, she teased, "Sounds like true love to me." Zach Sharper had met Raiker investigator Caitlin Fleming on a case in Oregon last summer, and it had been sparks at first sight.

A rare grin split his expression. "Don't kid yourself. I'm in it for the cookies. She's going to owe me big time for this one." He jerked his head toward the compact car idling behind him. "I set up a meet with your lab scientist outside

Denver. Tell me where to park this beast, and I'll return his car to the airport. I've got a flight back to Eugene tonight."

Macy turned to check the progress of Cramer and the security guard manning the gate. They were still checking the undercarriage of the vehicle. "They'll do a thorough check inside, too. Maybe you should switch vehicles now. This could take a while."

Needing no further encouragement, Zach leaned over to grab a parka on the seat beside him and opened the driver's door to jump lightly to the ground. "Thanks. I don't want to miss my flight. I've never seen Cait under the weather before." There was an anxious light in his whiskey-colored eyes.

"And you're worried?"

He shoved a hand through his shaggy sun-streaked brown hair. "Someone has to make sure the woman stays in bed. She seems to think the office will fall apart without her there to keep the thing running."

Smiling, she said nothing further. She'd only met him once, at Ramsey and Dev's wedding last month. But if ever there was a man in the process of falling hard and fast, it was Zach Sharper. "Give her my best and tell her I said to make you wait on her hand and foot."

He grunted as they strode back through the gate toward the car. "Like she'd allow it. Don't let her cover model looks fool you. She's got a mean streak when she's not feeling well." He stopped in his tracks as the man in the car got out.

Alfred Jones, more commonly known as Jonesy in the Raiker labs, was as brilliant as he was unconventional, and Macy couldn't help but wonder what Assistant Director Whitman would make of him. His stiff black Mohawk made a hat impossible, and she shivered just thinking about how the cold felt on the shaved sides of his head. Not to mention the multiple piercings that dotted his face and ears. As usual he was clad in complete black, with a hooded sweatshirt that proclaimed LAB RAT in bold white letters, baggy black pants, and . . . her eyes dropped to his feet. Thongs.

"Uh, Jonesy, you've seen snow before, right?"

"Hey, Macy." He swept by her like a man on a mission.

"What the hell are they doing? They absolutely are not allowed inside the lab. Hey. Hey!"

She and Zach turned to look at him running to accost Cramer and the other guard, who were yanking at the door of the secured lab. Macy gave a little sigh. Just the thought of the upcoming battle depleted her strength for a moment.

"Buck up." Zach patted her on the shoulder. "If it comes down to a fight, I'd put money on the little weird guy. He looks unpredictable."

"Yeah." She gave a sigh and started toward the men. "That's what I'm afraid of."

———

"Tell the truth." Cramer folded his arms over his impressive chest and scowled at her. "You guys still don't have dick."

Their earlier altercation hadn't improved the man's mood, Macy noted. He especially hadn't liked the fact that she'd had to call Stephen Mulder to resolve the argument. The man's agreement to allow the lab on the property without an interior search had clearly infuriated his chief security officer. Even though he'd been allowed access to it once Jonesy had it parked inside the employee garage and had handed the guards sterile gowns and shoe covers to put on before entering.

"We have several leads we're pursuing."

He made a rude noise. "The only thing you've got is your suspicion of Nick Hubbard. And if that were going anywhere, you wouldn't still be questioning me."

"Do you know his girlfriend?"

Cramer's gaze narrowed. "What do you know about Denise?"

"Enough to ask you about her," Macy snapped. And she'd thought Kell was irritating. Although the men were clearly annoying in different ways. "Had you ever met her?"

He shook his head slowly. "No. And I only know her first name. I got the feeling she had some backstory, some reason to keep things quiet. Nick didn't offer the details, and I didn't ask."

"So you never met her?"

"No." His look sharpened. "Why, does she have something to do with this? Maybe she can shed some light on where Nick is. Because I can guarantee you he isn't holed up somewhere with that kid."

It was on the tip of her tongue to tell the man that Denise Temple hadn't seemed so certain, but she swallowed the impulse. "So where do you think the kidnapper is holed up with Ellie? He couldn't have gone too far that first night in that blizzard. After the AMBER Alert, law enforcement was checking cars mere hours after she went missing."

He gave a hard laugh. "Are you kidding? There are enough remote areas in this state to hide out indefinitely. And I can guarantee you there are people in the mountains doing exactly that." But he seemed to give it some thought. "I've done my share of personal protection gigs in the past. Same thought behind it, really. Stash the client out of sight for an indefinite amount of time. You want remote but accessible. Around here, you get too remote, and you might not be getting out until the spring thaw. There are some passes I don't know if I'm going to get through until July or August. I can guarantee the kidnapper doesn't want to chance that. But maybe he's not relying on cars either." He squinted hard, one index finger tapping against his biceps. "Right off, most of the spots I'm thinking of would be in one of the national forests. Especially the Uncompahgre around Ouray or Ridgway."

Macy was already shaking her head. "There's no way he's going to take the chance of being discovered by tourists or rangers . . ."

The smile that Cramer flashed held genuine amusement. "I'm not talking Central Park here. Colorado still has spots that have never been explored, like the West Elk Wilderness area in the center of the Gunnison National. The Weminuche Wilderness area is situated between Silverton and Wolf Creek Pass. No highways through it, only logging roads. The Maroon Bells and Snowmass Wilderness area near Marble is another possibility. Of course, you're banking that the kidnapper would go to the trouble of keeping the girl alive long enough to need a secluded spot to keep her."

The matter-of-fact tone the man used had Macy's blood running cold. "You don't think he would?"

He gave a roll of his massive shoulders. "Depends if he needs her. Has there been a ransom demand?"

When he was met only with stony silence, he gave another shrug. "If ransom is the motivation, yeah, there's a possibility the girl's alive, although he doesn't necessarily need her to collect. Brings on a whole new level of risk. But I can see him keeping her as his ace in the hole. What if he has to provide proof of life to collect? So if ransom is behind this, there's a chance she's alive out there somewhere."

His final words echoed and reechoed hollowly in Macy's mind. "But your chances of finding her in an area like those? Slim and none."

———

"I can't work like this, Macy. I *refuse* to work like this."

Jonesy was nearly quivering in indignation. And the headache that had spawned a couple hours earlier sprang forth full force to rap at the base of Macy's skull.

"I have my orders." Nellie Trimball, the tech sent from the state crime lab, was tall and spare, and even given the extra height provided by his Mohawk, towered over Jonesy by a good six inches. Her long thin legs were sensibly covered in wool, and her feet encased in knee-high rubber boots. She began to unwrap a yard-long gray scarf from a cranelike neck as she continued. "I preserve the chain of evidence and provide quality control on all tests run."

"Quality control!" Jonesy's eyes nearly bulged out of his head. "Listen, lady, I *am* quality. I invented quality. The day I need some CBI drone hanging over my shoulder like a human ostrich critiquing my work is the day they'll be kissing my powder white ass in hell."

The visual image that obligingly flashed across Macy's mind at his colorful words did nothing to make the pounding in her head subside. "Now, Jonesy . . ."

"I'm lab manager at the state lab in Denver," snapped the other woman. Macy blamed Jonesy's apt description for making her think Nellie's long thin nose and neck made her resemble the ostrich he'd mentioned. "Whatever your experience is, I can match it and then some." She yanked off a loosely knit cap to expose brown hair sensibly fashioned into a bun at the back of her head. Macy had the errant thought that Kell would hate the hat even more than he did hers. "If your scientific expertise matches your fashion sense, you're going to need all the help you can get."

Jonesy hooted at that, raking Nellie with a withering gaze. "Fashion sense? It just so happens . . ."

"Enough!" Macy's raised voice held enough snap that they both stopped and looked at her. Taking a deep breath, she resisted the urge to rub at the pain throbbing above her nape. "CBI Director Lanscombe verified Ms. Trimball's credentials and her orders. He's adamant that she"—here her voice faltered for a moment; Lanscombe's word had been *oversee*, but there was fat chance of that occurring—"provide cooperative assistance on each test." Both Jonesy and Trimball began protesting loudly at this, and she raised her voice to be heard over them. "I can't believe either of you would turn down an extra pair of hands. Do I have to remind you what's at stake here?"

Jonesy and Nellie quieted simultaneously, although Jonesy still looked sulky.

Macy continued in the sternest tone she could summon. "We're under deadline. So far we've gotten little for test results." Trimball's cheeks flushed, but she said nothing. "So I suggest you both figure out a way to work together and have something solid ready for Raiker when he returns."

"When will that be?"

"Tonight or tomorrow."

The two exchanged a look. "That's not much time," observed Trimball. Her eyes, Macy noted, were a surprisingly lovely shade of bluish green behind thick lenses.

"All the more reason for the two of you to get to work." Shifting her focus to Jonesy, she noticed the expression of defiance lingering on his face. "Unless either of you want to call Raiker and Lanscombe to voice your objections to them."

Jonesy's defiance faded abruptly, to be replaced by chagrin. "As long as she remembers whose lab it is, we'll be fine."

"And as long as he realizes my expertise at least equals his, I'm certain we can get along well enough together," Nellie added stiffly.

Certain she'd merely achieved the calm before a storm, Macy decided it was time to beat a hasty retreat. "Good. I look forward to hearing about your findings. You have my number?" This to Jonesy, who nodded. "Great. Give me a call if you need anything."

Losing no time, she headed back in the direction of the house, the sound of voices following her. "Is this your conversion van? You can leave your coat and things in the front seat. The garage is heated. Where's the transferred evidence? In the back?"

"You aren't touching any of it until you're gowned and gloved appropriately. Where'd you learn your sanitary habits, a high school biology lab?"

"Look, lady, let's get something straight . . ."

Macy walked more rapidly until she could slip out of the garage side door and the rest of the words were blessedly lost behind her. It occurred to her that she'd had to deal with more controversy today than in all the time since they arrived.

Pulling the phone from her pocket, she checked it again for messages and found nothing from Kell. Despite the frigid nip in the air, she yanked off her gloves and shoved them in her pockets while she sent him another text, not bothering to couch this one in polite language.

She could blame the headache on her surliness, but there was no doubt that the lack of response from Kellan Burke was playing its hand in her temper, as well.

Chapter 10

Macy was in the middle of diagramming Becker's statement when her cell rang. Without looking up from her work, she sent out a searching hand for the cell phone, and brought it up to check the caller ID. Not even to herself did she admit the quick flare of disappointment that it wasn't Kell. It was too much to hope for that the man would take a moment to update her on the raid when he'd failed to do so for Adam.

The number was unfamiliar. And it was surely her recent conversation with her boss that had her answering warily, even after mentally assuring herself that Enrique Castillo wouldn't have access to her cell number, even if he had access to telephone privileges.

"Reid," she answered crisply.

"Very official sounding," came a familiar teasing voice. "Hard to imagine that this is the same woman who melts into a puddle of ecstasy at the very smell of Henri's cordon bleu."

The tension streamed out of her. "Ian." She sank down on the corner of the bed, genuine enjoyment suffusing her. "Where are you calling from?"

Her stepfather rarely stayed in the same place for long. Perhaps he'd been born with wanderlust or maybe it was a logical affliction stemming from his years working British embassies across the world. From South America to the Middle East, she'd traveled with him after her mother's death to wherever he was posted, until she'd attended boarding school in her teens. Since his retirement five years ago, she'd bet he hadn't spent more than a few months at a time at any of his homes.

"I'm at the villa in Naples, feeling jet-lagged and exhausted." His merry voice sounded anything but. "Thinking of staying awhile and wondering if I can convince you to come for a visit. It's been much too long."

A flicker of guilt stabbed her. "I'm sorry my Christmas visit got postponed. A case came up . . ."

"And you were needed." She could almost imagine his negligent shrug. He wouldn't try to make her feel guilty. Ian had always understood. As a former workaholic, he should. "But I know you'll want to make it up to me, and you do love the villa."

"I do," she agreed, smiling. "Will you still be there next month? I think I can arrange some free time by then."

"If it means getting you to myself for a week or two, you'd better believe I'm staying put. When you nail your arrangements down, let me know so I can arrange for a bangin' knees-up."

"I don't need a party. I'll welcome some quiet time with just the two of us."

"Maybe you'll stay long enough for a short cruise," he mused. She could almost see the wheels in his mind working. "I have some people I want you to meet, and there's nothing more relaxing than a few days at sea."

Giving up, she let him plan. Ian needed people around him the way she needed occasional bouts of solitude. They each had their own methods of coping. "Whatever you plan will be fine. I'll try to get away for ten days so we can have plenty of time together."

"Ten days." His voice was pleased. "I'll count myself among

the luckiest men on earth for ten days with the loveliest woman in the northern hemisphere."

Amused, she said, "Flattery has always been wasted on me, but I appreciate the effort."

A small sound alerted her, and she looked behind her. Kell stood in the doorway, his expression grim. Abruptly, her stomach did a nosedive.

"Listen, Ian, can I call you back? I have to get to work."

His voice was good-natured. "Of course you do. Don't forget to update me about your plans, say in a couple weeks? And I'll have everything ready for you. I'm looking forward to this, Macy-kidder. It's been too long."

The familiar nickname would have softened something inside her if she weren't so concerned about Kell's unexpected appearance. "I will. Promise."

"Love you."

"Love you, too." She disconnected and wondered when Kell's face seemed to grow even darker. "I didn't think you were ever getting back. Would it have killed you to update me?"

"Sorry to cut your phone call short," he drawled, his tone sounding anything but apologetic. "Hope your boyfriend is the understanding sort."

She stared at him blankly for a moment before comprehension filtered in. If he wanted to think she'd been trading sweet nothings with a man friend, she certainly wasn't going to burst his bubble. It was none of his blasted business anyway. "The raid," she reminded him.

He walked farther into the room and dropped, for once, into a chair rather than on the rumpled bed. "The family in the residence is headed by a single mother. There's also an elderly grandmother in the home, not exactly the desperado type, who spent most of the time threatening to call the police. A teenage boy who looks like his major interests in life are gory Wii games and reconnecting with his estranged father. All were scared out of their wits by having their door caved in, in the middle of the night, as you can imagine."

Impatience rose. "Do they have a computer?"

He gave a slow nod. "A Dell laptop with wireless access that isn't secured. It was confiscated, much to the teenage boy's dismay, but a quick check by one of the agents found nothing in the sent mail to indicate the ransom note came from that computer."

"It might be buried," she reminded him. "Or hidden somehow. Remember how long it took them to get information from the computers running the cameras on the estate?"

"Maybe." He stretched his legs. "Maybe we'll discover that Nancy Elliott—that's the single mom's name—is yet another girlfriend of Nick Hubbard, who allows him to use her computer to send threatening notes. But more likely we'll find that whoever sent the damn thing just cruised the streets with an unregistered computer and paused in front of a house that had an unsecured network to send from."

"Did you at least get written samples from everyone in the house for me to compare to the ransom note?"

"I did." His eyes glinted. "How could I not, when the order you texted to me was phrased so delicately?"

She felt the heat rise in her cheeks. "I had something of a trying day."

"If it can top having Whitman spend the day trying to remove you from the investigation, I'm all ears." To her dismay, he toed his boots off and stretched, looking for all the world as though he were settling in for a time.

"Not surprising, given his past history. I spent the last few hours smoothing over one confrontation after another." She gave him a shortened version of the showdown between Jonesy and Nellie Trimball. "I haven't heard from him since. I only hope they don't kill each other before getting us some results, finally."

"Jonesy's here?" Kell perked up at that. She recognized his reaction. For all his quirks, and the man had more than his share of them, he was the most brilliant forensic scientist in Raiker's employ. "Maybe we're going to get some answers at last."

She checked her watch. "Probably should give him a few hours." Guilt flickered. She hadn't mentioned food to the technician, although he'd seemed far more interested in getting his lab set up than in eating. "Maybe you can give him a call and find out if he's hungry. You could get him something from the kitchen and take it out to him."

He eyed her. "You're full of suggestions today."

Impatience reared. "Look, if you aren't here to contribute something helpful, head back to your own room. I've plenty of work to do. Did you bring those written samples I asked for?"

In answer, he merely reached inside his unzipped coat and withdrew some folded sheets of paper. "Copies of them, anyway. The originals went to Whitman."

Macy pushed away from her chair to cross the few steps over to take them from him. "Great. I can get these done tonight, as well. Did you get anything from the raid at all?"

Kell stifled a yawn with the back of his hand. "The kid saw a car drive off the night before last, about the time the ransom e-mail was time-stamped. It'd been parked in front of the neighbor's house across the street, but when we talked to them, they were clueless about it."

Disappointment reared. "So they didn't see it."

"Didn't see it, but also verified that it wasn't a guest there to see them." He lifted a shoulder. "Chances are, the kid was closer than any of us have been to the sender of that note." His smile was dour. "And his description was pretty worthless. All he could say was that it was silver."

She went back to the desk and sank down in her chair. "That's not much."

"That's shit," he agreed, slouching farther down in the chair. "Which is exactly what we've got on this case so far."

Macy eyed him carefully. If anything, Kell was usually annoyingly cheerful. She wondered if it were tiredness or something else that had him down. "Is Whitman holding a briefing soon?"

A corner of his mouth lifted. "If he is, I'm not invited. He and I . . . we're not going to end this thing as BFFs."

"We have every right to be there," she reminded him. "But if you have nothing else to do, my conversation with Cramer today got me to thinking. He named off several areas he thought might be good areas to stash a kidnap victim."

His voice was reasonable. "Like if he's in this thing with Hubbard he wouldn't be steering us exactly in the wrong direction."

"The thought had occurred to me, but it still bears checking into. What are the chances the kidnapper is going to head into Denver, or into any surrounding town, and keep the child in a place where neighbors could possibly spot her?"

Crossing one stocking foot over the other, he appeared to give it some thought. "Cooper did it, didn't he?" he said after a moment. "I mean, since he had Ellie for almost two years, and Raiker was the one who nailed him, I assume no one ever called in the information that a blond, blue-eyed young girl was living in his house."

"There were actually a couple instances when people mentioned later that they'd seen a girl in the window. They said he'd explained it away by saying a niece was visiting. But with the media frenzy surrounding this AMBER Alert, that'd be hard to explain away. The entire nation is reporting on this story."

He was quiet for a moment, enough of a rarity to have Macy wonder what he was thinking. "Okay. Let's say he wants to stash her somewhere out of the way. We're already located in the foothills. How far is he going to want to travel—in a blizzard, no less—to get her to a safe place?"

"Cramer says there are no end of spots remote enough to never be found. Areas that haven't even been fully explored yet." She rattled off the places he'd mentioned from memory. "But I did a little research on them, and all are three to five hours' drive from here. It's hard for me to believe he's going to chance driving that far, especially when he couldn't count on having that much of a lead time."

Kell looked like he was getting into the discussion. "Okay, given the state of the roads, and the need for speed after snatching the girl, we figured he used a snowmobile. He could have had one stashed nearby in a wooded area, out of sight. After scaling the estate wall, he'd only need to carry her a quarter mile or so to the vehicle and make his getaway."

Macy nodded. They'd had this conversation with Whitman upon arriving, but there'd been no way to validate the supposition. The snow had still been falling when they'd gotten there, erasing any trace of the kidnapper's exit.

"The road crews had been pulled off the road, so who would have seen him other than crazies out there snowmobiling in the blizzard?"

"But hauling the child with him would be pretty unwieldy on a snowmobile." She leaned back in her chair and thought out loud. Not even to herself would she admit how liberating it was to bounce her ideas off Kell. "If he heads for Crawford, Marble, Ouray, Ridgeway . . . all are three to five hours, by car. Where can he go that's closer, but still remote?"

He stared at her for a moment. "You know I've been here for the same amount of time as you, right?" When she only stared at him, he sat up, as if finally getting the idea. "So start researching it. Right. Sort of bossy today." His head was already bent over his palm pilot. "Not sure I like this side of you."

She'd already turned back to her work. "Somehow I'll manage to live with the disappointment. Have you eaten?" If he hadn't, she couldn't believe he wasn't already whining about it.

"Caught something on the way back."

"Good." She smiled into the computer screen. "Then there's no reason we can't work uninterrupted for a few hours."

———————

In the end, of course, her words were almost prophetic. There was a call from Raiker, and they'd taken turns updating him on various aspects of the day. Another from the pilot, verifying her plans for the trip to Chicago the next day. And yet another from the driver who was taking her to the airport. Macy could only assume that Mulder's employees were trained to check and double-check every last detail.

She still had time to run a test on each sample she'd gotten that day, including the ones Kell had brought her. And while David Elliott's had given her pause, if only for the sheer lack of writing coherence evident in his sample, none of the written communications provided a match for the semantics of the ransom note.

"Bloody hell," she muttered, glaring into the computer screen at the last result. There were still the files of threats Mulder had received that hadn't been delivered yet. Any one of them might match the ransom note.

But she couldn't get past the feeling that she was on a fishing expedition. In most of her cases, the authorities had a suspect in mind before she was called to run comparison samples. The process was much shorter. She'd already fed in dozens of samples, with no success.

And time was running out.

"No matches, huh?" She was surprised to find Kell right in back of her. His approach had been silent.

"No." And the word felt like a personal failure. She twirled around in the chair to find him much too close. "How about you?"

"Tomorrow we have to stop by a national parks office." He peered more closely at his palm pilot. "You only have to go an hour or two to the west or northwest to hit forests. We could get more information about the parks and wilderness areas in the state."

"You can go. Tomorrow I fly to Chicago, remember?"

His pale green gaze arrowed into hers. "Oh, yeah, that trial testimony. How long will that take? Just there and back, right?"

Macy hesitated. Just there and back. No reason to stop in Terre Haute along the way. No reason, because Raiker had already determined Castillo was just pulling their strings. Trying to get alone time with her by pretending to have information they'd find interesting. He was hardly credible.

And the thought—just the thought—of being alone with the man, even surrounded by prison walls, made her flesh crawl.

One, two, three, he's coming for me. The familiar chant, the childlike voice, echoed in her mind.

"Yes," she said firmly, muzzling that inner voice with an ease born of long practice. "Just there and back. I'll return by dinnertime, at the latest."

And she refused to feel like a coward for the words. She was needed right here. And although she'd face down Castillo if Raiker had asked—*she would, of course, she would*—he hadn't asked, had he? Because he knew it'd be a waste of time.

"What's wrong, Macy?"

It was the gentleness of his tone rather than the words themselves that had her freezing. Her gaze flew to his, saw the emotion reflected in his eyes, as well. "You look . . . scared to death."

Because the words arrowed much too close, she turned back to the desk to tidy up the samples she'd diagrammed. "Pretestimony jitters, I guess. I'll be fine. I have the plane ride to prepare." She was as prepared as she ever would be for the testimony she'd be giving, but the explanation was a plausible one.

It rattled her to realize how easily he'd read her emotions. And since she was afraid of what he'd see if she turned around, she busied herself putting the samples back in files and clicking out of the database of samples on the computer.

Then froze, when she felt his hands on her shoulders, as whisper soft as his voice. "Mace . . ."

An alarm jangled in her mind, shrilled through her head. There was danger here, of a kind she wasn't used to dealing with. Didn't want to deal with. Experience had taught her what to expect if she softened toward Kellan Burke. The time she had was proving damn hard to carve from her memory.

The alarm shrilled again, sounding louder this time. And when his hands abruptly left her shoulders, her eyelids snapped open. The sound hadn't come from her mind at all. It was his blasted cell.

Shaken, she rose and paced several steps to put some distance between them. That's what she got for thinking about Castillo at all. Just the thoughts weakened her. And being vulnerable around Burke was never a good idea.

Belatedly, she began listening to his end of the conversation. ". . . else do you have? C'mon, it's been all day. Did you check all the agencies that submit data to Coplink? Uh-huh. Hell, I don't care how far away. Wait. What?" Kell turned to wave wildly at Macy, leaving it to her imagination to figure out he wanted a pencil and paper. Crossing to the desk, she retrieved a pen and legal pad and thrust both at him. "Yeah, I'll take the latest blotter information, too." He scribbled in silence for a couple minutes, silent but for a couple, "Slow down, would you?" Then finally he set the pen down, staring at his notes pensively.

Tired of waiting for an explanation, Macy sidled close enough to cock her head and try to decipher his scribblings. He'd listed what looked to be a bunch of crimes. But it was the word *HOMICIDE???* that gave her pause. Who the heck was he talking to?

She waited impatiently for him to finish. "I appreciate it. No, really." His sincere tone would have been more convincing if Macy didn't know how easily he could feign the emotion. "It is a help. And if anything you give me pans out, I'll figure a way you get credit, too." He winced a little, and held the phone away from his ear. Macy could hear a raised woman's voice on the other end. In a flash, comprehension struck.

It was Denise Temple. Giving another look at the list, she wondered just what Kell thought a list of crimes in the surrounding area was going to tell him.

When he hung up, she leveled just that question at him.

"I don't know." He was staring at his writings consideringly. "I just hoped maybe something would pop. Crimes rarely happen in isolation. A perp steals a car to commit a crime. Or purchases a gun. Buys a plane ticket. I'm just wondering what else the kidnapper did that might be the one thing that provides us with the lead we need."

"The files Whitman prepared showed that he's had agents following up on reports of stolen and recently purchased snowmobiles," she reminded him.

He grimaced. "Which only reminds me that there are some jobs even less exciting than tracking down Hubbard's phone contacts."

"What'd she say about the homicide?" It was simple curiosity that drove her to ask. The Denver metro area alone was home to over two million residents. The homicide rate would reflect its population.

"She said a body was found in Jefferson County, in the Clear Creek Canyon Park." He lifted a shoulder. "Animals had been at it, so identification will be a bitch. Apparently a couple cross-country skiing happened across a half-eaten human femur. Sheriff's department found the rest of the body with cadaver dogs. Temple said they think it's a missing tourist. It'll be difficult to tell. It's minus part of the face and some of the . . . ah . . . appendages."

Macy felt a little queasy. "Just proving how easy it is to get rid of a body in these parts."

His gaze caught hers, and she knew he understood what she hadn't said. What she refused to let herself think.

With the plentiful remote wilderness areas in the vicinity, an eleven-year-old girl's body would be all too easy to dispose of.

Her cell sounded then, and she was grateful for a chance to focus on something else. She looked at the incoming text, and adrenaline shot up her spine. Without another word, she crossed the room to jam her feet into shoes and headed for the door, calling over her shoulder, "It's Jonesy. He's got something."

It was clear that Assistant Director Whitman wasn't sure how to react to Jonesy. It was equally obvious that he was mad as hell the lab was here in the first place.

"Ms. Trimball, can you verify the accuracy of the test results run today?" he was barking as Kell and Macy slipped into the conference room.

Nellie Trimball was once again wrapped up in the winter wear Macy had seen her wearing earlier. Jonesy still wore the sweatshirt he'd arrived in, but at least he was wearing boots rather than the thongs from that afternoon.

"Yes, sir, I'm confident they're accurate," she said primly.

"I don't need anyone verifying my test results," Jonesy snapped. He slapped the file folder he held onto the polished mahogany table before him. "I would have had them done in half the time if she hadn't been dogging my every step."

The woman sniffed audibly. "It certainly wouldn't hurt you to review established lab protocol and procedures. One can't take the chance on shoddy workmanship when lives are at stake."

The two of them squared off again, and Macy said a silent prayer of thanks that she'd been spared their bickering for the duration of the tests. "Shoddy?" Jonesy's voice went lethal. "Just who do you think—"

"We're grateful to both of you for your quick work," Macy inserted smoothly. Moving toward the conference table, she looked at Whitman, who appeared as though he'd swallowed a particularly nasty-tasting lemon. "Assistant Director Whitman, I assume you've been introduced to Alfred Jones? He's one of Raiker's finest scientists, lured away from Quantico a couple years ago."

Whitman's eyes narrowed so much they nearly disappeared. "He was with the FBI?" He raked the man with his gaze. He was no doubt wondering how Jonesy's Mohawk and piercings had gone over at the bureau's crime labs. Macy had often questioned that herself.

"I'm certain Adam sent you Alfred's credentials." Certain, because her boss had cc'd the document to her that very afternoon.

"Alfred? Don't call me . . ."

A firm sideways kick had the rest of Jonesy's protest sliding down his throat.

"Yes." The special agent glared at her. "Your boss is good about presenting information after the fact. Has friends in high places, doesn't he?"

She smiled blandly. "Lucky for us. With the cooperation of scientists from our labs and the CBI's"—she nodded toward Nellie—"we're no longer at the mercy of backlogs in the state lab in Denver. You must be excited about that."

Excited didn't seem to be in the man's vocabulary, but

something eased a bit in his expression at the reminder that CBI still had a hand in the lab results, thanks to Trimball's presence. He reached for the file folder, and Nellie picked it up and handed it across the table.

"We ran tests on the bloodstains found, both on the bedding and in the suspect's house," she began. "The results do indicate one positive elimination."

Macy and Kell exchanged looks. "Elimination of who?" he asked impatiently.

"Of the victim." The woman looked vaguely surprised by the interruption. She took the glasses off her nose and wiped them vigorously on the end of her scarf. "Neither result matched the DNA of Ellie Mulder."

Macy felt her knees weaken in relief. So the bloodstains on her bed and those found in Hubbard's bathroom didn't belonged to the girl. It was little, much too little, to pin hope on, especially in light of the threat assessment she'd run. But it was something.

"Who do they belong to?" Kell asked.

"The sample from location B was tiny," Jonesy put in, "which impacted the tests that could be used."

Nellie shot him a look that could almost pass for approval. "Minuscule, really. Which of course meant PCR DNA analysis, which was once thought not to be as accurate. However in recent years . . ."

"Can either of you get to the point?" It was plain that Assistant Director Whitman was even lower on patience than usual.

"We were able to match the samples found at location B with the employee DNA profile of one Nicholas Hubbard," Jonesy finished hurriedly.

Her earlier relief gave way to frustration. The tiny stains found in the man's bathroom could be explained by any number of reasons. "Any way of determining how old they were?"

Nellie Trimball looked down her long nose at Macy. "We weren't requested to make that determination."

"The bloodstains weren't degraded." Jonesy shrugged. "Repeated cleaning of the area over time would have eliminated them or at least deteriorated them to some degree. More than that I can't say. Also, the photographs show they were drops, not clotted, circular in shape."

"Meaning they came from a ninety-degree angle," finished Macy. But at this point, that determination meant exactly nothing.

"Let's go back to the bloodstain on the sheets," demanded Kell. "Were you able to match it to Hubbard?"

Jonesy shook his head. "We only compared it to two DNA profile samples, that of the suspect and the victim. It didn't match either."

Shock jolted through her. Hubbard's prints had been found in the girl's room. The CBI crime lab had determined that much. But if the stained bedding couldn't be attributed to either the girl or Hubbard, where did that leave them?

"Maybe that's an indication Hubbard wasn't working alone," she suggested slowly.

But Whitman's thoughts were clearly channeling in another direction. "Tomorrow I want those bloodstains compared to the DNA profiles we have on file for every employee on the estate. But first start with the parents." His glare dared either Kell or Macy to object, but both remained silent. It was hardly surprising that his suspicions would immediately return to the Mulders. Macy doubted they had strayed too far from his mind as suspects since the case had begun.

At any rate, the comparison samples had to be run, if only for elimination purposes. But she'd hoped the bloodstains would have yielded more telling information.

"You said the stains in the bathroom weren't degraded. How about the one on the sheet? Could it have been there awhile?"

"If it was, the sheet likely hadn't been washed since it was stained." Nellie had her glasses back on her nose. "There was no evidence of deterioration."

Which made Macy even more certain it had occurred the

night in question. It didn't seem likely that housekeeping would have put a stained sheet back on the girl's bed. More than likely it would have been disposed of.

But that didn't help explain how it had gotten there in the first place.

"Before they start the tests tomorrow, let's run the DNA profile result through CODIS." She saw Whitman's answer on his face before he even opened his mouth, so she said more firmly, "We save time by doing them simultaneously. As a matter of fact, we'll probably know whether or not there's a hit on the Combined DNA Index System before Jonesy and Ms. Trimball even finish the tests."

"I'll have the sample submitted into the state and national system," the assistant director surprised her by saying. His gaze traveled back to encompass the scientists once again. "Did you discover anything else?"

Jonesy looked a bit crestfallen. Clearly he'd expected more fanfare over the results he'd presented. "I only had time to run the two tests. If someone hadn't been underfoot every time I turned around, always yammering on about her research, or proper technique—which, for the record, I don't need to be reminded of—"

"It's the height of arrogance to think we can't all benefit from an occasional reminder—"

"Occasional." Jonesy snorted.

Before the two came to blows, Macy inserted herself between them. "This has been a big help. We're grateful to you both. Jonesy, I assume you want to stay in the lab." The large mobile station was equipped with a bedroom and small bath in back, separated by a double partition from the lab itself. She'd never known the man to stray too far from it when on location.

"I've got my things in there. And someone told me that we could call the kitchen at any time for meals."

"That's right. Be sure to do so. As a matter of fact, you could head there now and grab something to eat. I can vouch for the chefs. They're top-notch." She included them both in a smile that felt strained at the edges. "And, Nellie, if you ask in the kitchen, I'm certain they can find a housekeeper to direct you to the room Mrs. Mulder had prepared for you this afternoon."

Feeling a bit as though she were herding cats, she led them both toward the door. "Thank you again for all you accomplished today. We can talk about priorities for tests run tomorrow in the morning."

"I could eat," Jonesy said, stepping out of the room. "Is the kitchen to the left?"

"That's right." Gently she eased the door shut again, resisting the urge to lean against it. Instead, she turned to find the CBI assistant director agent wearing something suspiciously close to a smirk.

"Something tells me you've had practice at that."

"My stepfather did a stint at a number of British embassies. I learned the skills of diplomacy at an early age, and those skills came in handy today."

"Raiker will be back tomorrow. But it's a good idea to start running elimination samples on the bloodstain." Kell folded his arms across his chest, tapping his index finger against his biceps as he thought. "After that . . . what about the trap in Hubbard's bathtub? Probably not a priority to check it for more blood. Maybe we should concentrate on having them test the fibers found in the girl's room."

Whitman flicked a look at Kell, and his expression settled into its familiar near scowl. "You have an annoying habit of forgetting who's in charge of this investigation, Burke. I'll make those decisions myself."

Macy's heart sank. For a moment there, the CBI assistant director had seemed almost approachable. Really, the controversies of the day were getting a bit ridiculous. She could see Kell's response in his expression even before he opened his mouth.

"Can't say that I care for some of the decisions you've made so far," he said with a mildness that heightened her instincts. Like Raiker, the quieter Kell's tone, the more dangerous his temper. "Like the one when you tried to remove me from the incident response."

"You were a distraction." Whitman's face was reddening. "And you don't take orders worth a damn."

"Not from you, anyway."

The assistant director set his balled fists on the tabletop and leaned his bulk on them. "You'd never work for me, Burke. You have no respect for the chain of command. No understanding of what's required to be a team player. I know your type. Always the rogue, always wanting to go his own way."

Kell's smile was grim. He placed his hands on the table, leaning across toward the other man as if restraining himself from leaping across it. "You know nothing about me, but you've got one thing right. I'd never work for you."

———

Dusk was slanting long shadows through the trees, and with every step, determination grew inside him.

He was going to kill the little bitch. Put a single shot right between her eyes.

No. Gut her like a rabbit and leave her body in the snow for the animals to feed off her intestines. Or slice her throat. One horizontal cut, matched with another splitting open her torso from throat to cunt. Different scenarios each time, all ending with an agonizing death.

And he wasn't going to wait for the okay from the man who hired him either. Fuck him and his plans. What difference did a couple days make anyway? He could still collect the extra fee because no one had to know the little bitch was already dead.

It'd been a long time since the thirst to kill had been this strong. Not since he'd shot his crazy-ass father, the bullet going through the heavy Bible he held and into his heart. The daily beatings had always started with that Bible, before it was exchanged for the whip or belt. Men like that shouldn't have kids. They should recognize what lived inside them and spare their offspring. Like he had.

He ducked his head against the fucking wind that blew up here all the time. The gusts made it hard to walk sometimes, even with the trees as a shield. But he had to be careful anyway, because a couple times he'd heard shots. In the distance but still in the area. And once he'd thought he'd seen the flash of hunter orange nearby. The bastard was screwing up his trail.

When he found the snowshoe prints, it was hard to tell whether it was the kid in his boots and snowshoes or the hunter. The damn blowing snow obliterated a lot of the tracks.

Maybe the kid had seen a hunter, too. The thought made the ball of rage in his chest burn hotter. Maybe she'd found some stranger and been whisked off to safety. Maybe the cops were on their way already.

He wasn't worried. With the cover of trees and the stashed snowmobile, he didn't doubt his ability to lose them. And he wasn't going leave the job undone. Not after he'd invested so much time and effort into it.

There was his future reputation to consider.

Halting, he slid the pack off his back. Opening it, he pulled out the night vision goggles he'd used when he'd snatched the kid. Everything about that night had gone like clockwork. He could see now that it had been too easy. Almost charmed. Something had been bound to go wrong.

But he'd never expected the little bitch to get away.

He fitted the goggles over his eyes and slid into the pack again. The snowmobile was worthless in this terrain, which was why he'd stashed it farther downhill that first night and hiked the rest of the way to the cabin, pulling the kid on the plastic he'd had rolled up and knotted around his waist.

He'd responded rashly when he'd found her gone. He could admit that now. Running out clad in only the remaining clothes he'd brought had been damn little protection against the blasted cold and snow. The fucking forest made clear vision in any direction impossible. And plunging into it for long with no winter protection would have had him freezing in under an hour.

So he'd taken the time instead to hike to where he'd hidden the sled. To cruise down that damn mountainside and look for a place to break in. He'd been about frozen through when he'd come upon that general store. A quick entry through the back, and he'd found everything he needed. And then he'd headed back to hunt.

He was still hunting. The clothes weren't as high quality and insulated as the ones the kid had stolen, so he had to go back to the cabin occasionally and unthaw. The goggles painted everything in a weird green glow, but they afforded him vision, where she'd have none. He also had food. And water. The kid would be getting weak. Cold. Maybe the little bitch was already dead, a human Popsicle.

The thought brought a rare smile to his face.

Whichever it was, he needed to find her. And after all the trouble she'd put him through, he was hoping to find her alive. Maybe he'd skin her like a rabbit and dry the flesh to keep as a memento.

The thought cheered him. This kill was going to be the one that changed everything. All the trouble she was putting him through would just make it more satisfying.

And when it was over, he'd feel again. He was almost certain of it.

Chapter 11

"Well, at least we're getting somewhere. Finally." Kell was glad for once to have the frustration in Raiker's voice directed somewhere other than at him. He'd e-mailed his boss the results last night after the meeting with Whitman. "I didn't argue when CBI Director Lanscombe insisted on sending one of his own scientists because there's no way Whitman can contest the lab results. Saves us time in the long run."

"It will if she and Jonesy don't kill each other along the way. When will you be in today?" Kell balanced the phone between his shoulder and chin while he finished pulling on his socks.

"Depends on whether we run into weather. I have one more stop to make and then I'll be flying back to Denver. Should make it by dinnertime. Did Macy get off all right?"

"I assume so. I heard her moving around in her room well before dawn." He stopped then, not wanting to give his boss the mistaken impression that he'd been lying awake thinking about Macy on the other side of the wall. Nothing could be further from the truth. After no sleep the night before, he'd gone to bed early and had awakened at his usual time, that's all.

He straightened, looked around for his belt. Spotted it on the dresser. He had an internal alarm clock. That's what had kept him from falling back to sleep. Not wondering about the flash of fear that had crossed Macy's expression the evening before. The one she'd blamed on pretestimony jitters.

Which was, he thought grimly, as he threaded his belt through the loops one-handed, a bunch of shit. Whatever had put that look on her face, it hadn't been the thought of flying to Chicago for a few hours in a courtroom.

With effort, he shifted his focus from thoughts of her to the conversation. "Oh, you'll probably hear a few complaints from Whitman about me. He's not a fan."

"Hard to believe."

"I know, right?" He went to the drawer of the bedside table and withdrew his holster and weapon. "He almost . . . almost smiled at Macy last night, though. She's got this thing, people respond to it."

"It never pays to underestimate Macy Reid," Raiker agreed dryly.

"I was wondering . . ." Okay, there was no easy way to secure a shoulder harness with one hand. After he shrugged into it, Kell finally left it open until after the call ended. "How is it exactly that your cases on Castillo crossed? Because I was thinking, she must have had some sort of written communication from him and that's what put him away. But when I asked her, she got testy so I just . . ."

"Burke."

He winced a little, recognizing his boss's tone. "But I guess it doesn't matter."

"We'd all be better served if you kept your mind on the case at hand." Adam sounded a little testy, and this time it *was* directed at him. Which to be fair wasn't unusual enough to mention. Kell decided he could always request a copy of the court transcript from Castillo's trial to satisfy his curiosity.

"I figure Whitman will send us out to complete those interviews of Hubbard's phone contacts. But I want to stop and get some maps first." Briefly he filled Adam in on his thoughts about the remote areas nearby. "There's no end of places people can hide out indefinitely without having to leave this vicinity. And Hubbard was born and raised in the state. He'd be familiar with the area." There'd been some sporting equipment stowed in the man's basement, Kell recalled, as he rummaged through his closet for a sports coat. Skis and ski boots and snowshoes, although none of them had looked as if they'd seen recent use.

Raiker's voice was noncommittal. "She could be any-where. It doesn't hurt to take a look at the maps, but until we get a lead that pinpoints a specific location, we're spinning our wheels. She could even be out of the state at this point."

Kell shrugged into his jacket silently. That was true enough. She could have been moved just long enough to wait out the blizzard and then again to a more remote spot.

A familiar sense of frustration filled him. It was day five since the abduction. Three more days until the ransom dead-line. "I still think she's in the area," he maintained stub-bornly. He crossed to the chair on which he'd hung his winter coat. "There's going to have to be at least one more contact regarding the ransom. He can't be certain the Mulders are going to comply without establishing proof of life."

"Which can be done digitally and transmitted from any-where. Go ahead and cover all the bases. Just don't ignore whatever tasks Whitman assigns you." There was a danger-ous edge to Raiker's tone. "I already have enough to discuss with him when I get back."

Kell grinned. "At least you won't have to worry about him trying to steal me away from Raiker Forensics."

"That eases my mind no end." The call was abruptly dis-connected, and Kell tucked his cell phone inside his coat pocket then set to buckling his holster.

It felt strange to be preparing for the day knowing Macy wouldn't be at his side. The thought brought him up short. They'd worked together for a handful of days. Not long enough for the woman to be habit forming, for chrissakes. But he'd be lying if he denied there was something about her that had wormed its way into his consciousness months ago. Made thoughts of her difficult to shake.

Newly determined, he headed for the door, yanked it open. That train of thought was definitely not the way to focus on the day. Turning out of his room, he saw Travis rounding the corner ahead of him and quickened his step to catch up. He needed to come up with a creative reason for the agent in charge to take a few detours when they set out today. And if he couldn't completely banish thoughts of Macy, he could at least relegate them to a distant part of his mind.

———

"That's the last one on our list, right?" Kell surreptitiously glanced at his watch as he pulled open the vehicle's door and ducked inside. The wind chill was a bitch. It was as if Mother Nature felt the need to make up for the lack of snowfall today with a wintery blast of icy air that hammered from all sides. If he spent much more time in this climate, he was going to have to invest in a hat, which would only give Macy ammunition since he'd given her so much grief about hers. He checked his earlobes with his gloved hands, half expecting to find icicles hanging from them.

Travis slid behind the wheel and slammed the door shut after him. Ponderously, he took off one glove to reach into his coat for the folded-up sheet of paper listing contacts on Hubbard's LUDs. While he waited, Kell entertained himself by trying to blow vapor rings when he exhaled. With a little practice, he was pretty sure he could pull it off.

"Yep, that was the last one." He slanted a glance at Kell as he started the car. "I'm almost glad Macy wasn't here today. She didn't need to hear Zimmerman's profanity."

Turned out Gary Zimmerman couldn't be numbered among Hubbard's friends. Hubbard had sold him a snowblower the month before that Zimmerman claimed was a piece of shit. The two men had traded a couple phone calls that had left Zimmerman irate when Hubbard refused to give him his money back. Which only went to show, Kell thought, as he reached forward to jack up the heater, that snowblowers were the root of all evil. Georgetown had a handful of snowfalls all winter, and even that was enough to make him willing to man the next satellite office Raiker started, as long as it was in the South.

"I'm sure she's heard worse," he said belatedly, as the agent checked his mirrors before pulling slowly away from the curb. And he didn't necessarily appreciate the man summoning memories of Macy again. He took a chance on the coffee he'd bought before their last stop and brought it up to his mouth to sip cautiously. As expected, it was ice cold. He set it down again.

"I guess you'd know." Something in the man's tone alerted him. "What with the two of you working together all the time."

Travis was as transparent as glass. "Raiker has several investigators. We aren't paired together that often. I think it's been nearly a year." And over six months since the one time they'd *paired* in the way that continued to haunt him.

"Really?" Something about his answer seemed to lift the man's spirits. "So you're just coworkers. Like Dirk and me."

"Dirk?"

"Agent Pelton. I've worked with him a couple times. Know him fairly well as a colleague."

Something in the man's dogged persistence was starting to wear on Kell. "Yep. Sort of like that."

"So . . ." The man braked carefully, well ahead of the light in front of them, which was turning yellow. "Do you happen know if she's involved with anyone?"

Kell feigned a yawn. "Who?"

"Ms. Reid. Macy."

"Look, Travis, I'm not one of her girlfriends, okay? She isn't likely to tell me if she is." He'd never known a more closemouthed woman than Macy. She'd revealed far more to Whitman yesterday about her family life than she ever had to Kell. And the dearth of information he knew about her was starting to bug the hell out of him. "Although . . ."

Travis looked at him. "Although what?"

Horns sounded behind them. "The light's green."

The agent nosed the car through the icy intersection. "You were saying?"

"She was talking to someone on the phone yesterday when we got back from the incident response. I heard her telling someone she loved them, that's all." It made him feel a bit weasely to be gossiping about Macy when she wasn't there, but he figured she'd thank him for anything he could say that would discourage the agent's pursuit of her. He was actually doing her a favor.

"Could have been her mother," Travis offered after a moment.

"Her mother died when she was young." And he only knew that much because he'd overheard her mention it to a client on the last case they'd worked together.

"Or a father. Brother or sister."

"Maybe." Kell was sorry he'd brought it up. It was nothing to him if she had to fight off Travis's clumsy advances before the case was over. But it was telling that he'd never considered before that she might have been talking to a relative. The possibility eased something inside him.

And he didn't want to examine the reason for that too closely.

"So do you—"

"Sorry." Kell dug into his coat pocket and brought out his cell phone. "It's still on vibrate," he lied, tugging off his gloves and pretending to answer it. "Adam," he said with false enthusiasm. "Uh-huh. Just finished, as a matter of fact. Well, I suppose we could. I'm not sure how far away that would be but . . . really? Well, I'll let Agent Travis know. That's right. I'll give you a report tonight when I see you."

Slipping the phone back into his pocket, he eyed the CBI agent to see if he'd bought it. "That was Raiker."

"I heard."

"Since we're done with the tasks Whitman gave us, he wants us to swing by and check out a tip he received."

His words elicited a cautious tone and look from Travis. "What kind of tip?"

"Did Whitman say anything about a body being found in the Clear Creek Canyon area?"

"A girl?"

"No, no," he hastened to soothe the other man's immediate alarm. "A man. At least they thought it was a man. The animals had gotten to him so it was hard to tell right away. Raiker wants us to swing by and check it out."

"I don't see why." The agent frowned. "Doesn't sound like it has anything to do with the case."

"Wouldn't be that far out of our way, would it? Raiker said it'd be in the Jefferson County sheriff's department jurisdiction, so likely the body would be with the coroner there." A few minutes on the Internet last night had elicited enough information to draw that conclusion. "They're handling the AMBER Alert leads from this case, aren't they?"

Travis still hadn't answered. Kell shrugged. "But if you don't want to go, I guess you could always explain it to him when he gets back tonight. Although I think he and Whitman will be holed up most of the evening, comparing notes."

The agent was silent long enough to make Kell nervous. "How would Raiker get a tip from a sheriff's department here?"

"He has contacts everywhere. The man's a legend. Even people who don't know him are anxious to cooperate when they get a chance. You heard about his last case for the bureau, right?" He hadn't met a law enforcement officer yet who failed to be impressed by the story.

"I looked him up when I heard he'd been called in on the investigation," Travis admitted. "Caught by the child serial killer he was trailing, right? Freed the victim but was tortured for days before escaping and killing the guy?"

"That's the short version."

There was another silence. Then the agent put on his blinker and headed for the exit to the interstate. "Don't see what it can hurt. Like you say, it's not that far out of our way."

Jefferson County Assistant Coroner Deanna Evans was plump, blond, and businesslike. Peering closely at Agent Travis's

ID, she said, "My supervisor has the day off. But he didn't tell me to expect CBI."

"News of your John Doe just reached me today." Kell was filled with appreciation for the way Agent Travis could think on his feet. "I have reason to believe it might be connected to a case I'm working."

She nodded. "Well, come on back. The body still hasn't been identified and we haven't autopsied it yet. I've spent the last couple hours piecing it back together."

Kell pulled off his gloves and shoved them in his pocket, content for the moment to allow Travis to take the lead, since it'd taken the man's authority to get them in there. He studied the painted brick walls and institutional tile in the hallway they walked through. Morgues throughout the nation must use the same decorating scheme.

After they'd donned the sterile garb Deanna handed them, she opened a heavy metal door, and the familiar scent drifted out to greet him. He'd never been at a coroner's station yet that didn't carry that same odor. Swallowing hard, he stepped through the door, his gaze immediately going toward the corpse on the stainless steel gurney.

The man—and it was difficult to tell that it had been a man—was literally in pieces. It looked as though some of them were still missing. The abdominal cavity had been torn away, and to his inexperienced eye, it appeared much of the internal organs were gone. The skeleton was exposed in several places. After one look at the mostly missing face, Kell focused on the limbs.

"Too early for cause of death?"

"Too early for much of anything," Deanna said cheerfully. She rounded the table to stand on the side opposite the men. "But I'm told that they found the bulk of the body under a foot of snow, so chances are he was there at least since the blizzard."

"And I'm told he was found nude." Kell felt the agent's gaze boring into him, so he made sure not to catch his eye.

"I didn't have to cut any clothes off him." The woman pulled on some latex gloves. "They found large pieces of plastic sheeting near the body. My orders are only to assist with identification at this point. I've taken scrapings from under his fingernails. Tomorrow when one of the deputies gets here we'll probably fingerprint him if they still haven't identified him."

Kell crouched down to stare at the partially complete arm lying loosely next to the body. The last two fingers were still attached to the hand. "How many fingers left over there?"

"Listen, Burke . . ." Travis started uneasily.

"Everything but the thumb." Obligingly, Deanna held up the intact arm to show him.

The CBI agent peered closer, his objection forgotten for the moment. "Interesting. Maybe the animals got scared off before they did more damage on that one, huh?"

"Oh, animals didn't do that." Deanna brought the hand up close enough to the agent's face to have him taking a hasty step back. "See how smooth the bone is where it was separated? That was done with a sharp blade. Amputation, maybe?" she mused, reaching for a pair of surgical loupes and studying it more carefully. "Fairly recently, too, as the tissue hasn't healed."

"Why would someone have a thumb amputated?" Travis was peering over her shoulder while maintaining a safe distance.

"Infection. Frostbite." But she was already shaking her head. "No, this wasn't an amputation. The doctor would have sewn the blood vessels shut and probably sewn muscle over the bone for padding." She straightened, setting the loupes down. "And that, gentlemen, is why we don't rush to decisions about what we find on our table. I'm afraid I won't have anything to share with you for several days."

"We might be able to help with the identification," Kell murmured. He rose to look at her. "But we need to fingerprint him now."

Her eyes went worried. "Maybe I should call the sheriff's department. Or at least my supervisor."

"Okay." Kell's gaze had returned to the corpse's hand again. With the severed thumb. "But although we all try to play nice together, we both know CBI trumps local law enforcement." He flashed her a smile. "Do you need to see Agent Travis's ID again?"

———

"And what kind of verification process do you have in place, Ms. Reid?"

The attorney for the prosecution had been grilling her for fifteen minutes to no avail. Regardless of what she'd told Kell yesterday, Macy was unflappable on the stand. "The database has a ninety-five percent validity rate," she repeated patiently.

"But what about the work you explained earlier? You have to detect the patterns in the writing samples, you said. You . . . diagram the samples."

"It's much like diagramming sentences, yes. When I finish, it's those results that are matched to the samples in the database."

"But that part is subjective, right? I mean, what sort of reliability measures are in place to make sure you did that part of the job correctly?"

"It's not really subjective, no. Gerunds are gerunds. Participles are participles. Parts of speech don't change depending on who's looking at them."

The prosecutor, a buoyant stocky man barely topping five feet, was something of a showman. He made a flourish toward the jury. "I don't know about that. Seems my high school English teacher's opinion of my homework differed from mine." A few members in the jury box tittered.

Macy smiled pleasantly. "Exactly. Opinions differ but not the patterns or parts of speech themselves."

But still the man persisted. "So we're to believe you get it right the first time, all the time. There's no one validating the patterns you claim to find, no quality control of any sort. It's just your opinion." His gaze encompassed the jury box meaningfully. "Just one person's opinion. No more questions."

As he headed back to his table, the defense attorney, Rob Chapell, rose. "I'd like to redirect, Your Honor." Approaching

Macy, he spread his hands. "What's the difference between what you do and what our esteemed prosecutor's English teacher did to his high school essay?"

Laughter sounded in the courtroom, Macy's with it. "The major difference is I'm not passing any sort of subjective judgment on content or structure. While I'm going to give his teacher the benefit of the doubt, and assume she graded according to a rubric of some sort, she might be looking for sentence structure, original thought, adherence to proper rules of attributed quotes, and so on. But there is a window of subjectivity when she grades on the author's voice and style. She could show it to every English teacher in the department and get slight variations in the grade given. That's not true with my work. Five trained forensic linguists could analyze the content of that note, and all five would determine the exact same pattern. No matter how many pairs of eyes look at a verb phrase, it's still a verb phrase. The database does the rest."

When he returned to his seat, the judge looked up. "If we're done with this witness, let's take a fifteen-minute recess."

"Ms. Reid." Chapell fell into step with her as she passed his table. "I'll walk you out." They made their way through the throng of people in the courtroom and out to the less-populated hallway. She headed for the coatrack. "I want to thank you again for your testimony."

"Your client didn't write that bomb threat," she said simply. Setting her purse down for a moment, she reached for her coat and pulled it from the hanger. He took it from her and helped her into it.

"I agree. I was worried that the jury wouldn't be sophisticated enough to understand your testimony, but I'm glad I took the chance." He smiled a little. "Can't let a little fear get in the way if there's the slightest possibility of making a difference."

His words struck a chord with her that was vaguely disturbing. But there was no reason it should remind her of Castillo. There was a difference between taking a chance and letting a monster manipulate you, wasn't there?

"Listen to me," Chapell was saying, looking vaguely embarrassed. "I sound like Perry Mason."

"You sound like an attorney who works hard on the behalf of his clients," she corrected firmly, offering her hand. "Good luck with your case."

As he walked away, she retrieved her purse and pulled out her cell and called for a cab to take her back to the airport. Without traffic delays, there was no reason she couldn't be back in Colorado in a matter of hours.

It would take approximately sixty minutes to detour to Terre Haute from Chicago.

As if to outrun the thought, she hurried across the hallway to the wide stairway. Her heels seemed to tap a familiar rhythm.

One, two, three, he's coming for me.
Four, five, six, he'll be here next.

She reached the stairs, quickened her pace. And tried to believe that she wasn't hurrying from that childish inner voice that had never been completely silenced.

"Adam Raiker."

After returning FBI Agent Tom Shepherd's handshake, Adam cast a jaundiced eye around the cramped office, with its metal government-issued furniture, circa 1950, and said bluntly, "This is a shithole. You're wasted here."

"Well." The man looked none the worse for wear despite his two years in virtual career exile. "I'd say welcome to my castle, but you don't appear impressed."

He closed the door of his office and motioned Adam to a chair. The quarters were so close that when Tom pulled up his own chair and sat, they were nearly touching.

Adam leveled a look at him. "How long are they going to keep you here?"

The agent rubbed his jaw and gave a wry smile. "I'd forgotten how direct you are. The master plan hasn't been shared with me. I'm just doing my job and hoping my stint in purgatory passes quickly. How'd you hear about this?"

"Landry. He has his finger on the pulse of everything that happens in the bureau, even after all the years since he left it."

"Joe." The other man nodded. "He was gone before I started, but lots of people mention him. So." Pleasantries over, the FBI agent spread his hands. "Haven't seen you since the trial. What are you working on?"

Adam studied the other man for a moment. On the surface, he hadn't changed. Still had the golden pretty-boy looks and aw-shucks charm that opened doors with witnesses and women alike. But he was a solid agent, and it was typical bureau petty politics to punish him for not having a lead role in solving the high-profile kidnapping case of Ellie Mulder two years ago.

"I'm working for Stephen Mulder. His daughter is missing."

He nodded. "I heard. It's made national news, although someone is doing a damn fine job of keeping details out of the press."

"That would be the CBI assistant director. At least he's been earning his keep in that respect."

Shepherd leaned forward, clearly intrigued. "After losing her once, I can't believe Mulder took any chances with her."

"He didn't. High-tech security all the way. Someone still managed to snatch her out of her bed and off the property."

"Inside job?"

"Looks like it. I've been reinterviewing the perps caught up in the kiddie swap. All are accounted for, but I was looking for someone with an interest in the girl. Maybe with friends on the outside. Nothing has panned out yet. I wondered if you had any thoughts on it."

"Me?" Shepherd managed to look surprised and pleased at the same time. "I never had anything to do with those you prosecuted." He made a face. "Wish I had. But that was your angle. We pushed hard on the gardener they'd fired, if you recall. Never could quite hang it on him." He made a dismissive gesture. "Once you were on the scene, I discovered why."

"They moved halfway across the country and have all new household employees. But some of the friends and associates remain the same." Adam flexed his fingers on the polished mahogany knob of his cane. "I just wondered if anything came to light about the Mulders' finances, their business dealings, enemies . . . or of their friends that might be of use to us. Something that wasn't included in the case file."

The man gave him an amused glance. "Don't tell me you managed to get a copy of the case file from two years ago."

Adam inclined his head. "I still have a few friends in the bureau." He'd studied the thing on the long plane rides and every evening as he'd made the rounds, and nothing had surfaced for him. He was hoping the man next to him had something to offer.

But Shepherd was shaking his head. "I can't think of anything that wouldn't be in the file. You don't think this was another pedophile snatching?"

"More likely motivated by revenge or greed. Or both."

The buzzer on his old-fashioned desk phone sounded. "Excuse me." Shepherd got up to stab at the intercom button impatiently. A disembodied voice sounded.

"State police on the line, sir."

"In a minute." He turned with an apologetic expression on his face, but Adam was already rising.

"I appreciate the time. Good to see you again."

"Same here."

Adam was at the door, his hand on the knob, when Shepherd stopped him. "There was one thing . . ." He looked half-embarrassed, as if he wished he hadn't said anything. "I left it out of the case file because it has absolutely nothing to do with the investigation. Ancient history."

Interest sharpening, Adam said, "What's that?"

"I discovered it by accident and saw no reason to share it with anyone else involved in the case. God knows those people were handling enough misery. But Althea Mulder . . . years ago she and Lance Spencer had an affair."

———

Adam was still mulling over the information on the way to the airport. Ancient history, as Shepherd had said. And dredging up that sort of information was always distasteful. Neither Althea nor Spencer had included that detail in their statement. Why the hell would they? He didn't blame them. But that didn't mean he wouldn't have to find a way to question them about it, discreetly of course, and maybe set Paulie to digging on the details.

He scowled out the window at the bleak flat snowy landscape. It was enough to make him wish he'd never stopped here at all.

His cell rang then, and he dug the phone out of the pocket of his cashmere overcoat, checking the number on the screen. Finding it unfamiliar, he answered, "Raiker."

The news on the other end of the line elbowed aside his earlier irritation. It took a moment to decide whether to go with honesty or a lie. In the end, honesty lost. "Yes. I did. I'm sorry I didn't call myself, I just walked out of a meeting." He listened for a moment longer. "I appreciate you arranging it. Thank you."

He disconnected, clenching the phone so tightly he could feel the individual keys of the touchpad against his palm. A deep breath didn't help. Adam knew he had a fierce temper. Which was why he kept it so tightly leashed.

It was threatening to break free now.

His teeth gritted so tightly his jaw ached. And when the Bismarck airport came into sight, he still hadn't figured out what the hell Macy Reid thought she would accomplish at Terre Haute Penitentiary.

———

It took far more courage than it should have to not bolt for the exit from the private conference room the warden had arranged. If Adam found out she'd defied his orders, he'd be livid. And Adam Raiker in a temper was something to be avoided at all costs.

A small sound had her turning wildly. It took a moment to realize the noise was from her fingers on the table in front of her, engaged in that rhythmic tapping she couldn't quite shake under stress.

One, two, three. One, two, three.

Deliberately, she stilled the movements. And felt a new-found courage in the anger that seared through her. Castillo had cost her six years of therapy. Another decade on anxiety medication. And she weaned herself off both because she'd refused to be a victim anymore. She'd decided to do something proactive with her life, and her work had always been rewarding.

Helping put Enrique Castillo behind bars had been an unexpected bonus.

And had provided the kind of therapy one couldn't pay for.

But facing him again at that trial had been harder, far harder, than it should have been. Which meant he still had a hold on her. She'd be a victim of sorts until she broke free of it.

The clock on the wall ticked loudly. Macy could feel the blood pounding through her veins. She couldn't swallow around the boulder-sized knot in her throat. If she craned her head, she could see the profile of the guard stationed outside the door she'd been led through. She could leave. Now. Before they brought in Castillo. No one would have to know.

No one but her.

She moistened her lips that had gone suddenly dry. Ever since she'd left the courthouse, she'd been making those kinds of deals with herself. She could call the warden. He might say a visit on such short notice was impossible. Raiker had just been there, after all. What could they possibly need to follow up on already?

But the warden had agreed with an alacrity that had taken her aback.

The ride to the airport had been spent engaged in the same sort of mental warfare. The pilot might not agree to the change in plans. It was Stephen Mulder's jet. This stop hadn't been on the itinerary.

But the pilot had readily adjusted his flight plan.

No one was going to save her from her decision. And it took a true coward to hope to be delivered from a plan of her own making.

The other door into the room opened. A ribbon of cold sweat rippled down her spine. And then he was there, filling that doorway. Devouring her with his dark gaze in a way that had her hurtling back in time.

"My prayers have been answered."

"Apparently no one else's have been, or you'd be six feet under," she managed to say crisply. She pressed her knees firmly together to keep them from knocking. To the guard behind him, she gave a nod. "Thank you. This won't take long."

He waited for Castillo to seat himself across the table from Macy before he withdrew. And she managed, barely, to avoid screaming for his return.

"Your boss, Adam Raiker, surprises me."

"How so?"

"I did not think he would send you here. He said that he would not." His expression grew sly. "I wonder why he changed his mind."

"In the States, that's known as looking a gift horse in the mouth, Enrique." The name sounded foreign on her tongue. Tasted bitter. "You asked for me." She shrugged with a nonchalance she was far from feeling. "Here I am."

"Yes, you are here. *Mi rosita inglesa.*"

My little English rose. She couldn't prevent her flinch at the familiar phrase and knew he'd noted it.

"I could not believe my eyes at the trial. Little Macy Reid, all grown up. It was as if you had walked out of my fantasies and back into my life."

She managed to hide her shudder. The stuff of this man's fantasies was dark indeed. Looking him square in the eye, she said, "And seeing that you went to prison for the rest of your life was *my* fantasy."

There was a jangle of chains as he sat back in his chair, hands loosely clasped in his lap. "I thought of you often, Macy Reid. It is only fitting that you have thought of me, too. Our past binds us together. Our fates are entwined, yours and mine."

She tried for an expression of cool amusement. Hoped she

pulled it off. "Our fates? Your fate is to spend the rest of your life behind bars, remember? I can assure you, I have a very different future in mind for myself."

It was his turn to shrug. "But whatever your future holds, your past is always a part of it, *es verdad*?"

The words struck her with their clarity. And she finally recognized the strange compulsion that brought her here today.

If there was a way, any way at all, to free herself of her past, facing down this man, alone, was it.

Her watch was a dainty silver band, the face fussier than she would have liked, with encrusted diamonds. It had been a Christmas gift from Ian three years ago. She made a show of looking at it now. "Thirty seconds, Enrique, before I walk out that door again. So if you really have something to tell me like you claimed to have when Raiker was here, I suggest you start talking."

His eyes glinted and the false friendliness was gone. In its place was the mercenary pedophile he'd always been. "You were spoiled growing up. Had you been left with me, you would have learned your place."

"You'll forgive me if I don't share your views on child rearing." The old anger was there, a hot bubbling cauldron of rage. She'd never know the names of the children he'd savaged. Never be able to tell them that their tormentor had finally been brought to justice. And right now, at this moment, his sentence seemed much too lenient.

Life in prison. When so many lived in a prison of his making, filled with memories they could never forget.

Sickened, she pushed away from the table and rose. Adam had been right. This was merely one more act of blatant manipulation. And the time was long past that she'd engage in this man's games.

"Given the environment where you'll spend it, I wish you long life, Enrique."

"I am a man of my word. I promised Raiker I had things to share that he would find interesting, and so I do. You must sit down."

She laid a hand on the chair back. "I prefer to stand."

He gave a slight shrug. "Your boss, I am sure he does not know this. But that man—the last enemy that he fought—he had a son."

Nonplussed, she could only stare at him for a moment. She'd expected that he'd bluffed about having information. And certainly hadn't expected him to know anything about Raiker's cases. "What man?"

"The one who cost him his eye." A beatific smile crossed his face. "If the man were alive, I would ask for the details of that moment. I enjoy thinking of Adam Raiker in much pain."

"John LeCroix."

"That was his name. Our paths crossed from time to time, much earlier in my career. I remember there was a boy child. I do not know what became of him. But it is my hope"—he leaned forward with a suddenness that had his shackles jangling—"it is my dearest hope that he is even now plotting revenge on Raiker. That would be justice, I think. And make many, many people happy."

"If there was a child, Adam already knows about him."

"I am sure you are right. But he will think this child, this man now, is gone. Dead. That is not true. This much I know. I heard it from LeCroix's lips the last time we spoke. His mother took him away, and LeCroix spent many years trying to find them."

Bitterness filled her. "A belated attempt at fatherly devotion?"

"Probably not." He rolled his shoulders. "A man does not change what is inside him. We talked, he and I, about the convenience of fathering many children, giving them a few years to grow. Alas, it was not to be, for either of us."

Revulsion filled her. She'd heard of pedophiles who had families for the sole purpose of molesting their own children. To hear this monster express regret, as if his dearest dream had never come to pass, had her stomach threatening to revolt. "I only wish Raiker had met you earlier. Maybe you would have ended up like your friend."

His gaze went hot as he raked her form, and there was a lurch in her belly when she recognized the expression in his eyes. "Many years have passed, and never have I forgotten you. In my dreams I would think of finding you again. Making many girl babies with you. Blue-eyed, with curly dark hair and soft white skin. So very soft."

Blindly, she turned to the door. Whatever she'd hoped to accomplish here, she'd reached her limit. She raised her hand to summon the guard outside when his voice sounded again.

"How is your dear stepfather? Does Ian's knee give him trouble when it rains?" His laugh raked over her nerves. The contempt in it shot her spine with steel. Macy turned to face him.

"He's fine. Free to feel the ocean air on his face whenever he likes. He'll be happy to learn of your life here. I'll be sure to describe how you look in manacles."

His face was a mask of hatred. "Of course he is fine. He has always been fine, dear Macy. A cowardly cheat who could not keep a bargain, but fine, just the same. Tell me, have you ever once seen his knee?"

Echoes of the screaming from the room next to her cage swarmed her memory. She'd heard those screams in her nightmares for years. Seen for herself what the torture had cost her stepfather. "Your life is not long enough," she whispered hotly. "Your sentence is not nearly enough."

He cocked a brow. "You were young. And so very innocent." The last words were delivered slowly, as if he were savoring them. "You could not understand then, but I think you can now. Colombia was a dangerous place at that time, especially for foreigners. It was not unusual for wealthy families to pay insurance against the kidnappings that occurred so frequently."

"I'm well aware that you and your friends became rich off the ransom." She stared at him stonily, the most loathsome man she'd ever met. Given the numbers she'd helped put behind bars, it was a dubious distinction.

"We got but a pittance." His fist came down on the table to punctuate his words, causing Macy to start. "Half for the men who employed me, which we would all share, half for your saintly stepfather. That was our deal. But Ian arranged for our share to be stolen away from us, and you, my English rose, are the reason. You told him . . ." He shook his head sadly. "Things I warned you not to say. He ended up keeping most of the money himself and within hours of your release both of you were out of the country with the entire five million dollars." He spread his hands, anger in his expression. "I ask you, does that seem fair, after all our hard work?"

It was as if his words summoned a tiny movie reel, which fast-forwarded through still frames of those moments. The row of filthy cages, fashioned with boards and chicken wire. The hideous shrieks from the next room, following the sickening thud of the sledgehammer they'd used on Ian. The way the sun had seared her eyes when they'd released her to huddle, clasped to her bruised and bloody stepfather for the duration of the car ride to the drop-off point.

Those memories would always be a part of her. And coming here had done nothing to erase them. Her gaze lifted to Castillo. But she'd be damned if she'd allow the man to inflict more damage.

"You're a liar. A human trafficker and child rapist. What makes you think I would believe anything you had to say?" She turned back to the door and banged her palm against it. "Done here."

"See for yourself. Even after the best surgeons in the world—and surely he will say he saw only the best—there would be scars. Look for them, Macy. Examine his 'injured' leg, and you will see who the liar is."

The door was unlocked, and she slipped out of it before it had even opened all the way. But she wasn't running. Not this time.

Not ever again.

Chapter 12

"Tell me again why we're waiting out here." Agent Travis was slapping his folded gloves against his thigh in a rhythm born of anxiety.

"You don't have to stay," Kell explained for what felt like the dozenth time. "I want to see what Jonesy comes up with on those fingerprints." The employee garage was well lit, spotless, and at least as warm as the agent's SUV. He'd shed his coat shortly after passing the fingerprint cards over to Jonesy an hour earlier. "As a matter of fact, maybe you should go in and report to Whitman on the results of our day."

"I don't think so." Dan folded his arms and leaned gingerly against the SUV they'd driven that day several feet away from where Kell had his hips propped on its bumper. "He's going to want answers, and I want to be damn sure I can give them to him."

"It shouldn't be much longer." But in truth Kell had no idea what the timeline on this sort of thing was. How hard could it be to match a set of prints? He hadn't even asked that they be submitted to AFIS, the automated database that would compare them to millions of prints on file across the nation. He figured he'd leave that to the locals in Jefferson County if it came to that.

"Maybe you should ask him when he'll be done."

Kell gave a slight wince at the suggestion. His last friendly inquiry had elicited a ten-minute profanity-infused diatribe from the man. He didn't mind the obscenities, but all the scientific jargon in the rant had made his head hurt. "Why don't you ask this time?"

The two men looked at each other. Finally Travis crossed his booted feet. "I guess we can wait a little longer."

"I guess we can."

It was another fifteen minutes before Kell heard the sound of one of the automatic overhead doors opening. He straightened, turning toward the Suburban driving in. The SUVs were the most practical vehicles to drive in this locale. From their drives to and from Denver, it appeared Conifer always had about six inches more snow than the city.

But when he saw that it was Raiker behind the wheel, he ambled over. "Hey, boss. How was the trip?" His step faltered when he got a look at his employer's visage.

"Is Macy back?"

"Uh . . . no." He glanced around but recalled she'd been driven to the airport in one of Mulder's cars. "I don't think so. But I haven't been in the house yet."

Adam went around to open the back of the vehicle, reached in, and grabbed his bag. Kell sprang forward. "Let me get that for you."

The look in Raiker's eye stopped him in his tracks. "Have I suddenly become incapable of carrying my own suitcase?"

"Not that I know of." Kell tried to recall the last time he's seen Raiker this pissed. Certainly a few times since a punk managed to swipe his briefcase, back in his bureau days. The suppressed temper was rare enough to intrigue him but familiar enough to have him treading warily. Was it directed at Macy?

Falling into step beside the man, Kell figured he had to be wrong. He couldn't figure a reason Adam would be furious with her. How much trouble could she have gotten into in the time she'd been gone?

"Care to explain what you're doing hanging out in a garage?"

Kell gestured to the lab. For Travis's benefit, he explained, "Got prints from that body you told me to check out today. When you called this afternoon." He liked to think he had nerves of steel. It'd taken balls all those years ago to stand right next to the mark he was planning to rob. And after earning his detective's shield, he'd racked up an impressive number of commendations from his undercover stint in vice.

So it was a measure of the man standing next to him that one assessing gaze had Kell wanting to shuffle his feet guiltily.

"The call from me."

"With that tip you wanted me to check out?"

There wasn't a flicker of expression on the man's face. "The tip. About the body. Of course."

"Uh, maybe you wouldn't mind asking your, ah, Mr. Jones, how much longer he thinks the tests will take."

When Adam shifted his attention to Travis, Kell felt a flicker of relief. "Who are you?"

"That's Agent in Charge Dan Travis. Of the CBI. Adam Raiker."

"Doesn't seem all that difficult." Raiker crossed to the RV door and pounded his fist twice on it. A response wasn't long in coming. Moments later the door swung open. Adam ducked aside to avoid getting hit with it.

"Okay, that's it. I told you once, Burke, that I'd let you know when I was done. Do I do this to you, huh?" Jonesy bounded down the two steps from the RV, visibly incensed. "Follow you around on the case, constantly push you for results? You want genius, it takes time."

"And so, apparently, does mediocrity." Nellie Trimball followed him out the door to fix them all with a jaundiced eye.

He turned on her with a suddenness that had the woman rearing back reflexively. "You'd know all about that, you self-important, elongated shrew."

"Jonesy."

Kell felt a stab of pity for the man when he heard the softly spoken word. If possible, his normally pale skin went even whiter.

"Adam." His voice was weak as he swung around again. "You're back."

"What do you have for me?"

Visibly brightening, he said, "A lot, actually. I was just going to tell Burke I finished the test and we have a match."

Excitement rocketed through Kell's veins, but it was filtered with equal parts dismay. His hunch had paid off, but where did the news leave the case?

Raiker spared him a glance, before demanding, "Details."

"A match?" Travis sounded relieved. "You ran the prints through AFIS then?"

"No, Burke said to run a comparison on your suspect. I ran it twice. Only six digits were intact, of course, but given the results, we can still be reasonably certain the body belongs to Nick Hubbard."

————

"He wasn't involved at all." Driven to move, Kell had forgone a seat at the conference table to pace the room.

"We can't know that," cautioned Whitman. "There's still the matter of his fingerprints in the girl's room. And in the room next to hers. Remember the security specs you found taped to the back of the drawer in his filing cabinet. He may have had an accomplice who decided to get rid of him when his usefulness had ended."

"The prints and the specs could have been planted. I'd say his usefulness ended about the time *his accomplice* severed his thumb. What did the kidnapper need to accomplish this goal? An employee's thumbprint and his face."

"There wasn't much left of Hubbard's face," Travis put in from his seat next to Whitman. "But it didn't look like anything human had been at it."

"Ever seen one of those silicone masks?" Kell gestured to his head. "High-end ones sculpted by artists can cost thousands of dollars, but they're as good as anything you'd see from a Hollywood's special-effects team. The silicone moves with the facial expressions, and I'm telling you, they look real. You can even have hair attached, eyebrows." He turned to his boss, sitting across the table from Whitman. "Remember that armored car heist in Las Vegas last year?" He didn't wait for the man's nod before going on. "The two perps had masks made to look like a couple off-duty cops from that command area who had busted them years earlier. The witnesses all ID'd the cops as the culprits, and neither had an airtight alibi."

"I remember." In an aside to Whitman, Adam said, "Kell very likely saved those policemen from life terms in a federal penitentiary."

"If the perp needed Hubbard's thumb, he'd also need his face. If he had his face, he doesn't need Hubbard. And don't forget that message left for us on Hubbard's machine. Did Hubbard make it under duress or to deliberately throw us off?" Kell was on the move again. He always thought best when he was moving. "It'll be days before we get anything useful from the autopsy. But if Hubbard was in on the abduction, why would someone need his thumb? Even if his accomplice wanted to off him and keep the ransom for himself, let him do the heavy lifting first, right? He completes the abduction, hands over the girl, and *bam*, he's out of the picture."

"Maybe Hubbard was getting cold feet." It was the first time Agent Pelton—Dirk—had spoken. "He gets his hands on the specs somehow, but when it came time for the actual crime, he goes soft. Doesn't want to follow through. The accomplice turns to plan B."

"Too much preparation had to be done up front," Kell corrected him. "Those masks are works of art. Unless Hubbard went in and voluntarily had a life cast made of his face—and why would he?—then the other guy had it done from pictures. That's what the Las Vegas perps did. Shot rolls of film of the policemen from different angles using high-powered cameras with zoom. Handed the pics over to the sculptor and got the masks. But that process took nearly a month."

"There was substantial time and money invested in this," mused Raiker. He was staring at the ceiling the way he did when he was concentrating fiercely. "First the patch on the video surveillance. My best cyber operative estimated that would run over fifty grand, and something that complicated might take months of work. Then weeks to make the mask. Add in finding a spot to stash the girl . . . hard to believe one person is responsible for all that."

"I'm still not convinced Hubbard didn't contribute to the crime," Whitman muttered. "And you didn't speak to everyone on his call logs. There's still the number we couldn't trace."

Kell sent Adam a quick look. But as usual, his boss caught the fly ball neatly. "As a matter of fact, I was able to trace the number. It belongs to Hubbard's girlfriend."

"What?" Travis looked abashed at his outburst, but his emotion was reflected on the other CBI agents' faces. Except for Whitman's.

The assistant director gave Adam a grim smile. "I believe you failed to mention that."

"Did I?" The two exchanged a long look. "How neglectful of me. Especially in light of the full disclosure you've been practicing."

Uh-oh. Kell resisted the urge to grin like a fool. There were fireworks coming, and dammit it all, he knew he was going to miss them. Raiker would reserve his cutting assessment of the assistant director's tactics for when the two of them were alone. But he'd never been more inclined to bug a room just to hear the outcome.

"My people should have been allowed the opportunity . . ."

"To screw up the woman's life? I don't think so." Adam's tone was final. "There were reasons, good reasons, to keep her identity secret. Her background checks out, and so did her story. As it's looking less likely that Hubbard was even involved, it was the right decision."

"But it wasn't your decision to make—What is it?" Whitman barked, when the knock sounded at the conference room door.

The door eased open, revealing Trimball and Jonesy. "Sir, we have more results to report," the woman said diffidently.

But Jonesy was already bursting into the room to hand the file folder he held to Adam. "It just came in a few minutes ago. We got a CODIS hit for the blood found on the bedsheet."

Whitman looked nonplussed. "We never submitted the CODIS paperwork."

"I did it." All eyes turned to Jonesy. He looked a little uneasy at the attention. "Burke told me to this morning, but I never got to it until later this afternoon, after we finished some of the comparison data."

Trimball sidled around the table to hand an identical folder to the assistant director. He took it, but his eyes were on Kell. And the look in them wasn't forgiving.

Recognizing it, Raiker snapped, "All my labs are recognized and CODIS-participating." He flipped open the file. "Now if we could spend less time engaged in a pissing contest and more on reviewing the facts of the case . . ." His voice trailed off abruptly as he read. Kell headed toward him to view the contents of the folder for himself.

"Vincent Dodge," he read aloud over Raiker's shoulder. A sense of incredulity seized him. This wasn't just some match to a random unsolved crime: they had a name. "So he's in the system?" Damn, but they might have just caught their first break in the case, and it even came with a criminal record on file.

"He's in the system." Raiker shot a look at Whitman, who gave a short headshake to indicate that the name wasn't familiar to him. "He did wet work for the Giovanni family in New Jersey in the late nineties. Beat a murder rap when the witnesses on one of his hits all turned up dead."

"Maybe it's a mistake," Pelton said doubtfully. "Unless . . ." His head swiveled toward the assistant director. "Does Mulder have any enemies that are connected? Anyone on the threat list?"

Adam was already shaking his head. "Dodge is a free-lancer now. Was living in South America the last I heard of him. But he'd know all about masks, and other ways to alter his appearance, or else he'd be caught on the facial-recognition software so popular in some countries."

A feeling of foreboding settled in Kell's chest. "A free-lancer?"

Adam's face was grim. "That's right. For over a decade Vincent Dodge has been working as a hired assassin."

———

It didn't make sense. Kell lay on the bed, tossing an apple in the air, only to reach out and snag it with the other hand. Why bother with an assassin for a kidnapping case? There were plenty of scumbags out there willing to do worse, for a lesser fee.

Maybe it had to do with association. Whoever planned the abduction knew Dodge. Had a relationship with him and that's what led to his inclusion. He pondered the thought.

Whitman and Raiker were already at work putting in the necessary requests to get a list of Dodge's known associates. But if the man worked from outside the United States, that list wasn't likely to be recent.

Scowling, he lent a spin to the apple on the next toss. He'd almost suspect the man's DNA had been planted on the sheets to throw them off course. But imagining the perp of this case having access to Dodge's blood was a bit of a stretch, even for Kell, who was usually all too willing to ride a hunch.

The man's history didn't bode well for finding the girl alive.

A greasy tangle of nerves knotted in his stomach at the idea. If it were Kell, the kid would be kept alive as an ace in the hole. Things went wrong in these operations all the time. Ransoms sometimes weren't paid, especially without proof of life.

But an assassin on the scene meant she wouldn't live long.

A renewed sense of urgency filled him. He should go to work. Maybe go over the newest information from Coplink and the Denver crime blotters that Temple had sent. Look for anything that might connect to the dumping of the body or other happenings in the vicinity. They couldn't count on Dodge being dumb enough to keep the girl in the same vicinity where he'd dumped the body, but there'd be a team of law enforcement at the site tomorrow morning, regardless, looking for anything that might tie Hubbard's body to his killer.

Kell planned to be elsewhere. With Raiker back, he had more leeway in his assignment. At least if his boss's mood had improved by then.

That thought led, inevitably, back to Macy. He scowled up at the ceiling. She hadn't returned by the time they'd all been banished from the conference room to leave Raiker and Whitman alone. It was after midnight and the two men must still be holed up in conference because he hadn't heard Adam go to his room.

It was damn certain Kell wasn't going to get any sleep—he was too wired for that. He should forget about warning Macy about Raiker's mood and get to work. He straightened, intent on doing just that, when the door opened quietly.

"Macy," he hissed.

He had to give the woman credit. She had some vertical. She jumped at least a foot at the sound of his voice. "Shut the door and turn off the light." She'd flipped the switch on as she'd come in, but the lamp on the bedside table was turned on and suffused part of the room in a soft light.

"Get out now." She flipped the light switch off. "I mean it, Burke. I'm not in the mood."

"Raiker's looking for you." Although he was having trouble identifying the expression she was wearing, he recognized the wariness that slid over it easily enough. "Unless you're in the mood to face him tonight, shut the damn door."

She closed it gently behind her. "Did he mention why?" Her tone was guarded.

"No." And he saw no reason to tell her that wondering

that very thing had been eating him alive for the last few hours. Kell watched her carefully. "But he was well and truly pissed when he asked about you, so I'm thinking you'll want to give him some more time to cool off."

"Good plan." She crossed the room to hang up her coat. "Thanks for the warning. Good-bye."

The dismissal in her voice was lost on him. He was too busy trying to identify what else he heard there. Tension. That was evident enough. It was reflected in the rigid line of her back and shoulders. Her tone was brittle. Her movements so tightly controlled they looked slightly awkward, as if she were afraid she'd spring apart in a thousand pieces.

Whatever the hell was bothering her, it damn well didn't have anything to do with testimony she'd given in Chicago today.

"You missed some big breaks today." She was taking clothes out of her dresser drawer. "Remember that body I told you about? Turns out it was . . ." His voice trailed off as she went to the bathroom with pajamas in hand. Closed the door.

"Hubbard's," he finished. What the hell? The sound of the shower turning on stunned him as much as if she'd done a striptease right in front of him. Well, maybe not quite that much, and it really wasn't a good time for his mind to go *there* at any rate, but Macy was modest to a fault. The lights had stayed firmly off the one night they'd spent together.

But that had only heightened the sensation of taste and touch. He'd mapped every inch of her body with his hands. With his mouth. The memory was seared on his mind like a brand.

And the next morning, when he'd awakened to her cool little dismissal of their *lapse*, she'd been completely dressed. Coolly composed.

Under normal circumstances there was no way she'd be standing naked in the next room, knowing he was still out here.

She hadn't even ordered him out again.

That fact, coupled with her appearance, had concern mounting. And there was no way in hell he was leaving without finding out what was wrong.

He preferred to think of it as helpful rather than pushy. He couldn't offer any suggestions for stemming Raiker's anger if he didn't have all the facts and she should be grateful for his assistance. No one had been on the receiving end of the boss's temper more than Kell had over the years.

Fifteen minutes later he was rethinking that decision. Because when the door finally opened and she exited the bathroom, all the logical arguments he'd practiced fell completely out of his brain. He wouldn't have been able to utter them anyway because he was having a hard enough time just keeping his tongue in his mouth.

Her hair was still dry, a cloud of midnight curls, recently brushed, rioting over her shoulders to contrast starkly with the pajamas. As nightwear went, they weren't sexy. He told himself that over and over and tried to make himself believe it. The simple white top and pants were plain white cotton, cut much like a set of long johns. Except of course for the inch of lace at the hems of the sleeves and pant legs, and marching down the vee of the top.

He didn't need the beaded nipples pressing against the soft fabric to remind him of the weight and feel of her breasts in his hands. Of the velvety softness of her nipples in his mouth. Then even that memory was shoved aside by the expression on her face.

"What are you doing here?"

Something was very wrong. His gut clenched reflexively. Keeping his voice low and soothing he said, "I've been here. We talked, just now, remember?"

The shower hadn't done its job because the tension was back. And the blank mask that settled over her face had nerves scrambling in his chest. "I need to be alone. I have to . . . I can't . . ." A deep shuddering breath shook her. "Just once, Kell." Her voice was a whisper. "Just once. Do what I ask. Please."

If the last word hadn't done the trick, the suspicion that

tears were responsible for turning her eyes bright and glossy should have. There was little Kellan Burke wouldn't do to avoid dealing with a crying woman.

But the tears never materialized. She just stood there, statuelike, oozing a vulnerability that normally would have had him looking for the nearest exit.

He was as surprised as she was when he rolled from the bed to snap off the lamp. And then strode over to her, scooping her off her feet from where she'd seemed rooted.

"Don't . . ."

"Quiet," he said gruffly as he crossed to the bed and pulled the covers back. He laid her gently down and tucked the bedclothes tightly around her. When he rounded the bed, banging his shin painfully on the bedpost in the process, he'd never know what kept him from continuing out the door and back to his own room.

Instead he climbed into the other side of the bed and rolled over to snake an arm around her waist. Pull her closer so her back was pressed against him like a couple spooning.

"I need to be alone." Her whisper wasn't as fierce as it should have been. And told him that, as much as he might regret it, he was doing exactly what he should.

"Baby, that's the last thing you need. Go to sleep."

But even after her breathing slowed and a measure of the tension had seeped from her body, he knew she didn't sleep. Doubted he would either. Neither of them spoke. And they both ignored the soft knock that sounded at her door an hour later. Listened soundlessly until Adam had crossed the hall to enter his own room.

The lack of rest didn't bother him. As Kell lay there awake, he figured there were far worse ways to spend the midnight hours than with Macy Reid in his arms.

————

In the end, though, she slept. They both did. He came awake before dawn, aware that she was trembling violently against him, her breathing labored. He skated a hand over her stomach, soothing. Could feel the skin beneath the pajama top quivering beneath his touch. "Nightmare?" His face pressed to her hair, he could feel her nod.

A sense of helplessness filled him. "Mace, where'd you go yesterday? After Chicago?"

For a time he thought she wouldn't answer. When she did, her voice was barely audible. "Terre Haute."

He frowned in the darkness, his mind searching for the thread of familiarity. "Castillo is confined there."

"He told Adam he had more information, details that would help the case that he'd give only to me." The words were so thready he had to lean closer to hear. "We both agreed he was lying. Trying to arrange a meet and using the case as a lever."

He tended to agree. "So why go?"

She was quiet for a long time. "Because in the end, I couldn't be sure what was stopping me, disbelief or fear. And I decided long ago I wasn't going to let fear rule my life."

The pieces still weren't coming together for him. "That case? The one you worked that involved Castillo . . ."

Her breath streamed out in a long sigh. "I didn't work a case. Castillo was working with the men who kidnapped my stepfather and me when I was eight."

Kell stilled, the news hitting him with the force of a vicious right jab. And then comprehension crowded in, making bile rise in his throat. He remembered what Castillo was. What he'd been imprisoned for.

"Ian was stationed in the British embassy in Bogotá. We'd been there eight months when we were walking home from the park one Saturday. An enclosed jeep pulled to a stop beside us and men with rifles poured out of it.

"We were blindfolded, but I could hear them fighting with Ian, hitting him until he was slumped over me, quiet. I still don't know where they took us. A sort of barn, I think, far out into the country. We were kept separated and there were more children there, all of us kept in individual cages, bound and gagged. They took turns guarding us and I remember the first night when Castillo went on duty. He had kind eyes, I thought. Maybe he liked little kids."

Her voice went flat. "And I was right. He especially liked little girls."

His chest was too tight. It was a struggle to haul oxygen into his lungs. "He raped you?"

"He'd choose a different child every night. Only the girls. There were eight of us held there. Three boys. It was like a game with him. He'd walk up and down between our cages, talking about our various . . . attributes. Stop in front of one door. Move slowly to the other. And afterward . . . each time afterward, he'd stop by my cage. I'd be curled up in a ball, trying not to see, to hear anything. But I'd always hear him. 'I'm saving you for last, my little English rose.' I spent all my time certain my turn would be next. Hating myself for being glad it wasn't. That it never came."

The vise in his chest squeezed painfully. There was a fire in his gut that threatened to devour him. A thirst for revenge for a long-ago crime committed against helpless children. A crime no life sentence could ever pay.

"We were ransomed after a week. All the diplomats paid for the insurance, because the kidnappings happened too frequently. I never knew Castillo's name until I saw his face in the newspaper when the story of Raiker's case broke. I contacted Adam, told him what I knew, and he arranged to have me testify."

There was no emotion in her voice. But he felt it in the shudders that still shook her body at occasional intervals. "What was he waiting for? Men like him . . . they aren't good at overcoming their urges."

"I never knew. Never had a clue why those poor girls were savaged night after night and I was spared. But now I think I do. Five million dollars, he said. I don't think the others knew what he was doing at night. He was probably afraid he'd mess up the payoff if I was . . . damaged."

She pulled away then and he let her go. Rolled to his back and tried to beat back the emotion that was teeming and rolling inside him, battling for a way out.

But it was useless, all of it. There was no way to undo the terror that Macy had gone through. No way to undo the psychological damage, a form of survivor's guilt that must have ravaged her for years afterward.

Nothing to do with the rage that frothed and foamed inside him at the thought of the cruel shattering of innocence.

When she didn't return to the bed, Kell felt a sense of foreboding. He grabbed his glasses from the bedside table and put them on, getting up to pad to the bathroom door. Listened, and when he heard no sound, pushed it open with the palm of his hand.

She was leaning her palms on the counter, the fingers clenching the edge so tightly that her knuckles shone white. And when he saw her expression in the mirror, a sense of déjà vu struck him hard.

He'd seen that look before. She'd worn it after their one night together when she'd told him it would never happen again. Dismissing him, and their time together, with an ease that should have come as a relief.

He'd spent a lot of time in the intervening months telling himself he felt exactly that. But that lie had been exposed as soon as Macy had walked on that jet a few days ago and sat down at Raiker's other side. Relief was the last thing he was feeling. Then or now.

"Don't do it again." He'd meant the words as a demand. Had no idea why they sounded so much like a plea. "I know what you're thinking. That what you revealed leaves you vulnerable, and now it's time to draw back, rebuild your defenses or whatever." Hell, he should be familiar with the ploy. He'd invented it. "Don't."

"You should leave. Before any of the others wake up."

He hated her flat tone. The deliberately blanked expression. And he'd do about anything to rid her of it.

Kell started unbuttoning his shirt. Her eyes widened, and she swung around, taking a step back. "Are you crazy? What are you doing?"

He tore it off to clench it in one fist while he pointed to his scar with the other. "You asked about this, remember? The night we spent together. Didn't see it because you didn't want lights, but you felt it and asked me about it."

Memory flickered in her eyes, and her expression softened. Her gaze moved over him, lingering on the old injury, and he felt his skin heat. "I lied to you then," he said bluntly. And watched her gaze flash to his.

"You said you were shot on the job. When you were working undercover for the BPD."

"I got it when I was seventeen. A couple days home after I got out of juvie. Carrie . . . my mother, shot me." He steeled himself for the horror, the pity, the avid interest. The lie was infinitely easier than dealing with any of them, which is why he'd gotten in the habit of telling it.

But he wasn't prepared for her to close the distance between them. Put her soft palm against the old scar as if to heal it all over again.

He forced himself to continue. The story was ancient history, better off unsaid, but she'd stripped her vulnerabilities bare for him, and he knew she'd hate him for that. So he reciprocated. His story was more pathetic than tragic, so they were hardly equal.

"Seems she spent the six months of my lockup searching for my stash of money. Pretty damn pissed when she couldn't get at it, too. I had it in a lockbox at a bank. She'd found the key but had no idea which bank it was." A corner of his mouth kicked up, and he looked down at her. "I like to think that drove the crazy old bat nuts while I was in juvie." Although she hadn't seemed crazy. Drunk or stoned most of the time he spent with her, but not crazy.

"First time I went home I was going to get that key and find myself a different place to live. But she already had it, along with the gun." No reason to mention that the gun was his, too. Living that life, in that neighborhood, it had been a necessity. He lifted a shoulder. "She demanded the money; I told her to go to hell." His hand came up to cover hers as the wound throbbed with a phantom pain. "Close range, I was hard to miss. The bitch nicked my heart. Damn near killed me." In masterful understatement, he added, "We don't exchange Christmas cards."

His hand tightened around hers, and their eyes met. "The

thing is, Macy, I don't know where she is. I don't care. And if I knew, I wouldn't try to find her, wouldn't stir up that old poison. There's no point. What's in our past is the past. It's a part of us, but it doesn't define us."

Understanding lit her eyes. "Poison," she murmured. "Yes, that's what Castillo was after. Taking the chance to spread a little more pain. But if the past has too tight a hold, it's important to face it, isn't it? To prove, at least to yourself, that it *hasn't* defined you. And that you don't fear it. Not anymore."

He recognized suddenly what had driven her to face Castillo. What it had cost her. And what she'd gained in return.

"You're one of the bravest women I've ever met." His throat felt full, so he cleared it. "I thought so on our first case together. Remember when we were chasing down that suspect in Louisville and he turned on us with that knife. Didn't even have my weapon sited before you'd dropped him with one hard kick to the balls. He never saw it coming." His eyes dropped to her mouth. Full and gently curved. "Things are always scariest when you don't see them coming."

She moved away then. He'd known she would. So there was no reason to experience that clutch in his heart.

A heart that stopped in the next moment when she slowly pulled her top over her head.

Lust fogged his brain. He couldn't move. Couldn't think. Here, then, was the vision that had been denied him their one brief night together. As his eyes traced the curves and shadows of her torso, his palms itched to follow.

Delicate. She looked fragile somehow now that he could see the slim arms and narrow waist topped with the sweet curve of her breasts. Need clenched in his belly like a fist. She hadn't felt fragile in his arms that night, and he hadn't been slow and careful. But she deserved that much, to be tasted and touched and savored, every inch of her explored and exploited.

He closed the distance between them. As if of its own volition, his hand raised and his fingers entangled in her hair.

Fine and baby soft, just as he remembered. His face lowered to hers. And then stopped.

Memory wasn't necessarily selective. Thoughts of what she'd revealed earlier crowded in and summoned uncomfortably chivalrous urges. Maybe he knew her a little better than he realized. She'd avoided him for months after they'd slept together.

He wasn't eager to repeat that.

Kell rested his forehead against hers, tried to rein in his galloping pulse. "I don't want you to regret this."

"The only regret I'm going to have is if you don't quit talking."

It was the hint of annoyance in her words that had the tension easing and his lips curving. The last thing he wanted to do was add to the lady's regrets.

Cupping her nape in both palms, he kissed her then, long and hard. It was crazy to feel this sense of homecoming. She shouldn't taste so familiar when their time together had been so limited. But her flavor was sprinting through his system, summoning a response that was much too swift, and a bit too desperate.

He traced the seam of her lips with the tip of his tongue before demanding entrance. There was nothing of the hesitancy he recalled from their first time. Her tongue met his in a long velvet glide that kick-started his pulse and ignited a simmering heat.

Closer. Unconsciously his arm tightened around her. He could feel her nipples pricking his chest, begging for attention. But he was determined to draw this out, make it last. And this time, if she drew away again, he'd have more of her to remember. Enough to sate his hunger for her, finally.

The thought restored his fraying restraint. He took his time, deepening the kiss, taking his fill. There was sweetness there, with an underlying wicked heat to entice him to take more. Because if there was one thing that he'd learned their first time together, it was that Macy had layers she kept well hidden. And stripping them away, one at a time, would be primitively satisfying.

He scored her bottom lip with his teeth, was rewarded by her indrawn breath. One of her hands went to his back, traced his spine in a slow, languorous sweep. Tearing his mouth from hers, he found the pulse at the base of her throat, where it beat madly, and pressed his lips against it before cruising up the slender arch of her neck.

Her fingers dipped below his waistband, tracing light rhythmic strokes across his lower back. He widened his stance, brought her hips into closer contact with his. And reveled in the sensation as the increased pressure sent sneaky little demons from hell firing through his veins.

There was a temptation to push too hard, ask for too much, too fast. He knew better now. Knew enough to lure her in, soothe her nerves before pressing for what he needed from her. A demand for everything she'd willingly give him in return. And then more. For everything she sought to hold back.

Unable to deny himself any longer, he cupped her breasts, relearning their shape and weight. Wedging a breath of space between them, he flicked his thumbs over her nipples, urging them into tighter knots. Urgency licked up his spine, sped through his veins. It was difficult to take it slow when every instinct he had was whipping his need hotter. Faster.

Giving in to those instincts, he bent to take one nipple in his mouth and was rewarded by her sharply drawn-in breath. Her hands moved to his biceps, nails biting lightly, and the slight sting of pain only fanned the urgency higher. He lashed the taut bud with his tongue, gratified by her low moan.

It had seemed too easy for her these last months. Simple for her to forget the hours they'd spent wrapped around each other. Which had maddened him, because he hadn't been able to shrug it off so quickly. He had his share of experiences. Welcomed a woman who didn't try to throw strings over every roll in the sheets. But it didn't take a wealth of experience to recognize that Macy wasn't the sort of woman to take intimacy lightly.

Maybe that's why it had burned when she'd seemed to do just that.

In a hunger for flesh, he drew her nipple more deeply into his mouth, scraped it lightly with his teeth. Any satisfaction he got from her shudder was immediately lost when her hips did a quick grind against his. And he knew then that he'd been fooling himself earlier.

Slow wasn't going to be an option.

He moved one hand to her butt, torturing himself for a few moments at the feel of the soft cotton over warm flesh before greed reared up. With less finesse than normal, he pushed the bottoms down her legs, lingering to stroke the smooth thighs he'd bared, with the whisper of muscle beneath the sleek flesh. He released her breast to raise his head, lifting her a little to kick aside the pajama bottoms, and then walking her backward until the wall was at her back.

And then he feasted. Her breath was coming rapid and hard, and it mingled with his when he pressed a deep open-mouthed kiss against her mouth. He couldn't tell which of their hearts was hammering the hardest. Was very much afraid it was his. His lips streaked over her jaw, down the sensitive cord of her neck, where a quick nip made her shudder. Over the rounded curve of her shoulder. Across the delicate angles and hollows made by her collarbone. And then lower.

Her hands clutched in his hair, but he was only dimly aware of it. He'd never before experienced this primitive greed for flesh. His lips followed the curve of her breast, and he traced the shadowy under curve with his tongue. He wanted to touch her everywhere again. Taste her everywhere. To explore the gentle sweep of curves from breast to hip, the indentation of ribs, the smooth warm curve of her belly.

Her hands grew a little frantic on his shoulders as he knelt before her and indulged in the sensual exploration. He cupped her bottom in his palms, kneading the smooth flesh as his tongue delved into her navel. The muscles in her belly jumped and quivered beneath his lips, and he felt a measure of control return at the evidence of her desire.

If he'd been marked by their lovemaking months ago, this time he was intent she would be, too.

He traced the crease of her thighs with his fingers then repeated the action with his tongue. And when he parted her soft folds to settle his mouth over her moist heat, the only sound he was aware of was the thundering of his blood.

The sweet musky scent of her went straight to his loins. Whipped his passion to a fever pitch. The taste of her slick flesh had hunger rising again, faster and hotter, snarling and snapping like a caged beast.

Her hips jerked against his mouth and every movement drove the fire just a little higher. He should have been alarmed by this fever snapping in his blood, fueled by the taste and feel of this woman. His appetite for her couldn't be assuaged. Refused to be sated. The realization should have set off an inner alarm. He had well-developed instincts for self-preservation. But his mind, his senses, were steeped in her.

He worked a finger into her dampness, began to stroke. The dual assault had her hips twisting against his mouth in a primal rhythm. And when he heard her cry out brokenly, felt her go boneless against him, the fierce exultation he felt was tempered only by desperation.

Rising, he took more of her weight, as she leaned heavily against him. With one arm banded around her waist, he used his free hand to stroke and smooth her trembling flesh, all the while attempting to regain his rapidly flagging control.

When he felt her hands at his zipper, lust rocketed through his veins. Her movements were torturously slow, the descent an inch at a time. Perspiration beaded on his forehead as he battled the overpowering urge to strip himself and end this in a way that lacked restraint or finesse.

Kell dragged his eyes open and tried to focus. Oxygen seemed to razor in and out of his lungs. And what he saw in her expression had need spiking through his system.

Her gaze was still a little dazed, a little slumberous with satisfaction, but there was knowledge in her expression. She was purposefully trying to drive him out of his mind. And doing a damn fine job at it.

Releasing her, he propped his hands on the wall on either

side of her, as much for the support as to allow her freedom of movement. He wouldn't have expected teasing from her. Would have felt a greater appreciation for it if he weren't so ready to throw his head back to howl.

He leaned forward to string a trail of kisses along her jaw-line, lingering to worry the sensitive spot behind her ear. Her fingers faltered for a moment, then renewed their maddening pace.

There was a roaring in his ears, a fever in his blood that would only be quenched by this woman. There was no way to hide his reaction. It was there in his labored breathing, the muscles that jumped and quivered beneath her touch. And when she'd finished the task, and released him from his briefs, there could be no mistaking his response.

She took him in her hands to stroke, and his vision grayed at the edges. His jaw clenched as he battled back the savage need for completion. Every clever clutch and slide of her fingers seemed destined to shatter his resolve. To bring him to his knees in a quivering, quaking pool of hormones.

He reached blindly for his pocket, searched for a condom before she pushed his trousers and briefs over his hips. Kicking out of them, he had just enough reason left to stretch for the controls of the walk-in shower. To sheathe himself and then, with an arm around her waist, move them both inside it with a smoothness that owed more to luck than to dexterity.

The water was initially cool, and she jerked against him. But the multiple jets felt wondrous on his heated skin. He pressed her against the shower wall, his mouth going in search of hers, the last vestiges of control spiraling away.

They were seamed together. Mouths. Chests. Hips. And still it wasn't close enough. He was dimly aware of her re-mounting desire. The way she lifted one slim leg to glide along his thigh. And the dam of his restraint abruptly crumbled.

Mouth eating at hers, he lifted her, urging her legs around his hips. And when the position opened her to him, he entered with one deep stroke that had them both groaning.

The water pounding from the jets around them, above

them, had warmed. But he was aware of nothing but her. Of her inner muscles clenching and releasing around his shaft. Her heels digging into his hips. Her mouth under his, frantic and desperate.

Her hips rocked against his then, and conscious thought fragmented. He withdrew partially to surge against her again in a hunger that wouldn't be denied. His grip tightened on her hips as he pounded into her, in a brutal greed that was beyond his control. Her arms wrapped around his shoulders, one hand clutched in his hair. He heard her moan as she crested again, released her mouth to bury his face in her throat as his hips jackhammered against hers, the need inside him a raging ruthless beast.

Sensation crashed into sensation. With one last thrust, his climax ripped through him, a violence that shattered everything but thoughts of her.

Chapter 13

It was hard to tell what time it was, but the sky seemed to be lightening. Ellie trudged farther, her steps sluggish. Or maybe she wanted to think that because she was exhausted. And so sore from that tumble she'd taken down that rocky slope a couple hours ago that it was difficult to move at all.

She stopped. Swayed a little as she tried to get her foggy mind to *think*.

Traveling at night had seemed to make sense because he wouldn't be able to see her. But she couldn't see either. There hadn't been a clue a while ago that the ground had been about to give way before she'd fallen. She'd been dizzy and disoriented as she'd made her way to even ground.

All sense of direction had been lost.

If she had the energy, she'd cry. It was tempting, so tempting, to just sink down right here and give up. So what if he found her. By the time he did, she'd be dead anyway. Stiff and so frozen his knife wouldn't work on her anyway.

Two years ago she would have done just that.

She'd been frozen then, too, but not by the cold. Numb, the

way you get when your feelings hide somewhere deep inside just so you can get through the days. She hadn't wanted them to come back, even after she'd gone back with her mom and dad.

It was so much easier when she'd felt nothing.

Scooping up some snow, she brought it to her mouth. She hadn't found anything edible but a handful of berries, but the snow would quench her thirst. Even if eating it just made her colder inside.

And she also realized if she didn't stop now to build her shelter, she wouldn't have the strength later.

Stumbling forward, she began looking for a drift of snow at least four feet tall. They were easier to find in a spot where the trees were less dense, and the wind was free to shape the snow into swales. She lost track of time as she searched. But pink was edging the sky when she finally found what she was looking for.

Clumsily, she removed a snowshoe and fell to her knees. It worked like a shovel as she began to dig. She'd been more careful the first day but she didn't have the will to dig the trench the way her dad had taught her on their winter camping trips. Likewise, constructing the raised sleeping area was beyond her. This time she just dug, arms feeling as heavy as stones as she hollowed out a compartment deep enough to crawl into.

When she'd finished, she took another careful glance around before putting the snowshoe back on and hiking over to the nearby evergreens to break off some branches. Thoughts of soon being able to stop and sleep filled her with new strength. She returned and spread the branches on the floor of the cave, removed the snowshoes and dragged them after her when she crawled inside. The boughs would keep her insulated from the snow floor.

Collapsing against the prickly branches, she lay still. Her muscles began to tremble, not from the cold but from exertion. Closing her eyes, she willed herself to sleep.

And it was hard, so very hard, to care whether she ever woke up again.

"Okay, here's a quick rundown on what you missed yesterday." Intent on not giving her a chance to feel awkward about the their time in the shower—both of them—he focused on a subject sure to distract her. "That body Denise Temple told us about—the one in Jefferson County—turned out to belong to Hubbard."

"Will you give me the towel?" The annoyance in her tone sounded normal enough to ease his fears that she'd try to withdraw from him. "I'm perfectly capable of drying my— Hubbard?"

"That's right." Finished with her, he swiped the towel carelessly across himself before letting it fall to the floor. Giving her a friendly pat on the ass to get her moving, he urged her out of the bathroom to stand before her dresser. "Jonesy matched the fingerprints. Helluva a deal, and still not sure what it means, although I'm betting he was just the sucker the kidnapper needed for a thumbprint that would get him inside here."

Her head snapped to his as he started opening drawers and going through her things. "His thumb was missing?"

"It's like that commercial says. Miss a little, miss a lot." He found a filmy camisole—damn if it wasn't a dead ringer for the one in his fantasy—and thrust it at her. Her fingers closed around it reflexively so he went in search of underwear for her, and got sidetracked. She had what could only be described as a delectable, mouth-watering selection.

She was dragging on the camisole so her voice was muffled. "Did you let Denise Temple know?"

"Damn." He should have thought of that. He settled on a scrap of white lace held together with two narrow strings on each side and handed the underwear to her. "I'll have to call her first thing." Although the news wouldn't be out until CBI deigned to release it, she deserved to hear it firsthand, not be hit with it on the job.

"That's not all." He crossed to her closet and opened it to contemplate the contents. It contained absolutely nothing low-cut, which seemed a shame, given the mouth-watering underwear she was going to be wearing beneath it. "Jonesy got a CODIS match on the bloodstain on the girl's sheet." He settled on a pale blue sweater that looked like it might cling and dragged it off the hanger to toss to her. "Turns out he's in the system. Vincent Dodge. Raiker says he's an assassin."

The news seemed to have stopped her in her tracks. "That makes no sense," she murmured, stunned.

He glanced at the face of the clock next to the bed. They might have awakened before dawn, but their interlude in the shower was going to make them late. And he was fairly certain Macy would want to face the boss before he came to find her. "We don't know what it means. Put on your sweater." He turned back to her closet. "Where are those black pants you wore the other day?" If memory served correctly, they'd hugged her ass like a glove.

"What pants? And why are you dressing me?" Belatedly she seemed snap out of whatever fog she was in. "Get out of my closet." She crossed over to elbow him aside.

"You didn't seem to mind. And I'd be happy to return the favor."

But when she ignored the invitation, he strolled to the bathroom to gather up his things. Pulling on his boxer briefs, he carried the rest of his stuff out into the bedroom. "You'd best get the meeting with Raiker over with before you go down for the morning. I'm sure a good night's sleep did wonders for his temper." Actually, he wasn't certain of any such thing, but he hoped for her sake that it was true. "I'll catch you up on the rest of it when you're done."

He wasn't sure what worried him more: that he recognized the flash of unease in her expression or that he knew exactly where it stemmed from. "Maybe I should go with you to talk to him this morning." The man's temper was always tightly controlled, but no one who'd been on the receiving end of it was anxious to repeat the experience. And Macy didn't need that. Didn't deserve it. Not after what she'd been through.

The fierce bolt of protectiveness that pierced him then should have alarmed him. Would have if he weren't distracted by her actions. She'd run a brush through her wet hair and, with a few quick movements, had it fashioned into some intricate knot at the back of her head. It left her slender neck bare. He wondered when he'd started finding necks sexy.

"I should have spent last night catching up on the case."

Recognizing the self-reproach in her voice, his attention narrowed. "Give yourself a break, Mace. Anyone would need to regroup after a day like you'd had." It frustrated him that she didn't respond. And he knew she remained unconvinced.

Concerned, he yanked his pants on, leaving them unfastened. He was shrugging into his shirt when she selected a jacket from her closet that matched the pants she wore, pants similar enough to the ones he'd been searching for to satisfy him.

"I'll go speak to Adam while you"—she risked a quick glance at him, seemed relieved to find him partially dressed—"change your clothes."

He watched, fascinated, as a flush rose up that lovely line of her throat to suffuse her cheeks with heat. It told him better than words that she was thinking more clearly now, and embarrassment was setting in.

He wasn't going to allow it to cause her to throw up more obstacles between them.

"This . . ." Her index finger was tapping a nervous rhythm on the edge of the dresser. One, two, three. One, two, three. She cleared her throat. Couldn't meet his eyes in the mirror. "We should put this . . . last night . . . on hold. We have a job to do. We can't afford to get . . . distracted."

The words might be slightly different from those she'd uttered the last time they'd spent together, but the meaning was the same. And it lit a fire in his belly that had been simmering for the last six months.

"I'm sure you agree . . ."

He closed the distance between them and took her elbow in his hand. Watched her start at his nearness.

"Why are you so close?"

"This only works when I'm close." With a quick tug, he had her in his arms, and his lips on hers for a thorough kiss. It took effort to temper his frustration. And then to not get sidetracked when her lips parted. Returned the pressure.

Lifting his head after a moment, he murmured, "I have more faith in our ability to focus than you seem to. But if it makes you feel better, put us out of your mind for as long as you need." That was better, he figured, than having her brood about last night until she worked herself up to another dismissal. "Just know that after we bring Ellie Mulder home again, this is still going to be between us. And you're going to find me a bit harder to get rid of this time around."

Because he didn't trust himself to say more, he headed for the door. She'd been right about one thing; he had to get back to his room before others started rising. And he needed to give her some time to get her thoughts together before she faced Adam, especially since she wasn't going to let him accompany her for that meeting.

Easing open the door, he checked the hallway before slipping out and heading for his room. And tried to shake the feeling that he was leaving her when she needed him most.

————

Macy tapped gently at the door across the hall. Adam's familiar growl invited her to enter. Taking a deep breath to calm her rollicking pulse, she opened the door and walked in far enough to stand in the doorway.

He was seated on the edge of the bed, dressed more casually than usual in black slacks and a matching sweater. His feet were bare. The sight took her aback. She'd never seen the man less than totally dressed. Would never have guessed that the tops of his feet bore the same deep scars and furrows as those on the back of his hands and across his throat.

Her gaze bounced upward. His dark hair was still damp, and she took a moment to hope that he'd arisen very recently. "I know you wanted to see me."

"I wanted to see you last night." His ruined voice was always hoarse, but there was an edge to it now that didn't bode well. "I knocked. You didn't answer."

"I must have been asleep," she lied without batting an eyelash. There was no way she could have faced him last night. She'd still been too raw. Felt too exposed. Adam had a way of seeing right through people to the core. She hadn't been up to that last night. She questioned whether she was even now.

"Too bad." He picked up the socks from their spot on the bed beside him and yanked each on with barely restrained force. "Because I had the night to try to come up with a reason not to fire you." The pause was imbued with more threat than his words. "I didn't find one."

A fist squeezed her heart while her spine went to ice. It took all her strength to stand motionless before him, her face hopefully arranged into an expressionless mask. His gaze drilled holes through her, probing for a weakness. She was determined he wouldn't find one. "Are you asking me to supply it?"

He made a rude sound. "You're turning into a helluva investigator." With the help of his cane, he got to his feet, went to the closet. "But after the training I provide, all my investigators are excellent."

"None of them are forensic linguists," she pointed out. Deliberately, she took a step farther into the room to remove the overwhelming urge to reach out her fingers for the nearest surface. She didn't need to give away her nerves with mindless tapping.

"You think I couldn't find ten linguists if I wanted to?" He turned back toward her so suddenly it was all she could do not to flinch. "You have a specialty I lacked in my firm, but it's not why I chose *you*, Macy. You should know that. I told you why I wanted you when I offered you the job."

The conversation was burned into her memory. It'd been weeks after Castillo's trial. Weeks she now suspected he'd used to learn everything there was to know about her. Past and present. "You said you respected me."

"I respected how you reacted to the trauma you were dealt." Shoes donned, he turned to face her fully, both hands clasped on the cane as he leaned against it. "You didn't dissolve into victimhood. Some do. You didn't follow your career path as a means to a vendetta, determined to spend your life hunting down a man who may as well have been a phantom. That would have been pointless and stupid. Until yesterday, you were never stupid."

The assessment stung. It also whipped up a bit of her own

temper. "I have skills that bring people to justice. Or prove them innocent. My job choice had little to do with Castillo. And my visit yesterday wasn't about what happened over two decades ago. Just the opposite.

"If there was a chance, however slim, that he had something to offer that might be useful to this case, I had to take it. That's my job. Not ducking to take the easiest out."

His gaze narrowed. "I told you I doubted he had anything of note to say."

And again, his assessment found its mark. "And you were right. But it's one thing to make that determination based on the certainty of experience. And quite another to question whether I was accepting your opinion because doing so required nothing of me." She couldn't quite hold his gaze then. "Judging by the overwhelming relief I felt when you ordered me not to go, I tend to think it was the latter. And I couldn't accept that. Not for this case. Not for myself."

There was a long pause. When she finally managed to look at him again, his expression was no less fierce. But the edge to his voice was gone. "You had nothing to prove. Not to me."

"Maybe I had something left to prove to myself." Seeing the understanding flicker across his expression didn't mean she was out of the woods yet. She'd just exposed a weakness to a man who had no tolerance for them. It'd be in keeping with everything she knew about him if he fired her on the spot, for that much alone.

No one had suffered more than Adam Raiker. And yet if that trauma had marred him in any but the most physical way, she'd yet to see evidence of it.

"And did you?" Her gaze flew to his. "Prove something to yourself?"

She hesitated, recalling how difficult it had been to face Castillo. To hear his voice again. To have the past raked up like an old wound, reopened and throbbing.

And to listen to him spew lies about the one person who had suffered along with her. The only parent she'd had for over two and a half decades.

At the end—and only the end mattered, didn't it?—she hadn't run. And that was a victory of sorts.

"Yes."

He gave a terse nod. "You'll have to catch up on the run today. Ask Kell to brief you. I've got a breakfast meeting with Whitman." His smile was humorless. "That never does much for my appetite."

Clearly dismissed, she started to go, then turned back. "He did have something he wanted me to tell you, too. Probably as worthless as the rest of the poison he was feeding me, but . . . he claims LeCroix had a child. A son."

She was unsurprised when her boss nodded. "He did. Disappeared over twenty years ago, though. I've always suspected he was one of LeCroix's victims. Probably resting at the bottom of one of Louisiana's bayous. The man knew every inch of the area."

It was disconcerting on some level to discover even a particle of truth buried in the conversation with Castillo. So she reported the rest of what the man had said about LeCroix, ending with, "Is that possible?"

Raiker lifted a shoulder. "That the boy's mother disappeared with him? Barely, I suppose. But LeCroix had the means to hunt them down, and it's doubtful there would be anywhere they could have hidden that his men wouldn't have found them. I think my theory is more likely."

She nodded, went to the door. It didn't escape her that he hadn't commented on Castillo's hope that LeCroix's son was not only living but would exact revenge on Raiker for killing his father.

Or whether he'd decided one way or the other about firing her. Since Adam Raiker didn't make empty threats, she knew she wasn't out of the woods yet.

Lon Pearce, the owner and operator of Denver's Halloween-EveryDay Mask Emporium, looked entirely too normal to have created the gory and gruesome creations that lined the shelves of his store. "Yeah, September and October are our busiest months," he was telling the trio as they moved slowly through the empty store, looking at his goods. "People will come in looking for something to build a costume around. But I stay busy with the custom orders the rest of the year."

"And where do your custom orders come from?" Macy asked. She stopped before one particularly eerie mask of an old woman. It looked lifelike enough to speak.

"My website business is starting to take off. And I've gotten some work from a small indie company in Hollywood." He gave them a broad grin. "I did some masks for this really cool low-budget alien film they were shooting for practically nothing, just to get my foot in the door. I'm hoping word will get around. I sure wouldn't mind getting a piece of the special-effects pie."

"Ever been asked to make a mask that's a replica of a living person? Like from pictures?" Travis asked. He slipped a mask off the mannequin head and held it to squint at it, seemingly unaware of the shopkeeper's concerned expression.

"Oh, sure." Pearce picked up his foam latte cup and took a swig, reminding Macy she hadn't even had a morning coffee before Kell had rushed her out of the house. "You have to do a life cast for that. I made two of my dad for my brother and me to wear at his sixtieth birthday party. It was a riot."

"So how does that work?" Kell seemed fascinated by a mask with a machete extending from the skull, which exposed very lifelike gray matter. "I get on your site, put in an order, send you the pics over the Internet. Pay with credit card?"

"Sure, or with PayPal. I take both."

Although the Internet would offer anonymity, it was unlikely that Vincent Dodge paid by credit card. Macy withdrew a picture of Nick Hubbard from her purse. "Were you ever asked to make a mask of this man?"

Lon peered closer at it before shaking his head. "Nope. Why, does he have a mask like these?"

"Actually he did, but he's not available for us to ask about it." Kell turned from the display he was perusing to saunter up to them. "We're not even sure if it was done locally but thought we'd check and see who in the area could manage a job like his."

Lon scratched his balding pate, then crossed over to take the mask from Travis, who was trying unsuccessfully to re-place it on the mannequin head. "There are dozens of places selling products like this, but there are only a few of us actu-ally making them in the area. Barry Fingle, but he works out of Colorado Springs, about an hour south of here." Repo-sitioning the mask, he continued, "He does nice work. Sam Masterson, here in town, but he works mostly with latex and I know he doesn't do any sculpting. Wendy Parker does. Norm Ellison, he's in Boulder. And then there's my mentor." He grinned again, as if at a private joke.

"Your mentor?" Macy eyed his cup as he tipped it to his mouth again and wondered if he'd object too much if she swiped it from him. After the nerve-grinding session with Adam, she could have used a jolt of caffeine, but breakfast had consisted of the apple she'd grabbed before following Travis and Kell into the conference room for an update of yester-day's events.

"I call him that. He's the reason I got interested in masks when I was a kid. He began working with sculpture before moving to latex. Potsy we all called him, because, you know, back in the day"—he mimed smoking a reefer—"he's who you saw when you needed some. I also heard he was the man to see if you'd lifted something you needed to get rid of."

"A fence?"

"I don't know if that's true, though," he said in answer to Travis. "But he was a man of many talents. He's the best in the business. His stuff is so lifelike they could talk on their own." His voice had gotten a little dreamy. "He's shown me a couple times how to attach the hair so it holds better. Never met anyone else in the business who could match his skills. But he does it for kicks, I think. He doesn't have a website. Isn't even in the phone book. Just has a cell number."

"But you know where to find him?" Agent Travis was already taking out a pad and pen.

"Sure. He's over on Colfax. I don't know the exact address, but it's on the eighteen hundred block. One-story brick building, no sign, except for the one in the window. Quinn's." Pearce shrugged and straightened some of the mannequins on the shelf. "Always sort of wondered how he stayed in business."

———

"Colfax." Kell slammed the door of the vehicle and turned down his collar, which Macy assumed had been upturned in an attempt to keep his ears warm. "Why does that name sound familiar?"

"Probably because it's one of the longest commercial strips in the country." Travis started the SUV and checked the heater. "It runs through a half-dozen towns in the vicinity."

"Did you make that phone call you mentioned earlier?" Macy asked Kell. They hadn't had a moment alone together since he'd left her room that morning. And while a part of her was relieved at that fact, he also hadn't had an opportunity to update her about the intended call to Denise Temple.

"I did." His expression took on a serious cast that she rarely observed there. "She was . . . understandably upset. But appreciative of the update."

"Burke, you've got more women problems than anyone I've ever met." The sun was out, finally, and traffic had turned some of the packed snow on the streets to dirty slush. Travis caught her eye in the rearview mirror. "At the incident response, he actually left the house during interviews to take a call from a girlfriend. Can you believe that?" He shook his head. "Whitman was fit to be tied."

Something inside her stilled at the words. Because they weren't as surprising as they should have been. Kell had been talking to one of his women the other morning on the way downstairs to breakfast. And she'd long suspected he had a line of them. Ramsey had mentioned as much when Macy had confessed a few months ago to having a hard time responding to the man's quips. Not even to her friend had she admitted her difficulty had been made worse by the one night they'd slept together.

Swallowing hard, she looked blindly out the window at the passing storefronts. She was too fastidious to enjoy being one of a throng, and the sooner she came up with a way to tell him as much, the better off she'd be.

Unfortunately, she hadn't shown herself to be particularly articulate around him when the situation called for it.

He turned around in the front seat as much as the seat belt allowed to murmur meaningfully, "I was talking to her that day, too. Our friend."

Her gaze flew up to meet his, something in her chest easing. So the call he'd taken that day was from Temple. Ridiculous to feel this flicker of relief. The knowledge changed nothing between them. And there was no *them* in any but a professional sense for the duration of this case.

After that, given what she'd heard of the man's attention span, it would be a moot point. She tried to convince herself that she wasn't disappointed by the certainty.

———

"Anyone else getting a bad feeling about this?" Kell muttered as they got out of the car and stared at the scene across the street.

A sense of foreboding settled low in her belly. "Bugger it," she muttered. The portion of the street they were on wasn't in the best of neighborhoods. Young toughs, who all looked like they'd fail a cursory pat down, stood on street corners, warming themselves in fires contained in beat-up trash containers. There was a transaction openly taking place between a driver in a Lexus and a young woman of questionable fashion sense before she opened the front door of the vehicle and got in.

Most of the police tape around the burned-out shell of a building across the street had been torn away and was lying on the ground. But the boarded-up windows and doorway told their own story.

The three of them stared glumly at the scene. Travis muttered, "Ten to one, we've found Quinn."

———

Denver Detective Ryan Summers was short and squat, with slicked-back hair and a nose red from continual blowing. "Damned cold," he muttered as he tossed a used Kleenex in the metal trash can next to his desk. "Impossible to shake in this weather."

"So the fire broke out a week ago?"

"Sometime after nine P.M." Summers drew another tissue and blew his nose loudly. Macy eased away from his desk imperceptibly. If ever she'd seen a man who needed to be home in bed, it was this one. "Arson, the fire investigator said. Given the owner, I immediately figured him for it, but revised my opinion when the coroner identified Quinn's body inside."

"He has a sheet?" Kell asked.

"Quinn's been around long enough for his record to have started on stone tablets." He looked up expectantly, so Macy smiled at the joke. "Moved through the system a few times, but he's been clean for a couple decades, which means only we couldn't hang a damn thing on him." Although his desktop was a cluttered mess that had her fingers itching to organize it, he settled on a file folder unerringly and pulled it free from the clutter to open it. "Did a five to ten in the eighties for receiving stolen goods, and had some minor drug busts prior to that."

"But you thought he was involved in something more recently?" Travis was unbuttoning his coat. Kell's was already unzipped. In a stark contrast to most police stations she'd ever visited, heat was blasting through the area.

"Oh, yeah, we knew he was still receiving. Just couldn't catch him at it." He opened his middle desk drawer, freed a throat lozenge from a pack, and popped it in his mouth. "But once I started poking around after the fire, I heard a few rumors that he was the guy to see for new IDs."

"Forged identifications?"

He sneezed loudly before nodding at Kell's question. "Supposed to be a master at it, too, which was news to us.

Hell, maybe he was doing it all along even before his stint in prison."

"Did anyone mention what was inside his shop before it burned?"

"Freaky-ass stuff. Weird sculptures and paintings. I guess he fancied himself an artist, too. Masks and costumes." He shook his head. "The kind of thing he couldn't have made a living at, you know? Not in that neighborhood. Had to be a front for something else."

"What was he doing at the store at that time of night?" When the detective's rheumy gaze met hers, she went on. "Was the shop still open?"

"Hell if I know. His sort of place didn't have hours posted, but he lived in the back. He would have been there twenty-four, seven."

"What'd your canvass turn up?"

Summers snorted at the CBI agent's question. "In that neighborhood? The usual. A lot of nothing. No one saw anyone going in or out of the building that night. No one saw Quinn at all that day. I have it figured for a robbery gone bad. Some meth head breaks in looking for something to hock, and Quinn confronts him. Gets shot in the head for his efforts."

Macy's interest was reflected by the immediate straightening of Dan and Kell. "So he died of a bullet wound and not from the fire?"

"That's what the coroner said. Execution style, right between the eyes." He plucked another Kleenex from the box on his desk. "Every punk has a gun these days, and they all think they're Dirty Harry."

Twice he heard the far-off echo of a shot, and each time he did, his finger itched. He didn't know what the crazy orange-clad motherfuckers were hunting, but they were clearly desperate to find their game. Enough to risk frostbite and just plain freezing their asses off on this godforsaken mountainside.

He was here, too, wasn't he? And his desire to find his prey was probably more desperate than theirs.

And then there they were, in the snow, like a gift bestowed for his patience. The animal tracks didn't interest him, but the snowshoe tracks did. They led away to the left, a bunch of them around a rocky slope and then up it, over the steep incline and across the small ravine. With renewed energy, he followed them, for at least a couple miles.

The distance didn't matter. His focus had narrowed to certain deadly intent. He could do her out here, among the dense trees, and bury the body in snow. She wouldn't be found until the spring thaw, much like Hubbard, and whatever the animals left of them would impede identification for much longer.

It didn't matter to him. He'd be back on his sunny beach under his umbrella, enjoying the heat on his skin. After this, he didn't think he'd ever take another job in the cold.

A rocky shale cliff loomed in front of him and he slowed. He'd traveled enough miles to be wary about an upcoming terrain change. The tracks before him seemed to disappear, which indicated a steep descent on the other side.

Anticipation loomed. Maybe the fucking kid had fallen and even now lay at the bottom of the slope. Thoughts of putting a quick bullet between her eyes vanished. He'd gone to far too much trouble to set aside his plans now. He'd take her back to the portable ice fishing shanty where he could spend some time with her.

His knife was in that shelter.

He took off his glove and slipped his hand in his pocket, fingers closing over the Glock he carried there. His breathing was coming faster. Not from exertion, but from the burst of adrenaline that sent shocks through his system. Making his way carefully, he topped the slope and started down the other side.

And then stopped. Cursed viciously.

A figure in hunter orange was at the base, walking along, as if examining the cliff carefully. A dog was ahead of him, running circles in the snow like a fucking lunatic.

The man was wearing snowshoes.

A headache spiked, brutal and keen, the kind he used to get as a kid after the first few blows from the holy book. His fingers tightened around the gun in his pocket. He'd kill the man where he stood. Him and the damn dog for making him waste precious time tracking them.

A hunter. Not the kid.

"Hey!" The man below him looked up. Waved an arm. "Hey!"

Vincent stopped. Considered. The man was inviting death to his door. It seemed a shame to disappoint.

He made his way down the slope carefully. The hunter was dressed much as he was himself, in full winter wear and an insulated mask and gloves that trapped body heat. Keeping a wary eye on the dog, who gave him only a cursory glance before continuing to frolic, he continued his approach.

"Just wanted to warn you," the guy called. "There are a few of us hunters out here. Mountain lion season. You really should be wearing some sort of reflective outerwear. Don't want an accident."

He drew closer before responding. "I don't look much like a mountain lion. And I'm very careful." So careful, in fact, that he scanned the area closely before determining no one else was in the vicinity. In his pocket, the weapon warmed in his fingers.

"When the dog's on the scent, you never know. Guy follows the dog into the trees, maybe gets a sighting, and the next thing that moves is liable to get shot. That damn near happened yesterday. And worst of it was, I think it was a kid I nearly put a bullet into."

Breathing slowed. "Wouldn't expect to see a kid out here alone."

The hunter shrugged. "Probably had parents nearby, but I didn't see them. If I had, I'd have told them the same thing I'm telling you. Take some precautions and avoid a possible tragedy." He cocked his head. "You camping out here? Are you the one been making those snow caves?"

Adrenaline surged. "Yeah, that was me."

The hunter made a gesture of disgust. "Man, it's important to make sure you include an air hole. Make a hole in the roof with a branch or something. Wiggle it occasionally to be sure the air is flowing. If the snow collapses, you don't want to suffocate."

A grim smile crossed his mouth beneath the mask. "No. I don't want that. I'm a bit new at this. Lost my way and can't recall where my last shelter was. Some things fell out of my pack while I slept, and I need to go back and look for them." The dog ran over then and sniffed the ground around him.

"No offense, buddy, but if you're inexperienced, you should be traveling with a friend." Shaking his head, the hunter pointed to a spot well in the distance. "The one I saw today was that way, probably four miles. See that evergreen that's split there at the top? Probably thirty, forty yards from that tree."

His fingers eased from the Glock. The man's information had him feeling charitable. "Thanks. You've been very helpful."

———

Ellie needed to pee. She kept her eyes tightly shut, willing the feeling away. It was a major pain when she had to do it because the coat and snow pants needed to come off and she nearly froze in the process. Willing sleep to return, she tried to think of something else. Anything else.

Lucky's image swam across her mind, making her sniffle. Stupid horse. Ellie blamed Lucky for making her feel again. How could she not when the animal's gentle eyes looked so full of understanding? Like she comprehended all Ellie's secrets. All the ones she whispered in her ear after brushing her. And even those that were still lodged deep inside her.

If it hadn't been for Lucky, she'd still be numb inside. And she would have hated the animal for that if she didn't love her so much.

Her bladder wasn't giving up. She dragged her eyelids open, tried to focus. When she did, her blood went to ice. I'm still asleep, Ellie thought wildly. Trapped in a nightmare.

The masked face seemed to fill the opening of the cave. Evil waiting. And although she stared hard, willing the nightmare away, he didn't disappear. She recognized the eyes, those tan empty eyes, even before he spoke.

"What are you feeling right now?"

Chapter 14

"This is supposition. All of it."

Macy assumed Kell ignored Travis's objection because it was true. But that didn't lessen her interest in his actions.

The waitress in the diner kept sending them black looks. They'd commandeered three tables for their small party. Kell had pushed them altogether and she'd cleared them off so he could spread out the maps he and Travis had picked up from the wilderness office yesterday. They were joined by the city map of Denver and its suburbs.

"Let's look at this logically. Crimes this big don't happen in isolation. There's a ripple effect, you know? Things that have to be enacted in order to carry it out. What did Dodge have to accomplish prior to murdering Hubbard? We can all agree that that's the probable way it went down, right?"

There were no objections, not even from Travis. "There's no way to be sure Quinn made the mask—the fire destroyed any evidence of that. But none of the other names that Pearce gave us checked out."

"Regardless of who made it, we can be sure it took some

time. Two weeks would be a rush job, a couple of them said." Macy gestured for the waitress. As long as they were there, she may as well get the coffee she'd been craving. "Assuming Dodge took care of the preliminaries, he needed pictures of Hubbard to get a mask made. Maybe he got them developed."

"Good thinking," muttered Kell. He jotted down a note on the legal pad in front of him. "Travis, call Whitman and see if he can round up some DPD officers to follow up on that."

The agent snorted. "I don't know how things work with your boss, Burke, but I don't issue directives to the assistant director."

"You don't have to. Just report in and mention it as a logical next step. Or we can text Raiker." Macy glanced up at Kell. "Let him broach it with Whitman."

Burke nodded. "I'll call him. He was going to contact the FBI and Homeland Security and see if he could get a line on Dodge's entrance into the country by checking the airports and passenger manifests. Who knows, maybe one of his known aliases will show up on one. That'd give us the start of a timeline, at least."

"He has to have been staying somewhere in the meantime," Macy mused. She broke off then as the waitress sauntered over. The woman didn't look any happier when the order was only a pot of coffee.

"Yeah, but showing Dodge's picture at every motel and B and B in the area is going to take an army of officers, something I doubt the combined weight of CBI and Raiker can summon. Doubtful he took the girl to wherever he stayed, so what's the point?"

"So where do we suspect he's been so far?" The agent reached over to stab a finger at one of the maps showing Conifer. "On Mulder's estate. Quinn's place on Colfax." He seemed to search the Denver map for a moment before giving up. "Somewhere in the Clear Creek Canyon area since that's where Hubbard's body was dumped."

Kell meticulously circled each of the spots he'd mentioned on the map. "Maybe see if we can get a lead on long-term rentals from the airport," he muttered, his head bent over the legal pad again. "He had to have transportation."

"He drove Hubbard's car to the Mulder estate to report for duty in the guard's place." Gratefully, she picked up the carafe of coffee the waitress set in front of her and filled her cup, since the woman didn't seem to be into full service. "If our suppositions are correct, he had a snowmobile stashed somewhere fairly close to the outside wall he went over with the girl."

"And there were enough snowmobile thefts in the surrounding areas to keep us chasing our tail on that end for weeks," Travis muttered. Wordlessly, he held out his cup. Macy took it and tipped coffee into it, handing it back. His smile of thanks held a little more warmth than she was comfortable with.

"He might be working with someone else," she said, sipping from her own mug. "Once he stashed the snowmobile until he needed it, how did he get back to his vehicle?"

"Unless another body shows up in the area, we can be fairly certain he's working alone." Setting his pen down, Kell reached for his own mug and poured himself a cup. "According to Raiker, that's his MO. And we've seen what happens to people who cross his path in the enactment of the crime. He had a fairly narrow window of opportunity to kill Hubbard." Kell blew gently at the steam rolling off the coffee. "Hubbard's girlfriend had spent the night with him the night before. They'd planned something for the night of the abduction, but Hubbard never answered her calls that evening."

"And where'd you get this information?" Travis's voice held an obvious edge.

"Uh . . . Raiker."

Macy hid a wince, but Kell seemed unconcerned with the lie.

"The man seemed to come across an awful lot of 'tips' while he was away."

"What can I say? The guy knows people everywhere." A bit more hurriedly, Kell went on. "Anyway, Hubbard was on duty the next day. Did Dodge also have access to the guard schedule? Almost had to. He could have staked out the estate and gotten it that way, I suppose. Chose the guard who would be easiest to utilize in enacting his plan. Hubbard was the only one on the security team who lived alone."

"And he was on the duty roster for two days running. Security tapes bear out Cramer's claim that he rode to work with Hubbard the day before the girl was taken. No way Dodge takes the chance of impersonating Hubbard more than the one day he needs to. Why take that kind of risk?"

Kell nodded at her assessment. "So we have the hours between one A.M., when a neighbor saw Hubbard's light on, and sometime before six A.M., when he was due back at the estate."

"Takes at least forty minutes to get from his house to Mulder's," Travis put in.

"Dodge was probably hiding in the house. Park the car on the street in back of the house and cross through the yards. I've already shown you his locks were a joke."

"One to six." Macy stared hard at the map, tracing the distance from Hubbard's house to Clear Creek Canyon with her gaze. "He'd have had to get right on it. That's a lot of traveling if he dumped the body before reporting to work in Hubbard's place."

With the tip of the pen, Kell indicated the maps. "So he kills Quinn several days before the abduction." He touched the spot on Colfax Avenue. "Shows up in Hubbard's house the evening before the girl was taken." He shifted to indicate the Denver street where Hubbard had resided. "Afterward he travels to here." He traced a path to Clear Creek Canyon on the next map. "About how long would that take him?"

The agent stared at the maps consideringly. "An hour. Depends on when the snow started that day. We're figuring he was driving Hubbard's SUV, right? It's equipped for the weather."

But Macy had had another thought. "If he planned to load up the body in Hubbard's own vehicle, how did Dodge get to the man's house? Either a cab or his rental was abandoned on a nearby street. Either way, we check with the Denver police and local taxi companies' dispatch logs, see if we can get a lead on him that way."

Kell gave her a wink. "I knew I kept you around for a reason. Okay." He jotted down the suggestion before returning to the maps. "From the Canyon area he heads to Conifer." He touched all the places on the maps lightly, in the sequence the man had been at each. "If it's me, I'm not going to dump a body near the same area I plan to hole up with the girl." Shifting his gaze to the wilderness maps, he said, "The rangers' office we stopped at yesterday said there are no snowmobiles allowed in the Rocky Mountain National Park. The terrain makes it a perfect place to hide out, but there are no structures allowed there, and the ranger we talked to seemed to think they'd find one pretty quickly if it were built. The park is better staffed with law enforcement officers than are the forests on either side of it. But any of them is in close enough proximity to conceivably reach by sled after snatching the girl."

He looked at Travis, and the man held up his hands. "Don't look at me. Like I told you yesterday, I'm not an outdoorsman. Who has the time, right? There are dozens of remote areas in the state where the girl could be stashed, if . . ." He left the rest of the words unuttered, but Macy understood his meaning.

If she were still alive.

"But not all them are in the vicinity of the crime. And I'm still betting on him remaining in the same area. He hasn't moved out of this locale yet." Kell punctuated his words by tracing along the spots they suspected Dodge had been. "So maybe we need to spend some time going over crimes reported for Denver and the outlying areas."

"We've got two days until the ransom is due." Finishing his coffee, the CBI agent got up and reached for the carafe to pour himself more. "We wouldn't be able to collect all the information in that amount of time, much less pore over it."

"Quinn's death was on the crime blotter in the tip I . . . that Raiker got," Kell corrected his near slip smoothly. "The discovery of Hubbard's body was fed into Coplink."

Travis eyed him suspiciously. "How do you know about Coplink?"

In an effort to distract the man, Macy put in, "What might seem a routine B and E could yield clues if we found, for instance, that only a girl's clothing was stolen." The warmth from the coffee mug was welcome, so she kept her hands wrapped around it. "Or maybe a key is missing to a couple's ski lodge." She looked at Kell soberly. "But Dan's right. We're running out of time."

He pushed away from the table. "All the more reason to mention all this to Raiker so he and Assistant Director Whitman can prioritize."

"And in the meantime?" Travis's reminder of their time-line had frustration sounding in her voice.

Burke flipped through some pages of his legal pad, study-ing it. "The estate is located in Jefferson County. Hubbard's body was also found there. I know of a B and E in Summit County, a rape that occurred in Grand, and an armed robbery of a gas station in Clear Creek County."

"Hard to believe Dodge took time away from the task at hand to commit any of those crimes," Travis observed. He picked up a menu. "Are we going to eat while we're here?"

"Good idea. Let's get something to go." Kell stood up, taking out his cell phone. "I'll check in with Raiker while you order. I need to update him on what we discovered about Quinn anyway." He was already walking away when he called over his shoulder, "Get me a double cheeseburger. Hold the onions."

"Where the hell have you been? I've called twice."

The recorder the caller was using didn't mask the lethal tone. Vincent Dodge stared out the window at the trees crowd-ing the cabin and couldn't find it in himself to care.

"Accidentally shut the ringer off," he lied. The noise behind him had him swinging around, gaze narrowing.

The fucking kid didn't know when to quit. She was rock-ing back on the stool and letting it come down to the floor each time with a thud. Like the noise could alert the person on the other end of this line.

She didn't know that person was the only one as interested as him in seeing her dead.

He had the outerwear stripped off her and she was duct taped to a stool in front of the wood burner, thawing out nicely. It was best to get the blood warm and flowing before he went to work on her. It wouldn't be nearly as satisfying without an arterial gush when he decided to quit playing with her and finish it.

"I thought you were a professional. Amateurish mistakes like that aren't acceptable. Now I'm behind schedule, because you can't follow fucking directions."

Vincent remained silent. His employer would really rage if he knew what had actually transpired. Not that he gave a damn about the man's *schedule*, but there was his reputation to consider. In his line of work, he survived on word of mouth.

So he made an effort at a conciliatory tone. "Sorry about that. What did you want?"

"Fuck, I should have taken care of this myself."

Derision filled him. If the person on the other end of the call had the balls to do so, he wouldn't have hired Vincent in the first place. In his experience, there were a lot of people who wanted murder committed, but few who had the stomach for it.

It had never bothered Vincent. It was, in fact, his only real strength.

But the next words managed to shock him. "I'll need to deliver proof of life in my next communication with the parents. Do you understand?"

"Yeah." Proof of life. Shit. Had things worked out differently, he could have screwed himself out of the second half of his fee. He was used to delivering proof of death, not of life.

He walked over to the chair. The kid's eyes were wide, not with fear this time, but defiance. Dumb bitch. The next time she rocked back, he kicked the stool over. Something approaching amusement flickered inside him when the chair went down hard, her head bouncing against the floor.

"What was that?"

"Tree branch hit the shelter. No big deal."

"Go get a daily paper. *USA Today* would be best. Don't pick up something local, for God's sake. Get a shot of the kid holding it, and get plenty close so you can see her face and the date. Have her read from a story on the front page so the parents will know the newspaper isn't faked."

He stared at the kid, lying motionless on the floor now. She looked a little worse for wear after her adventure in the outdoors. There was a bruise on her face, some scrapes on her legs, and her wrists were scabbed.

Giving a mental shrug, he figured that would just make better viewing. Lucky he hadn't killed her yet. That would have fucked up this man's plans even more.

"Send me the file recording when you finish. I want it in an hour's time."

That got his attention. "What? That's impossible. I'm not in downtown Denver, you know. I don't even know how far I'm going to have to go to find a damn paper."

"That's your problem. You would have had more time if you'd answered the goddamned phone. You can't afford another mistake. Don't make one."

He checked his watch, swore. He was going to have to haul ass down this fucking mountainside. Drag the sled out of its hiding place. And drive who the hell knew how long to find that damn paper.

"After you finish, sit tight with the girl until you get my next call. She stays alive until I give the word, do you understand?"

"Better than you think." The call was disconnected then and he looked at the phone for a moment. He knew something the man on the other end wasn't considering.

There was no way in hell he'd know one way or another exactly when the kid was killed.

Crossing over to the stool, he righted it before dragging it across the floor to her bedroom. He checked her bonds to be sure they were secure and went back for the tape. With quick, deft movements, he fastened the legs of the stool to the cot and then for good measure looped a couple more lengths around her to the frame.

Squatting down in front of her, he tipped her chin up with his hand, his touch almost gentle. "You got a stay of execution, kid. Know what that means? You die tonight instead of right now." He rose, already mentally preparing for the ride ahead. "Enjoy your last few hours."

————————

The Summit County General Store was on the corner of Highway Six and nowhere. But the parking lot outside the structure was still filled with a half a dozen SUVs and a couple pickups. Macy figured that meant business was brisk.

When they walked inside, the elderly man behind the counter looked up. "Be with you folks in a jif." Travis and Kell approached the counter, but she was content to look around first.

The merchandising was a cross between a 7-Eleven and Cabela's. Coolers stocked with milk, soft drinks, and beer lined the back walls. There were guns, hunting knives, and ammunition locked up behind a glass case on another wall. Outerwear in all sizes was crammed on racks scattered throughout the space. Another wall held shelves of Colorado souvenirs and, oddly enough, a selection of chocolates. A large bulletin board next to the entrance was covered with for-sale bulletins and business cards.

Apparently the place was meant to provide one-stop shopping.

When the customers headed for the exit, she joined Kell and Dan at the counter.

"That's right, I'm the owner," the man was saying. "Kevin McLellan. Been here since the birth of the Rockies. That's the mountains, not the baseball team."

It was difficult to resist the smile he aimed at them, delivered beneath a drooping mustache as white as the hair on his head. Macy didn't even try.

"Agent Travis, CBI." Identification was presented, but the agent got no further before McLellan's gaze went wide.

"CBI? And here I didn't think my little break-in was going to get any attention. Deputy Edmonds sure didn't seem too worked up about it. Course it takes a lot to light a fire under him. Often thought his wife should give him a hotfoot every morning, just to put some spark in the man."

"Would you mind running through the details?" Kell asked.

"Well, it's all in the report. Two nights ago someone broke in here and stole nearly a thousand dollars worth of equipment. Edmonds said it was probably kids, which I'm here to tell you is a bunch of bullshit. I've been in business fifty years, and that's long enough to know kids would have checked the register, and then taken beer and guns. I don't mind telling you, Edmonds would never have gotten on in the department if his wife wasn't cousin to the sheriff."

"So no beer or guns were taken?" Patiently, Kell led him back to the statement.

"Told him they weren't. It was a pair of snow pants, coat, gloves, hat, face mask, snowshoes, and backpack." As an afterthought he added, "Oh, and he smashed that case over there to take a knife."

Macy caught Travis's expression. She tended to believe his obvious conclusion that they were wasting their time here. "Pretty specific list."

"What kind of knife?" Kell asked him.

McLellan rounded the corner, surprisingly spry for his years. "Show you." He stopped in front of the case. "Actually got a glass company out here for the repair work almost as quick as Edmonds was to take the report. That has to be a first." He tapped the glass. "It's was a Browning big-game knife. A beauty, too. Bastard took the most expensive model I had."

"And he took nothing else?"

The bell on the door rang, and McLellan craned his neck to see who it was as he answered Kell's question. "Nope. I keep pretty good records of the inventory, but I'm not going to lie and say I'd know if he grabbed a candy bar on his way out."

"How'd he get in?"

"Back entrance. Would you fellows excuse me for a moment?" As if remembering her presence, he looked quickly at Macy. "Ma'am?"

"No problem."

He strode to the door and exchanged good-natured insults with the newcomer, who was obviously known to him.

"There's nothing for us here," Travis muttered, even as Kell started off toward the back entrance. "Someone went shopping for some new winter gear. Snowmobiler, maybe. Or a hunter."

Macy was inclined to agree. "We may as well head over to check out the gas station robbery."

"Better to stop at the sheriff's office first. We can read the report in half the time it takes a witness to tell the story."

"Well, I'll be damned." She looked up at McLellan's delighted voice. "I have to see this." Curious, she trailed him and the newcomer to the door to peer out at what they were admiring in the back of a red pickup.

Then wrinkled her nose when she recognized it. The carcass of a mountain lion was in the bed of the truck. Although she knew many people who enjoyed the thrill of hunting, she didn't pretend to understand their passion for shooting beautiful animals.

"I think we're done here." She started at Kell's voice close to her ear. And mentally damned the zing of warmth that zipped down her spine in response. "What's that all about?"

Grateful to have something else to focus on, she moved away imperceptibly, eager to put some distance between them. "One less mountain lion to threaten humanity."

He sent her a sideways glance. "Not a hunting enthusiast, I take it."

"I'd be out of place in this culture," she admitted. Pushing out the door, she descended the steps, taking pains not to glance toward the pickup again.

McLellan called them over. "Come over and look at this. Ever see such a beautiful creature? Owen here has the devil's own luck."

The hunter had his face mask shoved up to his forehead, revealing a broad face covered with a bushy red beard. "I was afraid the season was going to get away from me without ever bagging anything," he admitted. "This is the first time I hunted the Arapaho Forest. I've always stuck to the Roosevelt before."

She was edging away toward their vehicle. What was it about men and trading hunting stories?

"Well, as soon as your story gets around, everyone and their dog will be hauling ass to the Arapaho. Hope you didn't get the last one."

"Too many people out and about in the forest for my taste. Don't know why the snowshoers and cross-country skiers can't stick to the trails and leave the rest to us. Damn near shot a kid out there yesterday. Walking around in hunting season without wearing any orange is just plain stupid."

"What would a kid be doing out in the forest?"

The hunter shrugged his massive shoulders at Travis's question. "Who knows? I warned a guy just this morning about the very same thing. Claimed he was the one who had made those snow shelters I'd seen, which he was damn lucky didn't collapse on him in the night. But I got to thinking after I directed him back to the one I saw, they were awful small for someone his size." The dog in his pickup barked through the back window, and he looked over, snapped his fingers at it. "Just saying, the wilderness is no place for amateurs."

Macy turned back at the exact time Kell straightened from his stance against the truck. But she beat him to what she knew he was about to say. "Do you think you could show us to the place you saw the those shelters?"

––––––––

"Turns out the guy—Owen Redmond—wasn't all that motivated about being a good citizen. Took a hundred bucks to convince him to take us to one of the shelters he'd seen." Kell was rubbing his hands together as he told the story to Raiker and Whitman. Macy could understand. She was still frozen through, as well. "We also had to buy snowshoes from McLellan to make the trip. Lucky we did. I've never seen so much snow."

"Hats came in handy, too," she murmured. Kell threw her a glance, his eyes glinting. She'd bought one when they were trying on the snowshoes and presented him with it as they followed Redmond to the forest entrance. Had she known, she'd have bought a face mask, too. The wind had been vicious, swirling snow around so wildly that they may as well have been in a ground blizzard.

"We marked the spot so we could find it easily again. Then talked to the Summit County sheriff. He put us in touch with someone who volunteers for the search and rescue team up there. He'll have his trailing dog ready at first light." Kell hunched into his coat, which he still hadn't taken off. "I'll need to take a scent article from the girl's room. He said a toothbrush would be best. Then we'll see if he can catch the same scent at the shelter."

"The area seems to fit." Macy looked at Travis with surprise. His attention was on his boss. "Burke started marking maps with the areas we know Dodge has been. If he stays in a fairly close proximity and wants a remote locale, he could find it in the Rocky Mountain National Park or the Roosevelt and Arapaho Forests. The park is out. Shelters aren't allowed, and there's a much heavier law enforcement presence than in the forests. But temporary shelters can be erected in the Arapaho. I don't think we have anything to lose by checking it out tomorrow."

"Except time," Raiker murmured. He'd been silent during their account. "The girl would have had to have escaped. And then survived a day or two in the forests, in freezing temperatures. As much as I'd like to believe it, it's difficult to think of her outwitting someone like Dodge."

There was a sober silence in the room for a moment before Macy asked, "Has another note come?"

Raiker shook his head. "He'll leave Mulder—and us—as little time as possible to respond. The longer lead time we have, the more preparation we can do to track the payoff. He wants to avoid that at all costs."

"All the more reason to try to follow up on every possibility we have," Kell maintained. "What about the passenger manifests for the airlines?" He'd finally stopped rubbing his hands together and just shoved them back in his coat pockets. His face, Macy noted, was still reddened from the time they'd spent outside. She was sure hers looked the same.

"That's going to take a couple days," Raiker replied. "And since the FBI's new mantra is all terrorism, all the time, it's doubtful Dodge was on any kind of watch list."

"We've added a couple agents to follow up on the AM-BER Alert tip lines," Whitman put in. He was wearing a black suit she'd never seen before. Macy wondered if he'd sent home for it or had been saving it. "The Jefferson County Sheriff's Office is being bombarded with calls. Several supposed sightings come in daily." He made a face. "Of course the majority of them are from out of state."

"Did Jonesy have a report today?" Apparently warmed through, Kell unzipped his coat.

"They were able to match the fibers found in the trunk of Hubbard's car with the carpet in his house. Another match was found in the girl's bedroom and in the room next door."

Macy digested Adam's words in silence. A couple days ago the discovery would have been another sign of Hubbard's guilt. Now it painted another sort of picture altogether.

"Hard to say whether that was purposeful or not," Kell muttered, scrubbing his hands over his face so his voice was muffled. "Dodge had to have planted those prints in the girl's room. Likely did the same thing to the security specs I found behind that filing cabinet drawer at Hubbard's. But he could have transferred the fibers himself. He probably was inside the house, waiting for Hubbard to get home, and did him in the bathroom. A bullet to the head, he falls into the tub, chops the thumb off there. Minimal mess."

"Given the large piece of plastic found in the vicinity of the body, it's likely Dodge wrapped Hubbard's body in a sheet of it and hauled it out to the garage, dumping it in the trunk." Whitman was looking at his watch. "At any rate, the focus of the investigation needs to become more narrow in scope."

Raiker put in brusquely, "While you follow up with the

dog in the morning, we'll put others to work tracking
Dodge's transportation to Hubbard's house. If he took a taxi,
it's not liable to tell us a damn thing. But if he left a car in
the vicinity . . ."

Macy exchanged a glance with Kell. Discovering a vehicle that Dodge had used and then abandoned would be a rare
find, indeed. But she didn't like the odds. The man hadn't left
any trace identifying evidence in Hubbard's car that had shown
up yet. He didn't build a reputation like his making mistakes.

But his DNA had been left behind at least twice, she reminded herself. Once to land him in the CODIS system, and
again with his blood on Ellie's bedsheet. And if a miracle had
occurred and the girl had escaped, that would be another very
big error.

She was going to hold on to that thread of hope until they
were proven wrong.

And she wasn't going to think about how long an eleven-
year-old girl could survive on her own in the wilderness.

The briefing broke up shortly afterward, and Macy got up
and began to drift with the others toward the door. Kell fell in
beside her. "I haven't thanked you properly for the hat. Or for
the fact you put so much thought into it."

She smirked. "You didn't like it?" Tricolored, it had featured earflaps and a large tassel on the top.

"It did the job. But you obviously could use a few lessons
in selecting . . ."

"Macy." They turned to find Raiker approaching. "I've got
a couple interviews set up. I'd like your help with them."

"All right." It was useless to try to search the man's expression because it rarely showed any emotion other than
impatience. But she found herself doing so anyway. If he'd
given any more thought to what he'd mentioned that morning
about firing her, it didn't show. But then, it wouldn't.

She held back until everyone was out of the room, with
the exception of Whitman, who was on his cell phone. "Who's
the interview with?"

"Follow me."

Obediently, she fell into step behind him. He waited until

they were in the hallway and out of earshot before speaking again. "Althea Mulder is in her office waiting for us. I requested that Lance Spencer meet us in fifteen minutes."

"Okay." Mystified, she trailed along beside him until they neared the woman's office. "And we're talking to them because . . ."

"They've got a history of being more than just friends in the past. I want to get an idea of what they are to each other now."

———————

"Adam." Althea Mulder rose at their entrance, one hand seeking the desk beside her, as if for support. She wore lavender wool pants and sweater, with amethysts at her ears and throat. The color highlighted her delicate blond beauty. "I thought . . ." She took in Macy's entrance with a glance before returning her attention to him. "I hoped you had news."

"We're constantly sifting through news, Althea, and prioritizing where to best utilize our efforts." Raiker's ruined voice could never sound gentle, but there was a note of compassion in it. "Sit down. Please."

There was a slight slump to the woman's body, as if a tenuous thread of hope had just been snapped. "Stephen said you have the name of the man who did this. That it wasn't Nick Hubbard at all." She sank back down in her chair as Macy and Adam found seats.

"We're fairly certain we know who carried out the abduction."

And Macy knew intuitively that Althea Mulder hadn't been told who—or what—Vincent Dodge was. Raiker was probably more forthright with the woman's husband. But she'd seen how protective Stephen was of his wife. The information wouldn't have been shared.

"So it should be easier to find him," the woman said urgently. She looked from one of them to the other. "You have a name. That's more than we had the first time Ellie was taken."

"It gives us some avenues to follow, yes."

There was a glint in the woman's eye that might have been temper. "My husband treats me like a hothouse flower, but I'm stronger than I appear, Mr. Raiker. I know you're keeping him informed, but he filters what gets passed on to me."

"Does he have reason for that?"

She looked taken aback. Then as quickly as the temper had appeared, it vanished. "I didn't handle it well last time. Ellie's disappearance . . . she was gone so long. I was under a doctor's care for a time." The woman drew herself up with a faintly regal air. "That would seem like weakness to some. But I got through that terrible time and I'll get through this one. She was brought home safely once. *You* brought her home. She'll come home again. I cling to that certainty."

"A case like this . . . we're buried in information." Adam leaned forward, his hands clasped between his spread legs. "Most of it's meaningless. But each detail gets the same amount of attention because I never know where it might lead. I don't know at first what's important and what isn't."

"All right." Clearly, Althea was lost.

"So what I'm asking you now won't go outside these walls. There's no need for it to. But you have to be frank with me, because I'm the only one who can decide if this information connects to anything else in a meaningful way." He stopped, giving her time to digest his words. "Do you trust me to do that?"

Her gaze was clear. "Mr. Raiker, if we didn't trust you— both Stephen and I—you wouldn't be here."

He gave her a slow nod, as if her response was no more than he had expected. "Are you romantically involved with Lance Spencer?"

She recoiled as if she'd been slapped. And her hesitation was telling. "No, of course not. Why would you ask that?"

"Have you ever been?"

An arrow of sympathy pierced Macy when she took in the stricken look on the woman's face.

"Yes." Her voice was nearly inaudible. "I'm not proud of that. It eats at me every day. Realizing what it would do to

Stephen if he ever knew. I could offer you a hundred excuses but that's all they'd be. I take my marriage vows seriously. And there really is no excuse for infidelity."

"We aren't here to pass judgment," Macy put in gently.

"You don't need to. I already have." The woman's eyes were bright with unshed tears. "So the answer is yes. There was a time eighteen years ago, before Stephen and I became engaged. We'd had a terrible fight. We've never fought like that since. Not ever. I was devastated, certain that we were over. Lance was a shoulder to cry on. And . . ." She looked away, her lips trembling. "Things went too far. Stephen and I got back together two days later. I never told him what had happened. I couldn't have borne it if I were the cause his friendship with Lance ending. And maybe I was trying to spare myself, as well."

Something seemed to ease in Raiker. Straightening in his chair, he murmured, "Ancient history."

"Yes, that time." She drew in a shuddering breath, then met his gaze squarely. "But it happened again three years ago."

"This is none of your damn business."

Lance Spencer's Greek god good looks were as polished as ever. His diplomacy was not. The glare he shot them encompassed both Macy and Adam. "What's between Thea and me doesn't have anything to do with Ellie's disappearance. Or with either of you."

"She says there's nothing between you." Adam had instructed Macy to take the lead with Spencer. But the fierceness of his glare when it settled on her told her that he wasn't going to be any more forthcoming with a woman.

He recovered quickly. "There isn't. Stephen's one of my best friends. I felt lower than a snake about betraying him."

"Hard to imagine, then, you doing so again just three years ago."

He eased back, her words clearly taking him by surprise. "Why would you say something like that?"

It occurred to Macy that he should have been the lawyer,

as adept as he was at dodging direct answers. "Why do you think?"

He was silent for several moments. Then he muttered a curse under his breath. "You spoke to Thea?"

It was interesting that her husband didn't call his wife by the diminutive of her name, but this man did. Macy tucked the observation away to be considered later.

"I thought your outfit was brought in to help." This was directed at Raiker, with a look that would have scored metal. "How the hell do you consider it helpful to pile one more thing on a grieving mother?" As if driven to move, he lunged from his chair. Paced. "Neither of us is proud of what happened between us. Either time. But it has absolutely nothing to do with this case."

"But does it have something to do with you picking up roots and accompanying Mulder to Colorado?"

"Jesus." His look toward her then was almost appreciative. "Your appearance is deceptive. You don't pull any punches. Like I say, Stephen and I have been close for two decades. I did my stint with Wall Street firms out of grad school, made my rep and my first million, both on my own. I didn't need to take the job when he first offered it. I wanted to."

"But wanting to work with him in DC is a far cry from moving to the Rockies to continue that work."

He shrugged, slipped his hands in the pocket of his tailored trousers. "Maybe I figured I owed him, did you ever think of that?" There was a flash of something in his expression that might have been remorse. "He gave me options. I could have stayed put and done a lot of my work electronically, flying out here monthly as needed. But I let him down in the worst way possible. With Mark and Stephen heading out here, I had nothing tying me to DC. What was stopping me?"

"Maybe the question is, what drew you out here?"

At Macy's response, he seemed to choose his words carefully. "I'm not sure you can understand. But this guy has suffered more than anyone else I know. Unimaginably. I'm glad I could be here for him." He gave a wry smile. "And it doesn't hurt that I'm getting rich in the process. What happened between Althea and me . . . that eats us up. But it isn't going to stop me from being here for Stephen. As long as he needs me." He lifted an Armani-clad shoulder. "Make of that what you will."

Raiker took over then, leading the man through more questions, all of which Spencer fielded with the ease he'd displayed the first time Macy had spoken to him. She watched him speculatively until he exited the room.

"Impressions."

She smiled a little at the familiar wording. In the training classes they were required to take when not on assignment, he'd often present his consultants with a set of circumstances or film clip, ending with the same demand.

"Hard to tell who he's trying to fool." Her stomach growled, reminding her that she hadn't eaten since the limp salad the waitress had packaged for her at the diner. "I don't doubt that he feels a real connection to Stephen Mulder. Fueled partly by their long friendship. Strengthened by guilt."

Her gaze went to the closed door. "But that's secondary to his primary reason for sticking with the business. Uprooting himself to move to Colorado. He's in love with Althea Mulder."

Raiker made a disparaging sound in response. Positioning his cane closer, he heaved himself up from the delicate wingback chair he'd been sitting in.

"Primal emotions are often at the root of all motivations." She took pleasure turning some of his other oft-spoken words around on him. He hadn't mentioned their conversation of this morning. She knew he wouldn't, unless he came to the decision that she had become expendable with her decision of yesterday. In any case, it wasn't a topic she was going to broach.

Raiker would do as he saw fit, for his own reasons. Macy's palms grew damp just thinking about it. She decided, as she rose to move toward the door, that she was in no particular hurry to discover if she was going to be unemployed after this job. She had more than enough things to worry about.

Castillo's taunts about Ian were always there, scurrying

about her mind like vicious little ants. Even considering them felt like a betrayal of the man who'd raised her since her mother's death when she was five. She knew what Ian was to her. What he'd always been. Just as she realized what Enrique Castillo was capable of.

But there had also been some truth to the information he'd revealed about John LeCroix's son.

Resolutely, she shoved it from her mind as she followed Raiker out the door. Of course he'd couch the most outrageous accusation within a layer or two of fact. It was the habit of most liars.

But realizing that had her wondering if there was an element of truth in the man's claims about Ian. And Macy hated that, certain it was exactly the response Castillo had been seeking. Like the poison Kell had called it, the lies sought to destroy anything good that had survived him.

She didn't want it to taint the only family she had left.

Belatedly, she realized Raiker was speaking again.

"Love and sex just muddy the issue. Any issue. They lend an unpredictability to events and reactions that can be difficult to filter out when making conclusions about a case. People always see more clearly without either hazing their instincts."

For a moment she was taken aback, a splinter of guilt stabbing through her. Raiker was almost uncanny in his perceptions, so it wasn't necessarily paranoia that had her wondering uneasily if he knew about her and Kell.

In the next instant, she recovered. Although her boss defined the term *close-lipped*, he had no compunctions about rendering an opinion on the actions of his employees, as she'd learned just this morning. If he had a notion of how she and Kell had spent the night, or more exactly, the morning, he'd have called them on it.

Which would have been redundant, in any case. Macy had already done an excellent job of berating herself all day.

She just wasn't any closer to determining what she was going to do about it.

Chapter 15

Vincent Dodge finished redoing her bonds so the kid's hands would be free. He'd been overly diligent about securing her before he'd had to leave the cabin again for that paper. She was fixed tightly. In the end, he'd finally pulled out his knife to cut through them, pausing to relish the panic in the kid's eyes.

Her fear was mildly satisfying. But not as much as he'd hoped.

Maybe he'd wasted his time by taking this job. Perhaps adding a kid to his resume wasn't going to provide the spark he'd hoped for. This numbness had been spreading for a long time. What were the chances one job would change that?

"Here." He slapped the newspaper against her chest. "When I get ready to record, you're going to hold it up in front of you. Then when I point at you, you're going to turn it to read one of the stories on the front page out loud."

Her arms and torso were still tied to the chair, but she gestured toward her face with one of her free hands.

"Forgot. I must have been too busy enjoying the silence."

He went to her and ripped off the tape he'd had covering her mouth and then back to the bag he kept beneath his cot for the instructions for the phone. He wasn't a technophobe, but he made it a point to learn only as much as a given job required. Goddamned computers and cell phones were ruining the world. He could appreciate their usefulness and still be convinced of that.

He took the time to read over the directions carefully, to use the diagrams to figure out how to run the video camera feature on the satellite phone. Then he replaced them in the bag, eager to have this whole thing over with.

And start on the real highlight of this job.

But when he picked up the phone, the kid started talking. "I don't read very well."

"Don't fuck with me. Follow the instructions or we'll skip straight to the next step." He paused long enough for her to get his meaning. "I'm sure you're as eager as I am to get to that part."

It'd be more satisfying, he thought, if she'd cry. Big fat tears accompanied with pleading or screams of anguish. Or maybe it'd just be annoying. He'd eaten that up when he'd first started this line of work for the Giovanni family. But in truth, it had gotten old. Which is why he'd switched from knives to guns in the first place. Over quickly and tidily with little interaction with the target.

Maybe that had been when he'd started losing the joy from his job, too.

"You think I'm lying, but I'm not. I was kidnapped before and held for two years. I didn't go to school all that time. My tutor says I lost instruction during my formative years."

He stopped messing with the settings of the camera long enough to look at her. "I don't give a shit about your sad story or your mother-fucking tutor. Jesus." He walked rapidly over to her and took the paper from her, scanned it. "Here." He stabbed at a story and held the damn thing in front of her face so she couldn't help seeing it. "It's about schools and No Child Left Behind." He gave her a thin smile. "That's called irony, kid. You reading about the state of public education in the country today. Because you're going to be left very far behind." He put some distance between them and zoomed in on her. "Now hold up the paper."

She obeyed. About time she did something she was told. She wouldn't have lasted long around his old man. He'd have worn the Bible out beating some obedience into her.

He hit record. Got in close to get the date like he'd been told. And when he gave her the signal, the girl turned the paper over and frowned down at it. He was about ready to turn off the camera and go give her a slap upside the head to remind her who was calling the shots, when she started reading.

Slowly. Painfully.

He grimaced, continued filming. School hadn't been his thing. No interest, for one thing, and thanks to his old man, he'd missed his share. But he could still remember the embarrassment of having to stand up to read in front of his class, although he'd never been as bad as this kid, stumbling over words and switching letters around. You'd think with her family's money, they could have gotten her a tutor who could teach her something.

Really, he'd be doing her a favor by killing her.

In less than a minute, he was finished. He stopped and texted the familiar number. Sent the video.

Then put the cell phone back in his pocket and considered the kid.

Severing the carotid arteries and the jugular vein in one practiced slice would be a quick, almost instantaneous death. He knew enough to realize there'd be no returning thrill in that. She'd put him through too much to let her off that easily.

"You know what flaying is?" He watched her face avariciously. Her fear would feed his satisfaction, which in turn would fuel the returning joy. He needed that response from her. Demanded it.

She shook her head.

"It's a particularly brutal form of corporal punishment. Should be reserved for the politicians of this country, if you ask me." He reached in his shirt and withdrew his knife. Not the one he'd packed in his luggage, but the one he'd stolen from that store. It was a beauty, a far better sample than he'd expected to find in the mountains.

He admired it for a moment, held it up to the light so she could appreciate the glint of the blade. "This particular Browning is made for skinning big game. You're not as large as an elk, so I figure it will do fine. Ever peeled an apple?"

She was still, fighting to keep any expression from her face, he could tell. That wouldn't last long. He wouldn't allow it. "My granny used to do it real fast." He mimed holding an apple in one hand. "Round and round she'd go, until she had the whole thing off, in one single peel. That's what I'm going to do to you."

"That won't help."

He drew back. "Won't help you much, no. But you'll be dead soon anyway, so who the fuck cares?" Her eyes met his. Weird, weird eyes for a kid. Eyes that saw too much.

"It won't help *you*. You can't get feeling back that way."

"What the fuck do you know?" He tried to reach for his earlier anticipation, but it was slipping away. She wasn't reacting the way he'd hoped. The way that he needed her to.

"I know." Her whisper was almost too low to hear. "I know what it's like to be numb inside. And I know how to make the numbness go away."

———

Dawn hadn't even begun to lighten the sky outside his window. Because it was better than pretending he could sleep, Kell had gotten up, showered, and dressed. He'd been surprised last night when Denise Temple had sent an updated Coplink report to his e-mail account. There was nothing else. No personal note. No statement of grief.

And Kell had understood. She was furthering the investigation in the only way she knew how, and sometime when this was over, he'd have to be sure to thank her for that. Although Assistant Director Whitman had to be accessing the same information, it had yet to show up in any report he'd seen. It hadn't been until Raiker's return that they had

280 I KYLIE BRANT

gone back to at least the semblance of partnership with the man.

But nothing on the reports jumped out at him. If this dog trailing operation didn't pan out this morning—and even he knew it was a long shot—they were running short on time.

And so was Ellie Mulder.

Swearing, he shoved away from the computer and went in search of a heavy sweater to wear in place of a suit jacket. It was all too easy to recall just how cold it had been following Redmond up to that spot in the forest. He pulled one from his suitcase but didn't put it on yet. Wearing it inside would have him roasting in under ten minutes.

Instead he paced. Usually the movement helped him think. But lately he'd learned he thought even better when he was able to bounce ideas off Macy. Her commonsense practicality helped ground him, even though he gave her a hard time about it.

Cocking his head, he listened for sounds coming from her room. There weren't any. It'd been late when she retired last night. And although he was still up, he hadn't gone next door, hadn't made up an excuse to see her.

She'd requested time, and space. Although he'd failed miserably with his mother, he'd become fairly adept in adulthood at supplying women with what they wanted while still doing exactly as he wished. He was still trying to figure out the delicate balance of granting her the time she'd asked for and making it too easy for her to elbow him aside again once this case was over.

In the predawn hours, he made a point of not lying to himself, so he didn't bother pretending he had any intention of letting her walk away this time.

He was male enough to be scared to death about that.

The knock at the door had him starting. With the sweater grasped in his hand, he crossed to it and pulled it open. Saw his boss in front of Macy's door now. "Downstairs, five minutes."

Even for Raiker the message was short. He called after his retreating back, "What's going on?" But only one event could account for the palpable tension in the man's posture.

"Another ransom note just arrived."

———————

Raiker and Whitman were speaking to the Mulders when Macy and Kell walked into the office. Two CBI agents were already there. What little hair Dobson had was mussed in the back. Someone already had coffee in pots on the table with a sleeve of foam cups next to it. Macy made a beeline for it.

"The message came in twenty minutes ago." Whitman looked up as more agents entered behind them. "We've been monitoring the account in the duration. Dobson was on when this came in."

Forgetting about coffee for the moment, Macy joined the crowd around the computer screen. But expecting to see text, she was shocked to see a picture. She leaned forward for a better look. "Is that video?"

"Very poor quality. This is as good as I can enhance it without calling in the techies." There was an underlying thread of excitement in Dobson's usually matter-of-fact voice.

Poor quality was right. Macy squinted at the screen. If she'd been seated at the table, the distance would have made identification difficult. But this close it was impossible to deny. The girl on the screen was Ellie Mulder.

"Quality's not good enough to make out the newspaper's date." Whitman came up behind her. "But that can be verified. And he's making it easier for us. See for yourself."

The video was less than a minute. And Macy found herself looking at the girl more closely than she listened.

The pajamas she wore were likely the ones she'd worn the night of the abduction. Her hair hung dull and listless. It was obvious that she'd suffered in the duration. Her hands, holding the paper, had contusions around the wrists. There was bruising on her face.

But her voice was strong and clear, if emotionless, as she read from the news story.

At the end of the video, Dobson started it again without being asked.

"Proof of life," Althea Mulder whispered behind her. Macy turned to see a bright sheen of tears in the woman's eyes. "That's what I dreamed for. She's alive." Clinging to her husband for support, she repeated, "She's alive."

"How does she sound to you?" Macy asked.

"Traumatized," Stephen Mulder surprised her by saying grimly. He and his wife wore thick luxurious robes over their pajamas with matching slippers. They were the only ones in the room who hadn't bothered to change clothes before rushing downstairs at the news. "When we got her back the first time, it was like she'd forgotten everything she'd learned in school. Her reading was stumbling and broken like we're hearing here. The tutor we hired has done wonders. She's reading on grade level again. But now . . ." He pressed his lips tightly together for a moment. "It's like listening to her two years ago."

"She's scared." Althea stared at the screen with swimming eyes, one fist pressed to her lips. "It doesn't show, but she's so frightened, I can tell. Oh, my baby. My poor baby." She turned to her husband, whose arms opened automatically for her.

"I've got verification," Pelton called from the laptop he was manning at the conference table. For his audience's benefit, he zoomed in on the screen. "It's this morning's issue of *USA Today*. And that story she's reading from is below the fold, front page."

"This is good news, people," Whitman said. Macy wondered if he'd gone to bed at all. He was clad in the same clothes he'd worn the previous evening. "We can expect the video to be quickly followed by . . ."

"We've got another message," Dobson called out laconically.

This time Macy hung back as Whitman and Raiker peered at the computer. With a stab of a finger, Dobson had the e-mail printing out.

"Arrogant son of a bitch," Whitman muttered. Straightening, he made a gesture to Dobson, who passed out the copies he'd just run.

As you can see your daughter is alive for now. If you're smart she can be back home with you soon. Be at the bank tomorrow ready to move the money at three a.m. I'm sure you can arrange it. You'll be contacted again.

Remember her future is in your hands.

"How do we know he'll really let her go?" Althea's voice was barely audible. Pulling away from her husband, she said more firmly, "How can we be sure that he intends to release her tomorrow?"

"He hasn't given us a reason to believe he won't." Raiker looked down at the paper in his hand again. "He recognized that you'd require proof she was alive. This message was primarily to deliver that. By sending it the day before the ransom is due, he's trying to guarantee your cooperation, while still not leaving you any way to discuss or negotiate it."

Assistant Director Whitman looked over at Dobson, who was still hunched over the computer. "How fast will you be able to get the owner of the IP address?"

"It's different from the one used before, but it'll be a lot quicker than last time, since we placed that patch on Mr. Mulder's e-mail account."

Macy noted the answer didn't seem to pacify the man. "The sooner we have an owner, the sooner I can get a warrant. Although it's likely he just cruised a different part of town and found another unsecured network." His smile was grim. "At least we know the sender is in the vicinity."

Adam went to stand next to Stephen. "We'll take this as good news," he said bluntly. "There was no reason to send proof of life with the first note, because you'd be questioning at this point if Ellie were still alive. Too risky for him to wait until tomorrow, because without it you might balk at the final payoff or not work as hard at liquidation. He had two reasons for contacting you today. To deliver the proof and to remind you of what you stand to lose if you don't cooperate."

"I'd say he was successful on both points." He clutched the paper in his hand as if it were a lifeline. "He was hedging his bets, but we would have paid anyway." Macy found herself looking away from the raw emotion on his face. "How could we not?"

"Agent Whitman and I have been making plans for the payoff." Adam eased his hips on the corner of the conference table. On another person it would have been a casual pose. She knew him well enough to recognize that he did it to alleviate the pressure on his leg. "The timing of the transfer will be tricky, but with CBI's help we can arrange it with the bank. Whitman will have a team equipped and ready to follow the money if it's to be a physical drop. If it's electronic, I have a system in place to try to track the money, possibly even divert it if we find your daughter at the last minute."

"No."

All eyes turned to Althea Mulder. She looked brittle, as though she would shatter in a million pieces if someone touched her. "We don't want anyone trying to follow the money or whoever comes to pick it up. We just want to pay and bring Ellie home."

Whitman's voice was gruff. "We all want that. But as you mentioned earlier, we can't trust his promises for a safe return. Something could go wrong. We have to be prepared for anything."

And it struck Macy then that everyone in the room except for Althea knew what Vincent Dodge was. There was no reason to have shared that information with the woman. Even a whisper of knowledge could be more cruel than ignorance.

She'd recently learned that for herself.

"Can we have a copy of that video?" Althea leaned against her husband now, as if that objection had left her weak. "When you're done doing whatever you need to do with it, will we get a duplicate?"

"Of course."

She seemed to take Adam at his word, because when her husband said, "Come. We have to leave the agents to their work," she left without protest.

There was a moment of silence when the conference room door closed behind them.

"We have to find the girl before three A.M. tomorrow."

Kell headed to the table for coffee, his voice grim. "Unless Dodge has changed his specialty, she's dead as soon as the money gets paid."

Because she was close enough, Macy elbowed him. Hard. The movement jostled his arm so he spilled some of the steaming liquid on the table.

He sent her a reproving look. But before he could speak again, Adam put in, "Paulie Samuels put together a file on Dodge. Given his talent for information gathering, I suspect it's at least as complete as any that an individual law enforcement entity has on him. Dodge has a particular set of skills that makes him attractive for specific jobs, yes. But he's honed other skills to make the enactment of his jobs easier. He likes to stalk his victims, so he has the patience for this sort of task."

Kell surprised her by handing her the first cup he'd poured before filling another for himself. Macy sipped from it gratefully as Raiker continued. "Some of the jobs attributed to Dodge had him waiting inside the home of his victims, so he's got some talent in circumventing security. He couldn't have managed the patch on Mulder's video feed himself, and the specs he planted in Hubbard's house also indicate he had some help with the security. But Kell is right about one thing."

A feeling of foreboding trickled down Macy's spine, and she raised her gaze to meet Raiker's.

"There was absolutely no reason to pay the price for an assassin if he wasn't going to be used in that capacity." He looked around the room, his visage grim. "Ellie Mulder's chances of being found alive plummet drastically after the ransom is paid."

There was the sound of a throat being cleared. But the gravity of the prediction kept the room silent for long moments.

Whitman finally broke the quiet. "We've divided all agents into teams of two or three and assigned each team a specific task. We're going to come at this from as many ways possible, people. We've got less than twenty-four hours."

286 | KYLIE BRANT

"I've got one of my men on his way. He'll go directly to the bank Mulder will use. He and another operative have been working on this from headquarters for a few days. They've developed a dandy little spybot to install on a designated bank computer if this money goes electronically."

Raiker had to be talking about Samuels, Macy knew. There was little he couldn't do with a computer. He always joked that he was matchless in his prowess with technology and cards. Although he'd likely been working with Gavin Pounds, another of Raiker's cyber wizards, it would be Samuels on-site in Colorado. He was Raiker's right-hand man.

"Burke and Agent Travis will follow up with the dog and trainer, Macy." Raiker looked at her. "You'll want to do another threat assessment. Compare the notes, although there's no reason to believe they weren't generated by the same person."

Macy nodded, but the entire process would probably only take a couple hours. If there was a positive match on both notes, there was no reason to run this newest one against the written communication samples again. The threat assessment tests always took the longest.

And she was certain she'd discover the threat implicit in this note just as real as in the last.

An hour later, Macy had ascertained that the same person authored both ransom notes. It would be well over an hour before the database results were done on the threat assessment, however. At loose ends, she called Raiker with the results she had so far and asked that he have Ellie's video e-mailed to her.

When she downloaded it a few minutes later and watched it, once again she focused on the child's demeanor and injuries.

It was all too easy to guess where the bruises had come from but more difficult to figure the source of the scabbing around her wrists. Rope lacerations might be the cause, although tape was used for her other bonds. Macy puzzled over it a while longer, before starting it over and turning up the volume.

The halting, stumbling reading had her wincing, and her opinion of the girl's tutor, Becker, sank even further.

To be fair, of course, Stephen had indicated the poor reading was a thing of the past, brought out again by trauma. That was probably the case, she decided, replaying the video yet again. There didn't seem to be a pattern to the girl's mistakes, as there were for poor readers. Few reversals. No confusion between *wh* and *th* words.

Because she had nothing else to do for the duration of the test, she looked up the news story and ran it off on her portable printer so she could compare the oral reading of the story to the copy. There were substitutions and omissions of small words and word parts, she noted. But never the same one twice.

Idly, she began to mark her copy of the news story with the girl's mistakes, although she was becoming more sidetracked with the sound of her voice. There should have been fear palpable in her tone. In her expression. But she was strangely emotionless.

And that, too, was a sign of trauma.

Studying the copy she'd made with the girl's errors, she decided to save it for the tutor. When—not if—the girl was returned safely, he would have more remediation to do.

The first mistake was the girl substituting *for* for the word *from*. Then later she substituted a word ending. There was actually more stumbling and false starts than actual errors. She'd read *cable* for *table*. *A* for *the*. A reversal of the letter *b* for a *d* in a word. *In* for *on*. *White* for *when*.

Macy straightened suddenly, looked harder at the sheet. Getting a fresh page of paper, she jotted the errors down in order. When she was done, all she could do was stare incredulously.

The girl hadn't reverted to her earlier reading difficulties at all.

She'd been sending them a message.

Forest. Cabin. White.

She waited impatiently for the threat assessment to finish, taking it downstairs and presenting her findings to Raiker and Whitman, who appeared in the middle of a strategy session.

"The authorship on the two notes is the same." It would have been startling to find out otherwise. "And the threat issued is real."

That, too, was unsurprising. But she got more of a response when she showed them what she'd found by analyzing Ellie's reading errors.

Raiker's smile was fierce. "This little girl has some serious guts. I'm going to make damn sure I meet her."

Whitman stared at the sheet she'd prepared for a while longer. "What about the rest of the errors?" He stabbed his finger at the jumble of letters and words at the bottom of the sheet.

"I couldn't make any sense of them," Macy admitted. Excitement was still tripping in her veins. This was the same little girl that Becker, the tutor, had pronounced as being capable of little creative thought. Her estimation of the man, never very high, bottomed out.

"There are eleven forests in Colorado," Agent Whitman pointed out. His eyes had deep circles beneath them. "Over twenty million acres of forested land. And any heavily wooded area would look like a forest to a child. In this state, anytime you get out of the city you're surrounded by wooded areas."

"She'd understand that, having lived here for two years. It makes sense that she isn't being held too far from here, though," Macy maintained, her earlier excitement somewhat dimmed by the facts. She'd done a little research of her own. The combined Rocky Mountain National Park and Roosevelt and Arapaho Forests accounted for millions of those acres.

"It's a piece of information we didn't have before. But unfortunately . . ." Raiker nudged his laptop around so she could see the screen. "The weather forecast for this area doesn't look good. Another winter storm is on its way, and the areas closest to the mountains will be hit first." She followed the direction his finger was pointing on the screen to see the moving system he was referring to. "Kell and Travis are liable to find themselves right in the middle of it."

"Levi Feldman." After the introduction, the dog handler lost no time following Agent Travis's gesture to get in the vehicle. Pulling open the door to the backseat, he slid in and slammed the door quickly after him.

"Agent Dan Travis. Consultant Kellan Burke."

Feldman bobbed his head to each in return. "Colder than a bitch this early in the morning." He looked delighted when Kell handed back a large steaming cup of coffee he'd picked up at the general store. "Hey, thanks. This'll help."

"So let me give you the scenario," Travis started.

Feldman held up a gloved hand. "I'd rather you didn't. Sheriff Preske said you needed a trailing dog, and he called me. If I have too many details, I'd be afraid of prejudicing the dog." He sipped from the coffee before continuing. "Belle is one of the best I've seen, but these dogs are trained on the reward system. If she senses I want her to go a certain way and she figures that's what she needs to do to get her treat, it increases the likelihood of a false trail."

"Okay." Kell took the ziplock bag out of the heavy parka he was wearing and handed it to the man. McLellan had made out like a bandit on this deal. Like the salesperson he was, once he figured they were going on a search this morning, he'd started peddling the gear they'd need, at what he claimed was a steep discount. Kell was willing to guess that the hefty price tag they'd paid had more than made up for what the man had lost in the break-in earlier that week.

"Good, you got her toothbrush." Levi shoved the bag in the pocket of his coat. He was outfitted in a similar manner to Kell and Travis. The frigid wind on the mountainside was unforgiving. "It's always more difficult getting a scent with a kid. Lots of time a mom has folded their clothes, right, and put them away. Made the kid's bed. Too many competing smells. But a toothbrush comes packaged and the saliva is a good source of scent." He gave a quick grin that settled his face into deep vertical creases. "Let's just hope she didn't drop it."

"So." He took another quick gulp from the cup. "You've got a PLS?" At their uncomprehending looks, he explained, "A place last seen?"

"We have a possibility. Marked it yesterday."

The man nodded. "Snow trail is always more difficult, but Belle has logged lots of hours in this sort of weather and terrain. If the scent is there, she'll pick it up. How far away is the spot you marked?"

Kell unfolded a map of the Arapaho that he'd picked up in the store yesterday. Redmond had been prevailed upon to help mark the area where they'd flagged the shelter. "Okay, sure. Looks to be about ten miles from here. Why don't you let me keep the map, and I'll jump in the truck and lead you there. I want to get as close as I can before I let Belle out. In this sort of terrain and weather, she'll wear out quicker than she does normally."

"Do we need to stay back, out of the way while she works?"

Levi gave him another quick grin as he opened the door. "Naw, once I give her the scent article, she isn't going to pay much attention to you. You'll be fine. But we'll have to work fast. I hear another storm is headed our way and will probably hit the area by early evening." He stopped then, seemed to think of something, and headed back to their SUV.

"You guys are going to want your own snowmobile. We're going to be doing lots of walking." He pointed in the direction of the general store. "You can rent one at the store. Just ask for Kevin McLellan."

———

While Feldman waited, Kell and Travis came to an arrangement with McLellan. Then the agent drove the SUV back to where the dog handler waited, and Kell followed him on the sled. They trailed Feldman as he found an entrance to the forest and parked his vehicle at the side of the road several miles inside, backed up against a snowbank. Then he hopped out of the truck and went to the back, lowered the tailgate. He had a snowmobile in the bed, which he started up and slowly drove off the truck, onto the bank. Then he got off and went back to the truck to hitch up a small covered trailer he had there.

"Insulated kennel," he explained as he worked quickly to hook it to the back of the sled. "Helps save up Belle's energy as we move from spot to spot." He shot them a quick look. It was difficult to tell with the face mask he wore, but Kell was certain he was grinning again. "You guys will have to double up."

Since he'd expected no less, Kell nodded and followed Travis back to the vehicle. He zipped up the coat he wore over several layers, including the snow pants he'd acquired at McLellan's, and took the hat out of his pocket. He was certain Macy had picked out the one most guaranteed to embarrass him, but he wasn't worried about logging fashion points out here. He donned a face mask and then pulled the hat on over it, covered it with the hood. And tried not to think about how much he hated winter.

After what seemed like an endless ride, they pulled to a stop behind where the handler had halted. "This doesn't look like the same area," Travis muttered as they trudged up to meet Feldman. "Maybe he misread the map."

"Maybe he can't use the sled farther in," Kell responded. The deep hood on the parka was coming in handy. Although it impeded peripheral vision, it served as a windbreak for the wicked wind. He was still getting the hang of the snowshoes they wore. "Looks like the terrain gets a bit trickier."

But when they reached the other man, they learned they were both wrong.

"Ready. We're precasting," Levi said into a handheld radio as he snapped a long line on the dog and let her go. Belle bounded through the snow for a ways, and then paused to sniff the area. He tucked the radio into his pocket. "The sheriff sent the radio with me. We always report every stage of a search." Before they could ask, he went on, "She needs to get used to the different smells so when we settle down to work for good, she'll be focused."

"How long does it take to train a dog for this kind of

work?" Real interest was apparent in the CBI agent's words. He wore skier sunglasses that made Kell wish he'd remembered to bring his prescription sunglasses from the glove compartment of the SUV. Though the sky was gloomy, the unrelenting starkness of the white landscape, punctuated with decked-out trees, was hard on the eyes.

"Depends on the dog's age and what sort of work it's being trained for. But generally a year or two. It's very labor-intensive. My group trains two or three times a week." Feldman let the dog roam around for a while longer before whistling. When it returned, he bundled it back into the kennel and fired up the snowmobile again.

The next time he stopped, they were close enough to the shelter they'd been shown the day before to see the tree branch they'd shoved into the snow in front of it. "Am I close?" Levi asked as they caught up with him.

Kell pointed a gloved finger. "It's a half a mile or so in that direction. See the bough upright in the snow?"

"Let's get started then." He took his radio out again and took time to check in with the sheriff's office. "Casting now." Tucking it away in his pocket again, he went to the kennel and freed the dog, keeping a hand on its collar. He exchanged the collar for a harness and then stood up again, brushing the snow from his pants. "When she's in harness she knows it's work time." Straddling the dog, he pulled the ziplock bag from his pocket. He opened it and held it in front of the bloodhound for several minutes. "Check it." Then he put the scent article back in his other pocket and snapped a leash on the dog's harness. "Okay, Belle. Find her."

The handler and dog made a slow wide circle. Kell and Travis hung back a ways. Despite what Feldman had said, he didn't want to take the risk of distracting the dog. He wished he'd remembered to ask how'd they'd know that the dog had picked up a scent. It seemed lackadaisical to him, alternately scenting the air and the ground before it.

The handler called back, "Luckily it's dry snow. Easier for a dog to work in than wet and packed stuff."

After fifteen minutes only inching slightly closer to the

shelter, the agent said, "Belle doesn't seem to be picking up on anything."

"We'll give it more time." But his once keen hope was beginning to fade, as well. They'd known it was a long shot. But there hadn't been enough good leads in this case to overlook this one.

And he was very much aware of the ticking clock with the delivery of that most recent note.

"Maybe I spoke too soon."

But Kell didn't need Travis's words to call his attention to the changing scene ahead. The dog was pulling hard at the leash, forcing Feldman along in its wake.

It was heading toward the shelter they'd marked yesterday.

Adrenaline spiking in his veins, Kell moved more quickly in the handler's wake. The dog tugged at the leash as it charged ahead. "It's picked up the scent?" he called.

Feldman turned around enough to give them a thumbs-up. "Sure acts like it."

———

Macy heard the roar of the snowmobile and pushed away from the bumper of the vehicle to start out to meet it. Her movements were clumsy. This was her first experience wearing snowshoes and they definitely took some getting used to. Carefully, she began to sidestep down the embankment. Halfway down, one foot went out from beneath her. She slid the rest of the way down on her butt.

And of course fate *would* have the sled pulling up at that exact moment. Odd that she recognized the identity of the driver, despite his being covered from head to toe. There was something about the way Kell held himself that was immediately familiar.

Or maybe she was just too used to fate's warped sense of humor. Her ignoble fall earned her a thumbs-up from him.

"Is that so little to ask? You falling at my feet whenever you see me?"

She struggled up and brushed herself off. "Gentlemanly to the end."

Another man dismounted from the sled with him and they both headed toward her. "Are you all right?" It was Agent Travis's voice. "Easy to hurt yourself falling like that."

Kell reached her first. Tipped his head in to murmur in her ear, "I'd be more than happy to do that for you, but I'm easily distracted."

Didn't she know it. One snowshoe had come off with her slide, and she grabbed a low-hanging evergreen branch to steady herself as she attempted to put it on again.

"Leave them off. We're heading down the road to drive Feldman's truck and the SUV up here. You can help."

They all climbed into the vehicle she'd driven, a four-wheel-drive Tahoe supplied by Mulder. "Where'd you get the gear?" He asked as he started a careful Y-turn.

"It's Althea's." And the woman had been pathetically glad to contribute to the search. Macy couldn't even imagine how unbearable it would be to sit home and wait while others looked for her daughter.

"Raiker filled you in on our progress, right?" The palpable excitement in Kell's voice would be difficult to miss. "I didn't have any luck when I radioed the sheriff. Preske refused to send out a bigger team, but he has to. The dog is tiring, and we're close, Macy, I can feel it. Raiker has to work his magic and get this guy to cooperate."

Trepidation pooled in her stomach. She was already certain of his reaction to the news she'd brought. "Whitman and Raiker both talked to the sheriff. He isn't sending out a search and rescue team with air-scent dogs to broaden the search. He can't. The storm is supposed to hit within the hour."

His head whipped around to stare at her. She knew she was about to add to the shocked anger in his gaze. "Raiker sent me in person to make sure you listened. The sheriff wants us off the mountain now. And Adam doesn't want to risk having more people up here needing rescuing from the storm." Clutching the snowshoes more tightly, she wished she didn't feel like a traitor for putting that look in his eyes.

"He sent me to make sure you follow orders."

Chapter 16

"Bullshit. That's bullshit, Mace." It was more difficult than it should have been for Kell to tamp the rising tide of frustration and anger. "We're close. So damn close. Belle—that's the dog—she's only lost the scent twice. Each time she's picked it up again. Feldman has let her rest and drink a couple times because the terrain is getting more treacherous. But if we just had a little more time. A bigger party. We'd beat the deadline; I know we would."

"I'm as frustrated as you are." He could hear the bleakness in her voice. "But it'll be dark earlier than usual because of the storm. The search has to be over by then anyway. And we can start again at first light tomorrow."

"You know as well as I do that tomorrow will be too late." As if to punctuate his prediction, an arctic blast of wind swept snow from the evergreens that canopied over the narrow road and swirled it across the windshield.

"Dammit, quitting makes no sense when we're this close." Surprisingly, the words came from the CBI agent. "That dog is working magic. We just need a little more time."

"Raiker and Whitman were equally emphatic. I don't dare go back to the estate without the two of you. The last thing I need is to give Adam another reason to fire me."

Her words caught his attention, but after a moment he decided not to pursue it in front of the agent. Raiker had been royally pissed when he'd returned the other night and hadn't found Macy there. And this was the first inkling she'd given Kell about the results of her conversation with the boss.

From the sounds of things, it hadn't gone well. But . . . firing her? For going to see Castillo? It seemed an overreaction, and Raiker wasn't given to overreacting.

But Kell could easily imagine the man's response if they didn't follow the orders he'd sent with Macy.

The mood in the vehicle was dour, and there was very little conversation as they made the trip down the slope so each could drive a vehicle back up it. The ascent reminded him of how much ground they'd covered since this morning. Which just made him less eager to abandon all their work now.

Once back up the narrow road they parked the vehicles at the side of it before mounting the sled. With three of them, it was a tight fit. Kell drove it carefully back to where they'd left the handler and dog. "Maybe I can convince Feldman to give it another fifteen minutes or so," he called over his shoulder to Macy. He was crouched over the tank, leaving the seat to her and Travis. She didn't answer. Probably too busy trying to maintain her grip on three pairs of snowshoes—hers and the men's—while clutching the seat for stabilization. It was her first time on a snowmobile, she'd admitted when she'd awkwardly gotten on. He allowed himself a small grin as he recalled her slide down the embankment when he'd first driven up. He was willing to bet she wasn't much of an outdoorswoman.

He knew her well enough to realize that he'd better be out of reach if he made the observation out loud.

His amusement vanished twenty minutes later when they pulled up near Feldman. "Damn. He's loading up." The handler was crouched down in front of the kennel. Upon their arrival, the man handed a treat to the animal inside and closed and latched the door.

Kell killed the sled, and they all strapped on their snow-shoes before heading toward the man in tandem.

"Maybe he's just resting her again," Travis put in hope-fully.

But Feldman's words dashed that hope. "I was beginning to think you weren't coming back," he called. "We've got to shut this thing down. I just got a second message from the sheriff. He wants us off the mountain, now."

"If we had another half hour," Kell started.

But the other man was already shaking his head. "We don't. Belle's about tapped out. I've run her longer than usual, and this isn't easy terrain. Even if Preske hadn't ordered me to, I'd have had to quit soon anyway."

Digging in his pockets for the man's keys, Kell handed them to him, frustration riding him hard. "We appreciate all your help today."

"Our pleasure. I don't mind saying, Belle's one of the best trailing dogs in this part of the state. If you need us tomorrow to resume the search, have the sheriff give me a call again."

"How far did you get?" Macy had donned a pair of wrap-around sunglasses that Kell was betting was yet another piece of equipment on loan from Althea Mulder.

Feldman pointed to a particularly dense area of trees a mile in the distance. "Had a hard time pulling her off the scent, if you want to know the truth. Got in the middle of those trees, and she acted like it was still strong. That's when the sheriff radioed again."

Kell joined Macy to stare in the direction the man had in-dicated. "What's causing that trail of vapor above the trees?" She pointed. "See it?"

"That's smoke," Feldman answered. "Probably a shelter in the vicinity. Nothing permanent can be constructed, but port-able structures can be erected temporarily. Everything would have to be packed in and be removed again by the end of the hunting season. That'd be my guess."

"Like a cabin?" There was a note to Macy's voice that had Kell sliding a look at her.

"That wouldn't be allowed," the handler answered. "But

I've seen a variety of snow tents or ice-fishing shelters used. Some of the shanties can be made-to-order."

She reached out to grab Kell's arm, the tightness of her grasp apparent even through the heavy layers of fabric. "Maybe we should stay a bit longer. Just long enough to check out that shelter."

"No telling how far away it is." Agent Travis had come up on the other side of her, one hand shielding his eyes as he followed the direction of their gazes.

"It's about a mile to the copse of trees." Feldman fired up the snowmobile, pitching his voice above the noise. "Don't try taking the sled inside them. The trees are too close together. You'd get hung up for sure."

"How far inside them did you get with the dog?" Kell asked, his mind racing.

"Couple hundred yards. Didn't see anything or anyone in the vicinity. The thing is, guys, you really need to listen to the sheriff on this one. The trail could lead through those trees and past whatever structure there is and onward for a dozen more miles. You don't know how serious it is to get caught in a blizzard in these parts." His tone was urgent. "Even the people we rescue alive often end up with limbs amputated." Feldman stopped for a moment and surveyed them. "So I can tell Preske you're right behind me, right?"

"We'll follow you out in a minute," Travis assured him.

With one more glance at the sky, the man lifted a hand and roared off.

"How long do you think it'd take us to get close enough to that structure to be able to tell what color it is?"

Kell's head swiveled to face Macy. "What?"

"That video this morning. All those mistakes she was making?" The thread of excitement in her words spurred an answering emotion in him. "They were clues. Forest. Cabin. White. Ellie was describing the shelter. I'm sure of it. We know she was in the vicinity. The dog followed her scent all day." Tugging urgently at Kell's sleeve, she said, "I can't leave before we first check out the structure inside those trees."

He took little convincing. But he was prepared to argue

down the agent, who struck him as a rule follower of the worst order. Kell visually measured the distance to the sled in case he had to make a dash for it to capture the keys, which in effect would present the man with a fait accompli. "What do you think, Dan?"

"Twenty minutes." The man was already striding toward the snowmobile. "We'll check it out and still likely make it back before the weather hits."

As if to prove him a liar, light snow began falling. But all three of them were already heading for the sled.

The ride to where the trees became denser was thankfully short. They abandoned the sled and once again put on their snowshoes before plunging into the wooded area.

"How'd you figure those reading errors were a message?" The admiration in Travis's tone dissipated the earlier kindness Kell had felt toward the man for agreeing to spend a bit more time up here.

Macy gave them what Kell was certain was an abbreviated version of events. "Ellie's gutsy." There was an odd note of pride in the word. "After all she's been through, this little girl hasn't fallen apart. She'd never have been able to think clearly enough to plan something like this otherwise."

"Well, it was a good catch on your end."

Kell quickened his pace. This outing was going to seem longer than it should if he had to listen to Travis fumble through another attempt at gaining Macy's interest. Every time she came on scene, his whole demeanor changed.

Because the man pressed her, Macy explained in a little more depth how the patterns had caught her eye when examining the girl's errors.

"You must be great with pattern analysis. That's what you did with those notes, too, right?"

"Macy's good with analysis." Something was riding him that he didn't want to examine too closely. Which was never a wise time to speak, but that didn't stop him. "Sometimes she's too good. Examines things too closely when she ought to just let them be, see where they go. Sometimes people can overanalyze things, don't you agree, Travis?"

He stumbled then, nearly landing flat on his face. He shot Macy a look, certain he hadn't imagined her hand on his back.

"I've always preferred to know exactly where I'm stepping," she said blandly. "While it might be gratifying to follow whatever whim catches our fancy, I'm most comfortable making a conscious decision about my actions. That way, I'm less likely to regret them later."

Scowling beneath his mask, Kell shoved his hands into his pockets. Regret? Is that what she was afraid of? Because he could accept that she wanted to set aside what was between them until after the girl was found. Hell, he agreed with that. But past experience had taught him that the longer they put off talking about what was going on between them, the more time she'd give herself to regret giving in to it.

Damned if he was going to allow her to neatly set him aside once again as a regret.

"You know," Travis was saying, "It sounds like you're a planner, like me. Nothing wrong with that."

"Maybe we need to be quiet," Kell interjected irritably. "Sound travels out here." He was aware of the looks Macy and Dan sent him but was past caring. Damned if he was up for standing silently by while the other man broke out his rusty moves again. He'd never been accused of being overly endowed with patience.

Which made it doubly hard to wait for Macy to get over whatever the hell was holding her back with him.

They walked about a half mile. Even surrounded by the thick strand of trees, it was easy to see that the wind was picking up. Little arctic funnels of snow encompassed them as they moved through the forest. It was difficult to tell how much of it was falling from the sky and how much from the already heavily laden branches overhead.

One minute they were surrounded by trees, and the next he could see a break in them. "Is that a clearing ahead?" he murmured, slowing to free the strap of the binoculars from inside his parka.

"I don't see anything."

He brought the glasses up and surveyed the area up ahead

carefully. "The trees thin in another sixty or seventy yards. I can see the outline of a rooftop."

"We're close then. Good." Travis hunched forward a bit as another blast of wind encompassed them. "We're going to be lucky to get off this mountain before the storm kicks in. It might not be as easy as you think."

They trudged farther, more carefully now. As the area between trees widened, they needed to be concerned about maintaining cover as they approached. His earlier excitement at Macy's news had dampened, both by the worsening weather and from reality. Chances were Feldman was right, and the dog would follow the girl's scent for dozens of miles farther before leading them to her. Even more likely, whoever was cozily ensconced in the structure beyond the trees was likely to be another bearded outdoorsman like Owen Redmond. Hopefully whoever it was would be more cooperative than the hunter had been.

But when he stopped to lift the binoculars to his eyes again, those thoughts scattered like the snowflakes in the air around them. He stared hard and long. Long enough to have Macy reaching for the glasses.

"What is it?"

Kell ignored the agent's hissed words and wordlessly handed the binoculars to Macy. She seemed to have trouble sighting with them for a moment. He knew the exact instant when she'd seen what he had. Her body stilled.

"It's white. The cabin . . . or shelter, is white."

"Yeah." The fierce satisfaction mingled with adrenaline to flash and spark in his veins. "It sure as hell is."

———

"You know what I think?" The man pressed the tip of his knife beneath Ellie's chin. She could feel its sharpness. If she moved, even to speak, it'd break the skin.

"I think you've been feeding me a load of shit, that's what I think. Last night and again today."

A long moment stretched. She had to force herself not to look away from his eyes, although the emptiness she saw there sent cold chills all the way through her. "I've already figured a way to get the feeling back." His smile was like a steely fist closing around her heart. "Unfortunately for you, it starts with peeling the skin right off you."

"But you can't be sure." The words had the knife pricking her harder, and there was an immediate answering pain. The slow trickle down the side of her throat would be blood.

His face closed. "I'm as sure as I can be."

"Listening to me is like insurance, right? Except it doesn't cost you anything." Oh God, it *hurt* to talk. If he didn't move that knife, she wasn't sure she could force more words out of her throat.

To her relief, he eased the pressure on the knife a tiny bit. "Don't kid yourself. Listening to you has a price. On my patience."

Summoning her flagging courage, she shrugged. "But what if killing me doesn't make the numbness in you go away? You should listen to me so you'll know what to do next." She waited a long moment. "Unless you don't care about never feeling again."

When he moved away suddenly, it was all she could do not to go limp with relief. "I don't think going out and buying myself a dumb-ass horse is going to do the trick. Problem is, you're just a stupid little girl. You don't know anything about what people like me have gone through."

"*You* don't know anything about what *I've* gone through," she said hotly. And Lucky wasn't a dumb-ass horse. This guy was the dumb ass. Just thinking the words made her feel a teensy bit better. "It's not about a horse. It's the pretending that's important." She could have told him that she was only eleven in years. In other ways she felt as old as the Rockies. As old as the forces that had carved them.

"Pretending." His voice was contemptuous, but she could tell she'd gotten his attention again. "I'm not a lame kid. I don't get off on make-believe."

"No, you go through the motions." At least that's what her therapist had accused her of. Going through the motions of living. "But it doesn't get you anywhere because it's like you're a robot. No feeling. Everything's automatic." There had been many times since this man had taken her that she wished she could go back to feeling that way again. "But when I started to pretend, I'd think about what I used to care about. It was hard to remember." Really hard because she hadn't been that kid anymore. She never would be. "I'd watch movies that had kids in them and I'd try to pretend to be like them. To act like them. And then one day, you realize that you've stopped pretending. Not all at once. Maybe about just one thing at first."

She stopped, her mind going back to that time. She'd only asked for a horse because of watching those movies with her mom. The girl in the movie acted sort of stupid. Ellie didn't want to be like her. She didn't care about the kind of things the actress had. But she'd become an actress just like the girl in the movie, and pretended some of the same things were important.

Which meant she'd had to pretend to be excited when her mom and dad had bought Lucky. And to care about how quickly a stable could be built. She'd pretended to be interested when her parents had decided to fill it with a few more horses so they could ride together.

It was easy to pretend with her parents. But Lucky had known. He'd always seemed to know about the yawning empty place inside her. And he'd known how to fill it up. A little at a time.

"Maybe a dog would help. You could walk it. Teach it tricks."

That brought a smile to the man's face, but it wasn't the kind of smile that made her feel better. "I had a dog once. The first gun I stole, I used him for target practice."

Her stomach hollowed out, and she thought she'd throw up. Funny, how the thought of him treating a pet like that seemed just as bad as what he wanted to do to her. What he *would* do to her soon.

Would anybody understand what she'd tried to tell them in that video? Would it make a difference? Maybe not. She didn't know exactly where she was. Or even how far he'd taken her from home. Were they even in Colorado anymore? Maybe they'd just think that she was scared. Stupid and scared.

Maybe no one had seen it. Because no one had come.

And they probably wouldn't.

"So . . . what else you got?"

She swallowed and forced herself to keep her mind on the man. He was asking questions. Maybe he was interested in her ideas.

And maybe his interest would buy her a little more time.

———

"We're back in the vehicles, yeah." Kell wasn't about to claim he'd thawed out. It'd take quite a bit longer for that. But there was finally warm air chugging out of the vents. And as excited as he was about their find, it'd been a couple hours since he'd felt his toes.

He pressed the cell closer to his ear. Travis was on the phone in the backseat with Whitman and the other conversation made it difficult to hear Raiker's low brusque tones.

"Were you able to gather any more intelligence?"

He'd had to hike well out of the surrounding trees in order to get cell reception to call in their findings the first time. "Even if it weren't for the weather, you probably couldn't get a look at this place from the sky. It's small, no more than fifteen by twenty. Eight feet tall. One window that faces the back. And it's white, so it blends in with the terrain."

"Were you able to positively ID the girl?"

His enthusiasm dimmed a bit. "I could only get partial glimpses of a female inside. I saw long blond hair. There's a blanket around her. But she sits so still I have to believe she's bound."

"And Dodge?"

"If you can send me a pic, I got a good enough look at him to make an ID either way." It'd taken climbing a tree in the process and trying to keep his balance long enough to find a vantage point that allowed him to peer into that lone window. The man had only crossed in front of it twice, but one of those times had been to stare outside. The blowing snow had obstructed Kell's view, of course. But he hoped that the high-powered binoculars had allowed him enough of a close-up to at least tell whether the man matched any photo Raiker could send along.

"From the angle I had, I could see the interior. It's all one room with a small wood-burning stove in one corner. There's a built-in bunk on the opposite wall with another portable cot set up closer to the door."

Raiker was silent for a moment. "Tactical options?"

"Wait until they're in bed for the night. Flash bangs through the window to surprise him with a simultaneous breach at the doorway." And it still burned that he hadn't been able to chance a stealthy approach to check the security of that door. It had been much too risky in the daylight, with the chance the man inside could come out at any moment. "The problem is their proximity. He's got a good chance of getting to the girl as quickly as the entry team does, depending on how fast he recovers. I couldn't find a vantage point that would allow a sniper a good angle for the bunk."

"Dodge is an expert. I'd imagine he'd recover fairly quickly." Raiker stopped, and Kell could hear a muffled conversation taking place on the other end of the line. After a minute, Adam resumed speaking. "Our best bet might be to get a sniper in there. Get him positioned to take Dodge out—if it is Dodge—the next time he crosses in front of the window."

"Now that's an idea I can get behind." Macy moved closer, leaning across the console in an attempt to hear the other side of the conversation. "Question is, how fast can you get one in here? Because I have a bad feeling about this. The bank meeting is set for three A.M., right? What are the chances he'll keep her alive any longer than that?"

There was silence at the other end of the phone. "A team is being compiled as we speak. It'd help lend some urgency if you could give us a positive ID."

Kell tamped down the quick flare of impatience. "Well, there's sure no Internet reception up here, but send me a picture over your camera phone, and I can be sure. And we need night vision equipment so we can continue to monitor the girl's safety." Because there wasn't a doubt in his mind, not after what Macy had reported, that Ellie Mulder was inside that shelter. "With a team, we can split up and spell each other on the surveillance."

"Chances are he has orders to hold off until the money is safely on its way tomorrow."

A feeling of urgency was building inside Kell that wouldn't be denied. He looked at the in-dash clock. Seven P.M. They had eight hours. Maybe. How much doubt was there that Mulder was going to comply with payment? The family's desperation was honed by Ellie's first kidnapping. Whoever had masterminded the kidnapping had done his homework. He'd be counting on their cooperation.

"Take a look at the photos I'm about to send and get back to me immediately."

Familiar with his boss's abrupt sign-offs, Kell disconnected the call and waited impatiently for the incoming message.

"Are they sending a team up here?"

"I think so, yeah." Feeling a flicker of sympathy for the way Macy had to sit there in the dark about what was being discussed, he filled her in. "But I've got a bad feeling about this. Safest bet is a sniper, yeah. But by the time they get one up here, get him in position, chances are Dodge and the girl will be asleep. I was in those trees, remember? There is no clear shot to the bunk." Dread was pooling in the pit of his stomach. "And if the wind picks up any more, the sniper will have a hell of time getting a shot."

His cell signaled them, and he pressed the command to display the incoming picture. "How do you make this thing bigger?" he muttered, reaching up to turn on the overhead light.

"Give it to me." Macy snatched it out of his hands. Although not familiar with his phone—at least not that he knew of—she pressed a few buttons and had the first photo zoomed to fill the screen in a matter of moments. Then she handed it back to him, but not before taking a good look first.

He stared, tilting the screen up to the overhead light. Obviously a mug shot, as the person in the picture was holding a numbered placard before him. This face was younger than the one he'd seen, with a light scruffy smattering of whiskers to obscure the jaw.

But it was undeniably the man he'd seen through the window.

"Is it him?" Macy demanded impatiently from beside him. "Is Raiker sending more than one photo for you to check?"

"Yeah." Kell couldn't look away from the screen bearing that image. The man looked ordinary. Like someone you'd pass on the street. Except for those empty, empty eyes. "But I'm already certain." He looked up then to catch her gaze on him. "Vincent Dodge is the man inside that cabin."

"Excuse me, Agent Whitman?"

Raiker looked up in annoyance at the interruption. Ordinarily they'd get the feds involved, but neither the weather nor their timeline would allow it. Getting the op together took a mind-numbing amount of cooperation with all the various agencies in the area. The forestry service. A search and rescue team, given the fact the promised storm had settled on the area with a vengeance. Summit County Sheriff's Office, since it was their SWAT team that would be utilized. And all of the arrangements seemed to come together with the pace of an impaired tortoise.

Whitman was similarly impatient. "Dobson. What is it?"

The man entered the room with a sheaf of papers in his hand. Once the final decision had been made to launch a tactical operation, all other agents had been banished to another office to work in. "We did a little investigation on the owner of the IP address where that newest ransom note was sent from. Household members Hugh and Sara Jane Guenther, and teenage children Becky and Sam." The man consulted the top page of the notes he carried. "Hugh is a garage mechanic, no record other than traffic violations. Sara works as a clerk at the Denver County Courthouse."

"Where is the address in relation to the Elliott home again?"

"Both in Denver. About twenty miles, give or take."

Whitman had opted for a more low-key approach this time around, given the near certainty that whoever had sent the note had merely cruised around until he'd found another unsecured network to send it from. "The warrant arrived a couple hours ago. Take Pelton and head over there to interview the family. The scope of the warrant allows for the seizure of all electronics with Internet access." Order given, his gaze was already drifting away.

"There's something else, sir." Dobson crossed to hand a copy of the pages to the assistant director. "My team finished with the Elliott computer. We accessed the boy's Facebook and e-mail accounts and found plenty of saved messages to and from his father. There were also some messages of a slightly different nature."

Whitman and Raiker exchanged a glance. "Such as?"

"In his history we found evidence of visits to various chat rooms." He shrugged. "Checked them out and they appear to be teen hangouts at first glance."

Adam sat back in his chair. "And where teens hang out . . ." he murmured.

The junior agent nodded. "At least from the tone of the Facebook messages, it sounds like he caught someone's attention who isn't a teen. There's something else going on there. Just wanted to know what you wanted us to do about it."

"Check the Guenther's computers for something similar when you bring them in."

The man nodded, turned, and left the room.

"Too many prongs going at once," Whitman muttered.

Adam was inclined to agree. He had Paulie ensconced in Mulder's bank with its two chief financial officers. He'd drive there with the Mulders in another few hours and wait with Stephen for the next message to arrive.

"You have your team in place to follow up on a physical transfer?" he asked.

The agent's pale brown eyes glinted. "Everything's ready on our end. The team will meet at the bank. I don't mind telling you, the CBI director had to go have the governor himself intercede to get this after-hours bank entrance OK'd."

Reaching for his wallet, Raiker extracted a hundred, placed it on the table. "I'm betting the transfer will be electronic. There are dozens of places in the world seven to twelve hours ahead of us who don't embrace the international banking laws."

The agent eyed the bill. "Middle of the night transfer smacks of wanting to use the cover of night to make the pickup. You're on." He withdrew a money clip from his pocket and thumbed through the bills until he found a hundred to join Raiker's. "You must not be that certain. You've only got one man inside the bank."

Raiker gave a slight smile. "I only need one man inside the bank." If Paulie can't follow or disrupt the transfer, it can't be done.

His smile faded as he considered his next duty. "I need to go update the Mulders." Waiting for news was the cruelest sort of torture. He tried to spare them that.

He just hoped they weren't in for an even crueler sort of torture at the end of this thing.

———

"We've got a positive ID on the man in the cabin."

Althea gasped audibly, her hand going in search of her husband's. Stephen grasped it, but his attention was focused solely on Adam. "It's Dodge? You're sure?"

He nodded. "Kell got a good enough look at him to match him to a photo I sent."

"And Ellie?" The woman's voice was desperate. "Did he see Ellie?"

Raiker hesitated. "There's someone else inside the cabin, but he wasn't able to see a face. He's fairly certain the second person is bound to a backless stool."

"If we know where she's being kept, what's stopping us?" Mulder was emanating fury and something even edgier. Fear. "Let's storm the place and get her out. I can have my security force here and ready to move out in less than an hour."

"We're compiling a team to join our operatives up there."

And the last thing he wanted was to add men to the team who couldn't all be completely cleared. There was still the unanswered question of how the security specs had gotten to Dodge. "They're being hit with quite a storm. High winds and lots of snow. The rescue will be dicey."

"But not impossible?" The steel in Althea Mulder's voice for a moment reflected her husband's.

Adam gave her a small smile. "No. Not impossible. However, I'm here to present you with another difficult decision. With that storm up there, I can't give you a timeline on the rescue attempt. There are too many variables. And if you aren't at the bank ready to move the money at three A.M., the consequences could be dire." His gaze was on Mulder. "Do you understand what I'm saying?"

"You're saying we need to go ahead with paying the ransom," he said bluntly. "And not to count on the fact that Ellie can be gotten out beforehand."

"That's right."

Althea squeezed her husband's hand where it lay on her shoulder. "We don't care about the money. We're ready to let it go. All of it. We just want Ellie home."

"Why don't you call the driver, dear." Stephen patted her shoulder. "Make sure he's ready to leave at . . ." With brows raised quizzically, he looked at Adam.

"One A.M. should be plenty of time."

". . . One A.M. Given the weather, he needs to select one of the four-wheel-drive vehicles."

Althea rose, but she seemed to realize she was being dismissed. She looked from one man to the other. "I don't want you two hatching something once I leave."

"Honey . . ."

She made a dismissive gesture at her husband. "Don't honey me. I know how your mind works. I don't want any secret plans or bait and switch strategies to outwit the man who's behind this." Her tone was fierce. "Our plan is simple. Find my baby, and bring her home. Pay the money. That's all there is. Agreed?"

"That's all there is," Stephen told her gently. "I promise."

She looked at him and Adam closely, but when neither of them spoke again, she seemed to be convinced. And the air with which she exited could only be described as regal.

The moment she was gone, Stephen turned to him, all trace of husbandly indulgence replaced by a deadly expression.

"What's the latest weather report for the area up there in the forest?"

"Snow and blowing snow through tonight, possibly continuing into the morning."

"Decreasing a sniper's effectiveness."

Adam cocked a brow. Clearly the man had a rudimentary knowledge of tactical operations. "It will be a challenge," he conceded.

"Cramer has experience in that area. My security chief? Maybe you can use him."

"I'd assume any shooter the Summit County Sheriff's SWAT team has on the unit has more up-to-date practice, training, and experience." He wasn't surprised that the man would try in some way to insert himself into the plans. A man like Mulder hadn't amassed his fortune by allowing others to make decisions for him.

"I understand how difficult it is to sit back and let the author of those notes pull your strings." Stephen's look was sharp, but Adam didn't flinch under it. "That's what I would feel in your place. Helpless. Compliant. It wouldn't set well with me either."

After a long moment the man nodded. "Burns like a bitch, I have to say. But then I imagine you feel much the same way having your team up there where the action is while you accompany me to the bank." He gestured to Adam's leg.

The man had unerringly placed his finger on a wound that still throbbed. Most of the time he liked to think he'd made his peace with the physical limitations he'd live with for the rest of his life.

Some days he knew that was a lie. So he gave a slow nod in return. "Burns like a bitch," he admitted.

Chapter 17

"It's one thirty." Kell crowded around the propane heater in the center of the circle of vehicles on the road and tried to convince himself he could feel his fingers again. "One and a half hours until the money transfer. We don't have much more time to wait on a decision, Sheriff."

"You know, Agent Whitman warned me about you, Burke." Sheriff Preske's voice was snappish. "He didn't exactly sing your praises."

"That's only because he's not a karaoke fan. But I think he harbors a secret desire to have my baby."

"Burke's solid, Sheriff." Kell looked at Agent in Charge Travis with no small degree of shock. "Abrasive as hell, but solid."

That last was more like what he expected from the man. He hunched closer to the heater and withstood an urge to turn and warm his backside. In doing so, he cast another concerned look at Macy. Was once again taken aback by her foreign appearance.

They all looked like special op polar bears. The gear that

had been distributed had included two-piece white Ghillie Suits and gloves and matching helmets equipped with LED headlights. Those had gone on over their outerwear.

The armored vests had gone on under it.

Macy looked like a cub amidst the bears, but her suit fit surprisingly well. The sheriff had heard there was a woman on the team and had brought gear to fit her.

There were enough personnel in the area to make Kell more than a little jumpy. But the combined forces of search and rescue, Forestry, CBI, and the sheriff's office SWAT team meant they could afford to break into two teams, each on for an hour and a half, giving everyone a chance to at least partially unthaw around the heaters or inside a vehicle.

"Last weather report predicted no end to the conditions." Everyone's head turned when Macy spoke. She'd been silent, drinking a hot chocolate from the huge container that had been brought up with the rest of the supplies. "Wind speeds of thirty-five miles an hour with gusts up to fifty. I'm sure your shooter is good. But adjusting for those sorts of speeds is dicey at best. With the poor visibility because of the snow . . ." She left the rest of the thought unsaid, but there wasn't a man there who couldn't complete it.

Crosby, the sniper, would have been blown out of the tree he'd finally chosen if he hadn't tied himself to it. "Your man can't stay out there until morning." Kell felt compelled to point out the obvious. "The flashlight lanterns were turned off in the shelter nearly an hour ago." He and Macy had been on duty, and he'd been damn glad when he'd seen it. Maybe it meant the girl had been given a few more hours.

But hours were all she had.

"The weather up here is hard to predict." Preske pushed up his face guard and mask to wipe away the ice forming on his mustache. "It's a big area. It can be cloudy and snowing in one spot and ten miles away the sun is shining. There's still a chance the weather will calm before dawn. And as soon as the guy stirs, Crosby will have him."

Kell subsided. It wasn't like Preske would be making the final decision in any case. He was checking in regularly with

Whitman and Raiker, who were already on their way to the bank. The final decision would be theirs.

Kell edged his way over to Macy and silently she held out her hot chocolate for him. He took a long drink and handed it back to her. It was barely warm, although it had been steaming minutes ago. "How you doing?"

"Getting nervous," she murmured back. He huddled closer to keep their conversation between themselves. "I just can't shake this feeling . . . Dodge doesn't have reason to wait long. Why would he? Every moment he stays here is a step closer to getting caught. It's conceivable that he's waiting to be given the word before killing her. But after the money is paid, why wouldn't that word come sooner rather than later? You'd think he'd stand a better chance of getting out of here in the dark."

"This storm is going to slow him down as much as it does us."

"Little consolation if . . ." She stopped herself from saying it. But he knew exactly how the thought would end.

Little consolation if the girl was already dead.

"If it were just our group, with Raiker at the helm alone calling the shots, I'd feel a whole lot better about this," he muttered. But he'd been on multiagency teams plenty of times during his stint with the Baltimore PD. Too many chiefs, not enough Indians. Snipers that thought they were flawless. Tactical teams too ready to go in before negotiations were given a chance to work.

And most scary, heads from various alphabet agencies wrangling over the best course of action. Either delaying the proper response until it was too late or making a decision based on politics and turf rather than on the reality of the issue.

"We just have to wait and hope that Raiker does his thing." Unconsciously he tried to shove his hands in his coat pockets for extra warmth. Was reminded that the suit covered them. "He's the only one I trust to make a decision like this."

———

Paulie Samuels was entertaining himself by practicing card tricks. It went without saying that he had a deck on him at all times. It was a habit the man had to keep himself calm and Adam knew him well enough to avoid getting sucked into the showmanship.

Right now he was seated at a polished cherry conference table in the bank president's office, spinning cards on his finger and shaking them from his sleeve. Sitting down next to him, Adam watched for a moment before saying, "Have you had any more attempts to bypass the security on our financials?"

The man looked up. The ace spinning on his index finger never faltered. "How'd you know? Right after I sent the bastard a little virus that should have turned his machine into a crispy critter, it wasn't forty-eight hours before there was another attempt."

Adam drew a deep breath. It was only when a person had something to hide that this sort of news would be so disturbing. He had more to hide than most. "And . . ."

Paulie lifted a shoulder. His tie today was covered with miniature slot machines. "Didn't get any further than he did the first time. Not as far, actually, because I was ready for him and had a dandy little detour set up for him. It'll be weeks before he can rid his machine of the blizzard of spam and porn notices I sent him."

"How do you know it's the same person?"

"Because he doesn't have a big arsenal of tricks. I recognize his patterns." When Adam didn't answer, his friend looked at him in surprise. "Hey, you aren't worried, are you? I've got your back, Adam, always. Instead of destroying his hard drive, I thought I'd send him a Trojan horse. See if we can get a glimpse of who we're dealing with."

"Spyware?"

Paulie's expression looked pained. "For you less technical people, that's as close as you can probably come to understanding it. But if we're lucky, we'll get some idea of who we're dealing with. Because while he's busy getting rid of the spam I loaded him with, I'll be going through any e-mail accounts, online banking transactions, documents . . . just as good as sitting at his computer myself."

Adam gave his friend a faint smile. "Good job."

The man's gaze drifted back to the cards. He turned over his hand and showed the queen of spades cupped in his palm. "I'll remind you of that when we negotiate my next contract."

With a flicker of amusement, he said, "I'm sure you will." Adam noted Whitman come in the room and rose to join the man in the doorway.

"Sheriff Preske just reported in. Your man Burke is getting antsy."

"Hardly surprising. What's the weather report?"

"There's always the slight chance it could get better by morning. But the forecast calls for several more hours of snow and winds."

"Damn." Ordinarily a sniper was their best chance to avoid harm to the girl. It was hard to avoid collateral damage when a structure was breached. His gaze traveled over the man's shoulder to the Mulders sitting at a table with the bank president. The couple's hands were clasped.

"They've got to go in," he murmured and was relieved when the CBI assistant director nodded.

"I agree."

"And the sooner the better. We might have more time if the transfer is physical, but if it's to be electronic . . ."

It appeared that he and Whitman were on a rare similar wavelength. "Then the girl doesn't have much more time."

———

Preske walked back into the group huddled around the heaters, attempting to hook the radio onto the belt at his waist as he did so. "New game plan, people."

Kell and Macy turned at the man's pronouncement. They'd been readying with the rest of their team to head back into place surrounding the cabin, to relieve the men there right now.

"We're going in."

"Hallelujah." Kell flexed his hands. The pronouncement filled him with a sense of relief. The trepidation filtered in moments later. He didn't have to be told how chancy a breach was. But with both Dodge and the girl hopefully sleeping, they stood a decent chance of getting the girl out alive if they cut off Dodge before he could get to her first.

A big if.

"Burke!" the sheriff barked. Kell moved into the circle. "How good a look did you get at that door today?"

"Not as close as I wanted. But the whole structure is made to be portable. To knock down and set up easily. The door won't be reinforced. You could go with either a mechanical or ballistic breach." Looking closer, he saw that the man had unrolled the drawing he'd made of the structure. "What do you have for new intelligence?"

"Misha and Cody are on the ground in back with night vi- sion binoculars. No lights on inside. They haven't seen any- one through the window since they went on duty."

So in other words, no changes.

"They're our two most experienced members with the thunderbolt. They'll be the primary entry team." The man stabbed his finger at the drawing of the window. "Hillis and Voss will wait for the signal and use the bang stick to rake out the window and toss in the flash bangs at the same time the other two are going through the door."

"Santeen, Wilder, and Matthews serve on our secondary entry team." He looked up then, seemed to guess the thoughts of the others in the circle staring at him. "Don't worry, boys. You've got a spot at the party. Whitman says Burke and Travis will follow the secondary team in and secure the hos- tage. Morgan, Neely, and Sachs will bring up the rear and help provide cover as you clear the area. Make sure to pick up goggles from the gear we brought. The grenades will have the place full of smoke. You got the best look inside, Burke, because it was still daylight when you got there before the wind became such a bitch. You and Travis go for the girl. You've got weapons?"

"Yes." He and the agent answered simultaneously.

"Everybody make sure you take a whisper mic headset. We don't want anyone jumping the gun out there."

Men were already turning away to get their needed equipment and to find snowmobiles. Someone approached the sheriff. When Kell noticed who it was, his heart sank. For a moment, just a moment, he'd forgotten she was here.

"Sheriff, I believe you forgot to give me a duty."

The man stared at Macy. The heat thrown off from the propane had melted the ice on his facial hair, and now it dripped down his red jowls. "Not everyone is going in there, Ms. Reid. I'm not. The SAR team isn't. Neither are some of my . . ."

"But the rest of *my* team is. What did Raiker and Whitman tell you about *my* duties?"

Preske was getting irritated. "I'm in charge on scene. I say you're best suited for calming the girl once they get her out."

"Ooh." Kell winced. "Hope he's wearing a cup."

"He's right," muttered Travis. "I don't want to be worrying about where Macy is when we're inside."

"You're on your own with that one." He shouldered through the men and reached Macy's side as she began to speak again. "I'll have you know, my law enforcement experience can match or exceed that of . . ."

Firmly, he grasped her arm and tugged, nearly pulling her off balance. "C'mon, Macy. You can ride with me." And then he didn't release her, despite her desperate tugging, until they were next to their ride.

"Did you hear him?" She was still fuming, and this time when she tried to free herself, he let her go. "Insufferable. I can't believe there's still that much bias in law enforcement."

"Then you haven't had as much experience in its ranks as you claim. Get on." He knew better than to point out that her accent had been front and center when she was slicing and dicing the man. He'd half expected to hear a "my good man" come out of her mouth as she was speaking.

"You could have helped." Her arms were folded over her chest, her stance suspicious. "If you'd said something about Raiker wanting me involved, he might have listened."

"So I should have come to your rescue, but that wouldn't have been biased," he countered. "Can't have it both ways, Mace. Now get on."

She approached him rapidly. But she wasn't headed for the snowmobile. Because he'd seen her in action before, he covered up reflexively.

But when she drew closer, all she did was push up his face guard and the mask beneath.

"What are you doing?"

Moving her head, her light shone over his face. "I knew it. You *agree* with him."

It was on the tip of his tongue to prevaricate. But in the midst of the gravity of the situation they were about to embark on, he chose the truth. "Up here?" He tapped the side of his helmet. "No. I've worked with you, remember? But here?" This time he thumped his chest. "Yeah, here I'm relieved that you're not going to be heading into a smoke-filled room with a hired killer inside and a mass of trigger-happy men swarming around. So sue me. But that doesn't make me a chauvinist. It just makes me stupid."

And damned if he didn't feel like it, with the glow of her damn light in his face, revealing more, much more, than he'd ever meant to. He pulled down his face mask and lowered the helmet shield.

"Why did you say that?"

He ground his teeth at the bewilderment lacing her words. "Hell if I know. I guess I'm just not as good at distance as you are." Nearby, snowmobiles were starting up and heading off. He turned on the ignition of his. If she didn't get on, he was tempted to ride off and leave her.

But she did settle herself in back of him, after first slipping out of her snowshoes. He handed his back to her, and she took them silently. And for the first few miles at least, bucking and battling through the hellacious wind and blinding snow seemed almost a reprieve.

The sleds were run on low speed and then abandoned a couple miles from the shelter to avoid having the sound of their engines carry. The team walked into the thickening woods in sets of four, with line loosely wrapped around their waists, connecting them by several feet's length to the person in back of them. They'd shed the line once everyone was ready to get in place. Another team would follow in a few minutes to form an outer perimeter encircling the cabin.

It still burned Macy that she'd be part of that outer perimeter.

She wasn't averse to being the one dealing with Ellie when she was brought safely from the cabin. And she knew she would be good at dealing with the traumatized child. But that didn't make it any more palatable than when her boarding school roommate had tried to convince her she should make both their beds because she was good at it.

The whisper mic headset she wore beneath her white tactical helmet sounded. "Primary entry team position."

"Misha, check."

"Cody, check."

"Secondary entry team position."

One after another, the men sounded off, indicating readiness. Macy could feel her muscles grow tense. Her palms in the bulky gloves dampened, despite the cold. She held a heavy down blanket to wrap the girl in and was standing behind a thick fir, twenty yards from where Kell was stationed. He was another twenty yards from the front of the house. When the first and second wave of men rushed forward, she'd move up to take the place he vacated. And they'd know exactly where to run with the girl to hand her off. Macy in turn would turn and take the girl much farther into the trees, beyond them, to safety.

The men had all checked in. There was silence on the radio. Time dragged to an abrupt halt. And every single scenario that could go wrong began to play in her head.

Kell had never seen the girl alive through the window.

He hadn't seen her face.

Hadn't seen her move.

Ellie Mulder might be dead even as they waited out here. She might have been killed the moment she made that video.

Her instincts were heightened to a painful level. Raising the night vision binoculars she'd swiped from one of the men on the way up, she peered at the quiet cabin and tried to convince herself that they were in time. That everything would be fine.

That the child wouldn't be killed in the crossfire.

She let out a long stream of breath, forced the negative thoughts from her mind. It was the waiting. Long and painful. The wind howled around them, the gusts carrying a heavy slant of snow that made it difficult to see more than a yard in front of her without help from the binoculars.

The only sound was the constant whistling of the wind. Then the radio sounded. "Breach, breach!"

Macy brought the glasses up again, saw the men running toward the door with the battering ram. At the same time they went through, she heard the flash bang grenades detonate, two in quick succession. The entry team was through the door now. Kell and Travis after them.

Macy ran up to the spot Kell had been in a moment before. The secondary team was swarming the shelter, and from her radio came a jumble of noise.

"Put it down put it down put it down!"

Shots. Four in quick succession.

"Knife!"

"Where's the girl? Got the girl?"

"Put your hands behind your head. Now!"

Everything was a blur. More men were entering the house. Some were running out.

One of them was Kell. The body in his arms was coughing.

Macy dropped the glasses to bounce against her chest and sprang forward, wrapping the blanket around the child so she was covered like a mummy. Then she shoved up her guard and face mask. She didn't want to scare the girl even further.

Carefully Kell deposited Ellie in her outstretched arms. "Got her?"

"I've got her." The weight didn't seem enough for an eleven-year-old girl. Macy brought the child closer to her chest. And still the girl continued to cough. The flash bangs would have filled the interior with smoke.

She turned and began hurrying toward the trees as fast as the snowshoes would allow.

"Prisoner secured. Prisoner secured." Calls and commands were still coming through her headset. "Structure clear."

Blocking out the calls and commands coming through the headset, she murmured to the girl the whole way. "Ellie, you're safe. We're going to take you home now. Your parents are waiting for you at home."

Macy thought she saw the girl's eyelids flutter. "I understood your message," she whispered to her as they moved rapidly away from the commotion behind them. "You're the bravest girl I know. Much braver than I was. To escape from him and then send those clues. I wish I'd had half your guts at your age."

Ellie's eyes opened wide then and stared at Macy unflinchingly. Her voice was choked. "I wasn't brave, I was scared."

She gave the girl a quick hug. "It wouldn't be brave if you weren't scared." Macy took a quick glance behind her. But the shanty was hidden by the dense trees. Straightening, she continued to head to the edge where they thinned. She could dimly hear the sound of the sleds as the rest of the team approached over the chatter on the radio. Macy staggered up to the first headlight she saw, grateful when the person on it jumped off to run into the trees toward the the rest of the team. She set the girl down on the seat and turned to lean against it and take a breath.

Then recoiled as an earsplitting *boom* shook the area. A huge fireball burst skyward. She draped herself over the girl protectively, her eyes riveted on the scene behind her. The flames surged upward, dancing and swaying in the heavy gusts of wind.

"What was that?"

Macy barely heard the girl. "Bomb?" It had to be. He'd had the cabin wired? Had he somehow detonated it after the team had staged the rescue? Or had the breach set off a trigger he'd had ready for just such an occasion?

"Man down. Where's SAR?"

"All personnel check in!"

"Prisoner secured? Matthews, what's your location?"

Man down. The words had her organs freezing. Kell. Where was Kell? Fingers scrambling for the glasses, she held them up to her eyes. She could see a few figures running. Treetops already torched from the flames, burning merrily in the wind. But the trees were too thick for her to make out much.

"Need a medic here!"

"Need a location check on Matthews."

A vise was squeezing her heart. Her body was poised, ready to head back toward the inferno to check on Kell herself. Then the girl on the snowmobile moved.

And Macy was abruptly reminded of her primary duty. "Scooch up. You'll have to side saddle." She couldn't afford to unwrap the girl. She'd be hypothermic before she got her back to the base. So they'd ride slowly to be sure she didn't fall off. Macy got on behind her and goosed the motor. They started to move.

In the meantime, she strained to hear more details from the radio.

"Matthew's down. Need a medic!"

"Get me a visual on Crosby."

"Prisoner security, check in!"

She threw another look at the sky. The wind was spreading the fire quickly. Then she turned her focus to the semi-circle of snowmobiles they'd left with headlights on in the distance as a beacon to find their way.

From the sounds of the radio chatter, there was more than one man down. And her heart was doing a fast gallop as she worried about Kell's safety. The wind snapped and blew the snow at a slant in front of her, making it hard to see more than a few yards away at a time, even with the light on her helmet and the headlight on the sled. Some distance later, when a figure stumbled out of the woods she immediately slowed.

"Help!"

Assuming it was one of the team, she stopped and started to get off the sled to offer assistance. Belatedly, the details she'd heard earlier on the radio clicked into place.

Prisoner secured? Matthews, what's your location?
Need a location check on Matthews.
Matthew's down. Need a medic!
Prisoner security, check in!

Comprehension slammed into her. This man wasn't wearing a white suit. Or a flak vest emblazoned with Summit County Sheriff.

And he was aiming a gun right at them.

"Get down!" Macy lunged to knock the girl off the sled as she drew her weapon. The man's figure was hazed by the blowing snow. There, then gone and there again. It was like aiming for a ghost. She stood. Sited. Squeezed off three shots in quick succession. And then was spun completely around when one hit her in the shoulder. Another in the chest.

She fought to haul in a breath. Dimly she realized she was on her back. The radio was just a jumble of noise now. Cold. She was surrounded by it. The snow was in her face. On her lips. Rolling clouds of smoke lightened the dark sky overhead. And when she tried to move, agony rolled through her like a gleeful gnawing beast.

She didn't know how long she lay there before she heard the girl's voice in her ear. "You killed him but it's all right." The words danced through her head, through her mind as she struggled to fight the waves of unconsciousness that threatened to haul her under.

"He was already dead anyway."

Chapter 18

Macy opened her eyes. She was still on her back. But the cold had been replaced by a furnacelike heat.

Disoriented, she blinked. Tried to move. Then whimpered like a baby when her efforts resulted in various aches awakening in an agonizing chorus.

"What's the matter? Are you in pain? Do you need another pill?" The heat was abruptly gone.

Slowly, tentatively, she turned her head. Found that it might be the one part of her body that didn't hurt. Kell was standing at her bedside, hauling jeans up his long muscled legs to cover the form-fitting boxer briefs. Which seemed a pity. The man did have a glorious bum.

Her eyes widened at the totally inappropriate thought. "Have you drugged me?"

"Well, yeah. Doctor's orders."

He came back from the bathroom carrying a glass of water. And sluggishly, a few of the cobwebs cleared from her foggy memory. "Last night. Forgot for a minute."

He shook a pain pill from the bottle on the bedside table

with a bit more force than was necessary. "Good for you. Wish it was that easy for the rest of us."

Macy eyed him carefully. Was he always this grouchy in the mornings? Because by the light slanting in the windows, dawn had long passed. "Pain pills make me groggy." But she took the pill and the glass of water he shoved at her because his expression didn't look too tolerant. "How's Ellie?"

His expression softened. "Fine. Thanks to you, she's fine. Her parents . . ." He looked away for a moment. Cleared his throat. "They're grateful."

"He came out of nowhere." Gingerly, she lay back on the pillow. Despite her dislike for medication, she willed for it to work so she could move without discomfort. "I wasn't paying as much attention as I should have to the radio chatter. I was just trying to get Ellie out of there. All I could think of when they said man down . . . I thought it was you." His head swiveled toward her then. She took a deep breath. Winced when that hurt, too. "I was afraid it was you."

Kell sat on the edge of the bed and reached for the glass she still held to set it on the table. "Two men lost," he said quietly. "Matthews and Crosby. Several others were injured in the explosion."

There was a quick hitch in her chest at the thought of the downed men. And the families they left behind. "So Matthews had Dodge secured after the entry?"

He nodded. "Matthews and Wilder. But the explosion sent them all flying. Wilder was thrown several yards away and when he got back to Matthews, Dodge must have already managed to get the key from the man's pocket and unlock himself before stealing the man's gun and taking off."

A soft knock sounded at her door. She had the presence of mind to yank the sheets up to her chest, although someone had helped her into her pajamas last night. If she bothered to pursue the memory, she was certain she'd discover that someone had been Kell.

Adam entered. Stopped to give Kell's bare chest and proximity a long look. "Was it a bomb?" She addressed the question to both of them, still trying to puzzle through it. The idea still didn't make sense. "Did he have the place booby-trapped?"

"It'll be days before we know for sure." Her boss stopped a couple feet from her bedside and considered her gravely. "How do you feel?"

"Like an enthusiastic mule gave me a few good kicks."

There was a flicker in his expression, there and gone too quickly to be identified. "Even with Kevlar, taking a bullet hurts like a son of a bitch. You took two."

She gave a wry smile. "The impact packs a punch." Macy stopped, her gaze going involuntarily to the scar on Kell's chest. The one he'd had no vest to deflect. "I'm fine," she said more strongly. "I'd like to get up."

"Whenever you're ready."

"Not a chance."

The two men glared at each other narrowly. "The doctor Mulder got to come out here said she should rest in bed a couple days," Kell pointed out.

"Macy's the best judge of how she feels."

"Macy is going to try to prove how tough she is to you so you won't follow through on your threat to fire her."

"*Macy* is lying right here," she felt compelled to point out. "And doesn't need anyone telling her what to do."

Raiker was glaring at Kell now. "When did she become your business?"

There was no way she wanted *that* discussion to spin out right here and now. So she distracted them the only way she knew how. "Ohhh," she groaned in feigned pain. As expected, that shifted their attention. She smiled complacently. "That's it, now, focus. I appreciate the doctor visit. I appreciate the meds, I think." Although from what she could figure, she'd been given something that had had her sleeping close to twenty-four hours. "I also appreciate Kell stopping by this morning to see if I needed anything." She raised her brows at him, and he snapped his mouth shut, obviously steamed, but discreet for once. Memory was filtering back through the drug-induced fog, and she knew he'd been at her side all night. She didn't want to examine the warmth elicited by the knowl-edge.

To Raiker she said, "Nothing in Dodge's MO would lead me to believe he was an explosives expert."

"I didn't see anything in my brief time inside that would have caused the explosion by other means." Kell folded his arms over his chest. "There was a wood-burning stove. A battery-operated TV."

Adam placed both hands on his cane and leaned his weight on it. "Dodge wouldn't have had to be an explosives expert to place the bomb if its instructions were given to him. But why would he? He had a gun and a knife. And based on his file, he enjoys the close work. One theory would be that he was planning to detonate the place so the girl's body wouldn't be found."

"Another would be that someone else was planning to destroy them both to get rid of a loose end."

Raiker nodded at Kell. "Exactly. Plus once Dodge was secured, he had nothing on him to detonate the explosive. Given the fact that he didn't appear to be awake when the cabin was breached, we can bet he wasn't the one planning to torch the place."

Macy shuddered. If the rescue had been staged just a quarter hour later, Ellie, as well as most of the team, would have been lost. "Let's compare timelines. When did the money transfer take place? And what time was the explosive detonated?"

The approval in her boss's glance was cheering. "The pain meds haven't completely addled your thinking ability. The final ransom note came minutes after three and demanded that the money be transferred to a numbered account electronically."

"With the time difference, that leaves dozens of countries as the possible destination," Kell muttered.

"Paulie is still following the money. It's bounced around to four different accounts so far, so whoever is pulling the strings knows what he's doing. The transfer was complete—at least it looked that way—at three fifteen A.M. Preske said the detonation was at three twenty."

"Remote detonation?" Macy moved restlessly against the pillows. The pain was receding to dull aches. Then she automatically corrected herself. "Not a cell phone trigger. Reception is too spotty in the area. A timer?"

"It's doubtful." Adam straightened. "Whoever set this up had to have complete control over the timing. Too many variables to take into consideration. No, I'll guess he used a satellite phone as the trigger."

"Doesn't make sense." Kell looked at his boss soberly. "Why hire an assassin if you're planning to do the final kill yourself anyway?"

"This bastard is cagey." Raiker gave a feral smile. "Covers all his bases. He hired Dodge because the man had a particular set of skills. He could prepare the hideaway and stalk the guard, force him to record that message before killing him and chopping off his thumb. Then he could be counted on to snatch the kid and kill her if Mulder didn't cooperate. And we saw with that final scene with Dodge that he was compelled to see his job through to the end. But loose ends aren't tolerated. Once the money was in hand and the girl was dead, Dodge became a loose end."

"So not only does the mastermind want the girl dead, he doesn't want Dodge around to talk either," Kell noted.

"But there still may be a loose end," Macy said slowly. She paused, trying to push aside the drug-induced haze fogging her mind. "Those security specs found at Hubbard's. Where did they come from? And did Dodge have the talent to circumvent Mulder's alarm system himself?" There had been another thing nagging at her and she searched her memory for a moment until she recalled it. "Then there were the ransom notes sent from local IP addresses. Someone's moving all these people around like chess pieces, waiting for a ten-million-dollar payoff. And yet he's driving around town in the middle of the night, looking for unsecured networks to send the ransom notes from?" Macy looked from one of them to the other. "Does that sound like the same person to you?"

"If you can think that clearly, you can make it to the briefing downstairs in another half hour." Raiker turned to leave. "Burke, I'll expect you to find a shirt."

Kell waited for him to leave before bracing both hands on

the bed, effectively caging her. "Just how the hell do you think you're going to shower and get dressed by yourself?"

"I'm sure I'll manage." He could help, the way he'd helped get her to bed—her memory had cleared in that regard—but it was obious he wasn't going to offer.

"Go ahead and try," he invited, pushing away from the bed to rise. "Hope you got some return of strength to that arm."

So did she. Because she was damned if she was going to allow him to dictate her actions. If he didn't want to help so she could join the meeting, she'd do it on her own. She struggled to swing her feet over the side of the bed. Lay there a minute trying to figure out how she was going to get up.

When she finally managed to roll to the elbow of her uninjured arm, she pushed herself up, shot him a triumphant look.

He clapped derisively, made a point of looking at his watch. "Two minutes flat, Duchess. At that rate, you'll make it downstairs in time to grab something for dinner tonight."

She sailed by him to the bathroom, her resolve strengthened by his attitude. She wasn't in *that* much pain. And she damned well was going to that briefing, with or without his help. "You heard Raiker," she snapped, right before she closed the door behind her. "Put a shirt on."

Fifteen minutes later she was willing to admit that he might have had a point about the difficulty she was going to experience. Trying to use her left arm at all had her shoulder weeping. And her reflection in the bathroom mirror told the story. Her chest and shoulder were covered with wicked bruises that promised to turn a rainbow of colors in the coming days. There was also a good-sized one on the back of her thigh, which she could only attribute to her graceless first attempt at walking in snowshoes.

But the injuries weren't disabling. She'd managed perfectly well washing her hair one-handed. After toweling her hair and patting herself dry as best she could, she was winded but feeling a bit triumphant. At least until she considered the process required to get dressed. Her door opened. And her mood soured to see Kell coming in, fully dressed, hair wet, as if mocking her with what he'd accomplished in the time it had taken her to shower. "Get out."

He shut the door to lean against it. "Déjà vu. Except this time I'm not helping."

"Who asked you to?" She yanked open a drawer, considered the contents. Clearly a bra wasn't an option. And she wasn't any too certain she could raise her arms up enough to put on a sweater. In the end, she dragged on a jogging suit in soft black velour with a front zipper on the top. Socks were the easiest part of the ensemble and then she checked the time again. She still had six minutes.

Brushing her hair quickly, she squirted some mousse in her left hand and then scooped it out with the fingers of her right, worked it into her hair. She was going to look ridiculous in a few hours. When it dried, the curls were going to make her look like a crazed Orphan Annie. And it suited her to blame that on the man leaning silently against the door.

Going to the closet, she shoved her feet in a pair of black slip-ons.

"I wasn't trying to be a dick."

"Practice must make perfect, then."

She always forgot how fast he could move. One moment he was across the room. And when she closed the closet door and turned around, he was there in front of her.

"I forgot about the vest last night," he said abruptly. "Even though I was wearing one—we all were—I didn't remember that when I heard you were down. That you'd been shot. It took me forever to get to you, and I'd remembered by then. But was still worried the bullet might have hit you in the head. The femoral artery."

Her ire with him immediately melted away. Because it was all too easy to recall the bone-numbing fear she'd experienced when she'd heard there was a man down and had had no way to be sure it wasn't Kell.

"You said earlier you were worried about me last night, too, so I know you understand how I was feeling."

Her voice was softer than she would have liked. "I guess I do." Because if their situations had been reversed, she'd probably be moving heaven and hell to make him follow doctor's orders, too.

And she'd probably be met with even less success than he was.

The intensity in his expression sent nerves scampering down her spine. "That makes me believe when you aren't thinking about time and space and distance, you care more than you want to let on. To either of us." She opened her mouth. Closed it again when a hint of fierceness entered his gaze. "That was a gutsy move last night, but I already knew you had guts. You showed them again when you confronted Castillo. The question is whether you have the same nerve when it comes to taking chances in your personal life. And you're the only one who can answer that question."

He left as abruptly as he'd come in, leaving her to follow more slowly. He had all but called her a coward, and there was no greater gauntlet he could throw at her feet. Macy passed blindly down the hallway past the priceless artwork and sculptures. She'd thought that facing Castillo a few days ago took all the nerves she could summon, but she'd been wrong.

In some respects, it was even more frightening to face her feelings for Kellan Burke.

The conference room was full when she opened the door, and the applause that broke out had her looking uncertainly over her shoulder.

"Here's the woman of the hour." She decided she was more than a little creeped out by the jovial expression on Agent Whitman's face. It was just too big a change from its normally stern lines. Giving a weak smile in return, she thankfully sank into the seat vacated for her by Agent Pelton, who moved to pull another up to the table.

"I'm just glad we were in time."

"As are the girl's parents. They're waiting to thank you in person when you're free."

She nodded, willing the conversation to move away from her and onto the case. Macy only had moments to wait. Whitman indicated for Agent Dobson to speak.

"As I was saying," the slender balding agent said, crossing to hand her a file identical to that in front of the others crowded around the table. "We followed up on some irregularities that appeared in David Elliott's Facebook messages. And we found the same sort of messages in Sam Guenther's."

Momentarily confused, she slanted a glance at Raiker. "The second ransom note came from the Guenther computer," he explained.

"And both households have a teenage boy living in them?" When he nodded, her attention shifted back to Dobson.

"Copies of some of the messages we retrieved are in the file." Macy flipped the folder open and started to scan them. "Since we also found history on the computers to indicate the boys frequented chat rooms, that might explain the nature of the notes on the social network sites."

"Pedophiles will troll those sites, pretending to be teenagers. Gathering information." Raiker tapped the file with one scarred finger. "It's possible he posed as another kid, a girl maybe. Got the boys to say things, do things, thinking they were communicating with a girl, and then blackmailed them."

The thought had her stomach turning. "You think someone blackmailed the kids into sending the notes?"

Adam shook his head. "From the contents of the notes, it appears the sender was trying to leverage a meet. But pedophiles will go to great lengths to research their intended victims. Online anonymity isn't guaranteed, not when someone is well versed in stalking. It's not beyond reason to assume he learned where these kids lived. He tells them as much. In one of the notes to the Guenther boy, the man tells him he's sitting outside his house. Using a cell phone with Internet access to communicate with the the boys would tell him the home's network was unsecured."

Still not sure where all this was heading, Macy shrugged. "Sounds like the first thing we need to do is see whether the same person wrote the Facebook messages to both kids. Then compare the authorship to that of the ransom notes."

Her boss inclined his head. "Then we'll go from there."

Dobson put in, "The Elliott boy received a message from

someone the night the first ransom note was sent."

Kell slapped his palm lightly on the file. "That interview with Nancy Elliott. Remember?" Although Whitman nodded, Macy noted that the memory didn't seem to be a pleasant one for the man, given his expression. "She went on a bit about crime in the neighborhood. How she'd called the city several times to complain about the streetlight by them being burned out but nothing was done."

When no one said anything, Kell continued. "But when we questioned the kid in his room and he said he'd seen a car out front the night the first ransom note was sent, he said the car was silver."

"And how did he know the car was silver if there was no streetlight?" Travis put in slowly.

"Unless he was communicating with the man in it that night and had seen it parked out there other times when the same guy harassed him." Excitement was beginning to hum in her veins. "I can have an answer on authorship for you in an hour or less." At Adam's nod, she pushed away from the table and rose carefully to exit the room.

Once Macy left the room, the conversation turned much more generic. A general debriefing session, bringing all the personnel accumulated there up to date on the various parts of the case.

And it was easy to see from the direction of the talk that the team was in the process of being dismantled. At least on CBI's end.

"For the most part, the remainder of our involvement will be run from headquarters in Denver," Assistant Director Whitman was telling Raiker. "Agent Dobson will stay in house while the authorship of the ransom notes is being followed up on. Likewise, Agent in Charge Travis will remain to accompany your people on any further interviews. I'd appreciate being kept updated as things progress." His smile was thin, and obviously not often used. "I can continue to arrange multiagency cooperation as needed."

In other words, Kell thought, as he shifted in his seat, the agency already had its eye on costs. With the girl back, the ransom paid, the situation could be construed as successfully concluded.

Except for the matter of the person responsible still being at large. He pushed back his chair to rise. Caught Raiker's gaze on him.

"Where are you headed?"

Feeling trapped, he drawled, "I was going to see how Macy's doing."

"She's fine and doesn't need to be disturbed. Grab a coat and go see what Jonesy is working on today," Raiker snapped. "We need final results on all the evidence transferred back here."

"Can't you just call him?" When the man's expression darkened, Kell added hastily, "Okay, okay. I'll go out to talk to him." He didn't think it was his imagination that Whitman smirked during the exchange. Probably enjoyed seeing him taking orders from someone.

When he got outside a few minutes later, the snow had stopped and someone on Mulder's well-trained staff had the drive cleared of the most recent snowfall. He yanked the hood of the parka up and ducked his head. The wind certainly hadn't let up, and it whistled through the area between the home and the outbuildings, which were set an eighth of a mile away, he estimated, from the house.

He lengthened his stride. He'd heard someone mention that this was the longest-sustained cold snap in the Denver for over a decade. Figured it was his luck to be here to enjoy it for its duration.

Kell almost, almost was ready to thank Raiker for this errand. Because he'd been ready to go to Macy's room to push. That seemed to be a forte of his, so he usually went with his strengths. But he was willing to admit that after their last conversation, a little distance would do them both some good.

Which was easy to say while they were still working in close proximity to each other. Tougher to consider if it continued once they were back in Virginia.

He ducked into the side entrance of the employee garage thankfully. It didn't even bear wondering what this place cost to heat in this climate. It was huge. Easily large enough for two dozen vehicles. The lab took up four of those spaces, and he headed to it now, banged on the door.

Flipping his hood back for the moment, he looked around and pounded again. Jonesy had obviously taken the opportunity to sleep in, something that held more than a little appeal for Kell.

Trying the door, he was faintly shocked to discover it unlocked. He let himself in, half expecting to hear Jonesy's indignant screech. The man was a demon about wearing gowns and gloves in his domain.

"Hey, Jonesy, you in here?" He thought he heard a noise in the back of the RV where the man's bedroom was but didn't want to gown up to go back and check it out. "Jonesy?"

"Yeah, yeah." The man came out wearing a long red robe emblazoned with a huge dragon. When he belted it, the tie looked like the dragon had its tongue out, panting. "Haven't gotten going yet this morning. Raiker didn't call." Then his eyes widened. "Did he?"

"No, he sent me out to be errand boy instead." Gingerly, he propped his elbow on a counter to lean against, half expecting the man to chastise him for that. "He wants an update on every piece of evidence that was transferred to this lab."

Jonesy didn't appear to be listening. His eyes kept shifting to the closed door behind him. "Uh-huh."

"So I don't know where you're at on the tests." Kell narrowed his gaze as the man took yet another quick look in back of him. "But Raiker definitely wants . . . what the hell has gotten into you?"

"Mr. Komodo." A teasing voice drifted out of the back room. One that was vaguely familiar. "Have you regained your fire-breathing capacities yet?"

"Dude." Kell couldn't prevent a laugh. "You've got a dragon under that robe? Nice trick."

Jonesy looked panicked. "No. Listen, tell Raiker I'll get right on it."

"On . . ." Brows raised, Kell waited invitingly. "Does she know you're calling her an it?"

Desperation edging his expression now, Jonesy approached him, talking rapidly. "You've got to leave. Now. I'll call Raiker. Tell him we talked. Go on."

"Alfred? Maybe I'm the one who should breathe a little fire." There was a deep-throated laugh. "I'll bet I know a way to make Mr. Komodo stand at attention."

The scientist—who at the moment looked like anything but—frantically shooed Kell away with his hands. But Kell frowned. God, that voice was familiar.

Then his eyes widened incredulously. "You've got Trimball in there?"

"Shhh." The man's eyes were imploring. "Yes, it's Nellie. That's why you really have to go."

He needed no further urging. Kell straightened with an abruptness that had his head hitting the overhead cupboard. "Don't let her come out here." God, he so didn't need that sight branded on his mind.

Oddly enough, Jonesy seemed to take offense. "She's really quite lovely. And . . . uh . . . very talented."

"I'm going, I'm going." Kell practically broke a leg trying to get out the door. "Say no more. Please don't." Safely out the door, he slammed it and leaned against it for a moment for good measure.

But once outside, his sense of humor kicked in again. A wide grin split his face as he headed for the exit. That was a narrow escape. All women were definitely not created equal because he'd had a far different response seeing Macy naked this morning.

Ready for the wind this time, he ducked out of the garage and jogged across the pavement. She might have thought he hadn't appreciated the sight, but he'd been pissed, not dead. And he hadn't seen her naked often enough for the image of her, flushed and pink from the shower, to have no effect on him.

But it had been the bruises scrawled across her skin that had caught his attention at the time. He knew he should be concerned at the way she had of crawling inside his skin. Setting up camp there. But he was pretty sure concern would be a waste of effort.

Far better to figure out what the hell he was going to do about it.

———————

The soft knock at the her door distracted Macy from the incoming test results. "Yes?"

When it opened to reveal Ellie Mulder, Macy's lips curved. "Well, hello. Come in."

"Hi, Ms. Reid." As the girl entered, Macy saw her parents right behind her.

"Ellie has been asking about you since her return." Althea smoothed her daughter's hair. "But we wanted to be sure you were up and around before we let her bother you."

"I'm fine. I'm so happy things worked out the way they did." She got up from the desk chair she was using. "How are you?" Macy addressed this to Ellie.

She shrugged, looked up at her mom.

"The doctor was most worried about the scabs on her wrists, but he thinks she'll be fine. She'll see him again in a few days."

"We can't thank you enough." Stephen Mulder's voice, his expression, was full of emotion. "But we wanted to tell you how much we appreciated what you did for our daughter."

"You're welcome." Macy's gaze went to the girl's. Held it. "But Ellie did the hard part herself. The dog couldn't have picked up her scent if she hadn't been smart enough to escape. We wouldn't have continued the search if we hadn't known there was a shelter and that it was white." She was rewarded when the girl smiled, just a little. "I told her yesterday how much I admire her. That's still true."

She noticed the look between the two parents. "If there's something we could do," Althea started delicately. "Some way we could show our appreciation . . ."

Macy was taken aback for a moment. Then, eyes still on the girl, she said slowly, "Well, there is one thing." And observed that she had all three family members' attention. "I'd like you to ask Ellie's opinion of her tutor."

The girl frowned, clearly at a loss. She lifted a shoulder. "He's o—" Then she stopped. Looked from Macy to her parents. "I don't like him. And he doesn't like me. I don't want to work with him anymore."

Stephen and Althea looked nonplussed. Stephen recovered first. "Baby, all you had to do was tell us that. I would have gotten rid of him. But you wouldn't have been working with him anymore at any rate. He's turned in his resignation."

The girl sent a shy smile to Macy. "I want to be just like you someday."

"You'll be better than me," she responded, her throat tight. "Smarter. Braver. Stronger. I want to be more like *you*."

"Well, we can see you're working and don't want to disturb you any further." Stephen began herding his family toward the door. "Please don't leave without stopping to speak to us. I know Ellie would like to say good-bye."

"I won't."

When they were gone, she slid weakly into the chair again. Emotional scenes could be even more exhausting than the action-packed one of a night ago. Once again her attention turned to the computer. She printed all the results, lining them up to study them closely.

A familiar hammering of excitement started in her veins. Without a second thought she reached for her cell phone and dialed Raiker. "I've got a match."

"On which?"

She stared at the sheets of paper again. "The same person authored both boys' Facebook messages." She drew a breath, unable to tear her eyes away from the results.

"And the person who sent the messages to the boys is the same one who wrote the ransom notes."

"We appreciate your cooperation," Agent Travis assured Nancy Elliott gravely. "We just need to ask your son a few more questions about the chat rooms he frequents."

David Elliott's head came up swiftly. "It's okay, Mom. I'll talk to them."

She looked uncertain. "I'll stay, too."

"Mom." The boy managed to imbue the word with pained adolescence. "I've got homework tonight, and you were going to try to cook dinner early, remember?"

"It's all right." Kell gave her a smile. "We won't keep him long."

She looked torn, but eventually she gave a jerky nod and headed into the next room, leaving them in the dining room.

"Here's the thing." Kell turned to the boy, all semblance of friendliness gone. They had a lot to accomplish and not much time to do it in. "We know you hang out in chat rooms. That you were probably talking to someone who didn't turn out to be who they said they were."

The boy shook his head so hard it threatened to fly off. "I don't know what you guys are talking about."

"You do, David. And if you waste our time proving it to you, your mom is going to be back in here and she'll hear the whole sordid story. That's okay with us." Kell lifted his shoulders. "We're doing you a favor here."

David's gaze dropped to the oak tabletop. "Okay, maybe there was someone. I thought it was a chick though. She sent pictures. She's hot."

"And did she ask you to send pictures back?"

He gave a jerky nod.

"How long did that go on?"

Swallowing, the kid said, "I don't know. A few weeks. Then she started getting sort of weird and I didn't talk to her anymore."

"Except then you started getting messages in your Face-book account, right?" When the boy didn't answer, Agent Travis pressed on. "And they weren't from a girl; they were from a man."

David grimaced. "Yeah. I mean the guy's a freak. But he has me by the . . . uh . . ." He gave them a quick look. "He threatened to send the pictures to my mom. To post them on the school's web page. To all my Facebook friends. He said if I blocked him, he'd do it. And if I stopped responding to his messages. I don't want pictures of my junk sent to my mom, you know?"

"So he has nude photos of you?"

Nodding miserably in response to Kell's question, he said, "I was getting really freaked. Somehow he figured out where I live. That's why I thought you were here that night. Because sometimes he'd park outside and try to get me to come out to his car. He was parked outside that night for a while, too. He'd message me sometimes, saying he was out there thinking about me while he . . ." Seeming to forget he hadn't told them any of this the first time they'd spoken to him, David lifted his head to look at them imploringly. "You guys gotta help me. I mean, that's a crime what he's doing, right? I'm just a kid. He's not supposed to be trying to get me to meet him for sex and stuff."

"No, he's not." Kell stood and reached for his cell phone. "And I think we have a way to make him stop."

"We've got Elliott's Facebook account information, so it was just a matter of accessing it and establishing contact with the guy."

Raiker nodded at Dobson's explanation. "And we can do it anywhere, from any computer. I posted a response to his last message. Let's just hope this guy checks in with the boys he targets regularly."

"And that he takes the bait," Macy murmured.

Kell said, "Maybe we should double the odds by posting come-ons from both the boys' sites."

"Too risky. He might be suspicious if he gets two positive responses in the same day."

Agent Travis looked at Raiker in surprise. "Uh . . . you posted the message?"

"I have more experience with pedophiles than I'd like to

recall," Raiker said grimly. "And we have the boy's past responses to help capture the tone. I can handle this."

"Won't he think it's odd that David has been out of contact and now is back on Facebook?" Macy asked.

Both Kell and Travis shook their heads. "The kid has been using his friend's cell phone to access it. He hasn't been away."

"Enough chatter," Raiker ordered, waving them away dismissively. "Get some sleep. If he takes the bait, this thing is going down tonight. Do you have things arranged with the Elliott woman?"

"Yeah, she gave it an okay," Kell said.

The computer pinged. Adam's attention reverted back to the screen. Then he looked up, gave a feral grin. "He took the bait. Now let's give him some line before we reel him in."

In the end, none of them went to sleep. Kell had tried to persuade Macy to do so until he noticed the odd looks he was getting from Travis and Raiker. Then he'd shut up, fumed in silence. It wasn't his problem that the woman didn't have the sense that God gave a goat. If she dropped facedown on this assignment, she'd have only herself to blame.

They passed the time playing five-card stud. Not Adam, of course. He'd been typing away in his David Elliott guise, posting numerous responses to the man online, occasionally muttering an obscenity under his breath.

Travis was showing a surprising aptitude for the poker game. But it was Macy who was cleaning up. She had most of the contents of Kell's wallet in the pile of cash before her and she had the tender sensibilities of a loan shark.

"What's that?" She eyed the piece of paper he'd scribbled on suspiciously. He pushed it over to her, and she picked it up. Unfolded it. And immediately blushed. "An IOU? I don't extend credit, Burke."

"You didn't read carefully enough." Although from the color climbing up her throat, she'd read his meaning fine. "I didn't offer cash."

She crumpled the note in her hand and deliberately turned to Travis. "Looks like it's just between the two of us, Dan."

"Be gentle with me."

"Your game's suspended for now." Adam shoved back from the table and reached for his cane. His face was a mask of grim satisfaction. "We've got ourselves a meeting."

Chapter 19

"Check the wire again. I want to be sure it's in working order," Adam growled.

"This is a test," Macy said quietly.

Travis called out from the kitchen, "Loud and clear."

"See if you can draw him out. We don't want him clamming up when he figures out you aren't Elliott." If Whitman was mourning being pulled out of his bed the first night he'd gotten to sleep in it, it didn't show. But it was the first time she'd seen the man dressed in anything other than a suit. The jeans and Broncos sweatshirt were going to take some getting used to.

"I have a feeling we're going to know him," Macy said quietly. "And we'll have lots to talk about." But if she did, she had no idea how he'd managed to circumvent the authorship matches with the written samples she'd collected.

"We're going in at the first sign of trouble," Adam growled. He'd assured her of that no fewer than three times already, so Macy merely nodded.

The Elliotts had vacated the house after Kell and Dan's

visit earlier that day. They were being put up in a motel nearby for the night, leaving the place to law enforcement.

The lights were off, except for penlights held by Raiker and Whitman. The trickiest part of the evening so far had been putting on a bra before leaving the estate so there'd be somewhere to attach the microphone.

They'd arrived at the house two hours before the meet was to take place. According to the message "David" had sent, he was going to slip out of the house at two A.M. His Facebook friend would be out front to meet him.

Kell appeared at her side. "Ready to do this?"

Mindful of the microphone attached under her clothes, she kept her voice nonchalant. "Yes."

"So." He rocked back on his heels, his face difficult to read in the darkness. "CBI has men posted all around the area. If he takes off with you in the car, the GPS bracelet you're wearing means you'll never be far out of reach."

"I know." This, too, had been gone over several times. "I'm ready."

But in the end, it turned out she wasn't. Because after a quick look over his shoulder, he leaned in for a quick hard kiss. The heat of it zinged along nerve endings already poised and ready. But it held an edge of frustration, as well.

"Be careful." His voice was almost, almost normal. "I want a chance to win back that money you stole from me tonight."

It took a moment to regain her power of speech. Several more to calm her rollicking pulse. "Won. Not stole. Won."

He was close enough for her to make out the familiar quirk of his brow. "Semantics."

"And we've got a car out front."

Macy turned at the quiet announcement, pulling up the hood of the boy's navy parka. She was about his height but slighter. Hopefully that difference would be difficult to make out until she was inside the car.

"If you make an ID, say the name right away."

"Yes." They'd need that clue if the matter turned violent. Her hand went to the knob. "Ready."

Keeping her head down and her manner furtive, she pulled open the door and slipped outside. The wind from earlier than day had died, but the temps hovered near zero. She looked up and down the street the way she'd been instructed before approaching the car.

Her chest felt tight. She had no way of knowing where the CBI agents were stationed. Or whether they were close enough for help if she needed it. Easier not to think that way.

She tried to match her stride to that of a teenage boy's. More of a half lope than the careful steps she'd like to take to avoid slipping on the slick pavement.

As she closed the distance to the car, she avoided the figure in the driver's window by rounding the back of the vehicle. Coming up on the opposite front door. Keeping her head down as she pulled it open. Slid inside.

And waited.

The voice was male. Pleased and just a little breathless. "I didn't think you'd come."

When she recognized it, Macy's blood ran cold. Reaching into her pocket, she said clearly, "But I knew you would." And pointed her weapon. "Mark Alden."

"What? What are you . . . Put that away, for God's sake!"

The man who had been friends with Stephen Mulder since college. The man who had stood up with his baptized daughter. The one who Mulder had relied on for legal advice had betrayed him in a way that strained the imagination.

"You were her godfather," she said rawly. Thinking of what this would do to Ellie, one more deep slice for a girl who already had so little reason to trust, had her easing off the safety.

"Listen, I don't know what's going on here." The man's usual genial tones were strained. "But you have the wrong impression. Ms. Reid. Macy, isn't it? This isn't what you think."

"It's surprising. Disgusting and disappointing. But it's exactly what I think." She had to take a mental step back. Away from the emotion that wanted to accuse and punish, and do her job. Consciously, she softened her voice. "I understand why you did it. I really do. Ten million dollars would set you up for life."

"Ten mill . . . No." The man shook his head violently. "I don't know what you're talking about. I mentor troubled teens in my free time, that's why I'm here. But ten million . . . I didn't have anything to do with Ellie's kidnapping." Alden's tone was incredulous. "My God, she's my goddaughter."

"The notes you sent to David Elliott match the authorship on the ransom notes. Ninety-five percent validity for my program, Mark. You need to tell me why."

He moistened his lips. "My statement sample cleared me. Or else you would have been talking to me long before this."

She stared at him, her mind working furiously. The man was right. She'd run the statement taken from e-mail correspondence on Mulder's work e-mail account without a match. It almost had to be someone with access to the Mulder home. But the statements she'd run had cleared them all.

"You had someone else write it," she said slowly, trying to puzzle it. The truth slammed into her then. "A learning disability, Althea said. And Lance said your wife used to write your papers in college. You're dysgraphic, aren't you, Mark? I'll bet you don't do any writing at all."

The man was sweating now. Heat was coming through the vents but not enough to be responsible for the perspiration breaking out on his forehead. "That's ridiculous."

"Given your disability, at work you probably have a secretary to dictate your letters to. And for personal use I imagine you use dictation software." The rhythms and patterns of a person's oral language sample differed subtly from their written samples. Her databases relied on written communication. But because the samples she'd had from him had been dictated, they were actually products of oral communication. "See, I know *how*, Mark. You just need to tell me *why*."

His face crumpled. "I didn't want to. You have to believe me. I didn't know why he wanted the security specs or the alarm code. I thought a burglary attempt, right? And what were the chances it'd be successful against Stephen's security?"

She watched him stoically, feeling nothing but contempt. "Who?"

"I don't know!" The man wiped at his tears. "He just started sending me photos. Older photos, from a few years ago. They'd arrive in an envelope to my home. To work."

"Photos of you with teenage boys?" she guessed.

He nodded miserably. "He threatened to go public with them. You don't understand who my family is. It wasn't just me I was protecting. My father . . ."

"Was vice president of the United States. I remember." But that hadn't kept him from engaging in the sort of behavior that would devastate his family when it was made public.

Not to mention ruining the lives of the boys he used.

"Tell me who it is." Her voice was hard, but she couldn't play the sympathetic ear. Not with what Ellie Mulder had experienced still fresh in her mind. "Tell me who sent the pictures."

"I . . . don't . . . know. Don't you get that? The last batch of pictures had a trac phone with it and a phone number. I called it, and he told me what he wanted me to do. That's how he contacted me every time. A half a dozen times in all, starting six months ago."

"So it was a man."

"I . . . probably. He used a distorter. I swear to God I didn't know he'd go after Ellie. Not little Ellie. I've been in agony."

But he was here, she wanted to point out, suddenly sick of the whole thing. He'd been posting messages to at least two boys during Ellie's absence. Not exactly the picture of the grieving godfather. "Where are the pictures now?"

"Are you crazy? I destroyed them."

"And the phone?"

"He told me to get rid of it." Alden stopped, as if just recognizing how that sounded.

She stared at him, her hand holding the weapon steady. "That's unfortunate, Mark. Because you destroyed everything that might back up your story."

"Wait. I'm telling the truth."

"We're done here," Macy said clearly.

"We can search for the phone. I threw it in a sewer in Aurora."

She saw the shadowy figures of agents rushing for the car.

"You have to believe me."

"No." The doors were opened. Alden was pulled from the car, leaving Macy alone for the moment. "I really don't."

"But if he is telling the truth"—Kell threw a look at her when she made a rude noise—"that means there's someone else out there. Someone who got away with ten million dollars."

"Well, not the entire ten million, as it turns out." Adam rubbed the back of his neck. "Paulie managed to divert some of the money. He's been trailing the ransom payment, and every time the money bounced to another account, he managed to snag a piece of it." He held up a hand to stem their questions. "I'm not even going to attempt to remember his explanation of how he did it. But the kidnapper got away with just over three point five million, instead of the full ten."

"What will happen to Alden?"

Her boss cast her a considering look. "Mulder has political capital to squander, too. But probably not as much as Alden's family. I imagine he's going to make bond in a couple days."

"And then hire the best defense lawyer in the nation . . . spend years putting off a trial . . ." Kell's voice was dour. "If that guy doesn't end up in prison for life, there is no justice in the world. Even if he's telling the truth . . ."

"There's no way to be certain he is," she put in.

"He's an accomplice to kidnapping and attempted murder. Macy's matching the authorship of the ransom notes to the communication with the boys will put him away." Kell slouched farther in the conference room chair.

"There's still the accounts the money was wired to." Agent Travis had been silent up to that point. "We've got good electronics guys in the agency. We can put them on it.

If we can get the owner of the account, we have the kidnapper."

Adam's enigmatic smile told Macy exactly what he was thinking. There was unlikely to be any more gifted than Paulie Samuels when it came to forensic accounting. "Maybe."

Kell looked at him. "What do you mean, maybe? You don't think we're ever going to know for sure?"

His boss pushed the chair away from the table and hoisted himself to a standing position. "I mean cases aren't always wrapped up in nice neat little bows. You take justice where you can find it. It's better than not getting it at all." He grabbed his cane and headed for the door. "Now if you'll excuse me, I need to go tell Stephen Mulder that one of his closest friends, the man he trusted with both his business and his family, was instrumental in the kidnapping and near murder of his daughter."

Macy watched him go, already feeling for the man about to take one more hit. He'd gotten his daughter back in one day. And lost one of his best friends in the next. Thinking of the secret Lance Spencer kept, she couldn't help thinking that Stephen Mulder could use some new friends.

"I think I'll go to bed." As she got up, Travis rose, too.

"I'll walk up with you." Her heart sank as she heard the man's words. "I have something I want to talk to you about." Noting the intent determination on his face, she had a feeling she knew exactly what that conversation would entail.

There was a moment, just a moment, when Kell shoved back his chair to follow them out that she thought he'd save her from the upcoming scene. Or at least trail along, making it impossible for the two of them to have a private conversation.

But instead he passed them in the hallway. "'Night, kids. Don't stay up too late."

Oddly deflated, she stared at his back as he sauntered away. There was no way, none at all, of predicting that man's actions.

"I was wondering about your plans after this case." Her attention bouncing back to Travis, she smiled weakly. He was a nice man. And she very much didn't want to be having this discussion. "I have relatives on the East Coast," he said earnestly. "And I've been meaning to make a point to get out there and see them."

———

Feeling like she'd gone ten rounds with a verbal jouster, Macy let herself into the room and snapped on the light. "That was just mean."

But she was talking to herself. The room was empty. There was no Kell stretched out on her bed or bending over her desk to snoop through her work. No quick-witted barbs about Agent Travis's interest. No double entendres to make her blush and stammer.

Which was fine. Absolutely fine. She pushed away from the door and went to the nightstand. It was past time for a pain pill. She popped one in her mouth and went to the bathroom for a glass of water to wash it down with. The man was due some sleep, and after extricating herself, as gently as possible, from Dan Travis's pronounced affections, she was more than ready to fall into bed herself.

She brushed her teeth. Of course it was just like Kell to blow hot and cold, constantly keeping her off balance. At the Elliotts' place, he'd kissed her before she'd walked out the door. Then earlier tonight he'd casually walked by when he had to have known what Dan wanted to talk to her about.

Sometimes she thought he purposely tried to drive her crazy.

Macy headed back into the bedroom. She was too tired to struggle with pajamas so she was going to crawl into bed fully clothed, something she hadn't done since she was a child.

But she got to the side of the bed. Stood there. Then looked toward the wall that joined the rooms. She already knew there was absolutely no chance she'd sleep, despite the exhaustion that was turning her muscles to lead. The bed held no temptation for her because the one man she wanted to see in it was giving her the distance she'd asked for.

And wasn't it just like the man to give her what she wanted once she wasn't sure she wanted it anymore?

Macy dropped on the edge of the bed, shoved her hands into the pockets of the jogging suit. Felt the crumpled paper she'd placed in one of them. Her breathing quickened. It was telling that it took far more courage to get up and walk to that door than it had to confront Alden earlier that night.

Before she lost that courage, she went out into the hallway and knocked on the next door. And when there was no answer, she knocked again, more than a little chagrined. He was *asleep*?

The door pulled open then. He still wore his jeans, and his eyes looked alert, although they were minus his glasses. He leaned against the jamb, barring her entrance. "I'm sort of tired. If you need to get undressed, maybe Travis will help you."

She placed a hand in the middle of his chest and shoved. It didn't improve her mood to realize he'd moved only because he wanted to. He backed away to lean against the desk, and she closed the door behind her, her palms dampening enough that she wanted to wipe them on her pants.

He didn't say anything. Slightly panicked, she searched her mind for something to say. Came up with nothing. Damn the man, where was that glib charm when she needed it?

"Um . . ." She held out her hand, showed him the crumpled note. "I came to collect."

He studied her gravely. "Technically, you didn't extend me any credit."

"I've got the IOU. You signed it." The nerves in her stomach were doing jumping jacks.

Leaning forward, he took it from her, examining it carefully. "That does look like my signature."

She reached out to tap it. "Also your suggested payment."

"Well, here's the thing, Macy." He handed it back to her, his eyes intent. "I didn't expect that to be a one-time payment."

Something in her eased a bit. And the pounding in her pulse was no longer due to anxiety. "No?"

He shook his head. "Hard to believe I'm saying this, but I'm not in for the short-term repayment plan either."

She smiled slowly. "That doesn't leave many options."

"Long-term payments, spread out over the course of years." He reached out then, quick as a snake, and tugged her into his arms. "It requires a partnership, someone willing to help fulfill that commitment every step of the way."

His arms settled comfortably around her waist. And the position was much too familiar. "I guess I didn't read the fine print."

"If we're together, we're all the way together." The intensity in those pale green eyes was mesmerizing. "You don't get to choose to push me away when something scares you. When *this* scares you."

All teasing vanished from her mind. Unable to look away, she only nodded mutely.

He reached to touch one of her curls. Wrapped it around his finger. "The next time you need to prove something to yourself, I'm at your side."

She froze at the remark. That time was closer than he had reason to know. She might not have to meet with Castillo ever again, but she'd have to discover for herself if the man's claims about her stepfather were true. Her stomach knotted on cue. But the thought of Kell sharing that with her eased those knots infinitisimially. "Agreed."

His lips on hers then were hot and deep and devastating. Her bones melted, and she leaned limply against him. "You could tell me you love me," he suggested against her lips. "Just because a guy's easy doesn't mean he doesn't need the words."

Macy hooked a hand around his neck, her fingertips grazing his hair. "I do." The wonder of it was something of a shock. "I do love you."

"Some practice should get rid of your tone of amazement," he decided. "Try it like this." He cupped her face in his hands and stroked her cheeks with his thumbs as he gazed at her intently. "I love you. Inside me there's still a ten-year-old boy looking for a warm place to call home. And I sensed it in you the minute we met." He threaded his hand in her hair to cup her head. "Scared me to death."

Her lips curved as they met his. "We'll work on that to-gether."

———————

He slammed his fist on the laptop, but the numbers on the screen didn't change. They'd stopped decreasing. They'd stabilized. But they didn't change.

Fuck! The red haze of rage was crowding in, threatening reason. After all his planning. All the time devoted to this project. For a lousy three and a half million? He'd spent a million in expenses alone.

He ended up with a third of the payoff and the girl was still alive. Her life was unimportant. But the money . . . that was hard to forgive.

Shoving away from the desk, he took the satellite phone, the trac phone, and the distorter and dropped them in the trash compacter. Pressing the button, he listened to the pieces grind. Much like his emotions.

This plan should have been executed with the brilliance with which it was evolved. And he knew who to blame for its partial failure.

Adam Raiker.

The name had his hands balling into fists. The debt the man owed was mounting. It included far more than money.

And the only repayment that would satisfy was Raiker's death.

Turn the page for a preview of
the fifth book in Kylie Brant's
exciting Mindhunters series

DEADLY DREAMS

Available April 2011
from Berkley Sensation!

The figure did a macabre dance as flames leapt to engulf it. Screams knifed through the night shadows, hideous and agonizing. The smell of gasoline lingered strong and heavy in the air, mingling with the stomach-turning stench of seared flesh and hair. Garbled pleas for mercy interspersed the screams.

But there would be no mercy from the watcher.

Nude, he stood just close enough to feel the searing heat on his bare skin. The flames beckoned madly, enticing him to join them. Just a step closer, they seemed to hiss. Feel it. Share it. Make us one.

He withstood the furnacelike blast as long as he could before moving farther away, his gaze transfixed by the writhing human torch. Fire was endlessly fascinating. Unstopped, it would gild the body, melt skin, and singe bone until it was sated. By that time, the figure would be little more than charred fragments of teeth and bone. Flames purified, cleansed the act of evil until only the motivation mattered.

And no one had better motivation than he had.

He flung out his arms like a preacher inciting the heavens, his form silhouetted against the brilliant glow. Justice had been a long time coming. And it couldn't be evaded any longer.

Marisa Chandler fought through the weight of sleep in a desperate bid for consciousness. Rolling from the bed, she immediately dropped to the floor, her limbs unresponsive.

But the jolt yanked her firmly from dream to waking, and for that alone she was grateful.

A bit painfully, she pushed herself to sit upright, leaning against the side of the bed. Sweat slicked her body, as if the flames in her nightmares had emitted real heat.

It had felt real. They always did.

She took a moment to will away the shudders that still racked her body. It hadn't been the same nightmare that had plagued her for four long months. She could give thanks for that, even as she fought to shrug off fear of what the vision might portend.

Resting her head against the mattress, she closed her eyes. Dreams like this one didn't mean anything. Not anymore.

The recognition brought both relief and despair.

The peal of the doorbell shrilled though her thoughts. Risa opened her eyes. Thought about ignoring it. But there was faint light edging the shades over the window, heralding dawn's approach. Her mother would have just gotten off her cleaning shift a few hours ago. She deserved the sleep.

The bell rang again insistently. Heaving herself to her feet, she padded barefoot to the door, checked the judas hole. The image of the stranger on the front porch was tiny, but she didn't need a larger image to identify him as a plainclothes cop. Faintly intrigued, she pulled the door open, leaving the screen door latched in case she was wrong.

Her instincts hadn't been exactly foolproof recently.

"Marisa Chandler?"

She took her time answering, scanning first the detective shield he held up for her perusal, then, more slowly, him. Caucasian, six feet, about one eighty, all of it muscle. Black hair and eyes. Hard jaw, uncompromising chin. Only visible identifying mark was the small crescent-shaped scar above one eyebrow. And despite his lack of expression, impatience was all but bouncing off him.

"Yes."

"Detective Nate McGuire, Philadelphia Police Department." He slipped his shield inside his jacket. "I'm on my way to a possible crime scene. My captain passed along a request from the chief inspector of the detective bureau that I extend you an invite to ride along. In an unofficial capacity, of course."

A chill broke out over her skin, chasing away the remnants of heat that still lingered from the nightmare. "Why would he do that?"

McGuire lifted a dark brow. "I figured you'd know."

She shoved her heavy mass of hair from her face and shook her head. Risa hadn't looked up any old friends from the force since coming home four months ago. Had avoided news like the plague. That hadn't been difficult, given her mother's penchant for watching only game shows and inspirational broadcasting.

"Apparently your employer, Adam Raiker, spoke to Chief Inspector Wessels about it." His midnight-dark gaze did a fast once-over, clearly wondering what it was about the woman in faded yoga pants and an ancient Penn State T-shirt that would catch the attention of the head of the detectives. "So I was told to stop and ask if you're interested. I'm asking."

She swallowed, just managed to avoid shrinking away from the door. "No."

He nodded, clearly not disappointed. "Sorry to wake you." Turning, he began down the stairs, leaving her to stare after him, fingers clutching the doorjamb.

Raiker. Damn him, her boss wouldn't leave her in peace. Wouldn't accept what she'd already accepted herself. Guilt, well earned, had rendered her useless. To him. To his forensics consulting company. And certainly to this detective.

The small house didn't have a driveway or garage. McGuire was halfway to the street where he'd left his ride, a discreet black Crown Vic. He moved like an athlete, his stride quick and effortless. She had the impression she'd already been forgotten as he mentally shifted gears to his first priority, his response to the callout.

"What's the crime?" For a moment she was frozen, hardly believing the voice had come from her. She didn't do this anymore. Hadn't for months. Likely never would again.

But still she waited, breath held, until he hesitated, half turned to call over his shoulder, "Possible homicide. A burned corpse was found about fifteen minutes ago."

The air clogged in her lungs. Blood stopped chugging through veins. Organs froze in suspended animation. The figure in the dream danced in her mind again, the engulfing flames spearing skyward.

But those dreams had become meaningless. Hadn't they?

Oxygen returned in a rush. "Wait!"

McGuire had reached the car now. And he made no attempt to mask his irritation. "For what?"

"Give me five minutes."

His response followed her as she turned away to dash toward the bathroom. "You've already used three." So she paused only to brush her teeth, drag a comb through her hair, and shove her bare feet into sneakers. Then she headed out again, snatching her coat and purse in one practiced move as she passed the closet. Risa took a moment to lock the door behind her before jogging down the steps toward his vehicle, already regretting her decision.

She didn't do this anymore. *Couldn't* do it anymore.

Which didn't explain why her legs kept moving her in the direction of the car.

She'd barely slid inside the vehicle before he was pulling away from the curb. Shooting the detective a quick look, she pulled the door shut and reached for the seat belt. "What's the location?"

"Body was found in a wooded area in the northern part of the city," he said in clipped tones.

"So you're from the Northeast Detective Division? Or the homicide unit?" She busied herself buttoning her navy jacket. It had occurred to her that the day was likely to be long and chilly. The temps had been unseasonably cool for May.

"Homicide."

It was what he didn't say that caught her attention. "If you're homicide, the call must have sounded fairly certain that there was foul play involved. Or else the crime bears some resemblance to one you're already working. Which is it?"

Dawn was spilling soft pastels across the horizon, but the interior of the car was still shadowy. Even so, she would have to be blind to miss the mutinous jut to his jaw. "What's your story, anyway?"

His attitude managed to slice through her self-doubt and land her squarely into familiar territory. She was well acquainted with suspicious cops. They would be the one element of her job she wouldn't miss if she left it. *When* she left it.

"I assume Inspector Wessels told you whatever he wanted you to know."

The sound he made was suspiciously close to a snort. "The chief doesn't talk to me. And Captain Morales wasn't in the mood for details when we spoke."

She was sidetracked by his words. "Captain Morales? Eduardo Morales?"

"Yeah. Why?"

Surprised delight filled her. "When'd he get his bars? I hadn't heard about his promotion." If she'd looked up old friends while she'd been in town maybe she'd have caught up on department gossip. But first she'd been focused on recovery and rehab for the physical wounds and then . . . the thought skittered across her mind before she had a chance to slam that mental door shut.

Then she'd been licking her emotional wounds.

"How do you know Morales?" He did a quick right on red in an effort, she suspected, to avoid waiting for the light.

"I was eight years on the force here before joining Raiker Forensics five years ago. Worked out of the Major Crimes Unit—Robbery and Burglary." Amazing that the words would be accompanied by a tug of nostalgia. "Morales and I were tapped for special duty on a Violent Offenders task force for several months. He's a good cop. How long have you worked with him?"

"Just a couple months." And it was clear that he was nowhere close yet to deciding if he shared her opinion of the captain. He shot her another sidelong glance. "You don't look like a cop."

"Chances are if I'd been knocking at your door at the crack of dawn, you wouldn't roll out of bed looking much like one either." She gave him a bland smile. "Unless you sleep with your shield pinned to your . . . chest."

Amazingly, his teeth flashed, although he didn't shift his attention away from his driving. "So you were on the job. But not homicide. Makes me wonder why Wessels wants you tagging along for this."

"My experience has broadened since leaving the force." And now it was her turn to go silent and brooding. Nothing could be gained from this outing, unless it was ammunition for her ongoing argument with Raiker. She was done with this work. The only question was why her boss remained unconvinced.

Risa recognized the area of town he drove to as one that used to be the haven of young drug users who wanted a remote place to get high. But it was deserted now, save for the police presence. The crime scene unit van was parked next to an unmarked car, and there were four other black-and-whites nearby. They got out of the car and made their way through a heavily wooded area before entering a clearing. It looked like the scene was secured and taped off, but those details were noted with a distant part of her brain.

Her focus was fixed on the blackened corpse lying inside the police tape.

A CSU tech was snapping photographs, and another man was kneeling next to the body fiddling with a machine she couldn't make out from here. But those observations registered only dimly. It was the victim who consumed her attention.

Because her palms had gone suddenly, inexplicably damp, she wiped them on her pants as she walked with more than a little reluctance to the scene. And wished once more that she were anywhere but here.

"Which one of you took the call?" McGuire stopped outside the tape and scanned the half-dozen uniforms in the vicinity.

"That'd be us." Two men stepped forward, both of them casting Risa a questioning gaze. One was tall and beefy, a good six inches taller than McGuire. The speaker was several inches shy of Risa's five-ten height. With his thick neck, skinny limbs, and sturdy torso, he bore an unfortunate resemblance to SpongeBob, of cartoon fame. "Officers Tready and Lutz." A jerk of his thumb indicated his partner as the former.

"Detective Nate McGuire. Homicide."

The flash of Nate's shield seemed to only partially pacify the man. He was still eyeing Risa quizzically.

"So run it down for me." McGuire's tone held enough of an edge that it captured Lutz's total focus.

"The lady who found it—Heather Bixby's her name—was out walking her dog. Wasn't sure what it was, but the body was still smoking when she came upon it. She called 9-1-1. Tready took her statement. She's waiting over in the car there."

"Walking her dog in this area? Alone, while it was still dark?" Doubt dripped from McGuire's tone as he shot a look at the car the officer had indicated. Risa seconded his disbelief. Philadelphia had dozens of parks, many of them updated with miles of paved trails. There was one within walking distance of here. While this spot, if anything, had grown seedier since her time on the force. The trees and bushes were overgrown, and it didn't appear as if public dollars were going to be spent anytime soon on creating recreation paths for joggers.

Lutz lifted his shoulders. "That's what she claimed, and she's sticking with the story. Making noises about needing to get to work, so if you want to talk to her, might need to make it quick."

"Did you see anything else? Anyone else in the area?"

This time it was Tready who spoke. His low, rumbling

voice matched his craggy features. "No one. But the usual freaks who hang out here would have taken off first sign of a uniform."

Nate nodded and dug in his pocket for a card. Handed it to Lutz. "Take the other officers and canvass the nearest neighbors. Write it up and send it to me at the homicide unit." He headed in the direction of the witness, who was sitting on the edge of the backseat in one of the squad cars, feet on the ground, with the huge brindle mastiff planted squarely between them.

Risa hesitated. No matter how much she hadn't wanted to come, she was stuck for the moment. And following the detective took her farther away from the blackened figure in the scorched grass. The distance would be welcome. She trailed after McGuire, who was already speaking to the witness.

"Mrs.," she was correcting him, one hand on the dog's neck. "Like I told them officers, I brought Buster out for a run. I just live over on Kellogg."

If Risa remembered correctly, Kellogg was a street of tired row houses in a neighborhood still clinging to a fraying aura of respectability. Of course, that had been five years ago. Things changed fast in urban centers, and north Philly had long been one of the roughest areas of the city.

"You live there alone?"

Impatience settled on the woman's face. "I've been through this once already. I live with my husband. He drives truck. I work a split shift at Stacy's Diner, on Seventeenth and Spruce, and I'm way late. Hal—that's my boss—is going to be a total prick about it, too. So if you could write me something, maybe on police letterhead, telling him I was helping you, it would go a long way."

"We can work something out. So you were heading to work earlier?"

Letting out a stream of breath, Bixby leaned forward to give the dog an affectionate pat. "I came to run Buster like I do every morning. My shift starts at eight, so we left the house at five or so."

"And you always come here?"

The woman's hesitation was infinitesimal. "In winter we stick to the sidewalks. But yeah, when it's nice we come here sometimes."

"Reason I ask, it's not the best area." McGuire seemed impervious to the morning chill in the air, although it had Marisa turning up the collar of her spring coat. "This is a known spot for drugs."

The woman lifted a shoulder. "Users, not dealers. And not this time of day, anyway. Doesn't matter. No one bothers me when I have Buster with me." She gave the animal a vigorous ear rub, which had it closing its eyes in canine ecstasy.

The woman was lying. McGuire had to realize it. But his voice was easy when he asked, "Did you see anyone else around this morning?" When she shook her head vigorously, he pressed, "Even in the distance? Someone running off, maybe?"

"No, it was just me and Buster. He was straining at the leash, dragging me toward . . . that." Marisa resisted the impulse to turn her head in the direction the woman pointed. The longer she could put off looking at the victim, the longer she could dodge recalling elements from the dream. "I got close enough to realize it was something dead. Burned. Didn't know if it was human, but I called 9-1-1 anyway." Her heavily made-up eyes gleamed avidly. "It is, though, isn't it? Human. You all wouldn't be so interested otherwise."

The detective reached in his pocket and withdrew a business card to give to her. "If your boss gives you any trouble, let me know and I'll call him." He accurately read the doubt flickering on the woman's face. "The cell is department issued. It'll show up on his ID screen."

Shrugging, she slipped it into her pocket. "So I can leave?"

"Has a tech taken a sample of the dog's hair yet?" Risa asked.

McGuire slid Risa a narrowed look. Clearly she was supposed to be seen and not heard on this outing.

When the woman shook her head, the detective said only, "Wait here. I'll send someone over right away."

Bixby's voice was plaintive as Nate walked away. "But why? I really gotta get to work."

Following a hunch she didn't question, Risa stayed behind. "It's in case they find hair on the scene. They need a sample from your dog, so they can eliminate it in the identification process."

"I didn't let Buster get close enough for there to be any of his hair on that . . . thing." If Bixby didn't seemed resigned to waiting, the dog did. It flopped down on its belly, drooling copiously.

Risa shoved her hands in the pockets of her coat and gave the woman a knowing smile. "So what time were you supposed to meet him?"

"Who?" Heather Bixby frowned.

"The guy you were planning to meet this morning. What time did you have scheduled?"

She had the woman's attention now. "I don't know what you're talking about. I said I didn't see anyone. You heard me tell that to the detective, right?"

"But you were lying. Or least not telling the whole story." Risa squatted down on her haunches and offered the dog her hand to sniff. "If you left the house at five, you would have had to get up shortly after four. Because first you showered, dressed, put on makeup before taking the dog out to a place you had to know would be a bit messy." She nodded at the woman's attire. Her sneakers were muddy, as was the hem of her tight jeans. "You're not a runner, at least not today. You aren't dressed for it."

"Jesus, I got ready for work first, okay?" Bixby folded her arms over her ample chest.

"You said." Risa nodded. "Dressed and ready to go three hours before your shift. Stacy's Diner is only a few miles from here. Walking the dog for thirty minutes still has you back home at five thirty, two and a half hours before your shift begins. Plenty of time to sleep in for another hour or two and wait for daylight. So I'll ask you again, who were you meeting here?"

The woman smirked. "Can tell you're no cop. Your detective skills suck. And I know when a person is just fishing. So go to hell."

Buster was much friendlier than his owner. He gave her hand a lick and Risa stroked his massive head. "No problem. What time does your husband go to work? Maybe I'll have better luck fishing with him." She didn't relish the flicker of panic on the woman's face, but she'd also never been fond of being lied to.

"There's no reason to bother Hal. He drives all night and needs some rest before going on the road again."

Rising, she contemplated the other woman. "Then don't make me."

Moistening her lips, Bixby said, "He never even showed up. We were supposed to meet, but he was running late. I called him when I found . . . that. He said call 9-1-1 but he turned around and went home."

Instincts she'd thought lost and buried were humming now. "Because he didn't want to be around when police showed up."

"It's not like that." But she could tell from Bixby's expression it was *exactly* like that. "He's still on parole. Just a misunderstanding," she hastened to explain. "He used some of the company's money for a couple weeks, and even though he put it back later, when the head of accounting figured it out, they nailed him on it. Bastards cost him two years in prison."

Risa didn't point out that two years was practically a gift for embezzlement charges. "His name."

Bixby's mouth set in mutinous lines. "That's all I'm going to say. I don't want to jam him up. He wasn't even here and doesn't know anything about this."

"Your husband is Hal Bixby, right? On Kellogg Street?" Risa turned away. "Thanks for your time."

"Wait!"

When Risa faced her again, the woman was staring at her with open dislike. "You're a real bitch, aren't you?"

"You have no idea."

After several moments obviously spent waging an internal

war with herself, Bixby finally said, "His name is Sam Crowley. But I swear, if you make trouble for him, I'll hunt you down and kick your ass." She smiled thinly. "I can be a bitch, too.

"I don't doubt it."

It had been far easier, Risa thought grimly, as she approached the crime, to play Bixby than it was to force herself closer to the charred remains in the grass. With every step closer her heart increased its tempo until it was a beating a rapid tattoo she feared could be heard by the officers at the perimeter.

Was that nearby tree familiar, with its branches growing in an X shape, studded with leafy buds? Perspiration dampened her brow. Her palms. What about that building beyond the trees to the west, with its boarded-up windows and tar paper roof?

"Hey, lady, you can't go in there." The hand on her elbow sliced through the sticky haze of memory and had her jumping in surprise. The officer released her when she shot him a look, but stood his ground. "Crime tape is up for a reason. You need to stay back."

She was tempted, more than she should have been, to do just that. To wait quietly for the detective back at his car. To forget the dreams that seemed far too entangled with the scene inside the tape.

The dreams that had been blessedly absent for four long months.

Instead, she scanned the area for McGuire and pointed. "I'm with him. You saw us come together, didn't you?"

The officer, with a fresh, youthful face that pegged him as barely out of the academy, looked uneasy. "Well, yeah. But I thought . . ."

Mystified, Risa waited for him to go on. "You thought . . ."

The kid—and he really was little more than that—actually shuffled his feet. "Ah . . . look! The detective is waving you over." The relief on his face was almost comical. "Guess it's his call if he wants you to go inside."

Still confused, she gave a little shake of her head before

bending down to snag shoe covers from the opened box at her feet. Donning them, she grabbed a pair of latex gloves from the other opened box and ducked beneath the tape. She was halfway to where McGuire stood speaking to a slender blond man standing next to the remains—

—*charred bones, melted flesh*—

—when comprehension belatedly struck.

The officer had thought her presence here was due to a personal relationship with McGuire, rather than a professional one. Under normal circumstances, the realization would have had her grinning. But her chest was tight. Her throat closed. The closer she drew to the body, the more conscious effort it took to keep oxygen moving through her lungs. To resist the urge to sprint, far and fast, in the opposite direction.

". . . use an accelerant?" McGuire was saying.

"Like I was saying . . ." The man broke off as Marisa approached. "Well, hello-o beautiful."

Resisting an urge to look for someone he might be addressing behind her, she focused instead on the gas chromatograph the man was using. "What'd the VTA indicate?"

"Jett Brandau."

Because it seemed churlish to refuse the hand the man thrust out, she took it for a moment. "Marisa Chandler." When she would have pulled away, he made a point of squeezing her fingers for a moment longer before releasing them.

"Arson investigator?"

He sent a quick glance to Nate before responding. "That's right. For the PPD."

She nodded. As the fourth-largest police department in the country, the force was plenty large enough to employ their own arson investigators who were also trained police officers. "And the VTA results?"

Brandau patted the side of the vapor trace analyzer's heating element. "Did three samples of the air over and around the body. Each yielded a substantial bump in temperature."

"Meaning a flammable residue is present in the area," she murmured, intrigued despite herself. It made sense. Setting someone on fire—if that's what had happened here—was more difficult than it sounded. Fire required fuel. The fabric of the victim's clothing would provide some, but with the wide range of fibers used, couldn't be relied upon to burn evenly. If total conflagration were the intent, an accelerant would guarantee it.

"Let me know when you're done getting the samples you need off the body so I can let the ME in. Then you can take comparison samples in the area as we finish searching each grid."

"Will do." The investigator shot her a smile that was probably supposed to be boyish, but to her jaundiced eye looked more than a little smarmy. "You're welcome to stay and help."

"I'll pass."

Her response didn't seem to faze him. He set down the VTA on one corner of the concrete pad before approaching the body with an evidence kit. "Hey, where's Cass?" The comment was directed at Nate and brought, to Risa's mind, a definite reaction.

The detective's lips tightened momentarily before he turned away. "She's running late."

"Reason I ask, I thought maybe the lovely Miss Chandler was her replacement." Brandau deftly managed flirting with his other duties. He was already kneeling beside the body and opening his kit before looking up at her again. "It is miss, isn't it? As in unmarried? Or really, really unhappily married?"

"No, it's dis." When both men looked at her, she gave them a small smile. "As in disinterested."

"Ouch." But there was no offense in the man's tone as he carefully cut off a sample of charred fabric from the corpse and dropped it in a glass container. "On the other hand, I miss Cass."

"I'll wave Chin over since you seem so desperate for companionship." Nate turned and gestured toward a slight Asian woman leaning against the medical examiner's van who headed toward them with surprisingly long strides.

"No." The panic on the man's face was mirrored in his

frantic movements as he sped up his collection process. "Seriously, no. I'm going as fast as I can here."

"Concentrate," McGuire advised blandly.

"You try to concentrate when you've got a pint-sized she-devil standing over you . . . hey, Liz." His movements were almost a blur of motion as he quickened his pace even further.

The ME stared down at him with her hands on her hips, eyes narrowed. "How long are you going to be, Brandau? We've only got about a dozen hours of daylight. I'd like to start my examination before nightfall, so if you can just give me an approximate timeline . . ."

"A few minutes. Ten at the most."

The diminutive woman cast a quick look at Risa then at Nate. "Where's Cass?"

"Running late."

"Uh-huh."

Mystified, Risa was getting the distinct impression there was something in the air regarding the absent Cass, but it was apparent no one was going to enlighten her about it.

"I appreciate you coming yourself, Liz."

Nate's words spiked Risa's interest. Normally an assistant from the ME's office was sent to collect the bodies. The appearance of the ME herself was unusual. Not for the first time, Risa considered that this homicide might be one in a series.

He went on. "When Jett's done here, you can start your examination. Pinning down time of death would be very helpful to us, so the sooner . . ."

The medical examiner shot him a look that would have scorched metal. "You want me to pronounce time of death before I even get back to the lab with this? No problem, I'm a magician. I also pull elephants out of my ass in my free time. Which trick do you want to see first?"

"I don't have to eat sarcasm to recognize the flavor, Chin. I was just saying."

"You know I don't deal in assumptions. After I get the remains back to the morgue and do a proper exam, you'll be the first to know."

"But they're still warm, right, Jett?"

"Air around the corpse is about one hundred thirty-six degrees. Liz is going to have to use a shovel to transfer it to the gurney. You find the ID yet?"

"I just got here, remember?"

From the easy banter between them it was clear they'd worked together before. Risa was the outsider here. And that was fine with her. She was still regretting the impulse that had made her accept McGuire's invitation to begin with.

And fighting a similar impulse to gaze at the steaming remains on the cracked cement pad beside her.

Back in her rookie days, she'd responded to her share of house fires or fiery car accidents. It was impossible to forget the sickeningly sweet, metallic smell of burned flesh. She would have recognized it even had she not known the circumstances surrounding the callout today.

The pitted concrete square on which the body lay had once been roofed, and meant to hold a couple picnic tables. But roof and tables had disappeared long ago, leaving only skeletal wooden posts and rafters. The rafters were completely scorched, and fragments from them littered the cement pad. The pavement had kept the fire from spreading into the neighboring trees and brush. Risa wondered if the choice had been intentional.

She forced herself to gaze at the burned figure clinically. This close, there was no mistaking it for anything other than human. Its limbs were drawn up in a hideous fetal position, wrists and ankles close together.

Intrigued despite herself, she sank to crouch beside it. "Were the wrists and ankles bound?"

The ME threw her a quick glance. "You mean because of the positioning? I won't know for sure until I get back to the morgue. But the limbs will shrivel on a burn victim, and they'll draw up toward the body."

"Pretty damn hard to set someone on fire if they aren't bound," Nate observed.

She thought of the agonized dance of the victim in her

dream. From its movements, at least the legs had seemed to be unfettered. But those visions might have nothing to do with this homicide. Especially if this death were related to other similar ones.

"Even if his limbs were completely secured, he could still roll, trying to put out the fire." She nodded toward the area in question. "There's no evidence of that. Which makes me wonder—"

The detective followed the direction of her gaze, and her thoughts. "—if he were kept in place by a rope thrown over those rafters."

"We'll know more after the body cools down and I can examine all sides."

Risa nodded at the ME's words. Had the person been burned while lying down, it would be reasonable to expect the burns to be uneven. It wasn't unusual for burn victims to look relatively normal on the side pressed against the ground, where the flames had been unable to wreak their damage.

But the figure in the dream hadn't been prone.

She looked at the detective. "How many others like this have you found?"

At first she thought he wasn't going to respond. Instead he watched as the ME rose and strode rapidly toward the city van, snapping out orders to her assistants. But finally he responded, "This makes the third, although it's too soon to tell if it's connected to the others."

"What linked the first two?"

He shot her a grim smile as he rose. "The first victims were found in remote areas. A combination of gasoline and diesel fuel was used as an accelerant. Both had their hands bound with duct tape but not their feet. They weren't gagged." His frown sounded in his voice. "That's hard for me to figure. It's easier to control the victims if they're completely secured. Gagging them would ensure their cries wouldn't summon help."

"But neither would be as satisfying." Her voice was soft, but from the sharpness of his gaze she knew he'd heard her.

"The remote locations give a guarantee of privacy. And even if someone comes . . . by that time it will be much too late to save them."

"You think he needs that? Their screams? But that still doesn't explain why he wouldn't bind their feet."

"Maybe he needs that, too." The death dance, she thought sickly, her eyes on the charred victim once again. The frenzied movements of panic and agony. She'd felt the watcher's ecstasy as he surveyed the spectacle. The near-orgasmic exultation from seeing what'd he'd wrought. "It might be part of his signature."

Something shifted in the detective's expression, leaving it impassive. "Signature. You're a profiler then?"

She rose, scanning the area. "All of Raiker's investigators are trained in profiling, too." Memory of the dream skated along the hem of her mind, and she sought to gather it in, to examine the details more closely.

That had been the last thing she'd been thinking of when she'd wakened from it this morning. Although she had art supplies in her bedroom closet, she'd gotten out of the habit of keeping an easel in her room with fresh drawing pencils and paper, to sketch the visual elements.

The dreams had been gone for months. She hadn't missed them.

And although Risa was far from accepting this one as anything more than a subconscious mind bump, it was second nature to draw on it to wring any useful information from it that she could.

If it were the victim's death alone that had so satisfied the watcher, a gun or knife could have been used with far less effort. Her shoulder throbbed, as if in agreement. No, his pleasure had been linked to the particular type of death he'd arranged. The flames had driven him delirious with delight, and he'd stayed as close to them as he'd dared.

Like there was an affinity there. Not just a murderer, but also one who chose fire deliberately because it satisfied a need inside him.

"It has to be death by fire," she said finally. "And he needs to watch." To *experience* it, deriving a sort of vicarious thrill from the flames. One of the crime scene investigators was photographing the area. Another was sketching it. Two others appeared to be waiting for direction from McGuire. "What'd the crime scene techs turn up in the other two deaths?"

"No wallets but IDs were left nearby." When she turned to him, brows raised, he said, "Yeah, just far enough away to be sure they weren't destroyed in the flames. Whoever the son of a bitch is, he wants to make it easy on us."

His jaw was clenched, and Risa suddenly realized there was more going on here than a killer choosing random victims.

"So you've established a pattern in the victimology?"

Nate's face was a grim mask. "Pretty hard to miss. If this one follows the same pattern, we'll discover the victim is either currently on the job, or he used to be on the force."